THE FLESH CARTEL

SEASON 5: RECLAMATION

RACHEL HAIMOWITZ

HEIDI BELLEAU

Riptide Publishing
PO Box 6652
Hillsborough, NJ 08844
www.riptidepublishing.com

The Flesh Cartel, Season 5: Reclamation

Cover Art by Imaliea, http://imaliea.deviantart.com
Editor: Sarah Frantz
Layout: L.C. Chase, http://lcchase.com/design.htm

ISBN: 978-1-62649-118-2

First edition
September, 2014

Also available in ebook across four episodes:
ISBN: 978-1-62649-119-9 (Episode 15)
ISBN: 978-1-62649-120-5 (Episode 16)
ISBN: 978-1-62649-121-2 (Episode 17)
ISBN: 978-1-62649-122-9 (Episode 18)
ISBN: 978-1-62649-123-6 (Episode 19)

THE FLESH CARTEL
SEASON 5: RECLAMATION

RACHEL HAIMOWITZ
HEIDI BELLEAU

TABLE OF CONTENTS

THE FLESH CARTEL

SEASON 5: RECLAMATION

EPISODE 15: TWENTY-FIVE

CHAPTER ONE

For the first time all year, Mat's imagination had turned out to be much, much worse than his reality.

What a fucking novel concept.

The Lakewood Psychiatric Facility was actually . . . kind of nice. Sure, his room locked from the outside at night, but it was comfortable and he didn't have to share it with anyone, and nobody—not even the orderlies or nurses—barged in without knocking and waiting for a reply. And yeah, they were making him take . . . take . . . he couldn't remember the names of all the pills, and *Jesus* there were a lot of them. They left him a little uncomfortably fuzzy-headed and sleepy and slow but also kind of pleasantly mellow, and they seemed to keep the nightmares at bay more often than not, which was a decided improvement over the days before he'd gotten here. And there was a *lot* of talking—individual therapy and group therapy and social chatter during free time from people who couldn't take a hint and leave him alone to worry about what was taking the damn bounty hunters so long and what would happen if they never came. But even that . . . even that wasn't so bad. Maybe it was the medication, or maybe it was how *tired* he seemed all the time, or maybe it was Dr. Astley's earnest fucking face and endless compassion, but he found himself sharing things he'd never thought he'd be able to repeat if he lived to be a hundred. Found himself crying like a little fucking kid through way too much of it. But also found himself feeling . . . well, not *better* afterward, but maybe . . . lighter? Less stressed, somehow.

Sometimes he actually found himself forgetting what he was really doing here. That he wasn't really crazy, that he wasn't supposed to be sharing his fucking feelings and healing his fucking mental scars and learning to cope with his PTS-fucking-D. And *that* was fucking terrifying—more terrifying than jumping at every shadow, holding his breath while rounding every blind corner, waiting waiting waiting for some bounty hunter to snatch him. More terrifying than imagining what they might do to him once they had him. Because he'd come to realize these last few days how comfortable he could get here if he let himself, how complacent—lulled by drugs he didn't need and therapy he obviously, desperately did. And the thought of fading away here, of *forgetting* . . . *that* was the stuff of more nightmares than anything Madame or Nikolai or Allen had ever done.

Which was why he kept practicing, over and over and over and over and *over* again, the story he and Nate and Louise had concocted about what he'd told the FBI, what their investigation had revealed, why they hadn't believed him, why they'd thrown him in here. The story he knew he'd need to be able to recite under the worst kind of duress, the one he knew he couldn't afford to forget, or to deviate from even the tiniest hair. The story he'd need to convince the bounty hunters was true before they'd take him back to Nikolai.

Which was also why—through the heart-stopping panic of realizing he'd been *actually* drugged by the nighttime meds orderly, room spinning and eyes and limbs suddenly too heavy to move, tongue too thick to make a sound—he was actually plain fucking relieved when they finally came for him.

He woke briefly to the sensation of movement—wheelchair, restraints, night-dimmed hallway. Pipes, concrete, strange sounds in the distance—machinery clicking, water running—footsteps, lots of them, wheeling him along. Basement, maybe. Or maintenance tunnels. He tried to stand, to stop them, wasn't sure why. Wasn't this supposed to happen? Couldn't move anyway.

Why was he so afraid?

A heavy hand landed on his shoulder, squeezed hard. Nails dug into his flesh. Pain. He wanted to make it stop, couldn't move.

"Easy, tiger." Female voice. The fingers tightened. Sound bubbled up from his chest, a low moan, not the words he'd meant to say. "I told you you wouldn't like what happened if I had to chase after you."

Bounty hunter. Bounty hunter was good, right? This was good. He wanted this. Why was he so fucking scared?

"Y'r hurtinme," he slurred, tried to shake her hand from his shoulder. Wrists strapped to the chair. Couldn't move. Probably couldn't have anyway even without the straps.

The fingers tightened more. "Go back to sleep," she said. Snorted air through her nose. "Hurting you? Honey, I haven't even *begun*."

She wasn't lying about the whole haven't-even-begun-hurting-you thing. When he woke next, he was strapped to a chair, and the bounty hunter had a shiny metal tray on wheels, like the one in a dentist's office, and on that tray was a whole fucking array of torture implements that desperately made him wish he could crawl up somewhere warm and safe like his nuts were trying to do.

No teeth pulling, no fingers cut off, but that still left plenty of options that wouldn't compromise his value, and he was pretty sure she went through them all. Like finger*nails*—those were apparently in bounds. Toenails too. By the end of the first . . . day? night? who the fuck knew . . . of endless questions, endless *I don't believe you*s, the same story over and over and over again (and thank God, thank *God* he'd rehearsed it so much), he didn't have a single finger- or toenail left.

But hey, there was still electricity and waterboarding and good old-fashioned rape. Being female didn't stop them; they improvised fine with fingers and fists and off-the-shelf cocks. He begged for them, sobbed for them—no acting required, no lies about how desperate they made him. He swore upside down and backwards and sideways that he was telling the truth, he was *telling the truth*, and he clung to that with the teeth they'd so kindly left him because Jesus fucking *Christ* if they didn't stop this soon, if they didn't believe him soon, he *was* going to slip. To make it stop, good Christ, *anything* to make it stop.

But if he did that, it'd only get worse. One slip and it'd all be for nothing. No more chances to make up for those lives he'd taken. No more chances to free everyone. No more chances to wrap his bare hands around Nikolai's neck and make one . . . last . . . kill.

No more Dougie.

No, one teeny little slip and all he'd have left before him was endless penance, endless pain, until Nikolai broke him. And he couldn't right all the wrongs that'd been done—to him, by him—if he disappeared.

He couldn't disappear. Not to pills and therapy, not to Nikolai's transformation. He was a fighter, or he was nothing. Not to mention, this was one beating he'd *earned*. What he deserved for leaving Dougie behind, for killing those men, for trying to manipulate Nate with fucking sex, for failing everyone, including himself.

He'd earned the beating, but that didn't mean he could throw the match.

So he fought on.

When Mat woke again, it was to pain and peace and motion. He was cuffed to a narrow bed in an RV, tucked naked under a blanket, every toe and finger agonizingly tender but neatly bandaged. Rural scenery was flying by the window. He was hungry and thirsty and in frankly fucking unreasonable quantities of pain, but he still had to bury his face in his pillow to hide his smile.

He'd done it. He'd fucking *done* it. They'd believed him, he'd survived, he'd held on and stuck to his story and they'd *believed* him. And now they were taking him to Nikolai's.

He ever so subtly ran a bandaged fingertip across the tiny incision in his armpit, already healed and disguised by the hair there in any case. He couldn't feel the chip beneath the skin, not through the bandaging on his finger, but the bandage came away clean—no blood, they hadn't found the transmitter.

Thank God.

He closed his eyes, let himself drift, knowing that somewhere not far behind him, Nate and Louise and a whole fucking FBI SWAT team were tracking the RV. Smiled into his pillow again. Nobody was hurting him anymore and he'd been strong enough and he'd be free soon. He'd have his revenge. His penance. His brother.

And who knew? Maybe, when this was all over, he'd let himself have what Nate had once so shyly offered, before Mat had ruined it with Nikolai's poison. Maybe he still *could* have that. Maybe it'd be one more thing he'd march in, guns blazing, and take back from these fuckers.

CHAPTER TWO

Nikolai circled his desk, clear except for his computer and the neatly arranged rows of photographs. One photo for each day Mathias had been at large. Twenty-five days. Twenty-five photographs.

All of the same thing: Douglas.

Poor, innocent Douglas.

Certainly Nikolai had had a hand in hurting the boy before, but always for a higher purpose, always to teach and guide him so he could learn the true fulfillment and peace of service.

Never like this. Never with such callous, untempered cruelty and brutality.

Some of these photographs could have been mistaken for service to the untrained eye—Douglas on his knees, eyes slitted and his face drenched in semen, Douglas screaming and impaled on a fucking machine, Douglas with a fist and half a forearm wedged into his ass—but they weren't. There was no fulfillment or sense of duty in Douglas's expression, only stricken suffering the likes of which Nikolai had never seen on a trained pet.

And that was only *some* of the photographs. In the others, the fact that the boy was being tortured was only too apparent. Cruelly caged and covered in his own filth, eyes blackened, lips split, fingers on both hands swollen and crudely taped. Weeping as he ate food that didn't look fit for human or even animal consumption.

But Nikolai left the photos in plain view, covering his desk. A constant reminder of the price of his failure, the ongoing cost of his powerlessness. And a way to center his rage, to keep it fresh and hot and craving retribution out of Mathias's hide. Time to tame the beast at last, to shape and mold him as he should have right from the start. Nikolai had once seen beauty in Mathias's wild nature, poetry in his fierceness. Not anymore. He would cleanse Mathias. Train him properly to service. Make him crave it.

But first, he would have his revenge for Douglas's pain. He would *take his time.* He would make the animal *beg.*

It wouldn't be long now. He'd received word from the bounty hunters that Mathias had been found and collected, cleared of any danger to himself or the Cartel. The FBI hadn't believed him. Of course they hadn't. Paranoid delusions, or some such nonsense. Let that be a lesson to the beast: no help was coming, not ever again.

But three days had passed before the bounty hunters had cleared him for return to Nikolai. And with them, three new photographs of Douglas. Horrible images, so horrible that Roger had retched behind his hand and fled the room. Nikolai hadn't betrayed any emotion, of course, but those images were burnt onto the backs of his eyelids all the same.

Perhaps he'd kill Allen. Train Mathias to the task and end them both in one fell swoop—Allen to Mathias's hands, and Mathias to Allen's enforcers. He had enough money. He had Roger. He'd have Douglas. He could retire. He might actually be able to stay right here in Tennessee, claim it was all some terrible accident, nothing to do with him. The Cartel would believe an upstanding pillar of the community like himself, especially against the word of cultureless scum like Allen. They'd let him live.

Yes. Perhaps.

"Master?"

Nikolai tore his eyes from those terrible photographs, glanced up at Roger's tentative almost smile, the tea tray in hand.

Roger squared his shoulders. Afraid—the poor creature was always afraid these days. Not *of* Nikolai, though gods knew that would've been fair; he'd lost his temper plenty enough since Mathias had escaped. But *for* Nikolai. Always *for* him. "I thought you might be hungry," Roger tried. Soft, hesitant. His eyes darted to the tray in his hands, to Nikolai's feet. Not to his eyes. Not to the photos on his desk.

Nikolai shifted some of those photos to the side, gestured to the space he'd bared. Mathias was on the way; Douglas would be safe again soon. He could allow some kindness now—for Roger, for himself. "Thank you, Roger."

A big whoosh of air left Roger's lungs in a poorly concealed rush. He scurried over to pour a mug of tea, to serve Nikolai a scone with fresh jam and cream. He didn't try to touch Nikolai; he'd been scolded one too many times these last weeks.

Nikolai thanked him again, stroked fingertips across Roger's cheek. Only for a moment, but oh how Roger *basked*, leaned in, eyes closed, hands frozen in their task. His smile was less forced when Nikolai pulled away and took a sip of tea.

Nikolai let himself enjoy it briefly, then asked, "I trust everything is ready for Mathias's arrival?"

Roger nodded. "Yes, Master." Was that a scowl? A frown? Worry, or concern? For Nikolai, or for Mathias? Roger and Mathias had gotten . . . well, *close* wasn't the right word, exactly, but there were feelings there. Feelings he himself had encouraged. But they weren't of any use to him now.

He sighed, put his tea down, grasped Roger's arm. Hard, too hard; Roger stifled a grimace. "You *are* clear on your duties, yes?"

"Of course, Master." Quick, nervous. Nikolai squeezed harder, until Roger met his eyes, let Nikolai read every truth on his face. Yes, well, Roger didn't have to like it; he only had to obey.

Nikolai let him go.

It would all be set right. Douglas home and safe. Mathias punished. Allen's desire for a feral, half-trained slave cured.

Feeling calm for the first time in twenty-five days, Nikolai drank his tea, and ate his scone, and then walked out onto the porch to wait. He let Roger sink between his feet and free his cock from his pants, swallowing him down for the first time in nearly four weeks while he enjoyed the glorious summer day.

He was still swimming in the lazy afterglow of quite possibly the best blowjob Roger had ever given when his phone beeped. The perimeter alarm; he pulled up the video, saw the RV turning into his driveway. Nudged Roger with his knee. "Go wheel the cart into my office, if you would."

"Of course, Master," Roger said softly, his voice decidedly tentative.

This time, Nikolai felt generous enough to comfort him. "We're bringing Douglas home," he reminded, and Roger nodded with a smile before slipping away into the house. Such a soft creature, after all these years of pampering. Too soft, perhaps. These next weeks would toughen him up right alongside Mathias.

Nikolai waited another minute, until he could see the top of the RV cresting the final hill before the house. Then he turned and went inside, leaving the front door open behind him, and settled back in his armchair by the unlit fireplace. Roger stood to one side, head down, back stiff, face carefully blank. To his other side, a covered instrument tray sat on the cart. On the shelf below it lay every single photo Allen had sent him. He'd unveil both when the time was right.

Sneakered footsteps up the front stairs, across the porch, down the hall. The distinct sound of a body being dragged. The women didn't announce themselves, didn't have to. They knew he knew they were here. Knew where to go.

And here they were, all four of them: two on guard, Tasers at the ready, and two dragging Mathias between them. Blindfolded, gagged, hobbled, arms bindered behind his back. Bruised, bloody, naked, a bandage on every finger and toe. He was limp, quiet, but not unconscious. Breathing too heavy, shaking too much. Just exhausted then.

"Adriana." Nikolai nodded in greeting. Didn't bother speaking to the others; there was a hierarchy here, as in any well-run organization. To be honest, he didn't remember their names. Only their faces, their obedience to their superior.

"Nikolai." She dropped Mathias at his feet; he landed with a grunt, curled up as tight as his bindings allowed.

Nikolai gestured to the tray still on his desk. "Tea?"

Adriana huffed a little laugh. "What is it with all you guys and *tea*?"

Nikolai smiled back, carefully measured. "Nectar of the gods and all that." He pointed with his chin at Mathias. "If you'd be so kind?"

One of the women grabbed Mathias by the hair, hauled him to sitting. He cried out around the gag, scrabbled to his knees. So worn down already. Excellent, excellent. She pulled a key from her pocket, unlocked the headgear, ripped it off, left him blinking hard against the light, licking at chapped lips and sucking air through his mouth.

"The prodigal son returns," Nikolai said. "How are you feeling, Mathias?"

"J—" Mathias gasped and gritted his teeth, which was a relief because now Nikolai knew for sure that he still *had* teeth. Not that Adriana would've taken them on purpose—they didn't grow back like fingernails, after all—but accidents did happen, and gods forbid Allen found another reason to complain. "Just fine."

Nikolai raised an eyebrow. "Expert hostesses, these ladies, then?"

"No offense to them, but I'm glad to be back here. Better than I've felt all year, in fact."

That was . . . unexpected. The snark, the mouthiness, yes. But the word choice seemed strange, even for Mathias. "I see your ridiculous bravado has survived your adventures intact. But we'll see how good you feel once I show you the hell you've unleashed in your absence."

"Did your customer satisfaction ranking go down?" Mathias snarled, voice hoarse. It must have hurt terribly, and yet still he couldn't resist.

Well, soon Nikolai would correct his errors and break the bastard properly. That would be the end of the back talk and the disrespect. "Oh, if only it were that. As if the opinion of slime like Allen means a thing to me or my business. No, it's not *me* who's been harmed at all." *Except perhaps the part of me that feels affection and concern for precious things like your brother* . . . But Mathias didn't need to know that.

Ah, that seemed to put a little wobble in his composure. His brows drew in. Maybe curiosity. Maybe just pain.

"Someone free his hands, please." A nod from Adriana, and the same woman who'd removed the blindfold and gag stepped up to unbuckle the binder. Mathias's arms fell limply to his sides, his face crumpling momentarily as full circulation returned. Nikolai gestured to Roger, who took the stack of photographs from the rolling cart and placed them in Mathias's bandaged hands. "Tell me, Mathias, how many days has it been since you made your escape?"

"Fuck if I know," Mathias said, resolutely not looking at the photos.

"Twenty-five days. And in your hands are twenty-five photographs. Look at them."

Mathias stared up at him, eyes full of hatred.

"I said look at them!" Nikolai roared. And then he cleared his throat. Straightened his tie. Spoke again in a softer, more controlled voice. "It's the least you can do, considering you're the cause of them."

"The cause of . . ." Mathias murmured as his head lowered, and his eyes moved irresistibly to the top of the pile. Narrowed. Widened.

The photos slipped from his bandaged fingers. Spilled across the floor for all to see. All twenty-five of them, in all their horror.

"What the fuck is this?" he growled. "What the fuck *is* this? What did you *do*!"

Nikolai's brows twitched. "Ladies, you can take your leave. There's a meal prepared for you in the kitchen, if you like. Your money should be in your accounts already. Thank you."

Adriana and her bounty hunters left, shutting the door behind them.

Alone at last. Nikolai stood, strode forward, and lowered to one knee, grabbing Mathias by the hair and forcing his head down so that the photographs were in his direct line of sight. "What did I do?" he asked. "Nothing, Mathias." He grabbed Mathias's right hand, slammed it down on top of the pile, mashed the heel of his own hand into all those raw nail beds. Mathias howled, too weak to pull away. "This is your doing, and I assure you, I'm as furious and sickened by this as you are. Probably more so, because unlike you, I care enough about your brother to try to look out for his welfare."

"I don't—" Mathias sobbed, then retched, fingers spasming beneath Nikolai's crushing hand. The bounty hunters clearly hadn't fed him the last three days, probably had barely watered him; nothing came up at all, not even bile. "I don't understand. I don't understand."

"It's blackmail, you simple fool. He wants you back, and he wants *me* to want you back just as much. He's been sending me one photo a day since you escaped, with the intent of continuing in that fashion until you are returned to him. Twenty-five photographs, Mathias. He's been torturing your brother and sending me the evidence for *twenty-five days*." He couldn't help the choked emotion in his voice. Not when he was looking right at the photograph of Douglas in profile, broken nose streaming blood, face nearly purple as he choked down a cock with no way to get air. Nikolai could picture him so clearly, crying, unable to beg for mercy, passing out from lack of air. Allen, perhaps, continuing to fuck his unconscious throat.

"You're lying," Mathias choked out. Tried to rear back, shoved at Nikolai's wrist with the palm of his free hand. Nikolai ground down harder. Blood seeped through the bandages as Mat screamed, tears leaking from his eyes. Just like his poor brother.

"You're many things, Mathias, but *stupid* isn't one of them. You know I'm telling the truth. You know this"—he jammed his index finger twice against the stack of photos—"is *your* fault. *You* brought this down upon his head. *You*." He grabbed Mathias's hair again in his free hand, waited until Mathias pried his eyes open before he continued. "So here's how this is going to go, Mathias. I'm going to give Allen what he wants: you, back to him, fully trained, no more desire to escape, no more refusals to fight whoever he puts in the arena with you, no more lip, no more trouble. And he'll return Douglas to me because he won't need him anymore. By the time I'm through with you, no one will ever need to keep you in line again. You'll *ache* to please him. Do you understand me?"

The sadness, the pain evaporated from Mathias's eyes along with the tears, replaced by fury, hardness, something else Nikolai couldn't quite name. His jaw set, and with his free hand he grabbed Nikolai's wrist again, hit a pressure point, pried Nikolai's hand from his tender fingers. A flash of fear—Had he gone *completely* feral? Would he really try to hurt Nikolai?—gone in an instant when Mathias failed to press his advantage. The bounty hunters were only a shout away, after all.

"You tell yourself whatever you've gotta to sleep at night, you sick fuck. But this isn't my fault, because if it weren't for you and your whole sick business, he wouldn't be with that monster in the first place. I know your guilt trip games, and I'm not falling for them anymore. Everything that happens to him now is on *you*."

"You left him alone with a monster," Nikolai replied. "You valued your freedom more than his safety."

"My freedom is our freedom." Mathias glared up at him, tightened his grip on Nikolai's wrist.

That was all the bullshit Nikolai planned to take from him. He twisted free, grabbed Mathias's fingers again and squeezed as hard as he could. Mathias choked, folded over their tangled hands, forced himself straight again, teeth bared, chin trembling.

"Well, your *freedom* has come to an end."

"We'll see about that." Not afraid at all, in spite of his pain and degradation, and that fact infuriated Nikolai all the more. How could it be that those photos pained Nikolai so badly, but affected Mathias so little? It was a terrible upset of the natural balance.

"So what now? You gonna torture me? Make me suck your dick? Fuck myself with that electroshock butt plug again? I've seen all your little tricks, Nikolai. Allen's and Adriana's, too. You don't scare me."

Nikolai scoffed, regaining his composure. "No tricks," he said with an easy shrug. "Merely a simple tit for tat. Twenty-five days your brother—my dear pet—has been suffering thanks to your actions. Twenty-five days." Again, he nodded to Roger, who went to the medical cart and picked up the tray waiting on its top shelf. Brought it to Nikolai's side, where he stood silent and still as a butler. Nikolai took the tray one-handed, set it on the ground near Mathias without letting go of the animal's mangled paw, clearly in sight but safely out of Mathias's reach. "Twenty-five days," he said again. "I plan to take them from you in kind. Twenty-five." He liked the sound of it. Liked the neat arrangement of five rows of five auto-injectors he uncovered with a little flourish of fabric. "Twenty-five doses of your serum, Mathias. And once you've finished them all, *then* your reeducation can begin."

Normally, this would be where Mathias, for all his pride and bluster, would begin to beg. Even he couldn't suppress or hide the fear the serum induced. And yet he was holding Nikolai's gaze, his own eyes hard and unflinching and . . . smug?

"We'll see who's gonna get reeducated, you slimy fuck. Spoiler alert: it ain't me."

Mat kept waiting for them to crash through the door at just the right time. Kept waiting for the shouts of the SWAT team, gunfire, whatever, but nothing happened. Nothing except for Nikolai picking up an auto-injector, then slamming it down into the meat of his thigh before his brain had managed to process what his eyes were seeing.

He'd have fought, run, *anything* to buy a little more time, but those women had worked him over hard, left him slow and weak, and Nikolai's grip on his hand—raw nail beds bleeding afresh—had left his head spinning.

Fuck, this wasn't supposed to happen.

That was all the thought he could muster before the pain hit. Hardly even any time to panic.

Which maybe was for the best, because oh *fuck* was this ever panic-worthy. *Where the fuck was Nate?* He should've been here by now, should've been here by now, should've stopped this . . . Should've . . . should've . . .

Nikolai let go of Mat's hand, and Mat crumpled to the floor, curled up around the fire in his belly and chest, arms and legs, back and head. Screamed. Didn't help, nothing would, moving hurt, *existing* hurt and where was Nate, where was . . .

God help me. Help me. What if they're not coming? What if they've lost me? Maybe I don't have the chip anymore. There was no blood because they cauterized the wound. I'm lost. They're never coming back. Nikolai is going to break me, and I'm going to be a happy cocksucker just like Dougie. I'm going to kill a hundred more people on Allen's command. I'll be a dog. I'll be a good dog.

But not for at least twenty-five days. Nikolai wouldn't even let him give in before every last dose of serum was gone.

Agony. Absolute fucking agony. He'd forgotten how much it hurt, how much pain the human body was capable of enduring without losing consciousness.

He wanted to give in already.

Fuck, Nate, where are you?

CHAPTER THREE

Not for the first time, Nate swore at the lack of audio on that fucking GPS chip in Mat's armpit. Mat had stopped moving about half an hour ago—inside the house now, he must be—but they had no way of knowing what was happening there. No camera, no mic. Fuck, they barely knew the shape of the estate. All they had to go on were some sat images, far too often obscured by a heavy canopy of trees.

He huddled around the printouts with the rest of the occupants in the mobile command unit, parked far out of sight of the road. The place was huge. A warren of trails up and down the mountainous woods, several scatterings of outbuildings. Toolsheds, greenhouse, something that looked like an old hunter's cabin. That was probably where the groundskeepers were living, where the SWAT team was converging first. But it was a beautiful day, cool breeze, clear skies—those men were likely scattered all over the property right now. And they had to be rounded up before anyone could risk breaching the main house. Otherwise, it'd be just their luck to be surprised by some burly brainwashed woodsman with a shotgun. Only a few more minutes to wait, though, and the team would be reporting in.

And in the meanwhile, he would have to resolutely *not* think of what was going on in that house. Of what was happening to Mat. Of what *had* happened to Mat in those three days in some abandoned warehouse in the rural South before pushing on toward Tennessee.

They'd all known it wasn't going to be pretty. Mat more than anyone. But no one had said a word. Everyone had pretended it'd be fine. No other way to move forward, not for any of them.

God please be okay I need you to be okay . . .

Nate had never known impatience like this. Never. Until—

"He said there were eleven groundskeepers?" asked a voice in his earpiece.

"Affirmative. And three more captives on the inside, all assumed hostile, plus Nikolai himself. And Mat, of course."

"All right, well, we've got eleven men cuffed now, bringing them in to the transport van. They look to be in good health. Perimeter alarms are all disabled, but if there are more near the house, none of these guys are talking; they might already know we're here. Still, if your guy on the inside's right about this, we should be ready to move in. You trust his count?"

"I trust him completely," Nate replied, setting down his coffee cup. "Once they're secured, we move in on the house. Get your team ready. Secure the perimeter, and wait for my signal."

"Copy that," the voice in Nate's ear replied.

Nate gave his bulletproof vest a pat as he stood. Louise checked her weapon—a nervous tic that betrayed how invested in this case she'd become; she'd checked it plenty already—and followed his lead, giving her ponytail one last securing tug.

"He'll be fine," Louise said, with just as much conviction as the last fifty times. "He's a tough son of a bitch, and they wouldn't have brought him here if they didn't want him alive."

"I know." His rote answer to her oft-repeated reassurance. He tried to believe it as much as she seemed to. "Come on, let's get this over with." He flipped the channel on his mic back to the open frequency. "Remember, we need Petrovic alive."

"I promise we didn't sleep through the briefings, Nate."

Nate froze halfway out the van, snarled, "God *damn* it, Vicks, I'm serious."

Dead silence in his ear for a moment, then a gentle, "I know. We got this, man. On your signal."

Nate closed his eyes, indulged in one deep cleansing breath, and then unholstered his sidearm. He and Louise would be going in last, no need for assault weapons, but he'd never wanted one so much in his life, if for no other reason than to crack the stock across Petrovic's skull like the scumbag worthless criminal he was. "Copy that," he said by way of apology. Then he leaped out the back of the van and began his crouching run up the mountain, Louise by his side. All around him, the SWAT team converged on the house, snipers in the trees covering the windows and doors, a team approaching the front door with a battering ram. Which they didn't actually need, because the fucking door wasn't *locked*.

The balls on this guy. Nate could hardly believe Petrovic's arrogance, except for the fact that he'd been operating for at least a couple decades without a hitch.

Well, his run was about to end, and he wouldn't be getting the chance to up his security for next time.

"Adriana?" a voice called from somewhere down the hall. Masculine, smooth, cultured. Not a drop of Tennessee in that accent, but definitely the slightest hint of *something*. Nikolai, had to be, with that fine trace of his early-childhood homeland still in his voice. The SWAT team fanned out quietly, two agents heading down the hall toward the voice, two upstairs, two each to the right and left of the foyer. Nate and Louise followed the men down the hall to the first door on the left. "Did you forget something?" Nikolai added.

"Yeah," Nate snarled as the agents spilled into the room, assault weapons homing in on Nikolai Petrovic, lounging at his desk reading a book while a man knelt at his side. The kneeling man's head snapped up at the same time Nikolai's did, no doubt reacting to the unexpected voice. Nate smiled, cold and cruel. "White dude, about thirty, six feet tall, hundred and seventy pounds, kinda mouthy. Maybe you've seen him?"

The kneeling man's face twisted first into shock, then terror, then froze somewhere between the two. Handsome fucker—must be Roger. Nikolai's expression, on the other hand, didn't change at all from that smug, shit-eating smile. As gracious as any host, he gestured with one hand toward the corner of the room where—oh God—Mat was curled up naked on his side, squirming and panting, glassy-eyed and trembling like he didn't even have the energy to scream anymore. Retreated to the corner like a kicked dog, too beat up and defenseless for anything else.

It took everything Nate had not to run to his side. But he needed not to show his hand.

"Can I offer you public servants anything? Tea, perhaps? Although you may need to make it yourself, if you have my cook in your custody already. No matter, you have seven hours until Mathias can bear to be moved again, so please, make yourself at home." He smiled magnanimously.

Seven hours? Nate instantly knew what he meant by that. Remembered it from Mat's testimony, and confirmed it at the sight of the medical tray with the epinephrine-style auto-injectors.

The serum, Mat had called it. Nate could picture the remembered pain on his face when he mentioned it. For a fighter like Mat to think of it with such dread, it must have been excruciating.

And now he was seeing its effects for himself.

Mat, normally so strong and resilient, reduced to a softly weeping child, moaning and incoherent.

And Nikolai, calmly sitting there, one hand curled loosely on the desk, the other draped oh-so-casually on Roger's head, smiling at them like they were no more of an inconvenience than a door-to-door Bible salesman.

"You *fucker*," Nate growled. He felt Louise's hand brush his arm—supportive and warning all at once—heard her say something to Roger, saw him climb to his feet at Nikolai's nod and turn himself over to one of the SWAT members. Saw the fear, the worry on his face. The calm smugness on Nikolai's.

Suddenly Nate was across the room, no idea how he'd gotten there, gun snapped in its holster, a fistful of Nikolai's thousand-dollar sports coat in one hand, an auto-injector in the other. "You *fucker*!" he shouted, hauling Nikolai from his chair, *thisclose* to smashing the auto-injector in his smug fucking face. He settled for waving it in front of him instead, so close that Nikolai's eyes nearly crossed. "What did you give him? You tell me what's in this! How do you stop it?"

Nikolai shrugged with his smug fucking face, and Nate shook him, hard. Reminded him he was holding a syringe full of poison by jabbing it near his eye.

"Answer me, you fucker! What'd you give him? Where's the antidote?"

Nikolai very calmly reached up with one hand, curled it around Nate's wrist, and directed the auto-injector away from his face. Tried to, anyway. Nate caught motion from the corner of his eye, a SWAT member circling around the desk for a clear line of sight. He shook his head—*don't fucking shoot, we need him.*

"As I already told you, the only antidote is time. Seven hours, Agent. That's how long it will take to wear off."

A borderline hysterical laugh bubbled out of Nate's chest. Practically a wheeze. His eyes turned to Mat, beaten and burned and bloodied, bandages around every finger and toe, teeth bared, tears leaking from his eyes. No. *No*. This was *not okay*. "Seven hours? Okay, okay, seven hours it is." And then he twisted his arm and slammed the auto-injector into Nikolai's chest.

So much for Nikolai's fucking *composure*; he dropped like a stone, his scream nearly drowning out Roger's panicked "*No*!" from somewhere behind them. Nate threw the injector at Nikolai's curled-up form, nudged the fucker with his foot. Nikolai screamed again, rolled away, writhed like he'd been electrocuted. Nate wasn't a violent man, wasn't a cruel one, wasn't even a vindictive one, not really, but he allowed himself a long, long moment to soak this in, to fucking *enjoy* it.

When he finally looked up, every pair of eyes in the room was on him, wide and incredulous.

"What?" he demanded. "My fucking hand slipped, okay?" He stepped over Nikolai, maybe kind of accidentally kicked him along the way, heading toward Mat.

Louise held a hand out, palm up. "Yeah, okay, partner. No big. It happens." He couldn't remember the last time he'd heard her sound so . . . *careful*. Like she was afraid she'd spook him.

"He was grabbing my fucking wrist."

"We saw, sir." The SWAT member who'd circled around for the shot. He nodded, pointed his gun at the floor.

Nate knelt down beside Mat, wondering if it'd make things better or worse to touch him. From here he could smell the sweat, see it dripping off his skin, hear all the little moans and whimpers forming and dying in his throat. He'd probably screamed himself hoarse three days ago while Nate had been sitting in a fucking van. "Someone call a fucking ambulance, would you?" He reached out, brushed the very tips of his fingers over Mat's forearm. Mat moaned, shuddered, curled toward and then around Nate and pressed his face into Nate's thigh. Bandaged fingers fisted loosely in the fabric of his pants; teeth sank in a moment later. Nate's heart squeezed. "Mat," he said softly. "I'm here.

You're safe now. You've just got to get through this, and I'm going to be here the whole time. The whole time, okay?"

"We can't—" Louise's voice came to him through the haze of anger and grief and worry and powerlessness, and on the heels of that, Roger sobbing and begging, "Please, sir, let me go to him, let me go to him, you have to let me help him, please, sir, *please*." Nikolai's screams had faded to constant, soul-deep moans and whimpers. Nate wanted to do the same when Louise said, "Nate, we can't call an ambulance. Too dangerous, remember? We agreed. We can't let anyone know there's anything strange happening here. Somebody would notice an ambulance. What if the Cartel has someone in the system and sees the address for the call?"

"Well, at least get me a fucking blanket!"

Commands behind him, voices in his ear. The house was clear; they'd found Jeremy and Tim, had them in custody, no one was hurt.

Except Mat.

Someone handed him a blanket, which he laid as carefully over Mat as he could. Someone else sat down in Nikolai's chair, propped his rifle against the desk and began typing on his keyboard. Louise was issuing orders. She was right, he knew she was. They'd planned it all out. None of the . . . the vics? perps? could leave. Nothing could look amiss. They'd be keeping Nikolai's men in the locked rooms in the basement until they'd completed the sting. Mobile command. Taking over the house. Going through Nikolai's files. Interrogations, plans—

He startled at a hand on his shoulder, cursed himself and every-fucking-one else when Mat whimpered at the jostling.

"Heya, partner. Why don't you find him a bed? Won't help much on the scale of things, but it's gotta be a hell of a lot better than the floor. Medic's on his way, okay?"

"Okay," Nate said, distracted, staring down at Mat's pained face. He brushed fingers across Mat's sweaty hair, did it again when it didn't seem to hurt him. He wanted to hold him, hug him tight, cradle him to his chest and squeeze his pain away. "Okay, okay."

"You stay with him. I'll take over here. Get the house on lockdown, get all of the . . . captives tucked away safe downstairs." Her clothes rustled, and then she faded away again, like all the others. He shifted, got a foot beneath him. Worked an arm under Mat's shoulders.

"I've got you," he murmured. "Gonna get you someplace comfortable, okay? You go to sleep, man, I've got you." Mat's hand tightened on his pants. "Not going anywhere, Mat. Just standing. Taking you with me, okay?"

Mat moaned again. To be honest, Nate didn't really think he could hear him. He'd been shot once, two lousy fucking months into the job, clean and simple through and through, but it'd been a hostage situation and by the time they'd gotten him out of there, the pain had been fucking crazy, had made the rest of the world fade away into a roar of white noise and nonsense. Still, he remembered calm voices and gentle hands. Remembered feeling safe. He could do that for Mat.

He slid his other arm beneath Mat's knees and hefted him up like a child. Mat found his voice at that, and his cry nearly made Nate drop him. Didn't help that he was built like a brick fucking wall, but then all the tension flowed out of his muscles and he lay in Nate's arms, panting and shaking and slack, and Nate turned to Roger and barked, "Bedroom, show me," and Roger sniffed back his tears and nodded and led him down the hall, hands cuffed behind his back, SWAT escort gripping his arm.

"J-Jeremy's room," Roger said, pointing with his trembling chin through a doorway to a clean, simple bedroom. He darted in before his escort could stop him, ducked down and pulled back the blankets on the bed, which had been made with military precision. All this with his hands cuffed behind his back, like the poor guy couldn't stop serving even when the jig was so clearly up.

Nate lowered Mat into the bed, watched him curl back in on himself the instant he was able, fingers clutching at the sheets, face pressed into the pillow. Every bandage on his right hand was stained with blood. Jesus fuck, had they ripped out his nails?

Nate realized he was shaking. *I let this happen. I. Fucking. Let. This. Happen.*

God, he hoped it'd be worth it.

Could anything be worth this? He'd done some studying on torture techniques. Fingernails took months to grow back. Toenails about a year. What the fuck could be worth that kind of sacrifice and pain?

Mat tossed, groped blindly for God-knew-what. Solace he couldn't find. Nate took his hand, let him clamp down, oh-so-careful of his missing nails.

"You there. Roger. Is it Roger?" Roger nodded, sniffled. Trying so hard not to show his tears. Not, Nate thought, because he was embarrassed by them, but because his pain wasn't supposed to matter or bother anyone else. "Isn't there anything you can do for him? Please."

"Master wasn't lying," he said. Bit his lip. The tears came again, despite his efforts. "Please, sir. *Please*. He's suffering so much . . ."

And whose fault is that, Nate nearly snapped, but then he realized Roger was talking about Nikolai, not Mat, and he turned to Roger's escort and growled, "Get him the fuck outta my face before I do something we're all gonna regret." But then he sighed, scrubbed a hand over his head. Roger had been kind to Mat, rare solace in a dark place. It wasn't fair for Nate to take out all his anger on him. "Let him see Nikolai. I don't care."

"Thank you," Roger blubbered as they dragged him away. "Thank you, thank you."

They were alone again. Just Mat and Nate in this strange, sad little room. Voices and footsteps filtered in from the halls outside, from upstairs, as Mat clutched at Nate and Nate clutched back.

Minutes later the voices and footsteps faded, the house secured and the perps on lockdown at last, and it was safe for the medic to come on scene. He checked over Mat with only the thinnest veneer of professional distance. As Nate had suspected, every finger and toenail had been ripped out. There were burn marks where he'd been electrocuted. Deep-tissue bruising. Probably a cracked rib or two, and what the medic thought might be a minor wrist fracture from fighting restraints. Plus whatever the fuck was happening to him now.

The medic put him on oxygen, wrapped his wrist in an ACE bandage, had Nate hold his arm down long enough to start an IV—no easy feat given his dehydration. Taped it down good and tight and then stood to leave.

Mat ripped off both the IV and the mask the second the medic left his side. Nate tried to put the oxygen mask back, but Mat grabbed his hand, curled in tight around it.

"You can't . . . you can't sedate him?" Nate begged, though he already knew the answer. "Give him something for the pain, at least?"

The medic shook his head. "No idea what was in that concoction Petrovic injected him with. Too much risk of bad interactions for anything but oxygen and saline. Nothing for it but time, and if Petrovic wasn't lying, that means . . ." He looked down at his watch. "Six and a half hours. You want me to sit with him so you can get back to work? Or hell, just have a rest?"

Yes. I can't stand to fucking see this.

But Nate shook his head. "He's my priority. Everything else, Louise can handle."

The medic gave him a sympathetic look, but shrugged. "Okay. You're the boss. You change your mind, call." He dug a packet of oral rehydration salts and a bottle of water out of his jump bag, mixed them together and handed it to Nate. "Since he's not going to tolerate the IV and I'm not willing to strap him down again, see if you can get him to drink some of that. Nice and slow, okay? Don't want him choking or puking." Nate nodded. "I'm going to go check on Petrovic."

"You let me know as soon as he can talk," Nate said darkly.

The medic nodded. "Count on it."

He knew that voice. Knew that touch.

Knew this pain, too.

But knew that voice.

Drenched in sweat, exhausted, trembling through aftershocks of the pain—hours of pain, never-ending, lighting every nerve and capillary and cell on fire, pain that dunked him bodily in acid but never let him dissolve, never let him die—he turned his head on the damp pillow, toward that tiny, flickering flame of comfort.

The familiar face swam into focus: Nate, sitting at his bedside. Nate's hand wrapped around his own, his touch light but steady. Nate's voice, unintelligible but gentle, leading him through the hours.

"You came," Mat whispered through his scraped-raw throat, and slipped into painless oblivion.

CHAPTER FOUR

It took Nikolai so long to rouse himself from the grip of pained sleep that he was certain, for a moment, that he'd taken terribly ill. He couldn't open his eyes, not yet, not with the pain in his head and his sinuses and his eyeballs themselves, but he felt warm sheets beneath him, Roger's hand on his forehead, soft words of encouragement being murmured in his ear. Something was wrong, though. The sheets were damp, the bed too hard, and oh *gods* how he *hurt*, not only his head but *everywhere*, this wasn't some ordinary sickness, couldn't be—

The serum.

He'd felt it only once, at the age of thirteen, when his mentor had dosed him so he'd understand how it felt to his trainees, what it'd do to them, how pliant and fearful they'd become when it was over, how best—and how sparingly—to use it in future. He'd never, *ever* forgotten.

And on the heels of that memory, another one: men with guns and bulletproof vests and badges, looking for Mathias.

Nikolai had surrendered. What else had there been to do but guard his dignity and wait—and hope that perhaps his buybacks would come to the rescue, that perhaps the FBI hadn't rounded them up before storming the house. And when his men had failed to materialize, he'd thought perhaps he could make a deal with the FBI, let *them* take care of Allen, all the while never letting a shred of fear show. The Cartel would protect him anyway, no matter *what* happened. So he'd keep the upper hand. Maintain the illusion of calm control.

Clearly that hadn't happened. And now he was lying in Tim's room, left wrist handcuffed to the heavy headboard, Roger weeping silently beside him as two agents stood guard by the door. Someone had hooked him to an IV while he'd been buried beneath the agony of the serum. Someone had stripped him to his underwear. In front of *strangers*.

"Cl—" His voice cracked. He'd been screaming; he remembered that very clearly, suddenly. Remembered that beautiful black—mixed?—man with the hazel eyes so full of hatred and righteous fury, waving the injector in front of him.

Roger's hand slid under his head, lifted him a few inches. A bottle of water met his lips, trickled in slowly enough for him to swallow without coughing.

"Clothes," he tried again.

"Shhh, easy, Master," Roger said, petting hand sliding from Nikolai's forehead to his cheek as one of the guards peeled away from the door and disappeared down the hallway. "I'd fetch them for you, but . . ." Nikolai heard a chain rattle, let his eyes slide to Roger's other hand, which was chained to the headboard like his own. Just as well, perhaps. He wasn't sure he could move yet, not without screaming. But oh, how he hated to be without that layer of protection in front of these men. Especially when the guard returned with that beautiful agent in tow—and his equally beautiful partner, if women were your thing. The man's fury shone as brightly now as it had eight hours past.

"Get him up, and get Roger out of here."

"No!" Roger cried. "Please, he needs me. He needs me."

He needed a lot more than Roger could give him right now, and he owed Roger . . . well, nothing, not really, but he *wanted* to ease the man's pain all the same. So he sat of his own accord—a ghastly unpleasant process with one hand cuffed and his chest bare and the remnants of the serum in his system—and then took Roger's hand in his own. Swallowed down his pain and put on a small smile for the man. "I'm all right, Roger. You do as they say; I'd be very upset if they found cause to hurt you."

"Master—" Roger bit out, and the male agent snarled aloud.

"Go," Nikolai said, firmer.

Roger nodded. Didn't fight when one of the guards came forward, unshackled him from the bed, and led him away.

As soon as he'd gone, Nikolai leveled a look at the two agents. "Not very professional, hitting me with that serum. I think that would count as cruel and unusual punishment, don't you?"

The male agent barked out a laugh. "That's rich, coming from you."

Nikolai shrugged with one shoulder. "I don't represent or claim to uphold the law. You do."

The agent stepped forward, all bristle and menace, and jabbed a finger toward Nikolai. His pain was useful; he was far too exhausted to flinch. "Yeah, well, maybe you should've thought of that before you grabbed my arm and fought me while I was holding the damn thing."

"Indeed." So that's what the agent was telling himself. No doubt his compatriots would all agree to that sorry little story; no point in wasting precious energy to argue it. "Do I get a lawyer, at least?"

The agent stared him down for another long moment, then broke eye contact just long enough to snag Tim's desk chair and drag it over to the bed, unceremoniously scraping the legs across the hardwood floor. He practically threw himself onto the seat, leaned aggressively into Nikolai's space. The alpha posturing was patently ridiculous—a wild ram looking for a head to butt—but between the exhaustion and the (fading, thank the gods) pain, it was strangely hard to keep holding his gaze.

"If you still want one when we're done talking here, we'll take you and all your boys on down to lockup and get you counsel. My name's Agent Johnson, by the way, and this here's my partner, Agent Menendez, in case you need to know who to go crying to your lawyer about. But here's how I'm thinking this will go. See, much as I'd like to kill you, slow and painful, right where you fucking sit, the fact is, Nikolai, that you're a small fish." Nikolai must have showed some expression of distaste, because the spiteful shit smirked. "I can take you in right now, and yeah, I'll be saving Mathias, and I'll be saving all the sorry sons of bitches you've been keeping in captivity here, but to my mind, that's hardly a win. No, what I *really* want is to look at the bigger picture. I want Allen. I want Madame. I want the procurement team who took these boys. I want every last name you've ever dealt with in any way, shape, or form. And unless you want to learn what it's like to be someone's bitch for the rest of *your* life—prison's rough for guys like you, you get me?—you're going to help me."

Nikolai rolled his shoulders, leaning against the headboard of Tim's bed and trying to imbue the motion with more authority than his state of undress might otherwise command. "First of all, I am no small fish. I would liken myself more to a crucial gear in an elaborate machine. You'd do well not to underestimate my importance to this process." Now, Nikolai smirked right back. "Secondly, while it's true I most certainly have access to the information you desire, I also have fail-safes in place to make sure it never falls into the wrong hands, so without my complete cooperation, you may very well return to your Bureau empty-handed. Thirdly, I believe prison is in fact quite kind to men like me, despite your assertions to the contrary. I've never hurt a child, and what's more, I'm very rich and well connected. If I even *make* it to prison—I am, after all, a poor little child-trafficking victim myself in your system's eyes, more likely to be 'rehabilitated' in a minimum-security psychiatric facility than sent to jail—"

Ah, now there was a look of surprise bordering on threat. A piece of information Mathias, and thus Johnson, had not been previously aware of. A very *crucial* piece.

"In fact, I expect that I'd live quite comfortably in prison, with a whole new group of pets to train to my every whim, thanks to my substantial wealth, the myriad failures and inequalities inherent in your system, my superior knowledge of the animal psyche, and the fact that, oh, yes, the Cartel most certainly has people in positions of power within the prison system who will be eager to reward me for my loyalty to the cause. So what choice shall I make, hmm, Agent Johnson? If you were me, what would you choose? Undermine my life's work, or spend some insignificant slice of time in your system's delicate care? Decisions, decisions."

Johnson's nostrils flared. "So that's a no to a plea deal, then?"

"Unless you have something more compelling to offer me, then yes—it's a no."

"*I* have something more compelling to offer you."

At Mat's gravelly declaration, Agent Johnson's head whipped around to the doorway as surely as Nikolai's did. The man was half-slumped against the jam, looking as pained and exhausted as Nikolai felt, bundled head to toe in track pants and a worn hoodie, holding...

Allen's photos of Douglas. One of them, anyway, sealed in an evidence bag, clutched tight in his bandaged, shaking hands.

Satisfied he had everyone's attention, he shoved off the doorframe, stumbled across the room. Half sat, half fell onto the bed, heedless of Nikolai's feet, one of which nearly got crushed beneath him. He tossed the photo at Nikolai's chest.

"You want him back," Mathias said. Not a question, a statement. "Only one way to make that happen."

"It only takes one, perhaps two biddable men to exchange a few choice gifts for you and me," Nikolai said. "Right out from under their colleagues' noses. And then I could bring you to Allen in trade for your brother, as I'd intended."

Mathias didn't hesitate. "Maybe, if it was anyone other than Nate on the case. Too bad for you he handpicked every single one of these people; I guarantee you none of them can be bought. Not for the price you'd ask."

Johnson shot Mathias an awed look. No mistaking that expression, and ah, yes, Nikolai had indeed lost.

Mathias pointed at the photograph of Douglas. "You told him you loved him. You told him that by being your slave, he'd always be taken care of. You're still a monster, but you're a monster who believes his own bullshit. I'm pretty sure of that." Mathias clenched his jaw, the disgust plain on his face as he added, "So as his m—as his master, are you gonna make all that a lie? If you care about him at all like you say you do, you've gotta value his safety over everything else. That's the responsibility *you* took on."

Nikolai hated to admit it, but the animal had a point. The very first thing his mentor had ever taught him was that if you were going to make the choice to keep a pet, you had to *take care of it*. And yes, selling them on relieved him of those responsibilities. But once he bought them back . . .

"And not just him, yeah? What about Roger? Jeremy? Tim? All the rest of your buybacks, huh? You cared enough to bring them home. You gonna let them rot now? You gonna let Dougie be tortured to death? I mean, maybe you *can* buy your way out of this, and maybe you *will* only spend a few months in some cushy psych ward. But maybe you can't, and maybe you won't. Maybe you'll be in jail for twenty years. What's Roger gonna do for twenty years? Or Dougie? How're they gonna get on without you? You took on a duty to these men. You can't choose your loyalty to the Cartel over them. Not if you're half the man you say you are."

Damn the man for bringing this down on his head, and damn him twice for talking such gods-awful *sense*. Mathias wasn't supposed to be this clever, and Nikolai did *not* appreciate being cornered by his own truths. What *would* happen if he couldn't retrieve Douglas from Allen? What *would* happen if somehow his money and the Cartel couldn't protect him from a lengthy prison stay, however cushy said stay might be? None of his boys could care for themselves. None could survive in the harshness of the outside world. They *needed* him. They needed him to do everything he could to ensure their safety and security with as little interruption to their routines as possible. Even if that meant plea-bargaining to guarantee reduction of his own time away.

Because Douglas would surely die in Allen's hands if Nikolai didn't act.

Agent Johnson must've smelled blood in the water, for he picked up right where Mathias had left off, as if they'd planned this entire speech. "Look, we can get Douglas back, make sure he's alive and well. We can make sure Roger and Jeremy and all these other men are well cared for. Get you into that psych ward instead of a jail cell—" Oh, how his face twisted in distaste at that, at the perceived injustice of it all. "But only if you give us the tools we need to help you, and to help *them*."

"You want me to help you dismantle the Cartel," Nikolai said.

"Every name. Every address," Johnson affirmed.

"They'll kill me."

I'll kill you, Agent Johnson so clearly wanted to say. Such a volatile man, so full of feeling. Nikolai could do so *much* with him, given the right tools and time. But he'd have neither now, would he? Whatever this case was to Agent Johnson, it wasn't merely some vague armchair dedication to justice. It was personal, very personal, and that made him so very dangerous. "They can't kill you if they're all behind bars. We'll protect you, Nikolai. Get you safe and sound to trial, and when it's over, you can take all your money and go somewhere else. Anywhere. We'll help you disappear."

Nikolai nodded. "I'll give you access to my computer. Auction houses. Storage facilities. Clients."

The agent smiled, slow and cold. "You'll give us one better. You"—he pointed to Nikolai, for once not full of posturing and aggression—"are going to give Mat back to Allen, and bring all your lovely invited guests here to the celebration fight. It's gonna be huge. Anyone who's anyone will have to be there. *Everyone.* You're gonna throw one of your famous parties Mat told me about. I'm sure you can convince Allen how necessary that is, right?"

Nikolai shuddered, but then turned on Mathias, a sudden, twisted victory flaring up in him quite by surprise. And oh, it was *good.* "You'll have to play the perfect slave, of course. Allen will want to know he's making a good trade. He'll need proof. You won't get to be feral this time, you understand? You'll need to be naked. At my feet. Worshipping." He flashed Mathias a lurid look, one that he thought adequately suggested all of the depraved acts Mathias would have to submit to and play along with. "For your brother, for Roger, for Jeremy, for *my responsibilities*, I'll do anything. Can you say the same, Mathias?"

Mathias hit him so fast and so hard that for a moment, Nikolai couldn't understand why he was on his side, why his face hurt so much, why blood was spilling from his nose.

"Don't ever fucking question my loyalty again, asshole," Mathias spat as an agent cupped his arm and started leading him from the room. "And for fuck's sake, my name is *Mat.*"

Somehow, Nikolai laughed. He supposed that was as close to a *yes* as he was ever going to get from that beast.

CHAPTER FIVE

Nate had done his job, reached accord, and now he needed to get the fuck out of this room before he followed Mat's lead and rearranged Nikolai's face himself. He cast a glance at Louise, who nodded—*I got this. Go.* She'd get all the paperwork signed, get the experts in, get the interviews started. Nikolai hadn't asked for a lawyer, after all, so that, at least, was one headache they could avoid. But now that they'd committed to this plan of action, they had to fucking see it through, and that . . . well, that wasn't going to be easy.

He got exhausted just *thinking* about everything they'd have to do to fly under the radar for the next however long it'd take to make it look convincing that Nikolai had broken Mat. Keep every one of the . . . he still didn't know what to call them, vics or perps? . . . on lockdown at the house, get them psych reviewed, get them the care they needed while making sure they posed no threat. Until Nikolai had revealed every single mole the Cartel had—and frankly, it was a long stretch to think Nikolai *knew* every single mole the Cartel had—they couldn't afford to let anything seem amiss. Nikolai would still have to put on airs of conducting his business. And the FBI would have to let the bounty hunters continue on with theirs as well, keeping the tail back far enough not to alert the women to any potential trouble.

And Mat, God, poor Mat would have to stay here. Probably for *weeks*. With Nikolai under the same damn roof because where else could they put him while he was planning the fucking party? How long did it take to "reeducate" an escaped slave?

And what would it mean for Mat? When the time came, what would he have to do to play his part? How much more humiliation and torture would he have to bear?

None, if Nate had anything to say about it. Get everyone to the party and arrest every last one of them before the main attraction began.

Fuck it. Tomorrow—he'd worry about this shit tomorrow. He was exhausted, brittle, on edge. He'd watched Mat writhe and scream and sob for seven fucking hours and he needed . . . He didn't know *what* he needed. Food, probably. Sleep, definitely. And some time alone. Maybe some time with Mat *not* writhing and screaming and sobbing, if Mat would have him. Louise could take care of the rest, at least for now.

He stood. Left the room, wandered out into the hallway and just . . . leaned there for a while. Head back, eyes closed, wondering where to go next. Not for the first time in his life, he thanked fucking God Louise was his partner. Couldn't imagine doing this without her, or with somebody else.

Couldn't imagine doing this without Mat, either. The guy really had gone above and beyond for this case. Let himself be publicly discredited. Spent time in a mental institution under lockdown. Dangled himself on a fucking hook to be taken and tortured and degraded. And now he was going to play the perfect slave for a frankly way-too-gleeful Nikolai.

How many other victims would go that far to help get justice? How many *could*?

Justice. Revenge. His brother's safety.

What would it be like to be at the center of that dedication and passion and tenacity? Did Dougie even realize what an amazing thing he had? Nate's parents loved him, no mistake, and loved him well. But though he'd had no brothers or sisters, he'd never been an only child; he'd always had to share his parents' love with their causes. Had grown up understanding that some things were bigger than you, more important than you, that sometimes Dad couldn't come to your ball game because justice and civil rights needed cheerleaders and champions too.

Dougie . . . with a brother like Mat, Dougie had probably gotten to spend years and years and years of his life with the certitude that he came first.

"Hey."

Hand on his shoulder. He opened his eyes to Mat studying him with all the focus, the concern he imagined was so often pointed at

Dougie. He scrounged up his best attempt at a smile, but it felt pretty sad. "Hey yourself. You okay?"

Mat shrugged, grimaced. "Sore. Tired. Starving."

Nate realized Mat's hand was still on his shoulder. His eyes were drawn to it, to that buzz of warmth where nothing but a single layer of cloth was separating their bare skin. But he was afraid to look, afraid to make Mat notice. Afraid Mat would pull away if he did. He swallowed instead, cleared his throat a little. "Well, I can fix two and a half of those three things."

Mat raised his eyebrows, a genuine smile struggling onto his lips. "Two and a half, eh?"

Was Mat closer to him than he'd been a second ago? Why did he feel closer? "Uh." He was really pretty sure neither of them had moved. "Yeah. There's, um, food in the kitchen, and plenty of beds to crash in. And as for the—" he gestured vaguely up and down Mat's body, which still seemed to be trembling a little, like he was cold. "There's, um. Tylenol. And what looks like a really nice tub/shower upstairs."

Mat grimaced a little at that, and Nate wondered if he had bad memories of bathing or showering up there, or if he was unsettled by the overall prospect of staying in Nikolai's spaces. But then Mat seemed to shake it off, and the hand on Nate's shoulder gave a gentle squeeze before falling away, and he asked, "Come eat with me?"

"Yeah," Nate said. "Of course." Because there was no other answer to that question, not really. And then he shut up, because if he let himself say anything else, it'd probably end up being *And then come shower with me?* or worse, *And then come sleep with me?* And frankly, no damn good could possibly come of that. Not for either of them.

Mat had been dreading bunking down in Nikolai's old room—or worse, his own—but in the end, Nate found him a luxurious guest room with a huge king bed and adjoining bathroom and no sexual paraphernalia anywhere—or at least if it *had* been there, someone had been nice enough to clear it out before he went in. They'd shared a near-silent supper, and then Nate had walked him up to the room, given him a gentle pat on the shoulder, and said, "I gotta get some work done. You get some rest. If you need anything—*anything*—just ask."

And now Mat was sitting alone on this strange bed, too uncomfortable in this place to undress—though he really wanted to, really needed a shower—and too anxious to sleep. So he sat awake on the very edge of the bed, listening to the buzz of activity downstairs.

While Nate had been babysitting Mat, some techie had worked with Nikolai to pull information off his computer and the Cartel's servers. Louise was doing interviews with the various men they'd locked up downstairs. Making sure they were fed and cared for and knew what was up, although Mat would have been happy letting them starve down there in that maze of locked torture rooms, after what they'd done to Dougie. After what Mat had watched them do to Dougie, oh God, he wanted out of this fucking place, the memories were threatening to drown him, all of them coming back with perfect clarity, and it was like he was back, really back, and any moment now Nikolai would stride into this strange room and tell him to kneel and demand a blowjob or worse.

"Mat?" Nate called from down the hall. "You okay in there?" God, he was breathing so hard it'd probably carried to the next room, where Nate was doing God-knew-what for work. Setting up a base of operations? Cataloging evidence? Taking pictures?

Mat dreaded to think what the guy was going to find, which he would then of course automatically associate with Mat.

Sure, Mat had told Nate a sizeable chunk of his story, but that didn't mean he'd been forthcoming about all the little agonies, all the individual acts of degradation he'd experienced here. But now, Nate would know. Already knew too much, had seen him naked and worn down to nothing, to begging and tears and clinging incoherence by the work of the bounty hunters and the serum. And now, as a part of gathering evidence on Nikolai's sick operation, he'd see something like that fucking electrified butt plug, and he'd wonder if it had ever been used on Mat. Things that had been, things that hadn't . . . what did it matter, so long as the seeds of association were planted in Nate's mind? How could Nate ever look at him again and not see . . . What? A victim. What Nikolai had tried to make— No, what Nikolai *had* made him.

Was that perverted client's set of bunk beds still set up somewhere? That letterman jacket?

"Mat?" Nate called again. "Can I come in?"

Mat scrubbed a hand over his face, realized his eyes were leaking. Not quite crying, but dangerously close. He knew damn well he wouldn't stop for hours if he let himself start. So he wiped his cheeks clean with the gauze on his throbbing fingers—the Tylenol hadn't touched that pain, and the medic wouldn't give him anything stronger until his bloodwork was cleared, not after the serum—and tried to sit up a little straighter.

"Mat?"

No mistaking the worry creeping into Nate's voice. Mat was pretty certain he wanted to be alone, but it wasn't fair to leave Nate out there with his panic. "Yeah, I'm . . . Sure. Yeah."

The door opened a crack, and then wide enough for Nate to slip in, but not an inch past that point. He shut the door behind him.

"I'm sorry. You must hate this. Being here."

Mat shrugged, cast his eyes to his hands curled loosely in his lap, freshly bandaged by the medic after dinner. He'd tried not to watch, tried not to see what they'd done to him. But of course he couldn't leave well enough alone. Had to examine. To *pick*. He didn't know *how* to leave shit alone. And maybe that'd served him well here and maybe it hadn't, he couldn't even fucking *tell* anymore.

"Needs to be done," he said when the silence had grown too oppressive. "Doesn't matter if I hate it or not."

Nate took a step closer. Another one. Then one more when Mat didn't object, until he was close enough to touch. The hair on the back of Mat's neck prickled, but he felt no urge to move. Too tired, maybe. Didn't want to move even when Nate reached out with a tentative hand, cupped Mat's shoulder with almost painful care. "It matters to *me*," Nate said.

Mat was abruptly on his feet and halfway across the room, back to Nate, shoulders hunched. "Don't," he said. "Don't. I can't . . . you can't just . . ." He started to drag a hand through his hair, cursed his stupid missing fingernails when pain flared. Wished he knew what to say, how he felt, why this bothered him so much. Tried and discarded the next dozen words that stumbled to his lips, finally settled on, "I don't want your pity."

But that was wrong, too. Wasn't what he really meant, and worse, Nate looked wounded by it. Said nothing, just stood there and let Mat be cruel.

Mat sighed, ran his palm over his hair again, more careful this time. Tried to meet Nate's steady gaze, found it much, much harder than he should've. Realized he was *ashamed.* "I'm sorry, that's not . . . I know you aren't . . ."

Nate nodded, eyes soft. "Why don't you have a shower? If you want, I can, I dunno, stand guard."

The laugh that bubbled out of Mat's throat was so sick it nearly died there. He held up his hands, wiggled his fingers. "Can't hold the damn soap."

Join me, he almost blurted. Wanted to. *Help me. I need help.*

He didn't fool himself for one second into believing he was only talking about the shower. He actually missed Lakewood. Missed talking with Dr. Astley. Even missed group, missed sitting around saying nothing and listening to everyone *else's* problems. It had made him feel less . . . alone.

"It'd feel good to get some hot water on you. Or hell, wait here and I'll run you a bubble bath?" Nate tried. "Hot soak'll ease those sore muscles."

He couldn't. Not yet. Shook his head, helpless. "Maybe, uh." Licked his lips, slunk back to the bed and sat. Let him be dirty for one more day. Who the fuck would notice? "Maybe tomorrow."

Nate nodded. He looked so fucking *sad.* "Whenever you're ready. You take care of yourself however you need to. Just . . . do take care of yourself. Going to be rough times ahead, so you need to be ready. Need to build up your strength. Conserve energy. Uh—"

"I want you fighting fit," Mat murmured, echoing Nikolai's words.

He flushed when he realized what he'd said, and in front of who.

"God, I'm sorry." Nate flopped down onto the bed beside Mat and put his head in his hands. "I have no fucking idea what I'm talking about. No idea what I'm doing. Jesus, they can't train you for shit like this."

Mat huffed. "Believe me," he said darkly, "people can be trained for *anything*."

Nate's head snapped back up. "Training. God. Oh God. Petrovic, that sick fuck."

He looked so distraught for a moment that Mat found himself reaching out to touch the guy, soothe him, but the instant his hand landed on Nate's thigh, shit got awkward, and he pulled it back.

Nate cleared his throat, fingers brushing absently over the place where Mat had touched him. "Well, one thing I *do* know is that you don't have to fight anymore, Mat. Not ever again if you don't want to, okay?"

Nice sentiment, but, "*This* fight ain't over yet. And you can't win it without me."

"Well then, at least you won't have to fight *alone*, okay?"

Why, of all the things he'd been through, seen, heard in the last few days, was *that* the one to make his throat tight? He swallowed, cleared his throat, swallowed again. This time when he touched Nate's leg, there was nothing awkward about it. Just warm, comfortable, soothing, even when Nate's hand slid atop his own.

Their fingers laced together, Nate oh-so-careful of Mat's injuries, and Mat's breath caught.

"I can't—" Nate began, then choked up, coughed into his fist. "I can't fucking stand the thought of what he's gonna make you do to convince Allen the trade is good. I can't stand it. I can't stand the fact that he's so fucking gleeful about it, like even though he's lost, he still gets this one last thing, this one last humiliation. I hate that the FBI has to cooperate with him, and I especially hate that you're a part of it. This isn't what I signed up for. Making you do these things—fuck." He lifted his free hand to his face, rubbed the heel of his palm against each of his eyes. "Fuck. I'm being completely unprofessional."

Mat laughed. They were sitting on a bed holding hands, and Nate was stressing about his *anger* being unprofessional?

"What?"

The smile on his face felt damn good. "Nothing."

Nate's return smile was hesitant, but it was there. They sat in silence for a moment, just *looking* at one another, and it hit Mat like a fucking hammer between the eyes how badly he wanted to close that last little distance and kiss Nate. But he couldn't, not now, not after he'd ruined everything between them with his clumsy seduction back at that West Virginia safe house.

But not *everything* was lost. He really did need help, after all. He licked his lips, sucked in a deep breath, hoped he wasn't about to fuck everything up again. "You know, maybe I should have that shower after all. Maybe you could, um, help me?"

Wrong choice. Nate yanked his hand out of Mat's like it was on fire, and he shot out of bed just as fast. He seemed almost panicked when he said, "Is that what you're really asking for, Mat? *Help*?"

Fuck. "I . . . yes?"

Now Nate seemed downright pissed: shoulders tense, arms crossed, jaw clenched. Not pissed at Mat, though—Mat had gotten very, very good this last year at knowing when other people's anger was directed at him. "I *can't*, Mat. Because it *isn't* just 'help,' is it? First I'm washing your back, and then it's your front, and then it's—" He cut himself off hard, swallowed. Clearly aroused and very, very upset about it. Fuck it all, the last fucking thing in the world Mat had wanted to do was *upset* him. "It's not a good idea. And I'm willing to bet some part of you agrees. I know you're—"

"Don't psychoanalyze me," Mat snapped. "Yeah, I'm freaked out. Yeah, I hate being here, and having all these memories coming back, and knowing that downstairs there's the man responsible for raping and torturing me and my brother." *So excuse me for wanting a little comfort and a little fucking normality in the middle of all that.* But he wasn't angry enough to say that, and he didn't want to hurt Nate for trying to do the right thing. So instead, he let his head hang like a scolded kid a moment, plucked absentmindedly at his hoodie, looked up again. "You packed this for me, didn't you?" he asked gently.

Nate's posture relaxed somewhat. "Yeah. I . . . figured you'd probably need some clothes. And more than that, you'd need *those* clothes." The comfort those clothes gave him. The comfort Nate couldn't give him in good conscience.

"Thank you, Nate," Mat said. "I'm fucked up beyond recognition, but you don't let that scare you away, do you?"

"Never. Never getting scared away. And by the way? I recognize you. You're still that fierce, passionate, beaut—" Another swallow.

"Still the same man who never gave up, never stayed down, never stopped striving."

Mat wished they were holding hands again. Wished, again, to kiss him. "Will you stay with me tonight?" Added hastily, "No ulterior motives this time. I'll be fully clothed. I just . . . I don't know if I'm gonna sleep, otherwise. You're right. I hate this place. And you're the only thing here keeping me partway sane. But maybe if you stay close . . ."

Nate's arms fell loose to his sides, and he took a single step forward. "If I stay close . . .?"

Big breath. Another one. He wasn't afraid this time of upsetting Nate, so much as he was afraid of changing the way Nate saw him. Not fierce at all—just a scared little kid, really. But Nate was standing there, waiting, so open, so patient, so fucking *hopeful.* Mat couldn't hold back in the face of that. "Then maybe when I wake up in the morning, I won't think that I'm . . ." Fucking tears were creeping back again. His throat seized. He sniffed, swiped at his eyes with his knuckle.

"That you're still under Nikolai's thumb," Nate finished for him, and closed the little distance left between them. No pity on his face, no scorn, nothing but compassion and understanding and the same awed respect he'd shown Mat from day one.

When he sat down again, he put his arm around Mat's shoulder and pulled a little—an invitation, not a demand. Mat had no qualms giving in. He laid his head on Nate's shoulder and sighed.

"What we're doing, Mat, it's all an act. He doesn't own you. He has no power over you. I'm not going to let him forget that. I'm not going to let him toy with you or exploit you or any of it. In fact, you know, I think maybe I—" He shuddered; Mat felt it. "Maybe I'll be right there beside you, when the time comes. You thought I was . . . a part of all that when you met me. Why wouldn't other people believe it, too?"

"Nate . . ." Mat sat straight again, shook his head. The arm around his shoulder was suddenly oppressive, his skin crawling.

"Yeah, listen," Nate said. He turned to face Mat more directly, reached out with both hands to clasp Mat's, but let them fall to his lap when he caught Mat's flinch. "*Listen.* That way I can be right there. I can protect you. You won't be alone."

"Nate—"

"I'll be right there with you, shoulder to shoulder, just like this."

"Nate, *no*. Okay? No!" God, how it killed him to watch the passion drain so abruptly from that handsome face. "It's not . . ." He made himself touch Nate, a mere brush of bandaged fingertips over the back of one hand. That was good enough, would have to be enough. "It's not that I don't appreciate that, okay? And I mean, maybe if . . . maybe if there *is* some way for you to, uh, you know, to *be* there without having to . . ." He tossed one hand, a helpless little gesture. "You know, all of that. *Maybe* then it'd be okay. But I can't ask that of you—"

"You're *not* asking. I'm *offering*."

"And that's worse! Because you don't know *what* you're offering, I'm sorry, but you don't, and I can't . . ." He had to close his eyes for a second, shut them against the images flashing in his mind, swallow against the nausea burning up his throat. "I *can't*, okay?"

Nate's face fell. "I'm sorry. I'm trying to help, but I fucked it all up, didn't I?"

Mat smiled tremulously and gave his hand a squeeze, then went for broke, leaning in to press their foreheads together. "I told you how you could help, Nate, and you haven't fucked that up yet, not once. Sleep? With me? Please?"

He heard more than saw Nate swallow, lick his lips. Gentle hands settled atop his own, and it was Nate, not Mat, who finally broke the contact. "Yeah," he said. "Yeah, okay."

CHAPTER SIX

It was nearly time to head to Florida, and Nate couldn't find Mat. He tried not to worry about that—the house was big, the estate was *huge*, and Mat had taken to going on long runs through the woods when he needed out, which was often. No surprise, considering they'd been stuck here for six damn weeks already—six damn weeks in which Dougie had been stuck with *Allen*, though at least the photos—and, supposedly, the abuse—had stopped once Nikolai had proven Mat was back in hand. Still, it was hard to shake that constant state of nerves from being here, from Dougie being there, made so much worse by where they were about to go, what they were about to do. What Mat would have to do.

Louise was standing outside the master bedroom, shoulders tense, lips set. "You seen Mat?" he asked. When she shook her head, he went in without knocking, found a near-naked Roger dressing Nikolai in a summer-weight suit. He seemed to be having trouble with it; his hands were shaking, and he obviously didn't want to lift them from Nikolai's skin. They hadn't been allowed to see each other in some time—not since the start of the psych evals—and it had clearly taken its toll. Roger was thinner, pale, too quiet, clinically depressed according to Dr. Akers; he'd clung to his "purpose" throughout the last month and a half, offering silent, polite obedience to every command from every potential authority figure. It half broke Nate's fucking heart, but the other half couldn't forget what Roger had helped Nikolai do.

Nikolai had meticulously maintained his own appearance, but he'd become quieter, less smug. It seemed not even the thought of Mat's imminent debasement could raise Nikolai's spirits all the way, but he was obviously trying. Had to put on a good show for Allen, after all.

Which was the only reason Nate was permitting Roger to be with him, to serve him, now. Dr. Akers had made a stink about it—*harm his recovery, repress his fledgling sense of self, bad enough he's been forced to stay in the home of his abuser*, etc., etc.—but Nikolai had never gone anywhere without Roger before, and Nate wasn't risking the entire operation for six weeks' worth of whatever minuscule progress Roger might've made toward healing after twenty-something fucking years.

He realized Nikolai was staring at him, that Roger had given up all pretense of dressing Nikolai and was instead resting both hands on the man's torso, body pressed so tight to Nikolai's that there wasn't enough space between them to slip a piece of paper through.

Nate cleared his throat, averted his eyes. Too hard to watch this shit, to see a beaten dog fall apart for being kept from its abuser. "You know where Mat is?" he asked instead.

Nikolai arched an eyebrow and said dryly, "I am no longer his keeper, if you'll recall."

God, the *fucker*. "Yeah, and you're not Roger's anymore, either, so stop loitering and get dressed, both of you. We leave in fifteen."

He may or may not have slammed the door on his way out.

"Try the basement," Louise said to his tense, retreating back.

He nodded—she was probably right—but *God* how he hated going down there. The place *looked* pleasant enough—hardwood floors, expensive artwork on the walls, a high-quality hotel feel in the bedrooms—but it was hard to ignore all those locks on the doors, the lack of windows, the one room at the far end of the hall clearly designed as a dungeon. All the implements were gone from it now, bagged and tagged and cataloged, but Nate saw them every time he opened that door anyway. Saw Mat in his mind's eye, hanging from the shackles bolted to the wall or strapped to the naked wire bed frame, being whipped, paddled, belted, clamped, raped with any number of purpose-built objects, some bigger than Nate's whole fucking *arm* . . .

He shook his head, blinked hard. Somehow he'd made it to the top of the basement stairs, found himself just *standing* there, one hand clenched white-knuckled around the doorknob. Cold sweat was dripping down his neck. How was it possible that after all these weeks, the disgust, the *fury*, hadn't faded at all? How could he still feel it as keenly as he had the first time and continue to function in polite society—or whatever passed for it at this place?

Well, at least it'd be over soon. Just a little while longer, just two more days . . .

He opened the door, called down the stairwell. "Mat? You down there?"

No reply.

But there was noise down there. Some kind of mechanical whirring that at first Nate was too upset to place, but then he realized: a treadmill. It was the sound of a treadmill. And yes, there had been a treadmill in Mat's old room downstairs. The one with the boxing equipment. And the drawer full of terrible gags. And that giant electrified plug.

Nate had the weird urge to *run* to him, so he did. Pounded down the stairs. Flew through the various security doors until he found Mat's room, the door wide open.

Mat was inside, running full out on the treadmill.

Nearly naked in a pair of tight red shorts, socks, and sneakers. Dripping with sweat, panting hard but steady. Staring blankly ahead, focus turned so far inward he didn't seem to realize that Nate was here.

It was wrong for Nate to be watching him like this. He wasn't on display. Wasn't some soft-core calendar boy or sweaty porn star.

He was a human trafficking victim, and good God, he deserved better than this.

So Nate cleared his throat. Cleared his throat again. Finally stepped forward, setting his hand on the bar of the treadmill as he called out, "Mat. Hey."

Mat didn't startle, exactly, but he did look strangely spooked, like he was half-awake and half-dreaming. He hit the emergency stop button and stared at Nate like he didn't know who he was.

"We're leaving soon, so you should probably take a shower, okay? You need anything?"

Mat slowly blinked himself back to the present. Grabbed the towel hanging over the bar and mopped at his face. "I haven't come down here this whole time. I didn't want to. But I thought . . . since I gotta play the good little slave, maybe I should get into the headspace, you know?" He scrubbed at his face with the towel again, looked down his body, plucked desultorily at the waistband of those tight running shorts. The face he made was not pleasant. "Man, method actors losing a bunch of weight got nothing on me."

Nate winced.

Mat stepped off the treadmill, sat down on the side of the bed and began to unlace his shoes. He wasn't looking at Nate when he spoke. "You knew this was my room, right? When you came down here."

"The boxing equipment gave it away."

Mat nodded. "Right. Uh, well, this is how I lived. When I was here." He toed his shoes off, peeled off the socks. Stood and hooked both thumbs in the waistband of the shorts. "These shorts are the only clothes he let me wear. I did a lot of running. A lot of working out. And then he'd make me suck his dick or fuck myself on him or . . ." Mat shrugged. ". . . or worse."

Nate winced again, and then regretted it when Mat looked up to meet his eyes. Mat's face hardened, but Nate couldn't tell if it was in response to *his* response or because of what Mat was about to do—which was, apparently, pull his shorts down, leaving himself buck naked in front of Nate. Nate didn't know which one of them blushed harder, but they both resolutely held each other's gazes, not looking away, not looking at . . . other things.

Eventually, Mat scratched at his left collarbone and dropped his eyes. "Practice," he murmured. "I need to . . . you know."

Nate nodded. "Yeah. It's okay, Mat, it's going to be okay."

Mat shrugged like maybe he didn't believe Nate, turned and paced over to the bathroom door. Nate tried very, very hard not to watch the muscles in his ass flex. "Anyway," Mat was saying, "I don't know why I'm telling you this, but I guess—I guess I kind of want you to know the truth and hear it from my mouth instead of, I dunno, letting your imagination run wild. And I kind of want to say it to remind myself of what's about to happen to me. What you might see. This is a start, I guess. He used to wear me down, you know? Ask questions and twist my answers, poke all these little holes until I was a wreck. Tired and hungry and hurting and miserable and hating myself. And then he'd make me do things, when I was impressionable like that. Sometimes he'd make me beg." He shuddered, pushed through the bathroom door.

Nate followed—strange and wrong to follow him into the bathroom, but it seemed rude *not* to when Mat was still talking to him, so he leaned uncomfortably in the doorway.

Mat unfolded a towel, left it on the toilet by the tub. "You know, Allen would call me Dog, but I felt even lower than that. They *kept* me lower than that."

Nate's brain short-circuited and spun, like a radio dumped into a tub of water and a bike with a broken chain all at once. "D-dehumanization," he said, not sure where he was going with it, whether he was going to cite the textbook at the guy or relate to him on some other personal level (as if Dr. Akers hadn't tried both a thousand times with Mat these last six weeks). Maybe mention all those thousands of little moments in his life where he'd been forced to feel less-than, inferior, ugly, better off dead. Not black enough to be black, not white enough to be white, not selfless or inspiring enough to be his father's son, not clever or wild enough to be his mother's. He wasn't about to rate a lifetime of racism against months-long sexual abuse and imprisonment, didn't want to compare, didn't want to spend one single ounce of energy on such terrible mathematics, but at least *he* was okay. At least he had a partner who respected him and parents who loved him and a lifetime of built-up coping strategies to help him get through the accumulated shit of it all. Mat had none of that. Nothing but Dr. Akers and fucking *Nate*.

"It's okay, you know," Mat said, giving the taps a crank. "You don't have to say anything." And then he did something strange. He laughed. A soft, fragile sound, but a laugh all the same. "You look just like people did after my parents died, wanting so bad to say something but coming up with nothing. Nothing's *okay*."

Nate nodded, relieved and numb all at the same time.

Mat stepped under the spray, still facing Nate. Tipped his head back, eyes closed, raked his hands through his hair and swore; the nail beds had healed weeks ago, but with only half a nail grown back, they were still sensitive to touch and heat. Looked creepy, too, but Nate kept his fucking mouth shut about that. Kept his mouth shut about Mat's looks in general, actually, even the complimentary stuff. Like how beautiful he was right then, with his body stretched out like that, lean muscles taut and rippling, water running down his smooth, pale skin.

Fuck.

"I, uh . . ." Nate shifted subtly, trying to put a stop to whatever ideas his cock was getting. "I should, uh . . ."

Mat paused in reaching for the soap, shook his head. "Stay," he said, and for a moment Nate wondered if he'd ask him to join him again, if the last six weeks of that awkward push-pull, that weird are-we-friends-or-are-we-colleagues-or-do-we-want-to-fuck-each-other-against-a-wall tension, would come back to bite them once more, leave him floundering for excuses about conflicts of interest and PTSD and white-knight syndrome and whatever else he'd been telling himself lately to get by. But then Mat added, softer, "Please. I need to get used to people looking at me. I can't be ashamed. I can't hide myself. Nothing."

Nate winced. "Is that the way I look at you? Like them?"

Mat shook his head. "No. You . . . sure, you see this"—he gestured to himself, up and down—"and maybe sometimes you want something, but you also see *me*. And if you *do* want something, you want it *with* me, not *from* me."

Nate nodded dumbly, felt the heat in his face. He didn't deserve the trust Mat gave him, not with his cock trying so very, very hard to spring out of his pants at the sight of Mat soaping himself up.

"Those people, they don't see me. They don't see a person at all. They don't apologize for anything. They don't feel guilt, or remorse, or any of it. Only entitlement. You'll see."

"I don't want you to do this," Nate blurted out before he could stop himself.

"I know. Me neither, for the record. But we both know it's the only way." He scrubbed at himself, then reached for a piece of tubing that hung limp from the faucet. Flipped a switch so that water sprayed from the hose's narrow metal nozzle. The shower shot—and God, it infuriated Nate that he'd had to learn what the damn thing was called, what it was for.

"We're not going to let it go that far," Nate snapped.

"So you say. But if it *does* go that far, I need to be ready. Everything needs to look normal. I need to look like a good slave." He swallowed hard, then focused on the task of adjusting the water pressure and temperature against the palm of his hand. "It's not that bad anyway. The least of my problems, to be honest."

He'd told Nate to watch, but Nate still turned away and shut his eyes when Mat reached behind himself.

A few moments later, the shower turned off. When Nate opened his eyes, Mat was already out of the tub and toweling off. Just when Nate let himself think things were safe again, Mat gestured to the toilet. "I gotta, um . . . the shower shot, you know?"

This time, Mat was blushing. So finishing the enema with an audience was one step too far for him. Which was exactly why Nate knew he *should* stay. His stomach roiled. He stayed glued to the spot, staring blankly at Mat, who blushed harder, then nodded and sat. They stared at each other wordlessly, both of them so deeply hating every moment of this . . . and then it was over. Mat wiped, flushed, and stood, still blushing all the way down his chest and to the tips of his ears, finished drying himself off, and silently followed Nate back into his former room.

Nate thought that would be the end of it, but it wasn't. Because Mat was still looking at him with that pained expression, needing something but hating that he had to ask for it. Hating that he had to ask *Nate* for it.

Nate took a step forward, cursing his stubborn erection. Then remembered this was exactly what Mat needed: to reacquaint himself with how it felt to be objectified, to have others be heedless of his personal space. Nate took another step. A final one, which left him mere inches from Mat's naked body. Raised a trembling hand and cupped Mat's cheek, wanting so badly to be *kind*, to be *good*, to have Mat want instead of hate this. Mat sucked in a breath at the contact, closed his eyes, went so still and rigid that Nate jerked his hand back.

"No," Mat said. "No. I need . . ."

Nate touched him again, the same as before, palm cupping his jaw, fingers in his damp hair. Allowed himself to pretend, for a moment, that they were lovers, that soon he'd be naked too and they'd be pleasuring each other, and let his thumb drift across Mat's plump lower lip. Mat's lips parted, and his tongue traced across the pad of Nate's thumb, shooting sparks straight to his chest and dick, pulling a little moan from his throat before he could stop it.

God help him, he wanted this so bad it hurt.

"You really still want me," Mat said, his voice strangely smooth.

"I went to every fight of yours I could. The after-parties, too, if they'd let me in. I had . . . a crush." *Still do,* he didn't let himself add.

Mat sighed, and his eyes fell closed. He murmured against Nate's thumb, "I don't know whether to be happy you remember me before all this, or sad because I'll never be that person again. Sad that one day you're going to realize that, and then you won't look at me this way anymore. Because you're a good guy."

"I don't feel like a good guy," Nate admitted. Case in point, his thumb stroked of its own volition over Mat's lips again, back and forth, back and forth, as if it could make up for what his own lips couldn't have. "And we've had this conversation already, Mat. I told you how I see you. I'm not naive, and this isn't hero worship. I've seen you at your lowest, and you know how you looked to me then? You know what I saw?"

Mat's teeth closed gently around his thumb, and when his eyes met Nate's, they were shining with unshed tears. *What?* that look asked—begged. *Tell me something I can live with.*

"The same fighter I always saw. But now, a hero too. The bravest fucking man I've ever known." He tugged his thumb free, moist now, and caressed Mat's lips again. "Beautiful inside and out, and not in spite of his scars, but *because* of them."

Mat blinked, and the tears in his eyes spilled down his cheeks. He seemed frozen, lips parted, chest still, and for a long moment Nate felt the same, like he couldn't even *breathe,* like if the molecules he was made of so much as vibrated too hard, he'd fall forward into Mat's lips and mesh together until they wouldn't know *how* to separate again.

And then Mat closed his eyes, and sighed a warm gust of air over Nate's thumb, and said, "Hit me."

Nate almost, *almost* fooled himself into thinking he'd said *kiss me.*

But only almost. "What?" he breathed.

Mat pulled back, just an inch or so, just enough to crack the glue that'd held Nate stuck in the moment. His face had hardened, jaw tense, lips pursed, but there was no mistaking the pain, the desperation in his eyes. The new tears waiting to be shed. He looked *wrecked.* "You heard me. Knock me down. Put me on the floor. *Hurt* me. I can't . . . I can't *have* this now, you understand me? I need . . ."

"I *can't*, Mat. I can't give you that. I can't cross that line with you."

"Damn it, Nate, this isn't fucking about you! Or your morals, or your lines, or any of that bullshit." He tugged at his hair in both fists. "It doesn't *matter* anymore, don't you get it? For the next few days, none of that matters. It *can't* matter, and I *need you to help me* remember that. I need this, okay? I *need* this."

When Nate did nothing—only stood there helplessly, like an idiot, mouth hanging open as his heart struggled to catch up to the truth he knew, in his head, that Mat was speaking—Mat shoved him. Hard, both hands to the chest, caught him by surprise and sent him on his ass.

"Fuck you," Mat growled. He took two steps forward, straddled Nate's hips and *loomed* there, looking ten feet tall. Looked like he was contemplating kicking Nate while he was down and only barely stopping himself. "You say you see the old me. You keep saying I'm a fighter, strong, but you treat me like I'm made of goddamned *glass*. You won't break me with a little push, Nate. You can't. I'm—" He spun abruptly, stalked over to the bed and sat down hard, dropped his face into both hands. "I'm already ground into fucking sand here, man. You can't break pieces. You just . . ." He tossed his hands, let them flop to the bed, curled his fingers into the blankets. Laughed a little, shook his head. "You just put them where you need them. Add a little water and build what fucking suits you until it gets washed away again."

God, what the fuck was he supposed to do with *that*? Nate sat up, climbed to his feet, nice and slow. Buying some time to fucking think. Approached Mat, just as slow, clasped a hand to his bare shoulder. Mat was tense, trembling, too hot. Wouldn't look at Nate. "It's okay to be afraid, you know," Nate tried. "That doesn't make you weak, or broken. Fuck knows I'm scared to fucking death, and I'm not the one in the line of fire."

Mat grew somehow even more tense beneath his hand, and for a moment Nate was sure he'd said the wrong thing, that Mat would shrug him off, shove him away again. But instead Mat's hands lifted to Nate's hips, tentative at first, trembling like the rest of him, then settled there, grasping firmly. And before Nate's body could begin to betray him and pop another boner, this one in Mat's face no less, Mat—much to Nate's horror—slid off the bed and onto his knees. His hands slid to Nate's thighs, and now his face really *was* level with Nate's crotch. He was so fucking close to it Nate could feel the heat of his breath through the fabric of his pants. No way Mat could miss his erection now. The urge to press forward that tiny little bit into Mat's waiting mouth . . .

"Stop this," he mumbled—to Mat or himself, he didn't know, but God, he fucking disgusted himself right now—at the same time his hands settled on either side of Mat's head. Mat sighed with relief. Not pleasure, just relief as Nate tightened his grip on Mat's hair.

"I'm not afraid," Mat said. "Well, no, I am afraid. I'm terrified. But I'm not afraid of *you*." He fought Nate's grip, and Nate didn't have it in him to stop Mat from moving, from pressing his face into Nate's thigh and nuzzling there, his cheek warm, his mouth a scant inch from Nate's straining dick. Mat's hands slid around to the backs of Nate's legs, pressed tight, almost but not quite touching Nate's ass.

Nate *burned*.

He couldn't take this. He couldn't fucking take it. But he wasn't pulling away, either, both hands sliding through Mat's hair, cupped against his head. He was . . . He was . . . oh God, babbling. "Is this . . . Is this practice, then? Is that—" Talking talking talking, like he'd done when he was a kid, too afraid to let on how out of his depth he was, hoping to fill the world with words even half as elegantly as Dad could.

"Yes and no," Mat replied. The words vibrated against Nate's groin, made him gasp, made his fingers tighten against Mat's skull. If he wasn't careful, he was going to mash his crotch right into Mat's face. Now *that* would be practice. "You're the safest person here to practice with, yeah, but I'm not going to pretend that's all this is."

"Mat . . ." Half-warning, half-begging. They couldn't do this. They couldn't have this. So many reasons why it was wrong. "We *talked* about this, remember? We can't—"

Mat's fingers dug into the backs of Nate's thighs, and when he shook his head, his nose brushed the very edge of Nate's straining cock. "No. Listen. *Please*."

"Do I have to listen with you . . ." Nate's voice cracked, and he trailed off. All the ways he could finish that sentence—*on your knees, naked, so vulnerable, your face in my dick, looking so fucking gorgeous*—and he couldn't say a single one of them.

Thank God, *thank God*, Mat pulled back a few inches. Tipped his head back and met Nate's eyes. He wasn't crying anymore, and the hardness was gone, and the neediness there, the desperation on his face, could almost be mistaken for real arousal. Fuck, it probably was, and that was the worst part of all of this. "I know this isn't . . ." Mat blinked, sank his teeth into his lower lip, hesitated a long moment. ". . . *real*," he finally said, and it looked like it hurt Mat as much to say it as it hurt Nate to hear it, to have to admit the truth of it. "But it's . . . *you* are . . ." He averted his eyes, tipped his chin back down. ". . . good, you know? You're a *good memory* in a sea of flaming shit. Even in this horrible fucking room, you're like an oasis. I literally feel like we're somewhere else, or like this room doesn't have the same power anymore, and I . . . I'm gonna *need* that, okay? When I'm—When I'm on my knees at *Allen's* feet and he's not gentle or kind or calling me a fucking hero, I'm gonna need to open my mouth and be his fuckdoll, and I feel like maybe if I do this with you, here, now, maybe I'll have something to keep me from fucking up the whole operation, or hell, from completely losing my*self*."

Fuckdoll. "You're not just some slave to me," Nate said. Wanted to keep repeating it over and over again, until it had Mat shedding his skin like a snake and becoming the man Nate knew he was beyond all this. And partially wanted to say it to absolve himself of the guilt he felt for wanting this as much as he did.

The tears were back in Mat's eyes, and Nate could feel his own welling up too. Mat blinked them away, pressed his forehead to Nate's thigh, nodded his head. "I know. And that's why . . . that's why I need this so badly, you know?" He looked up again, blushing fiercely, both hands clinging hard to Nate's pants. "Something good to hold on to, to . . . to pretend it's not Allen, to be . . . *transported* again."

Fuck. *Fuck*. Nate's hands settled on either side of Mat's face, thumbs stroking twin lines beneath his eyes, wiping away the stray moisture there. The urge to kiss him, to sweep him up into his arms and hold him so tight they'd both forget *how* to let go, was back again stronger than ever. This situation . . . everything was so fucked up, so wrong he didn't know where to begin. But they were stuck with it, weren't they, and if he could give Mat some comfort, *any* comfort at all, help him through it even *this* way . . . well, who was he to deny Mat that? It wasn't like his body wasn't with the program, anyway. And so what if he felt dirty, disgusting, lecherous, and opportunistic? So what if every time Mat looked at him from here on out, he'd see just another pervert, just another man who'd used him? Wasn't that a small price to pay to ease Mat's pain?

"Okay," he whispered. His voice cracked, so he cleared his throat, tried again. His thumbs were still stroking, stroking across Mat's face. "Okay."

Mat's shoulders slumped. Not disappointment. Relief. "Thank you. Thank you, thank you, thank you . . ." He leaned forward, murmuring under his breath still, *thank you thank you thank you* over and over again as he kissed the hard line of Nate's dick through the fabric of his pants.

God, Nate wanted him. Wanted him so bad he couldn't even summon up the self-hatred anymore when Mat drew his zipper down. "Mat," he moaned softly, because Mat needed to hear it, needed to hear his name and know that that was how Nate saw him, and always would: as a person, not a fucktoy, not a dog, not a hole. "Mat, Mat—"

"Nate! Agent Johnson!" Nate startled so hard at Louise's voice calling down the stairs that he almost tripped over his own feet. "Did you find Mat? We're gonna miss our flight!"

"Plane's private, it's not leaving without us!" Nate called back, and Mat was still on his knees, hands still braced on Nate's thighs, looking up at him with a mixture of wanting and panic, as if he'd only now realized that they weren't alone, that someone might walk in on them . . . Fuck, *Nate* had only now realized that, what with all the blood having fled his brain since the moment he'd walked into this room. "We'll be right up!"

Fuck. He couldn't decide if Louise had the best or worst possible timing in the whole fucking world. He sure as shit knew what his cock thought, but the rest of him was iffy.

Mat huffed what might've been a laugh or a sigh, Nate couldn't tell, and then shook his head, lips twisted into an expression as confused as the sound he'd just made. He gave Nate's fabric-covered cock one last squeeze—Nate moaned, half-broken, knees almost buckling—and then zipped Nate back up. No easy feat, the way his dick was trying so hard to escape. Everyone would notice if he couldn't get himself back under control, and *fast.*

Just think of Allen standing where you are.

Oh yeah, that did the trick right quick.

Mat had climbed to his feet while Nate was scolding his dick, and was pulling on his comfort clothes—that worn gray hoodie, those old track pants. He wouldn't have to go naked until they reached the docks to Allen's. Didn't need to be cuffed, either—trained pets could travel off leash, after all.

He wasn't, Nate noticed, so much as a little, tiny bit hard. Probably hadn't been this entire time. Which made Nate's own dick lose interest even faster than thoughts of Allen raping Mat's throat. Nate had wanted this so, so badly, had even convinced himself it was a good thing, the *right* thing, while Mat . . . Mat had only been doing what he'd needed to survive.

Just like always.

THE FLESH CARTEL

SEASON 5: RECLAMATION

EPISODE 16: TO THE VICTOR

CHAPTER ONE

Douglas had never thought he'd see the day when he missed that cum-soaked, glitter-stained little bunk room full of mean, spoiled pets. Yet here he was, dreaming of one way after another to earn his ticket back there. Bargain after bargain, an endless list of pleasures and promises, each one as ignored as the last. Allen didn't care what Douglas could do, what he could offer, how much of himself he was willing to give. Allen only cared about what he could *take*.

And he was painfully, terrifyingly good at taking.

At first, Douglas had thought the worst of what Allen had ripped away was Penny. Nikolai too, of course, but that didn't count, not really, not when he'd been trained to leave the nest from day one. But Penny . . . she'd fit into his world, his duties, his purpose. Brought light and love and laughter, joy and passion. Just like Nikolai had. And now they were both gone.

But it didn't take long for Douglas to remember that, in the right hands, the body could be made to suffer just as much as the heart.

And worse, *his* body was being used to make Nikolai suffer, too. Douglas was no fool. He knew why Allen was taking all those photos. He tried to be strong, be brave, not scream or flash his teeth or let the tears fall, not huddle in his chains, trembling like a beaten dog every time Allen drew near.

He tried to be Nikolai's brave boy.

But the truth was that he'd *never* been very brave, and he'd been sure, *so sure*, that his days of suffering were long behind him. It wasn't *his* job to suffer—that was *Mat's* job. But the cowardly dog had run off with its tail between its legs and left its responsibilities in Douglas's lap.

Well, maybe that's what Douglas deserved for letting the dog off its chain in the first place. He'd been selfish to do it, thinking of himself, his own needs, his own desires. Thinking of Nikolai, instead of what Nikolai had taught him.

And look at him now.

He deserved this, but that didn't mean he wasn't going to keep begging for it to stop. He wasn't strong enough not to.

Beg Allen for relief. And then, in the darkness, when he was alone with his pain and suffering, beg Nikolai to save him. Pray to him, like the remote and unhearing god he was.

A knock sounded at Mat's door, startling him out of a decidedly unpleasant daydream. The hall door, not the one adjoining Nate's room. He stood, contemplated the robe tossed across the bed, but . . . no. The FBI had booked every room on the hotel's keycard access–only top floor and told the maids they wouldn't be needed today, which meant his visitor was most likely an agent. In ten minutes he'd be naked and giving a lecture to a whole room full of agents, some of whom would be naked themselves. Best to get used to it now.

The room was comfortably warm—he'd pushed the heat up before he'd stripped—but his bare skin still pebbled as another knock sounded. He stood, sighed, scraped a hand through his hair. He could do this. He *could*.

"Mat? It's me. Can I, um . . . is it okay if I come in?"

Just Roger. Mat's pounding heart settled, but he still checked through the peephole before undoing the security chain and dead bolt and opening the door.

"Just" Roger, like the man wasn't Nikolai's right hand.

Roger didn't give Mat's nudity a second glance as he took the invitation to come inside. He'd spent months seeing it every day, after all. Mat nearly even felt comfortable like this in front of the man, though it wasn't without bitterness that he noted Roger's fitted gray slacks, fitted baby-blue shirt, only hint of skin at the throat where a single undone button showed a tantalizing flash of collarbone.

Roger hovered beside the bed until Mat waved permission for him to sit. Mat's instinct was to pull up the desk chair for himself, but he made himself sit beside Roger instead. Something in him demanded he be kind and sensitive to Roger—gentle. But when too many seconds ticked by in silence, Roger staring at his hands fidgeting in his lap, jaw muscles working, Mat finally overcame his scruples and spat out, "Why are you here?"

And then immediately, irrationally felt sorry for it. Roger hunched in on himself, like he expected Mat to strike him. He looked so fucking miserable Mat seriously thought about hugging him.

"Sorry," Mat said. A reasonable compromise. "I'm sorry, I just . . ."

Roger nodded. "Yeah, me too." At last he looked up from his lap, met Mat's eyes. "I just . . . when we have Douglas back, when this is over, what . . ." His gaze drifted back to his hands again, to his fingers worrying the fine cloth of his slacks. "They won't let us go back, will they? What's going to happen to us? To Nikolai? To . . . to me?"

Again he met Mat's eyes, and this time, Mat's breath caught. The poor guy looked so fucking *guilty*, like asking after his own fate was somehow unbearably selfish, like he wasn't entitled to know.

Mat laid his hand atop Roger's, stilling the restless fingers with a squeeze. "I don't know, really. There'll be an investigation. Trials. I don't think they'll send you to jail since you're a victim too, but a psychiatric facility, maybe, where they can help you get your life back. Didn't they talk to you about this?"

Roger nodded, bottom lip caught between his teeth, green eyes bright with nerves and fear and maybe just a touch of hope. "My life?" He huffed, not quite a laugh, too needy and desperate for that. "Will Nikolai be there too, then?"

"You don't—" Roger flinched, and Mat realized he'd just crushed the poor guy's hand. He made himself unclench, brushed his thumb over Roger's wrist. "Nikolai *isn't* your life, Roger."

The *fear* in Roger's eyes when he said that . . . So wide, so lost, like a wounded baby animal. Half of Mat wanted to pull him into a hug again. The other half wanted to shake him until his teeth rattled, until he remembered how to be *human*.

And Roger must've seen that frustration, that anger in Mat's face, because he pulled his hand back, hunched his shoulders, asked, painfully soft, "Do you hate me?"

"No," Mat said, just as soft. Except, it wasn't really as simple as that, was it? Roger had *done things*. So many things, every last one of which should've been unforgivable. Mat shook his head as images flashed in his mind: Roger aiding Nikolai in branding him. Roger turning around in the driver's seat of what should've been their salvation and shooting Mat with a tranq dart. Roger giving him the serum. Giving *Dougie* the serum, even as Mat begged him not to. "I don't know," he amended. "Maybe?" Yet he winced at Roger's flinch, at the obvious pain it brought Roger to hear that harsh truth.

But Mat's confusion was evidence that it wasn't the *whole* truth.

He reached out, took Roger's hand again in both his own. So gentle. He realized he didn't want to hurt Roger. Not even a little. Ducked his head to catch Roger's gaze. Held that, too. "I mean look, you saved my life, you know? That day you came in and found me on that chair . . ." He had to stop, swallow. That long-ago moment of weakness still flushed him with shame. "I was ready. I was gonna do it, I really was."

Roger's free hand brushed Mat's cheek, and Mat closed his eyes, leaned into the touch. Let himself have that, just for the moment. Even from Roger. "I'm glad you didn't," Roger said. "Even if you do maybe hate me."

The joke Roger tried to turn that into fell very, very flat. No mistaking the man's pain for anything but what it was. Mat squeezed his hand again, looked him in the eye. "I know you think your world's ending, Roger. But you gotta listen to me. You're *wrong*. You're gonna go check in to a hospital, *away from Nikolai*, and they're going to get you therapy, and you're going to realize there's a whole world out there, and that you can have a life beyond all this. Trust me, I was there. Even if it was just a ruse, I spent a couple weeks in care and it did me a hell of a lot of good. I can only imagine how much better it would be if I was there for real. If people were treating me for what happened here, instead of for paranoid delusions." Mat's heart thumped in his chest, in his pulse points, at the realization. Being in that facility . . . it had helped. It had really helped. It could help again. There was a way past all this. If he believed Roger could eventually get better—even after decades of brainwashing and abuse—then he had to believe he could get better, too.

And just as importantly, so could Dougie.

Hope. He'd forgotten what hope felt like.

Like power. Energy. Happiness, even.

He pulled Roger into a tight, fierce hug.

"I'm scared," Roger whispered against the bare skin of Mat's shoulder.

"That's okay," Mat said, and squeezed tighter. "That's normal. I'm scared too. We can be scared together, okay?"

Roger shuddered silently against him for a moment, then mumbled, "Twenty-six years, you know?"

Mat did know.

"I was only eighteen."

Mat rubbed slow, firm circles on his back. "And you wanted to be a cop, remember? You wanted to go to school and earn a badge and stop people like Nikolai from hurting people like you, like Dougie."

"No, that's not—" Roger stiffened, tried to pull away, but Mat didn't let him. Just kept holding him, kept rubbing circles on his back.

"*Yes.* What Nikolai did to you was just as bad—worse, even—than what your dad did when you were younger. You were determined then not to be powerless anymore, Roger, do you remember? You don't have to be powerless anymore now, either."

And neither did Mat. Neither did Dougie. They'd end this. Put it behind them. Pick up where they'd left off. Dougie would go back to school. And Mat . . .

Mat wasn't sure what would become of him, but it had to be better than this.

Roger stayed still in his arms, not relaxing against him, but not pulling away, either. Giving in, then. Not accepting the truth, just avoiding conflict. Being a good slave.

So he didn't believe Mat yet about what Nikolai had done and how wrong it was. That was okay; Mat couldn't hope to undo twenty-six years of brainwashing in one conversation. He cleared his throat. "Look, forget the future. Let's focus on the now. You want to rescue Dougie from Allen, right?"

Roger nodded. He cared about Dougie. That was real. For now, it was enough.

Mat pressed their foreheads together in a show of strangely brotherly affection and solidarity. "So let's go get him back from that sicko."

Douglas yelped, his entire body bucking, but with straps at his wrists and ankles and waist all affixed to an unmoving wooden structure, there was nowhere for him to go.

Not that he didn't already know that after what seemed like hours of being bound and beaten.

Behind him, Allen was panting heavily, which meant the pain would ease now, for a couple of minutes at least. Not stop—it never stopped. Even his splinted fingers, broken what seemed like weeks ago, still throbbed above the restraints. But for a little while, Douglas would get to have awareness outside the pain.

Which wasn't as uncomplicatedly good as it sounded, because it meant Allen would start asking the questions that Douglas's life depended on him not answering. *Where did the dog go? How did he escape? What happened to the man you were with?* Those same questions, over and over again.

A deceptively tender hand cupped Douglas's sweat-drenched skin where his neck met his shoulder. "Why do you make me do this?" Allen—not his master; this violent brute didn't deserve to be called his master anymore—puffed. "Nikolai wants you back, you know that, don't you? All you have to do is tell me the truth, and I'll give you back."

Lies. All lies. If Douglas admitted to helping Mat, to standing by and watching Mat throw that horrible client overboard, he'd never be allowed to go back to Nikolai. Allen would want to punish him, and Douglas had no idea how much worse things would get then. Which was a terrifying prospect, because they were already so very terrible.

Permanent damage, maybe. His teeth. His balls. His eyes. His tongue. Allen would rip him apart, and Nikolai wouldn't be able to stop it.

He couldn't fall for Allen's ploy. Allen had nothing to offer him. Only Nikolai.

Nikolai. He had to survive this so Nikolai could bring him . . . back. Home.

He had to wait on Nikolai.

He suffered every moment of it.

"I already told you, Master. Mat knocked me out. You saw—you *saw*." He let the pain, the fear, the desperation bleed into his voice. He told himself he did it because Allen loved to hear it, and not because those feelings were genuinely all that he had left. He couldn't even remember what Nikolai's love felt like, not anymore. Could barely remember how it felt to hope that he might feel it again, might feel anything but Allen's endless tortures. "He hit me and I passed out and that was it, I don't know what happened, I woke up and you were there and they were gone and you know the rest."

The gentle hand *tightened.*

Douglas cried out.

"Lies," Allen whispered in his ear, voice still ragged, and then he pulled back, and the short whip thudded into the sorest part of Douglas's back. "Lies! Lies, lies, lies!" He punctuated his words with more hits, clumsy and uneven, nothing like Nikolai's calm, measured strikes.

Angry. Allen was always angry.

That was okay, because Douglas was fucking angry too. He was tired of hurting for no reason. Tired of paying for Mathias's "crimes"—if it even was a crime to want to get away from a monster like Allen. Douglas wasn't sure anymore. Wasn't sure if a slave's undying loyalty ought to be pledged to a petty tyrant who didn't care. Who didn't guide or protect or care for, only used and hurt.

Does Nikolai deserve your loyalty, then?

Mat. That was Mat's voice, not Douglas's.

He was cracking.

Yes. Even if Nikolai abandoned me here. Even if he's watched me suffer all this time and never come to help me and take me back by force. His hands are tied. He wouldn't leave me if he had a choice.

Mat had tried to save him even with his hands tied. *No matter what.*

Douglas squeezed his eyes shut, for the first time wishing that he could block out what was in his mind instead of the pain in his body. He'd take the pain gladly if it would silence this doubt.

But Allen had stopped hitting him. Had disappeared altogether. Douglas couldn't hear him breathing. Was it over for today, then? Except . . . Allen hadn't taken a picture yet. That wasn't right. That didn't follow the pattern. Questions. Abuse. Questions. Abuse. Picture. And then Douglas would be left, either to hang in pain, or to be used by Allen's household—never Penny, her touch was nothing but a memory now, as faint and distant as Nikolai's—or to the merciless punishment of a fucking machine.

No matter how harried and frustrated Allen got, no matter how sloppy, he *never* forgot the picture.

Which meant . . . this wasn't over.

And it wasn't. A moment later, the door to Allen's little torture chamber opened again. This time, though, Douglas couldn't hear Allen's panting because it was drowned out by louder noises.

Dog noises.

What did it say about Douglas that his first reaction to that wasn't fear or panic or revulsion—*he's going to have that thing tear me apart or fuck me*—it was . . . exasperation?

Before he knew what was happening to him, he started to laugh. A hoarse, embittered sound. Just like Mat.

Well, why not? Allen had certainly been treating him like Mat for long enough.

"What the—" The dog must have jerked on its leash then, cutting Allen off. "—fuck are you laughing at, you stupid cunt? Have you finally lost your fucking mind?"

"I'm just thinking how, if you make that dog fuck me, it'll probably be a better lay than *you.*" Douglas laughed again. "You're pathetic. No master at all. That's why Mat ran away. You don't deserve to master us, any of us, not even him."

"You— How fucking *dare* you? I should have your tongue cut out for speaking to me that way!"

Douglas laughed again, harder, hard enough to bring tears to his eyes. His back hurt and his ribs hurt and his arms and his fucking *everything* hurt and Allen was going to make it all a thousand times worse in a minute and he *couldn't stop laughing. Hysterical,* some part of himself whispered, but the pain-mad part of him just barreled on, harnessing the strength this anger lent him. "You should, but you won't! Because you need to keep me intact, don't you? In order to get Mathias back you need to keep me whole. You think you're the master here, but Nikolai fucking *owns* you."

"You think you're so precious!" Allen sputtered back, and the dog barked and snarled, but he didn't let it off the leash. Couldn't.

Douglas was right, Allen was keeping him whole. All this torture, all of it designed to hurt but never damage him too much. A fine line, and a brute like Allen must be *drowning* in fear to still be able to toe it. "So sure of yourself. So sure of Nikolai. You think he's better than me? That prissy fag in his fancy suits with his slutty manservant?"

Projecting. He's projecting. That whole thing he has about punishing slaves, dressing all his toys up like girls, he's drowning in internalized homophobia. He can't stand Nikolai because Nikolai is the person he wishes he could be.

Where the fuck had that come from? That was . . . that . . .

Allen's voice was bordering on hysteria. "You think he's so fucking special? That he cares about you so fucking much? Well then why isn't he here, huh? He dragged Mathias back in four weeks ago, did you know that?"

Four *weeks*? No. Not possible. No way. That was an entire extra month of terrible photos. A month of unimaginable suffering for Douglas. A month of fucking machines and whips and electroshock and waterboarding while being used by twenty guys in a single night.

Allen laughed. "Yeah, that's right, pup. He's had him this whole time. Could have brought him to me right then and there but gave me some bullshit instead about how he needs to 'reeducate' the dumb beast."

No, not bullshit. Mat had escaped once. He'd do it again if Nikolai didn't lay down the law. That took time. Douglas knew that. He *knew* that. Even if it did mean leaving him here at Allen's mercy.

"If he's so good at remaking people, how come it's taking him so long? You'd think he'd put a rush job on it considering I've been sending him horrible pictures of his favorite little slave every single day. Unless . . . you aren't his favorite? Maybe you're just a meal ticket like all the others, huh? Maybe his reputation's more important to him than you are. Or maybe he's not as good at *training* people as you think. Which is it, cunt? Is your precious Nikolai incompetent, or does he just not give a shit about you?"

Don't engage him. That's what he wants. Nikolai doesn't need you to defend him.

The next voice in his head wasn't his: *He doesn't need you at all.*

Shut up, Mat, shut up*!*

"It takes time!" Douglas roared. "It fucking takes time to break someone. Any tin-pot dictator could tell you that. In fact, why don't you ask one, since they make up your entire social group?"

Allen *tsk*ed. "*Break* someone, Douglas? I thought Nikolai was above all that barbarism."

"Just dumbing it down so a brute like you can understand it," Douglas bit out.

And then froze, because it wasn't true. Not remotely true. Allen had said "reeducate." That word, *break*, had come from Douglas alone. From Mat's fucking voice in his fucking head.

Nikolai broke you.

Transformed me, Douglas countered, but it was weak. He was arguing with his own head and he was fucking *losing*.

Brainwashed you. Lied to you. Never loved you. Isn't coming for you, not until he can profit from it.

You're nothing to him but a paycheck.

He didn't transform you with his love. He devoured *you.*

"Stop it!" Douglas screamed. The dog barked; Allen laughed. "Stop it, stop it, stop it!"

"He's not coming for you, cunt. This is the rest of your life. Your future. You want off that cross? You tell me what you and your little bitch brother did to my client."

He should've jumped. Should've gone with Mat. Maybe his brother didn't love him either, didn't really give a fuck about him, but in freeing himself, Mat would have freed Douglas too. Brought him along, if only for the future meal ticket. Just like Nikolai.

Or maybe he always loved you and it was all a l—

No. Douglas wasn't going there. Couldn't handle any more fucking *revelations* today. Didn't know what to believe in any case. All he knew for certain was that Allen was the enemy.

"I'm not telling you *shit*, jackoff. Do your fucking worst." *I've got nothing left to live for.* But when he spoke, it was Mat who spoke through him. "As far as you're concerned, I'm fucking invincible."

His hit landed. He knew it, because Allen was silent, and he kept the dog back.

The dog, who seemed scary, but couldn't be allowed to maul him.

So why didn't Douglas feel as confident as Mat's words had made him sound?

Oh yeah, he thought as Allen dragged him off the wooden X and down the hall to the room with the fucking machine. *Because Mat had nothing. No hope. No future. No greater purpose. Nothing but misery and suffering.* It was easy to be confident when you had nothing to lose.

But *did* he have nothing to lose? Or was Nikolai still waiting for him? Maybe he still had a future, and that was why fresh defiance died uneasy in his throat.

Or maybe there was no hope after all, no future but this, and Douglas was just a coward. Unlike Mat, he still feared pain. Feared it so very, very much.

Allen strapped him in face-first with some toothless barb about how he was going to shut Douglas's yappy mouth one way or another and leave his sloppy cunt free for every cock on the island to ride tonight. A monstrously fat dildo shoved past his teeth and halfway down his throat. He gagged, choked, for the first time in months had to suppress the urge to puke.

After all, just because you've got nothing left to live for doesn't mean you get to die. And if you're not dead, you can still suffer.

The dildo pulled out with a mechanical whirr, too slow, not far enough. Pushed back in. More gagging. Ropes of spit lashed down his chin and tears streamed from his clenched eyes. He *couldn't breathe.* It hurt. Worse than the waterboarding.

And with nothing and no one left to live for, there's no refuge from this pain. No Nikolai in shining armor. No Mat begrudgingly looking out for me.

He'd lost. Everything.

CHAPTER TWO

"No matter what," Mat whispered to himself in the mirror, his expression determined.

"What?" Nate asked softly.

Mat startled. Caught Nate's reflection and flushed. "Oh, uh, nothing. Is it time?"

"Yeah. Final check to make sure the Nude Crew is gonna pass muster. Nikolai's doing the inspection." His nose wrinkled in disgust.

Mat had spent so much of the last few days naked that he'd nearly forgotten he was flapping in the breeze; he was *more* than ready. The undercover agents who'd volunteered had all done the same, but then, they didn't have Mat's history. He could only teach them so much. What if someone slipped up?

Then their "master" will beat them, just like they all agreed. It'll be fine. Everything'll be just fine.

Mat swallowed, fell into step two paces behind Nate before he'd even realized he was doing so. He tried to take that as a good thing, as much as it disgusted him on a visceral level.

There were five agents posing as slaves, who'd secure the house from the inside during the raid. Fifteen agents posing as free men and women, some as slave owners and others as rich assholes eager to bet on the big fight, who'd secure the crowded arena. Nikolai had planned a massive party for Allen to host. Had invited a whole slew of his contacts within the Cartel and promised Allen a fiercely obedient Mat who would gladly fight to the death on command . . . but only after Douglas was back at his side.

It wouldn't get to the fight. That was the plan. They'd play their parts long enough for Douglas to make it out of Allen's clutches, and then they'd spring the trap. Twenty agents versus however many of Allen and Nikolai's combined guests. Backup coming in James Bond–style by scuba-suit to smuggle in weapons and neutralize the island's security.

As they slipped into the top floor's massive meeting room, where the five "slave" agents knelt too-awkwardly naked by their "owners'" sides, Mat couldn't help but be grateful Nate had finally given up on volunteering to join them. Whatever this . . . *thing* was between them, whatever it could or couldn't ever be, at least Nate would never really have to *know* what it was like to be on his knees at someone else's feet.

Mat gave the volunteers a long, slow once-over. He'd seen them all before—three women, two men, all as beautiful and believable as Louise and Nate when Mat had first met them—but this was their last chance to make the sell. They had to be perfect. Nikolai and Roger would be arriving any minute now to cast final judgments; Mat tried to see the volunteers through Nikolai's discerning eye.

"I could make magic with this lot, given time," Nikolai said from the doorway.

Mat jumped. Very deliberately didn't turn around to meet Nikolai's eyes. "Fuck you," he said—rote now, no real heat behind it, the ever-present anger banked. "No more *magic* for you. Just do your damn job."

Nikolai pressed into the room, commanding, magnetic, Roger dressed pin neat walking two paces behind him. The slave-agents' eyes all dropped to Nikolai's feet. Good.

He approached the men first. One was older, mid-thirties maybe, brown hair, beautiful hazel eyes. Skin was questionable, though; the makeup had covered at least one tattoo so well it was like it'd never existed, but there was nothing to be done for a collection of scars that spoke of years of messy combat. Mat would've nixed him on that alone if he weren't so damn attractive despite it, body lean and muscled, face an envious mix of pretty-yet-masculine. He was kneeling at the feet of a giant of a man—not so bad looking himself with his muscular build and gently curling dark hair—radiating quiet menace, but that didn't stop Nikolai from trailing fingers across the slave-agent's shoulder, chest, up his throat to grip his chin and tilt his head back.

"Lot of scars on this one," Nikolai said. The big man somehow bristled even more. Unless they were the best fucking actors in the world, he and his "slave" were close friends at the very least. "Tyler, is it? Does your master need to punish you so cruelly and often?"

Just rehearsal, Mat reminded himself. *It's a fair question.* But fucking damn, did Nikolai have to sound so fucking pleased to be asking it?

Tyler somehow managed to avert his eyes despite Nikolai forcing his head up. Good—this guy just might be able to pull it off. "It's from before, sir. My master saved my life, gave it meaning." And oh, the way Tyler gazed into the big man's eyes at that, the way the big man gazed back... if that was acting, they deserved a fucking Emmy. "I never give him cause to punish me, sir."

"If I commanded you to suck my cock right now, would you?" Nikolai asked, his voice dripping with gleeful pleasure.

Tyler nodded in the confines of Nikolai's grip. "If it pleases Master, sir."

The big man was growling, "It does *not* please Master," before Tyler had even finished his sentence.

Nate cleared his throat. "Easy, Zane. But good. That's good—you're doing great, Ty. We're going to do our best to keep everyone out of any X-rated situations, but there's no guarantees. We don't expect anyone to touch the . . ." His voice wavered. He cleared his throat, took a breath to try again.

"The slaves," Louise finished confidently, relieving Nate without commenting on his obvious discomfort. "Not without their master's permission, and we're going to try our damnedest to make sure that permission isn't granted, but if it *is* the only way to keep from compromising your cover..."

"You need to be ready for anything," Mat added, even though they'd all had this conversation what felt like a million times already. Couldn't be stressed enough, as far as he was concerned; these people had *no* idea what they were getting themselves into. "You can't flinch. You can't hesitate. You can't look disgusted at what people are doing or making one another do. And trust me when I say it can get pretty fucking horrible."

Nikolai's hand landed hard on Mat's bare shoulder, pressing down. *Lead by example, I suppose.* Mat sank to his knees at Nikolai's feet, in perfect position, and though his stomach was threatening to leap out through his throat, he somehow managed to keep his face blank, his jaw unclenched.

Nikolai's hand slid into his hair, deceptively gentle for a moment before forming a fist, yanking Mat's head back. "A demonstration, then?" he asked. "To test their readiness?"

Oh God. He'd . . . he'd known this was going to happen, he'd *known* it, and yet—

"Touch him again before we're on that island," Nate growled, "and I'll break every fucking one of the twenty-seven bones in your hand." He hadn't drawn his gun, but his hand was hovering.

Nikolai demurred with grace and humor, showing his palms in a gesture of surrender and smiling ever so slightly. The fucker. "Shall I continue my rounds, then?" he asked.

Nate's jaw twitched, but he nodded. Nikolai approached the other man—Hollywood pretty, young, probably hadn't been an agent for more than a couple years. He "belonged" to a couple perhaps ten years older than he was—well, probably not a real couple, but they certainly seemed comfortable enough around each other so the cover story fit—and boy, was he selling the meek, trembling slave thing. Maybe a little too well. Nikolai cupped his cheek, drawing out a nauseous moan, and moved on to the next in line.

She was beautiful too, of course she was: black curly hair no thicker than a layer of peach fuzz atop her perfectly shaped head, skin dark enough that her teeth shone by contrast when she offered Nikolai a demure smile. Nikolai smiled back, squatted in front of her, cupped her shoulder and ran his hand down to the tips of her fingers where they rested on her thigh.

"Show me your foot, darling," he practically purred, and Mat wanted to fucking hurl again, but the slave just shifted from kneeling to sitting—elegantly as fuck, at that, like a dancer or a gymnast—and extended one foot toward Nikolai's waiting hand, toes pointed for maximum grace.

Mat snuck a glance at her "owner," and saw nothing but pride on the man's face: *Isn't my pet perfect?* Thank God; they wouldn't be able to get away with too many possessive, angry masters. With the tendencies toward voyeurism among the sick slave-owning set, a universally hands-off attitude toward the slaves would give them away for sure.

Nikolai cradled her heel in one hand, stroked her smooth calf with the other as he tipped her leg up to expose the sole of her foot. His wandering fingers left her calf to trace the fake brand. The makeup was incredible. Even Nikolai looked impressed, letting out a low whistle. "And you're certain it won't come off as they walk?" he asked no one in particular.

"Not even in the water," Louise said. "Not even if someone gives them a foot massage. That shit ain't coming off until the layer of skin it's attached to does."

Nate coughed. "There's also a removal spray the FX people provided."

Mat wished they could use that on *him*.

"Too bad. I'd have enjoyed seeing who was dedicated enough to allow me to brand them for real."

You're on your knees. You're in character. Don't rise to the bait. Mat stayed still. Even when Nikolai laid the slave's foot in his lap, square up against his crotch—her bare toes curled in teasingly, God, she was *perfect*—and ran his hand up the inside of her thigh. Her pubic hair had been trimmed into a heart shape, her labia pierced with a gold ring Mat suspected had been there long before she'd volunteered for this job. When Nikolai's fingers neared it and she parted her thighs, Mat half expected her owner to say something, or at least for *Nate* to say something, but they all stayed still, watching, collective breaths held.

"My my my," Nikolai said, voice tinged with a touch of huskiness. "Such enthusiasm, my dear. But I don't swing that way."

She smiled, baring her teeth, and all her sultry flirtatiousness vanished in a blink. The foot curled in Nikolai's crotch pressed in hard enough to make him gasp and flinch away. "Neither do I, resident expert pervert. But I *did* minor in theater. And I'd suck even your fugly-ass cock if it means I get to bring your world crashing down around your ears."

Said ears might've been turning just a tiny bit pink, but Mat didn't let himself grin at that. Couldn't, not until this was over.

Besides, Nikolai recovered his composure awfully fast. He stood, brushed the wrinkles out of his pants. Rather than moving on to the next two slave-agents, though, he turned back to the man he'd passed by before. "And you?" he asked. "Would *you* suck my cock?"

The man turned his gaze to the floor, throat working, no answer coming out. The couple behind him shifted uneasily; the woman laid a reassuring hand on his shoulder. "I . . ." he began, then stopped again. His fingers curled against his thighs, trembling. Nikolai's leering grin turned into an outright sneer. "I, uh . . ."

This wasn't going to work. Not this guy. He'd ruin everything. Even if he didn't blow their cover, Allen and his guests would smell his fear like blood in the water, and it'd be open season. He'd be ripped to shreds.

Nate must've seen it too, because he put himself between the guy and Nikolai, squatted down to eye level, and said, "Hey, it's okay. This is so fucking above and beyond, man . . . you don't have to do this."

"I . . ." The guy looked past Nate's shoulder, up at Nikolai, and practically turned green. "I have to. I have to do this. If I don't, who will?"

Nate grabbed him by both shoulders, and shifted to block Nikolai from view. "I will."

"No!" Mat shouted. Fuck staying in character. Fuck playing the perfect slave and setting an example. "Nate, no!"

Nate rounded on Mat, still grasping the young agent with one hand, the other pointed angrily at Mat's face. "Mat Carmichael, you are an important part of this mission, but you are *not* in charge of it."

Fuck that. *Fuck* Nate scolding him like some fucking *child*. He shoved to his feet, shoved *Nate*, hard enough to send him stumbling back. Followed it up with a pointed finger to the chest. "You gonna go without me, huh? How'll *that* go over?"

"You'd give up on saving your brother just to one-up me?" Nate shot back.

"I'm trying to *protect* you!"

Silence. Awkward, heavy, cricket-chirping silence, broken only by Mat's and Nate's harsh breathing. Mat realized everyone was staring at them. Realized what he'd just done, what he'd just implied: those five volunteers . . . *they* were disposable enough to be fed into the meat grinder, but not Nate? Why had he *said* that?

He swallowed. Averted his eyes. He was the one who'd fucked up; he was the one who should look away first. "I'm sorry," he whispered. Cleared his throat, said, "I'm sorry," again, stronger now. Not just to Nate, but to those other brave agents, naked on their knees with fake brands on the soles of their feet. "I didn't mean . . ."

Jesus fuck, what a mess. Tears burned his eyes, the back of his throat. He was such a fucking *mess*.

"Now there's an interesting development," Nikolai said, smug.

Nate jabbed a finger at him. "You shut the fuck up." He turned back to the kneeling, pale-faced agent. "Louise, take Williams back to his room so he can take a hot shower or get dressed or raid his minibar. Whatever he needs." And then he reached for the buttons at the collar of his pale blue dress shirt. He undid them, adding, "And get that makeup artist in here to do my foot. I'll be going in his place."

Nikolai chuckled.

Mat blinked away the hot tears in his eyes and lowered himself back to his knees.

CHAPTER THREE

Nate fucking hated the water. Being buck-ass naked on an impounded craft purchased with the spoils of the heroin trade didn't exactly make it any more appealing. Having no place to hide a weapon was just the sugar-free icing on the shit cake—though Ty had not-so-jokingly suggested a few ideas in that regard.

Yeah, no. He'd pass.

Mat paced the deck, back and forth, back and forth, over and over and over again. Nate wanted to join him, but stuck with the undercover crew, going over the plan one last time, trying one last time to account for all the ways this could go sideways.

At least he was ninety-nine percent sure that an agent balking wasn't one of them. He took in the Nude Crew, pride swelling in his chest. Ty, draped casually against a deck rail and Zane's sturdy chest, looking utterly ridiculous in a cowboy hat pulled low against the sun and nothing else, not even socks or shoes. He'd been . . . twitchy, no other word for it, when they'd boarded the boat, but now he was all easygoing confidence, not a care in the fucking world. Ty and Nate had been friends a long time, way back from when Nate had first been assigned to the DC office, before Ty had left for Baltimore. Which was why Ty and Zane were here now, backing him up—they knew how important this was to him. He'd had a crush on Ty, maybe, once upon a time—fuck, who hadn't?—but this was *not* how he'd wanted to learn the guy was circumcised.

Beside him, looking weirdly tiny by comparison, was Megan, using Ty's big body for shade. She was way too fair-skinned to be up on deck buck naked for more than fifteen or twenty minutes, all cream and freckles and strawberry blond hair that was obviously natural, if the neatly trimmed landing strip at her crotch was any indication, but shy she was not. No reason for her to be, either, not with a body like that. Sure, all of his agents were fit, but there was a difference between fit and pinup model, and Megan definitely landed on the pinup side of things. He didn't envy her those breasts when she had to run, though.

Desiree and Angie were sitting at the nearby table with their "owners," studying the map of the property—or at least what they'd been able to put together of one from satellite imagery and Mat's and Nikolai's recollections. Neither of the women seemed to notice they were naked. Their owners didn't, either, which was just as important: the fifteen "masters" might not be putting their asses at *literal* risk, but they had just as much of a show to put on as the "slaves." Acting like this whole sick enterprise was normal or even preferable; it was a tall order for anyone not as evil as Nikolai or as broken as Roger.

And Nate really needed to get his shit together. He was *not* going to be the weak link in this chain, especially not after butting heads with Mat over his right to take this position.

Agent Holt, the leader of the amphibious team, came out of the wheelhouse and headed toward Nate, very deliberately keeping his eyes above chest level. He hadn't been working with the undercover team very much, and it showed in his discomfort around all the casual nudity.

"Um," he said, coming to a stop at least three feet further away from Nate than he probably would've if Nate were dressed. But then he cleared his throat, tugged at the zipper on the sleeve of his wet suit, and met Nate's eyes directly. "We'll be coming into view of the island in five. Time to put your game faces on."

Well, at least they'd be wearing *one* thing, eh?

"We're diving now."

"Chopper ready?"

Holt nodded. So nice of their drug lord to have bought a boat with a helo pad. "It'll go up at 20:00 on the nose. We'll have the grounds secured by then, and all the other boats too. See you on the other side, yeah?"

Nate wished him good luck, watched silently for a minute as Holt's team slipped into the water, as natural and deadly as a school of sharks. When they'd disappeared from view, he turned to Mat, who was already on his knees, uncomfortably close to Nikolai's feet.

It made Nate's blood boil.

Get it under control, Johnson.

He couldn't compromise the whole damn mission by getting angry every time he saw Mat being debased or abused. Happy. He was supposed to be happy in his position, and completely oblivious to the fact that there was anything wrong here. Just like Roger, the poor bastard, who Nate had spent plenty enough time around this past month to emulate convincingly.

Nikolai ran his hand through Mat's hair, and Mat shut his eyes and leaned into the touch like a convincingly happy cat, yet still Nate's hands clenched into fists.

"Tsk tsk," Nikolai said with a smirk. "None of that. Mathias loves his master's touch, don't you, Mathias?"

Mat opened his eyes, his expression blank. "Yes, Master," he replied, voice rough.

"I think I'm seasick," Nate bit out and headed for the edge of the boat.

Louise was at his side immediately. "You sure you can handle this, partner? We can cut the Nude Crew down to four if you think you can't hack it. Better a no-show than a fuckup, right?"

"No. Four's not enough in that house. Even five's playing it tight. I'll be fine."

"He just needs to kneel," Mat said softly, and yet somehow his voice broke through the waves and the engine. "Come kneel beside me, Nate. Get in the right headspace."

Nate flashed Louise an ill look and then padded back to Mat's side, where he promptly lowered himself to his knees—not a comfortable prospect on the hard deck. "Thought you'd be happy to see me turn tail," he whispered, because yes, being on his knees made him feel like he should. Like he should be seen and not heard. Not speak until spoken to. All those rules his parents had never raised him with. All those centuries of ugly history colored into his skin regardless.

Mat didn't look up. Didn't make eye contact as they spoke. His hands lay perfectly posed and still on his knees. "On one level I would. But this is what you want, and I was wrong to challenge you. Especially in front of your agents, who are putting themselves through this to save *my* brother."

"I appreciate that," Nate replied, trying to follow Mat's lead by not looking at him when he spoke. He couldn't stop himself from smiling, though, inappropriate as it might've been right now. A stress reaction, nothing else. "But in the interests of transparency, it means a lot to me that you cared enough to. And in case we don't get out of this alive . . ."

I'm falling in love with you.

"Don't," Mat said. "These people, they're cowards. They don't know how to stand up to people who fight back. We're gonna be fine. *All* of us."

"Silence," Nikolai commanded above them. "We're approaching the dock."

Nate looked up, and yes, they were. The rest of the Nude Crew had lowered to their knees at their owners' feet. Were staring into some middle distance, psyching themselves up, going through whatever pre-mission rituals they usually did. Louise would normally be checking her weapon now, but it was in a waterproof bag along with everyone else's weapons and radios, being snuck onto the island by the amphibious team. It terrified him to think they'd all have to wait and hope to pick up those guns one by one out of a toilet tank—what if the drop-off agents were caught?—but they had no other choice. No way to carry in past security. And really, if all else failed, he knew at least half a dozen of these guys could *take* a weapon off one of Allen's security.

The island rolled into glorious view. Another time, another situation, Nate would've loved to visit a place like this with Mat—a perfect blue-and-green Caribbean jewel, gleaming in the sun. They motored toward the docks nestled in a sandy cove dotted with palm trees, the manor house visible in the distance, bizarrely out of place in its heavy Victorian finery. Other boats were already docked—a *lot* of other boats, several of them much, much nicer than even this little floating five-star hotel they'd requisitioned from evidence. Man, it seemed when Allen and Nikolai planned a party, they planned a *party*.

Ah well. The bigger the party, the more sons of bitches they'd have in custody by the end of the night. They hadn't limited themselves to the island, either. Right now, all around the world, teams of agents and local LEOs were poised to make *their* raids too. Auction houses and their attached prisons. Owners. Trainers. Those fucking bounty hunters who'd tortured Mat. Nikolai's "little black book" was extensive and detailed, and in this first-wave attack, the FBI was going to take down as many as man power, intel, and international law would permit before too many of these rich creeps had a chance to disappear. Nate wasn't kidding himself, they'd never catch them all, but they'd make a dent. Maybe even a big one. Save some lives. Prevent any more twisted tragic cases like Roger.

But right now? Right now, Nate was mostly concerned about *one* young man. About the promise he'd made to Mat. *We'll get him back. I swear it.*

The boat began its final maneuvers into dock, which was swarming with naked deckhands, liveried footmen, and armed security. Guests, too, chatting and drinking and laughing by the water. One group two berths over was fucking, noisy as could be, not a care in the world who was watching. Gangbang, and Nate was ninety-nine percent certain the woman stuffed full of cocks was not there of her own free will. He averted his eyes as quickly as he could, tried to erase what he'd seen.

Jesus, there wasn't enough bleach in the whole fucking *world* for that.

A deckhand tied their boat off. Nate stood when the other slaves did, walked two paces behind his masters, gaze down, shoulders back, trying to think of *anything* but how naked and on parade they all were, about the eyes raking over him, measuring and assessing. Security wanded master and slave alike before letting them leave the docks. Even Nikolai submitted to a cursory pat-down.

Allen greeted them—or rather, greeted Nikolai—on the strip of beach right off the dock.

"Mr. Petrovic, finally!" he called pleasantly, like they were neighbors sharing a fence.

"Allen," Nikolai replied, much less pleasantly. "I believe I have something that belongs to you."

Mat, standing behind him, didn't move. Not a single muscle. He didn't even twitch.

Nate marveled at his self-control. It wasn't submission or surrender, it was *power*.

It made his heart ache.

"I believe you do." Allen gestured at the boardwalk leading off the beach toward the house. "Shall we discuss it inside? Over drinks and a fuck, perhaps?"

"Sounds heavenly. I've missed my Douglas's sweet mouth."

Allen's smile was cruel, knowing, and a little too in control for Nate's liking. "Would your guests care to join the others out back? There's a barbecue on the beach, live music, dancing, play. Got to keep everyone entertained until the big fight, after all."

Another cruel, knowing look, this time directed at Mat. Mat kept his head down, his shoulders back, his mouth shut. Like he hadn't even *heard* Allen. Allen squinted, stepped forward, lashed out suddenly and tangled his fingers in Mat's hair. Pushed Mat to his knees with a hard twist; Mat went down silent but for a little *whoof* of air.

"Finally neutered the damn dog, did you, Petrovic?"

Nikolai said nothing. Allen shoved Mat's head away, put the sole of his dress shoe to the center of Mat's chest and knocked him over. Left his foot perched there, heavy enough to blanch the skin.

"Please," Allen said to Nikolai's "guests," all gracious host again. He gestured behind him, to a patiently waiting footman. "Percival here will show you to the party. You too," he added, staring pointedly at Roger. "Your master and I have some things to discuss in private."

Nikolai nodded at the assembled group, and though Nate didn't like it one bit, they'd planned for this, hoped for it, even—it'd be easier for them to pick up their weapons in several small groups than one big one. They split off and began to follow Percival.

Nate followed too, behind his masters like the good slave he was fiercely reminding himself to be, when Allen's hand shot out and grabbed his arm. "Not you, Horse Cock. You come with me."

Fuck you, he thought, but managed to keep it off his face when he realized this would mean he'd be able to keep an eye on Mat. Better the devil you know . . . "Yes, sir," he croaked.

"We'd prefer to keep him with us, if it's all the same to our generous host," Agent Ballard said, lacing the fingers of her left hand through her "husband's" and draping her right hand possessively on Nate's bare shoulder. Jeez, she was just acting and he wanted to scrub that shoulder with steel wool.

Allen's mean eyes narrowed. "Oh come now, Mrs. . . . ?"

"Stephenson," she ground out.

Allen nodded, fake smile plastered in place. "Mrs. Stephenson. Don't be a poor sport. I'll return him to you in one piece."

"My wife is quite possessive of that cock," Agent Rickson tried. "Even I can't touch it half the time."

"Well, I promise not to touch it at all, then," Allen said. He sounded like he meant it, too. "He's just so lovely, is all. Those eyes. I'm sure you understand."

Ballard and Rickson hesitated, the silence stretching thin and brittle, Ballard's fingers uncomfortably tight on Nate's shoulder. This . . . wasn't going to end well. Not if he left it to them.

He swallowed, ducked his head a little further—a half bow toward Allen. "You honor my master and mistress with your kind words, sir." Shocked by how steady *his* words came out. How infused with what sounded like genuine gratitude. Fuck-all knew how he managed to add in the same tone, "If it pleases them, I'll honor them further by serving you."

For one brief, terrifying moment, he was *certain* he'd puke on Allen's shoes.

But then the nausea passed and Ballard's hand gave one final squeeze and slipped from his shoulder. She laughed, a quiet, nervous little sound, and said to Allen, "He always was a flatterer, this one. Go on then, Nate. Be good."

"Always, Mistress," he said. Not so nauseous this time, like it was getting easier with each sickening word that spilled from his lips.

Thank God.

Mat cast him a blank glance under his eyelashes as they fell into step together behind Allen and Nikolai.

No reading him. Was he angry? Terrified?

I'm right here, he wished he could comfort, but maybe that was no comfort at all.

Allen led them through the house, into a study. Far from prying eyes. He poured Nikolai a drink and waved him into an armchair. Mat settled immediately at Nikolai's feet; Nate followed suit on the other side.

"I don't see my boy here, Allen," Nikolai said, sipping calmly at his brandy.

Allen's veneer of *good host* slipped instantly away, replaced with *shrewd businessman*, or possibly just *pissed client*. "Impatient for a man who waited eight weeks already. You'll get your boy back, Petrovic."

He smirked. "As soon as I have ample proof that this dog is sufficiently tamed. I won't have him run away again, Nikolai. I *won't.* I had to relocate my entire household until the bounty hunters cleared him. It was incredibly inconvenient. My wife has been inconsolable."

Nikolai rested a casual hand on the back of Mat's neck, then used it to shove him forward, toward where Allen was sitting. Mat took the hint and crawled on hands and knees to Allen's feet as Nikolai said, "He won't run away again. Too hungry for a master's cock, now. Too eager to please. And *far* too aware of what happens to *bad dogs*. Isn't that right, Mathias?"

"That's right, Master. I'm sorry for ever running away. I was . . ." He licked his lips. "Ungrateful."

Allen sat forward in his chair, reached down, and closed his hand around Mat's flaccid dick. "Is that so? Care to show me how grateful you are now, Dog?"

Mat didn't buck up into Allen's hand, didn't even move, really, but somehow his body language screamed eagerness, openness, readiness to serve. Even when Allen's hand tightened hard and cruel around Mat's cock and balls. Mat whimpered but made no attempt to pull away, let alone strike back. "Anything to make it up to you, Master."

"Anything?" Allen purred. "Well then. Nikolai, relax, help yourself to my bar. Dog, suck my dick. Horse Cock, fuck my dog's hungry cunt so I can see for myself just how *eager* he is now."

There was . . . no way Allen had just said what Nate had *heard* him say.

Was there?

But Mat was leaning in toward Allen's crotch, and Allen was staring at Nate, impatient. Waiting.

Nate shot a glance at Nikolai, desperate for reprieve from someone—*anyone*, even Nikolai. But none came. In fact, Nikolai looked downright pleased. But then, why wouldn't he, the sick creep, to see the two men responsible for bringing his empire down reduced to . . . this.

Nate turned back to Allen, slunk close on all fours like a kicked dog. Remembered to speak to the monster's feet rather than his face, let the slow creeping terror in his chest seep into his voice. "I . . . sir, I would obey you if I could, but Mistress said—"

Nate had been slapped harder in his life, had certainly felt worse pain, but couldn't remember a time when he'd *ever* burned with quite so much humiliation. "Your *mistress* isn't here right now. I'd hate to have to tell her you got so eager for sloppy dog cunt that you fucked him *without* my permission."

"I'm afraid I'd have to back him up," Nikolai added, downright gleeful.

Not that it mattered in the slightest; he wasn't a real slave and nobody was going to beat him for doing anything. Except for the part where actually they probably would because he was stuck here away from the rest of his team and the sting wouldn't go down for some time yet, and he *had* to play along.

And it was really quite strangely easy to draw on that fear, that sense of hopelessness, that clarity of powerlessness. To remember the stories his grandfather had told of his harrowing time on the Freedom Bus, that his parents had told of being run out of stores and parks and once out of an entire fucking hillbilly town at the feet of a violent mob because a black man had dared to stick his cock in a white woman. To remember how small he himself had felt far too many times, even after he'd earned his badge, when some bigoted jackass had judged him on sight.

He kept his eyes down, and his voice soft, and his cowering fear at his fingertips, and said through the horror, the disgust, "Yes, sir."

Mat sighed. A soft sound that could have been mistaken for arousal, but that Nate understood as relief. Or maybe Nate just needed to *believe* it was if he had any hope at all of getting through this. Of even getting an erection, let alone using it to *rape* Mat.

Shit. Getting an erection was going to be a serious problem.

Allen took a seat and spread his legs. Nate took himself in hand, staring down at Mat's pale muscular ass with its faint pink scars.

Even in the best of circumstances, Nate wasn't one for topping. Yeah, he was equipped for it—though not as equipped as Allen's racist "Horse Cock" jabs implied—but that didn't mean he loved it. He'd only done it twice, actually.

Never mind that this wasn't the best of circumstances. No, those would be with Mat and him in his bed, laughing and kissing, him rubbing Mat's shoulders and wrapping his legs around Mat's waist.

Not . . . not kneeling here watching as Mat melted like wax and poured himself between Allen's spread thighs, reaching with steady hands for Allen's fly.

Not watching Mat nuzzling into Allen's crotch, moaning like it was something he actually wanted.

Allen believed the lie, leaning back and half-shutting his eyes. "Get on with it, Horse Cock. If you don't come in his ass before I come on his face, I'll tell your mistress you prefer my dog's cunt to her undoubtedly lush pussy."

Fucking disgusting.

Mat moaned again, stuck his ass up and wiggled it, though whether for Allen's sake or for Nate's, he couldn't tell. Didn't matter—Mat's fake eagerness wasn't helping Nate's stubborn flaccidity. "L-lube, sir?" Nate managed. His fucking hands were shaking. He was going to *ruin everything*, Jesus Christ, why hadn't he *listened* to Mat—

"Spit on his cunt. He can take it. Deserves it for running away. Right, Dog?"

Mat hummed an affirmative around Allen's cock, wiggled his ass again, even as Allen planted a hand on Mat's head and shoved him down, chin to balls. As if this could get any worse.

Nate spat into his hand, rubbed himself, tried to summon up that image of himself wrapped around Mat's hard body, clutching his nape and kissing him and kissing him and kissing him.

They'd never have that now, but at least his dick was at half-mast. He shuffled directly behind Mat, touched him on the hip for strength—not sure who needed the comfort most. Spat onto his fingers again, surprised he even could considering how dry his mouth was. Stroked his hand over Mat's cheeks, working up the courage to part them, trying to convey the depths of his feelings, his regrets, his . . . his *love* through that gentle touch. Slid his fingers down Mat's crack—amazing how Mat didn't flinch at all, *moaned*, in fact, like he *wanted* this, though that wasn't possible, simply wasn't possible, Nate had no illusions about how badly he was going to hurt Mat. Parted those firm cheeks, reached for that tight little hole with two spit-slick fingers—

And found himself on the floor, cheek stinging something fierce. Allen had *slapped* him again.

And, great, what little erection he'd managed to coax from his unwilling body was gone now.

"I said spit *on* him, not *in* him," Allen said, just the tiniest bit breathy from Mat's ongoing ministrations. He grabbed Mat's head again, pushed Mat into another deep-throat. "Bad dogs don't get prep."

Oh God. No. He couldn't do this, he couldn't, there was no way even the *head* of his cock was going to fit inside an unstretched hole, he couldn't do that to Mat, he *couldn't.*

Mat wiggled his ass again, and Nate realized: the wiggle wasn't an attempt at seduction, or an act for Allen's benefit. He was telling Nate to get the fuck on with it.

"I'm sorry, sir," Nate said, buying time despite Mat's urgings. "I uh, I serviced Mistress twice on the way over, and I . . . um, it seems I'm having trouble, um . . ." He gestured at his flaccid dick, hoping, hoping.

Nikolai laughed aloud. "Poor stud cock! What a hard life this one has. Why don't you have the dog suck him, Allen? Just to get him hard. I for one would most certainly enjoy the show, wouldn't you?"

Man, Nikolai was enjoying this way too fucking much. Fuck the plea bargain. Nate was going to do everything in his power to make sure they threw the fucking book at this sick creep.

"Go on then, Dog. More cock for your hungry little gob."

Allen shoved Mat off him, nudged him in the ribs with his foot. Mat stumble-crawled around until he was facing Nate, still on his hands and knees, ass between Allen's legs. Allen took advantage of the new position and smacked him hard, first one cheek, then the other. Bright red handprints popped up on Mat's fair skin, and vomit-inducing glee popped up on Allen's ugly face. He hit Mat again. And again. Mat's hands clenched into fists and his eyes squeezed shut, but he nuzzled into Nate's crotch anyway, soft lips mouthing at flesh until he found Nate's cock and balls—which were still trying to crawl up into his belly—and took them in his mouth.

CHAPTER FOUR

Nate was actually doing worse than Mat had expected, and that was *really* saying something. Then again, Mat supposed that neither of them had expected *this.* Even before this new development, Nate had only barely been keeping himself together, his face flashing with a slew of dangerous emotions. Luckily, Allen was too busy being his usual sadistic self to notice. Nikolai certainly did, but he didn't give the game away.

It wasn't like Mat wanted Nate to be the perfect submissive slave. He definitely didn't want that dick inside of him without lube or prep—didn't want it inside him *period.* Getting hard in his mouth, finally, after Mat rolled out every damn trick he knew (and he knew a *lot* of tricks). If this were any other place and any other time, he'd have been impressed and delighted to be doing this for a guy like Nate. As it was, he just felt nauseous. And kind of wistful?

He couldn't put a name on the emotions running through him now. Only knew he hated Allen for taking this from him too. Ever since that last night at Nikolai's—and really before that, if he were being honest with himself—he'd fantasized about this, about wrapping his lips around Nate's dick, hearing Nate moan and feeling Nate's hands in his hair. And even before that night, he'd had a strange, fearful wanting for Nate. Nothing as simple as desire had once been for him, but undeniable nonetheless. And now it was all happening and being stolen at the same time.

But, no . . . That was something they were never going to have anyway, never *could* have had. Nikolai had ruined him long before Allen had unknowingly tainted this forever.

Not that Nate's dick stretching his jaw wide felt tainted. Certainly didn't *taste* tainted. But those pulled-back little stutters of Nate's hips, those stifled moans, those reluctant fingers threading through his hair . . . Tainted. Every one of them. Nate *hated* this. Would never feel about Mat how Mat felt about him, whatever the fuck that even *was*. Couldn't. Mat was his rape victim, now. Maybe always had been. And whatever this moment might've been to them without Nikolai and Allen watching, whatever strength Mat might've once drawn from it, whatever happy memories they might've made, that was gone now. Gone.

And somehow that might've been the biggest tragedy of all.

No wonder the guy had freaked out every time Mat had tried to come on to him. The fact that Nate wasn't freaking out now as Mat bobbed up and down on his dick like a good slave spoke to nothing but his self-control and his willingness not to blow the mission.

Nate had come to his fights. His after-parties. Mat couldn't remember him, not even as a face in the crowd, although God knew he'd fucking tried. Combing through his own memories, squinting at every blur. If only Mat had noticed him then. If only Nate had been brave enough to approach him. Mat would've traded any of his post-fight hookups—no, *all* of his post-fight hookups—for just one night with Nate. Back when he'd been a fighter and Nate had been a fanboy. Maybe they could have had wild sex, over and over again until they ran out of condoms or they just couldn't gather the stamina anymore.

Maybe they could have fallen in love.

Not just infatuation or lust, but the kind of love that would have had him bringing Nate home to Dougie, asking for Dougie's blessing. It could have been good. It could have been better than good.

Now it was just . . . sad. Forced under duress, with an audience, faking every moan but maybe not every whimper.

And even sadder? Mat *still* wanted it. Still found himself trying to lose himself to it, to let himself enjoy the hot heavy weight against his tongue, the pleasant ache in his jaw. Almost, almost tricked himself into managing it. But, no. Nikolai had ruined that too. Ruined *him*. Maybe forever.

"Look at that. They're *both* hard!" Allen crowed. "Maybe your six weeks was worth it after all. I've never seen my dog with a boner before."

Oh God, he was *hard*? Blood heated his cheeks and ears as well as his cock. Why had he let that happen, made Nate have to see that? What would Nate think of him *now*? When was the last time he'd gotten hard of his own accord, anyway? He . . . couldn't even remember.

Allen spanked Mat one more time, noise and heat like a firecracker, the pain ripping him from his little panic party. Then Allen's hand twisted in Mat's hair, pulling him off Nate's dick with a horrible *gluck* and a long, ropey string of spit. Allen spun him around by the hair and shoved his own cock back down Mat's throat before Mat could even think to take a breath.

"Go on, Horse Cock," Allen said over Mat's gurgled choking. Mat couldn't quite muster up the courage to shake his ass for Nate this time. He'd let stupid, dangerous thoughts into his head, and now they'd set up camp and wouldn't leave. He was choking and his throat hurt and his skin burned where Allen had hit him, and he was *afraid.*

Ruined. Everything was fucking *ruined.*

Trembling hands smoothed down his flanks, over his flaming cheeks, spread him wide. The head of Nate's cock slipped along his crack, nudged at his hole, slipped again. Too big to push in without help. Sure enough, one hand left his ass, and Mat squeezed his eyes shut and tried not to picture that hand wrapped firm around Nate's cock, guiding it forward. Tried to relax so he wouldn't have to traumatize Nate any further by bleeding all over him. But he was a fucking mess, and fuck-all knew how they'd even *gotten* here, and he just had to remember what it was all for, how Mat's wants and Nate's wants had nothing at all to do with any of this, didn't matter for shit. This was about Dougie, and Dougie alone.

Nate forced his way inside with a grunt quickly drowned out by Mat's cry, the pain so ugly he jerked his head out of Allen's grasp and off his cock lest he clench his teeth down around it. Not that he wouldn't have *loved* to bite the fucker's dick clean off, but they couldn't afford that sort of complication right now. Not until Dougie was safe. Not until Dougie was safe. Not until . . .

Allen smacked him, lighter this time, wisely didn't try to put his mouth back to use yet. "The dog's cunt is so tight Horse Cock can barely get inside!" Laughter. Ugly laughter. "Jesus Christ, Petrovic, you been saving him for the queen or something?" And then, to Nate, "Move it, Horse Cock. This isn't some flowering virgin seduction. *Fuck* him."

Mat sobbed and twisted, wishing he could escape but trapped on both ends. Was six weeks such a long time that he'd forgotten this pain? He'd taken the bounty hunters' *fists*, for fuck's sake. And now he was crying at Nate's timid intrusion?

Of course, the bounty hunters had used lube.

And he hadn't . . . he hadn't *cared* about them. They hadn't cared about him. They weren't being raped too.

Fuck, he'd *begged* Nate to stay away. Why hadn't the stubborn fuck *listened*?

"That's it, Horse Cock," Allen urged, mashing Mat's face back into his crotch by the grip on his hair. Mat pried his jaw apart and forced himself to suck again, choking on the pain *and* Allen's cock. "Faster, boy." Such an innocuous name compared to "Horse Cock," but for Nate, probably worse to bear. Yet Nate obeyed, hips pistoning, and something gave inside Mat with a sickening, burning tear, fresh blood slicking the way. How did Allen expect him to fight after this?

"Harder," Allen panted. "Make him *scream*."

Maybe he didn't. Maybe he expected Mat to lose. To die. To suffer and prostrate himself and beg forgiveness, and then make Allen a huge heap of cash on the way out. They'd be betting for him to win, all of them. Well, win or refuse to fight at all. His record was spotless, except for the one time he'd sat in the sand and said no. And after reeducation, there shouldn't be any more of that.

It's not going to get to that point. It's not. Nate promised.

Nate's as powerless as you now. See Evidence #5B: Cock in Ass.

Except Nate wasn't alone. And neither was Mat, not anymore. They just had to get through this. That was all.

Which was easier said than done. Allen gestured Nate to speed up, and the strokes went from punishing to downright brutal. Mat screamed around Allen's cock.

And Allen pulled out and came, shooting across Mat's forehead and nose.

Behind him, Nate moaned, his thrusts stuttering. He was close, thank fuck. Mat wanted this over with. Was so tired of hurting. Of fucking up. Of disappointing people.

Strangely, it was Allen who put a stop to it. Wiped his cock off on Mat's cheek and then shoved Mat to the floor, growling, "That's enough, Horse Cock." Nate didn't really have a chance to stop of his own accord; his cock slipped out as Mat fell, friction on torn skin like a gravel burn making Mat scream again as the head popped free. Mat curled up and lay perfectly still, praying Allen was done with him, hoping not to draw any more attention to himself. Couldn't stop his eyes from sliding up Nate's bare body, though: the round puckered scar on his right thigh that had almost certainly been made by a bullet, the blood smeared dark across his—still very, very hard—cock and trimmed pubic hair, the careful, desperate blankness on his face that Mat feared would slip and crack any second now.

"See?" Nikolai declared into the silence. "The dog's been tamed. You've had your fuck; now it's my turn. Where's my boy?"

"The dog still has a fight to win," Allen said, and though he was tucking his cock back into his pants, there was no mistaking the dick-waving contest going on between him and Nikolai right now.

Nikolai, still perfectly relaxed, took a sip of brandy and said, "That wasn't our agreement, Allen."

"Yeah, and neither was you sending me a dog that wound up *biting* last time. After the fight, Petrovic. You'll get your *precious boy* after the fight."

Fuck. *Now* what? The estate was huge and Dougie could be anywhere, anywhere at all. Fuck, maybe he wasn't even here. Maybe he was . . .

Maybe he was already dead.

No. No no no no no. Allen was a sadist, but he had a self-preservation streak a mile wide. He wouldn't cross Nikolai like that. He *wouldn't.*

"So be it," Nikolai said, and took another sip of brandy. He held his free hand out to Mat, crooked his fingers. "I'll just keep Mathias with me in the meanwhile. I'm sure you understand."

Mat didn't waste a single second crawling back over to Nikolai's side. God, he *hurt*. And not just between his legs. Couldn't even bear to *look* at Nate right now.

"Fine. Then *you* can get him cleaned up. And put Horse Cock away downstairs—not enough room in the stands tonight for everyone and their mother to bring a pet." Allen checked his watch, eyed up Mat again. "Fight starts in an hour. See you there, Petrovic."

And with that, Allen got up and left.

Mat curled into a ball at Nikolai's feet and wept.

CHAPTER FIVE

Nate left him alone for two, maybe three minutes, but Mat knew as well as anyone that the clock was ticking, and he couldn't lie here and wallow forever. Nikolai pointed Nate toward the en suite to clean up, and when Nate came back, he called Mat's name and handed him a warm wet washcloth. Mat didn't miss the way Nate carefully didn't let their fingers touch, wouldn't meet Mat's eyes.

"So, uh." Nate gazed off into some middle distance while Mat dabbed gingerly at his ass. He hadn't bled as much as it'd felt like he'd bled; that was something, at least, he supposed. "I'm going to see if I can meet up with the Nude Crew, find Dougie."

Nikolai made no response, just sat there sipping the remains of his drink. When Mat didn't answer either, Nate added, clearly at a loss, "It's, um, that way?"

Mat looked to where Nate was pointing, at the door in the corner that led to the slave halls. Just because Nate wouldn't talk to him didn't mean he couldn't man up and talk to Nate, so he said, "Yeah. And then down the stairs into the basement."

Nate nodded, but still wouldn't look at Mat. Turned to Nikolai instead. Cleared his throat. He seemed as awkward and uncomfortable as he had the night he'd popped a boner in front of Mat in the safe house. "If he's at the fight with Allen, you make sure you get him and bring him to the rendezvous site."

"I know, Nathaniel." Nikolai swallowed the last of his drink, put the cut-crystal glass down on a coaster on an end table. Mat briefly entertained the notion of smashing it into Nikolai's temple. "We have discussed this before; I'm not a child."

Nate bristled, but held his tongue. More or less. "Just get him out of there before any shooting can start. Eight o'clock, okay?"

A heavy, put-upon sigh. "I *know*, Nathaniel."

"And how many times do I have to tell you Nate's short for Nathan, huh?"

"Which is, in turn, short for Nathaniel," Nikolai said, and there was no mistaking the mischief in his voice. Why did Nate let Nikolai get to him like that over such stupid shit? Now was not the fucking time.

No. Now's time for fucking. For being *fucked.*

Snap out of it, Carmichael.

"And you," Nate said, pointing at Mat but not quite looking at him. "You promise me *you'll* get out before the shooting starts, too."

He tried to meet Nate's eyes, just to see how pissed, how horrified, how disgusted the man really was, how differently he saw Mat now. Couldn't. They kept darting around. "I will."

"Straight to the rendezvous site. No matter what. We'll get your brother, okay? I promise."

"Okay, Nate," he lied. No fucking way he was going *anywhere* without making sure Dougie was safe.

He was never entrusting Dougie's welfare to anyone else again. Not even Nate.

Nate was a good man, and he cared about Mat, but all the promises in the world didn't change the fact that if Nate had to choose between Dougie and the success of his mission, he'd choose the mission. He had to think of the bigger picture.

Mat didn't.

But at least he'd lied convincingly—or maybe Nate was too busy avoiding his gaze to catch the lie in his body language—because with one last look, one last nod, Nate slipped out the door.

Mat struggled to his feet, resolutely refusing to ask Nikolai for any kind of help. "You'd better escort me to the dressing room," he said.

"With pleasure," Nikolai replied. Mat was certain that Nikolai's *pleasure* had much less to do with keeping Mat in his place and much more to do with the hope of seeing Dougie at the fight.

Yeah, enjoy it while you can, you sick fuck. I'm never letting you touch him again.

Too bad he needed an escort, or else he'd have been seriously tempted to strangle Nikolai here and now. Warm up for his fight.

Nah. Fucker doesn't deserve such a quick end. Let him die alone in jail, a plaything for other convicts.

They walked shoulder to shoulder through the familiar maze of halls down to the dressing room; Mat couldn't follow the customary two steps behind because Nikolai didn't know the way. Nikolai kept up appearances, though, squeezing the back of Mat's neck whenever they came into view of any part of Allen's household.

No sign of Dougie.

When they finally made it to their destination, Nikolai didn't waste time on small talk. "I'll take my leave, then."

Even a mindfucker as practiced as Nikolai couldn't hide how distracted he was. How eager he was to find Dougie and get to him first.

"Don't get shot," Mat called, but showed enough teeth to make it plain how little he cared about Nikolai's survival. Even though they were alone, it was a damn foolhardy move to talk to a master that way, and yet somehow Mat couldn't bring himself to care. They were close. So close. He didn't want his last interaction with Nikolai to be one of submission.

"Good-bye, Mathias."

It'd better fucking not be good-bye. Maybe he cared about Nikolai's survival after all: they needed this fucker at the myriad trials to come—including his own. "I mean it. Don't get shot."

"And deny you the sublime pleasure of seeing me fall from grace? I wouldn't dream of it." He paused in the doorway, one hand resting against the jamb as he looked over his shoulder with a wistful smile. "But be careful what you wish for, Mathias."

Mat ran it over and over in his mind, but he couldn't find a single downside to an eternity of Nikolai dropping his soap in some prison shower.

Mat waited. And waited. Watched the minute hand crawl around the clock face. Wrapped his hands for show. *Or for just in case shit goes sideways and you have to fight.* He wanted to trust Nate, he did, but after how badly his whole "pose as a slave" plan had gone, Mat wasn't sure that was the wisest decision. The guy meant well, but that didn't mean he wasn't in over his head with how fucked up and twisted Allen and Nikolai's world could get.

7:30. Music started playing in the arena, some upbeat techno-funk to rile the crowd. He had no doubt liquor was flowing freely by now. Slave cock and pussy, too. Everyone would be beautifully distracted when the time came.

7:45. Someone came in to give Mat his fifteen minute warning. He mumbled "Thank you, fifteen," without even thinking. How easily he fell back into routine—but was it the UFC one, or the slave dogfight one? Even Mat didn't know anymore. Maybe he'd never know again.

7:48. His wrapped hands began to shake. He was sweating. Heard his heart start to pound in his ears. In twelve minutes he might have to kill someone. He'd sat in this room how many times before, living with that truth? He couldn't do it again. He *wouldn't* do it again, and no matter how many times he told himself an entire fucking SWAT team was about to descend on the island, his body just wouldn't get with the fucking program and *calm down*.

He wanted this over with. Wanted Dougie back, wanted his hoodie and sweatpants back, wanted to see Nikolai and Allen safely (or, better yet, not so safely) in jail, wanted to leave Nate and everything between them—good and bad—behind. Start again somewhere. Take his brother and just . . . build something new. Untainted. Untouched by all this *shit*.

Can't untaint that blood on your hands, Mathias.

God, there were so many fucking awful voices in his head these days, he didn't even know who was speaking anymore. Didn't know who to listen to, who to trust, what to believe. What if the amphibious team hadn't gotten the guns onto the island? What if Nate had given himself away? What if the Cartel had someone inside the FBI, someone who had already dismantled their entire mission? One fucking chopper wasn't going to help if everything else went to shit.

7:55. The stagehand came back with a five-minute warning. Mat paced. Took a drink of water in the fruitless hopes of settling the nerves in his stomach. 7:56. 7:57. Was this clock even right? What if things were going down already and he was just *sitting* here?

Where was Dougie? Had Nate found him? Or had Nikolai gotten to him first? Played the hero, gotten his claws back in? What if Allen had him chained to his side? Wouldn't let him go? Used him as a human shield or a hostage or just shot him out of anger when the SWAT team ruined his fun?

7:58. What if Dougie was already dead? Was that why Allen had held back? Was he planning on fighting Mat and then showing him and Nikolai Dougie's dead body?

Dougie's dead, tortured body?

Mat stumbled over to the sink and puked.

7:59. No. Dougie was okay. He *had* to be okay. No way they'd come this far, fought this hard, only to find—

8:00. The rumble of the crowd changed. Rose in pitch. Shifted from bloodlust orgy to chaos.

8:01. Gunfire.

Some suited security guy, one of Allen's meatheads, ran through Mat's dressing room with an automatic weapon clutched in both hands. Didn't even notice Mat—he was a fucking slave, who would notice him?—until Mat rushed him, dropped down to sweep his leg, and took him to the floor. Took his gun, too. Had no clue how to shoot the fucking thing, but that didn't really matter. He just slammed the butt into the guy's face instead.

Gun in tow, he made a run for it. In the chaos, nobody tried to stop him. He tore through the tight slave halls, rubbing shoulders with other naked bodies. The bunk room. The kitchen. The gym. Even the fucking storage closets. Room after room, and Dougie wasn't in any of them.

Had Allen brought him into the arena before shit had gone down? Did Nikolai have him now? Nate or one of the other FBI agents? Allen, still?

Dougie, clutched to Allen's chest, a gun to his head. Nate, making the choice: Dougie or the mission.

Mat nearly doubled back, right into the fucking fray, when he realized: Dougie had been tortured for *months*. Tortured, but presumably kept alive and whole so Allen could still make the trade.

He'd be injured. In need of basic care.

And Mat knew where injured slaves were sent.

He barreled up the stairs to the ground floor, out the first exterior door he found, onto the beach where the remnants of the prefight barbecue remained. No firefights here, but three men and one woman in evening wear were tearing across the sand, pursued by a pack of agents in SWAT gear. Where the *fuck* did those assholes think they were going? They were on a fucking *island*, for fuck's sake.

To the dock. They haven't realized yet that the boats have all been secured.

A helicopter circled overhead, spotlight glaring. Out on the water, silhouetted by the setting sun, boats circled like predators. FBI vessels? Local Coast Guard? Navy? Mat didn't waste time trying to identify them. He just pounded through the sand, headed for the stables.

I'm coming, Dougie. I'm coming.

No matter what.

CHAPTER SIX

Douglas huddled in a corner of his stall like the animal he was, arms over his head and eyes squeezed shut. The sound of a passing helicopter—no doubt one of Allen's fancy-ass guests making a fancy-ass entrance to his fancy-ass party-slash-re-debut fight—made him whimper and clutch his ears, as if that would ever help his screaming headache.

Allen would be here soon, he knew it. As soon as the fight was over, as soon as he'd made his triumphant reintroduction of his fighting dog to the world. Here to put him out of his misery. Word on the slave grapevine was that Mat was back. Mat was back, but word was Nikolai didn't even want to make a trade. Why would he? Douglas was damaged goods now. Ruined. Spoiled. Mat was back and Nikolai didn't want him, which meant Allen didn't need him anymore.

Which meant one thing: a bullet to the head. Put down like an animal. That was why they'd left him out here in the stables. They'd shovel out the bloodied hay and it would be like he was never here.

Douglas couldn't say he was terribly bothered by that thought. What good had he ever been to anyone anyway? Nobody wanted him. He'd never been anything but a burden, a drain. A bad foster son. A bad brother. A bad slave. A bad dog. Not even of any use as a hostage.

Frankly, putting him out of his misery would be the biggest act of compassion anyone had shown him in years.

Which, now that he thought about it, meant that Allen probably wouldn't even bother.

They'd probably leave him out here to starve and die in his own filth. He was far enough from the house that they wouldn't have to hear him begging.

Great. Just fucking *great*.

Someone screamed. Far away, maybe on the beach near the barbecue pit. Another noise, *loud*. Was . . . was that a gunshot? More than one—a whole volley of them. Who was Allen killing this time? What for?

Who cared? It had nothing to do with Douglas, unless maybe this was an organized execution and maybe Douglas was next. Maybe someone would come for him soon. Put a bag over his head like they did in old movies. Lead him to a post.

The door to the stall rattled. He was right. They had come for him. He forced himself to unfold his body and shuffle painfully to the middle of the stall, where he knelt.

Perfect position, just like Nikolai had taught him. Maybe he didn't know anymore what was true and what wasn't, what Nikolai had done out of love and what he'd done for money, but this one thing, at least, he knew for certain: *No resistance, no will. Give them no reason to hurt you anymore, until they hurt you for the last time.*

If he was lucky, it wouldn't hurt at all.

He just hoped there wasn't an afterlife, because he didn't think he could bear to meet his parents there like this. Mom or Dad *or* Pattie.

Hah. Like they'd let you into Heaven anyway. How you gonna get through that gate? Suck Saint Peter's cock?

Why not? Seemed to work for Mary Magdalene.

Key in the lock.

Douglas took a deep breath and closed his eyes, trying to find some calm center still left inside his pain-racked body.

"Dougie."

Douglas's eyes shot open—*Am I dead? Is this Heaven or Hell?*—and he saw Mat standing there. Right there in the doorway. Right there, close enough that Douglas could smell him. Shoulders low, stance wide, naked but for hand wraps, panting heavily with a gun in his arms. A gun which he quickly handed off to the stable boy-cum-medic, Reginald, who was skulking behind him.

"Dougie, oh God," he said, and tears streaked down his cheeks as he fell to his knees in front of Douglas, cupped Douglas's bruised face in two shaking hands. "You're alive, you're alive, you're alive . . ."

All at once, the calm left him. He shook, violently. His teeth chattered. Hot wet tears drenched his face. *No thanks to you*, he wanted to shout. Pound on Mat's chest and say, *See? See what they've done to me because of* you*?* But though the anger burned in his chest and his throat, something else, something cool and cleansing, flushed right overtop it, beside and between it, filling in all the empty spaces the lies and the doubts and the cruelties had left. He felt *small* again, like a child again—helpless and frightened and sad and lost and a hundred other things he'd buried beneath Nikolai's manipulations and Allen's violence. He felt like . . . like a *little brother*, looking up with surety and longing and awe and trust and belief.

He felt safe.

He felt . . . *loved.*

"You came for me," he murmured, and even his voice sounded young. So soft and unsure.

"Of course I did." Mat let out a broken laugh and crushed Douglas to his chest, wrapped strong arms around cracked ribs and Douglas didn't even care, barely even noticed the pain, lifted shaking arms and hugged him back, grabbed on and swore he'd never *ever* let go again. Not for anything. Not for *anything.*

"I promised I'd come back for you," Mat said. "You're my little brother. No matter what, remember?"

No matter what. Mat had said those same words at Douglas's darkest moments, at his least human moments, and now he was saying them again. Douglas knew he shouldn't believe them—knew Nikolai would advise against him believing them—but that was the funny thing.

Nikolai wasn't here.

Mat was.

No matter what.

The Flesh Cartel

Season 5: Reclamation

Episode 17: Boxed In

CHAPTER ONE

Mat had never realized just how nerve-wracking it was to be sitting on this side of the hospital bed. To be the one waiting and worrying and hoping, staring down at the evidence of so many months of terrible abuse and simultaneously praying for and dreading the moment your loved one opens their eyes. Opens their mouth and says something that won't crush your heart any further.

The doctors had sedated Dougie for two solid days. Not for the injuries, which were extensive but noncritical; no, for the state he'd been in when they'd brought him here. Frantic, terrified, unwilling to let go of Mat, to let anyone else touch him—not even Mike. Convinced they were all Allen's men here to kill him, Nikolai's men here to feed him more lies. Delirious, probably—three months of torture and malnourishment and dehydration would do that to anyone.

The docs had started weaning Dougie off the sedation this morning, but he was still sleeping. Still hiding from the horrors of the world.

Mat didn't blame him at all.

Dougie was growing restless now, though. Stirring and moaning in his sleep. Mumbling things Mat was certain he didn't want to hear. He'd likely wake soon. But which Dougie would open his eyes? Nikolai's perfect pet, Allen's wounded animal, or the brother who'd cried on Mat's shoulder the entire boat ride back to Florida? One thing was certain: it wouldn't be the bright young man Mat remembered from before all this.

When Dougie finally did come around, he woke up quiet. Confused, maybe, but calm. They'd pumped him full of fluids, nutrients, painkillers, let him sleep safe and uninterrupted for days—Mat's eyes stung with tears as he let himself hope, just a little, that maybe it'd done the trick. That maybe that'd be all he'd needed, and now he'd turn those big blue eyes on Mat and say *I want to go home*.

But he didn't. Oh, he looked at Mat, all right—blinked and blinked again and then furrowed his brow and maybe narrowed his eyes for a second and then just . . . let his gaze slide away. Didn't say a word.

"Hey," Mat said softly, so many anxious weeks of waiting and love and relief all stuffed into that single syllable. "You're safe now, Dougie." The first thing, the most *important* thing to say. He carefully didn't touch Dougie, though he wanted to—take his hand, squeeze his shoulder, brush the hair from his forehead—God, he wanted to. "We got out. We're free."

"Mat," he said softly, his throat rough even after two days of quiet. "It was you?"

Who else?

Mat flinched when he realized. He resolutely ignored the part of him that was trying to analyze those three little words and determine if they were . . . disappointed.

He played it off with a weak laugh. "Sorry, just me."

Dougie flushed and winced—or was that glared? Embarrassed? Angry? Maybe both. Suddenly, Mat felt ashamed for trying to be funny at all.

"I am sorry, Dougie. We tried so hard to get you out sooner."

That awful hint of hope in his eyes again; Mat knew damn well who Dougie was thinking of. Waited for his brother's inevitable, timid, *needy*, "We?"

It still made him cringe, though. "Had a little help from the FBI."

Crestfallen again. Of course he was. His precious Nikolai hadn't come for him.

Well, okay, he kind of had, but Mat sure as fuck wasn't going to mention that. That wasn't the kind of *help* Dougie needed right now. Sure, it might sting, but in the long run, it seemed like a little withholding of information was for the best.

Silence, long and awkward. Emotions flitted over Dougie's face so rapidly—and shallowly, as if he was half-numb, or too frightened to let them free—that Mat could barely begin to decipher them. Sadness—no mistaking that one. Shame, too. Disappointment. In between them, definitely that flicker of hope again. But mostly he just seemed . . . lost.

Yeah, Mat knew *that* feeling too. And he hadn't been even half as fucked up as Dougie when he'd broken free. At least Nikolai had let him keep his sense of self, his ability to be fucking pissed off and know he'd been wronged. Dougie didn't even have that.

But he did have one thing that *really* counted. Someone else who loved him, who'd guided him, whose memory might not've been tainted by Nikolai's machinations. "Hey!" he said brightly, reaching for Dougie's arm but then smoothing the sheet next to it instead. "Mike's here. He's really anxious to see you. Can I let him in? Just for a couple minutes. Or longer, if you want. Whatever you want."

Dougie didn't reply, not right away. The flitting expressions slowed, settled onto one or two very clear ones: Sadness. Fear.

Grief.

Dougie blinked tears out of his eyes and shook his head. Pulled his blanket up to his chin and turned his gaze to the far wall. Not sticking around to hear Mat's opinion on his reply—leaving the only way he could.

But . . . *why*? Aside from Dougie, there'd been no one in the world Mat wanted to see more than Darryl when he'd opened his eyes in his hospital bed. No one who'd offered more relief, no one who'd managed to calm and ground and soothe him so thoroughly. Mike had been to Dougie what Darryl was to Mat—more so, even, had taken him into his home for four years and raised him. If Dougie was searching for stability now, for a father figure to step in and guide him—and wouldn't or couldn't accept it from Mat after what Nikolai had done to them—then Mike should've been perfect.

"He was worried sick for you, Dougie. *He* was the one who wouldn't let the case rest, even after the cops closed it. He called in favors, got it to the FBI. He's half of why we found you, Dougie."

Dougie seemed to flinch a little—hard to tell, as blank and still as he was holding himself—and it took Mat a moment to realize . . . *Don't call me that. My name is Douglas.* And yeah, it *was* the name on his birth certificate, but they'd never, ever used it, and Mat couldn't stomach the thought of using it now.

"Dougie, please, let him see you. He won't . . . he won't *judge*, you know. He saw me too. Was here when I woke up a total fucking wreck. Stayed with me the whole time."

"Why?" Dougie whispered. "Why would he do that for you . . . or for me? We're not his kids. We're not his family. What does he want from us?"

"W-want from us?" Mat blinked. "He doesn't want anything from us! That's—that's Nikolai talking, Dougie. Not everyone in this world wants something from us. Sometimes people just care." He dropped his head. "The way I do about you."

Anger flashed briefly in Dougie's eyes, then faded into the dullness of disappointment. Mat knew the things Nikolai had told him. Had seen the security tapes in his six long weeks with the FBI at Nikolai's estate. Had heard the words from Nikolai's own mouth: That Dougie was Mat's meal ticket when he could no longer fight. That Dougie was Mat's burden. The albatross Mat only tolerated for its usefulness. And Mat could see how Dougie had bought it, too—exhausted, suffering, frightened, and isolated as a master manipulator played on his greatest fears. Preyed on the heart of that fourteen-year-old child whose world had imploded, who'd made beds and washed dishes and done all his homework and stayed seen and not heard like a good little foster kid so the new family wouldn't discard him like the last one had. Mike and Pattie had been a blessing, a boon, *real* parents to Dougie, but while they'd been the last, they hadn't been the first.

And then there'd been Nikolai, whose "love" really *was* conditional. Brutally so.

So he supposed it shouldn't have come as such a painful shock that Dougie was convinced the whole world was like that now.

Maybe the direct approach was best, then. "Mike loves you, Dougie. *I* love you. That doesn't come with a price tag. You could lounge around on the couch eating Cheetos and watching *Colbert* for the rest of your life and I'd *still* love you."

Dougie's eyes slid back to Mat's. Still so carefully blank, though the puckered mouth gave his cynicism away.

"I'd take care of you forever if you needed me to. I—"

"I'm not a *child*," Dougie snapped. Well. At least he was speaking. "When are you gonna figure that out, huh? You gonna . . . what? Dress me up like your own little living doll and suffocate me like you always did? For *what*, Mat? I don't *need* that bullshit. Just . . ." He snapped a hand at Mat, grabbed the covers, and pulled them up to his ears as he curled away, his back to Mat. "Fuck off."

Mat's hands curled into fists, but he wouldn't hit Dougie. Not ever again. "Okay," he said, softly. "Okay, okay. I'll tell Mike to come back another time, when you're ready to see him, huh? It's okay. He'll understand."

"Please stop talking," Dougie mumbled. "I can't take it anymore. Please."

He was on the verge of tears. So was Mat. Best, maybe, to let them both cry in peace. What had he been expecting, anyway? To swoop in like some white fucking knight and make everything magically okay? It'd taken Nikolai almost a year to mold Dougie into Douglas. Two lousy days wasn't going to put *that* mess back together again.

Mat squeezed his eyes closed, held them closed until the burn of impending tears faded. Laid his hand on the bed by Dougie's shoulder because he knew he shouldn't touch his brother but also couldn't not. Cleared his throat. "Okay," he said. "Okay. I'll, um . . ." He gestured helplessly toward the door, never mind that Dougie wasn't looking at him. "I'll just be outside with Mike. You call us if you need us. Or if you just want us. Whatever. Okay?"

Mat waited, but Dougie didn't reply. Didn't move. Didn't so much as make a sound.

Suddenly, *You're safe. We're free* felt like a pretty cold comfort.

Nate sipped his coffee and stared down the hallway at the psych ward waiting room, currently occupied by one particularly weary-looking Mathias Carmichael. Nothing new there; Mat had spent so much of the last four days in those waiting-room chairs that Nate wouldn't be surprised if they'd molded to the shape of his ass.

Mat shouldn't be there. He should be in Dougie's room. Or on a psychiatrist's couch, after all he'd been through himself. After what Nate had helped to put him through. Or in bed, resting, recovering from his own violence of the last week. Getting up, walking around, eating something that didn't come in a plastic wrapper.

It broke Nate's heart to see him like this.

Even worse to know he couldn't help Mat. Not anymore. Not after—

God, he hadn't even worked up the courage to *speak* to Mat since then. Not more than was strictly necessary, anyway, and those few painfully brief encounters had involved no eye contact on either side.

Then again, why *would* Mat want to look at him after what he'd done to the poor guy?

"Still pining, partner?"

Nate turned and nodded a greeting to Louise, who'd snuck up on him as effectively as she always seemed to lately, holding a breakfast sandwich in each hand. One half-eaten, the other still wrapped. She offered it to him—not to eat, he'd done that already, but to give to Mat—and he shook his head.

He'd learned these last few days to anticipate the look of reproach on her face.

There was an actual, physical pain in his chest as he watched her pace the last twenty feet to the waiting room, sit down in the chair beside Mat with all the comfortable freedom of a person who hadn't *raped* him, and hand him his food.

Well, at least she was making sure he remembered to eat.

At least she was caring for him now that Nate couldn't.

It wasn't your fault, Agent Johnson. You *were raped too.*

Yeah, thanks, Mister-Work-Appointed-Shrink. I wasn't the one left bleeding and covered in cum.

Fuck. Maybe the group home would be as good for Nate as he was hoping it'd be for Mat and Dougie. A whole building full of people who'd understand what he'd been through. Who'd been through so, *so* much worse for so much longer than that short little taste he'd gotten. Maybe they wouldn't mind if he sat in on the group sessions. He needed to help the DA prep for trial anyway, right?

Maybe with a therapist—one who truly understood this whole fucking mess—acting as a mediator between them, Nate could find the words to apologize to Mat.

Louise jogged him out of his little pity party by somehow ending up right in front of him again, instead of in the waiting room next to Mat. She touched a hand to his biceps, and he was ashamed to say he twitched a little. But he didn't feel the need to shake her off, and she didn't spook and let go, either. "You with me, partner?"

Nate swiped a hand across his mouth, took a swig of his cooling coffee. "Yeah." He nodded his head. "Yeah. I'm okay."

She was nice enough not to call him on his bullshit. "Mat's heading in to try visiting again. Mostly Dougie lets him if he just sits there quietly. I think he's hoping to desensitize the kid or something, I dunno. It's gotta be hard." She frowned, eyebrows drawing down. "Poor guy. All that sacrifice . . ."

"Yeah," Nate agreed, because what else was there to say. No words to describe how fucked up that particular situation was. "But I hear there's high hopes for the group home. They brought in the best."

Louise nodded. "You should tell them."

He should. He knew that. Louise had been there for Mat, sure, but she didn't have the trust, the connection that Mat and Nate did—or rather, had once had. Still, it'd be cowardly to pass this off to his partner. Even though he knew she'd do it for him if he asked.

"Yeah. Okay." He finished his coffee in one long gulp, tossed the paper cup in a trash can, shook out the tension in his shoulders and neck. Started purposely toward Dougie's room, into which Mat had disappeared a minute or two earlier. Louise followed close behind in silent support.

He knocked twice, gently. No way he was going in without permission. Wouldn't barge in on anyone anywhere ever again, if he had a choice.

"Come in," Mat called.

The minute Nate stepped through the door, that blanket of awkwardness settled over him again, nearly smothering him. "Uh, so . . ." He swallowed.

Dougie was lying on his side, his back to Mat. Mat was sitting at Dougie's bedside, staring resolutely at his brother's blanketed shoulder blades. They didn't look much like reunited brothers. More like strangers.

"The docs are going to discharge Dougie today," Nate said.

Mat nodded, eyes still on Dougie's back. "Yeah. They came in to talk to me about home care."

Home care? Just where did Mat think he'd be taking Dougie once they left this place? Had he even considered it?

Of course he had. Mat the big brother. Mat the substitute father. No way he hadn't spent the last four days racking his brain about their futures.

"So, um. About that. Dougie, are you awake?" He didn't want to talk about Dougie like the guy couldn't handle his own life. Even if he really couldn't right now. People had been treating him like a child, like a *thing*, for the last year and change. Nate wouldn't do that too.

At last Dougie said softly, "Yes." He rolled onto his back, as careful not to meet Mat's eyes as Nate was, and pressed the button to raise the head of his bed into a sitting position. He and Nate hadn't spoken at all, really, beyond basic assurances on the boat ride from the island—the docs had banned anyone from questioning him about his ordeal—but his gaze landed square on Nate's and held. "You're the agent who arrested Allen," he said. Not a question.

Nate nodded. "Yes. Me and my partner. I'm Nate. This is Louise."

Dougie's eyes flitted from him to Louise and back. "And Nikolai," Dougie added, carefully flat.

Nate nodded again, trying to decipher that empty tone, that empty expression. Was he angry? Relieved? Something else? "Yes."

A long, uncomfortable pause. Then Dougie dropped his gaze to his lap and said, soft and scratchy, "Thank you, sir. Ma'am."

"You don't have—" Nate began, but was cut off by the look of sheer despair on Mat's face, by the sick twisted feeling in his own gut. He cleared his throat, made sure to keep his voice soft, his eyes kind. "You don't have to call me sir, Dougie. Just Nate. Nate's fine."

Dougie didn't respond to that. Didn't argue, but didn't agree, either. Maybe that was for the best. He'd rather the kid *not* mindlessly obey his every request. The fact that he didn't had to be a kind of progress, right?

"All right. Well, I'm just going to come out and say it. You two have been gone a long time, and in that time your bills haven't been paid and the bank has repossessed your house. Now, the FBI Victim's Services can probably accommodate you with an apartment, but there's another option I'd like to discuss." He looked into Dougie's eyes, then quickly glanced in Mat's direction, trying to discern any reaction but finding nothing. They were both so horribly blank. "Along with rescuing victims and arresting the people who hurt you, the FBI also seized a pretty sizeable amount of assets. A good portion of that has been put aside for a victim's fund, and part of it is being used to create transitional housing and long-term care facilities for the Cartel's victims. You'd have a roof over your head, three square meals, exercise facilities, a TV, a game room, round-the-clock medical care—"

"And supervision," Mat cut in.

Nate nodded. "For people like Roger, supervision is the only way to go. Technically, they're guilty of crimes, but they're also victims themselves. Where to draw the line with that . . . well, that's something the courts will have to decide. But for now, we have a duty to care for them, but also a duty to protect society at large."

"You think we're dangerous?" Dougie spat.

"Not you. Not your brother. Not to other people, no." He hesitated, not sure if he was trying to let the truth of that last bit really sink in, or if he was just avoiding what he had to say next: "But maybe to yourselves."

Dougie looked . . . offended at that, but maybe also resigned. Mat just looked *betrayed*.

"Look, nothing's set in stone or anything. For some people, it may just be a short term thing, just until you get back on your feet and adjust to the outside world again, and maybe get a little bit of much needed therapy. For others, it might be the rest of their lives, but it's not *prison*. It's . . . it's a safe space to heal, and to help us prepare to prosecute the *real* bad guys here." Neither Mat nor Dougie seemed convinced, and Nate found himself scrambling to make them understand, to soften this blow some-fucking-how, to lighten the palpable suffering and despair that had settled over the room. "You'll have access to some of the best, most experienced psychiatrists in the fields of human trafficking and sex crimes. It's a nice place—a seized estate, all marble floors and canopy beds and meditation gardens and the whole nine. You'll be with other people who understand what you've been through, what you're still going through. No pressures, no responsibility but to *heal*, okay? I'm asking you both to trust me."

"I won't go," Dougie said. "I'm not sick. I'm not going to a hospital. I'm not letting them tell me what to do. You tell me it's wrong, what Nikolai did, but you just want to put me in a hospital where I'll be a slave to a shrink instead? Someone telling me when to eat, what to wear, telling me what TV to watch, locked doors and p-pills and—"

"Dougie . . ." Face as tight as his voice, Mat reached a hand out, almost but not quite touching Dougie's shoulder. Seeking permission, but Dougie didn't give it; he jerked away. Glared at Mat. "It's not *like* that, Dougie. I'll be right there with you, okay? It'll be good. It'll *help*."

Dougie's fist pounded the mattress as he shouted, "How many times do I have to tell you I don't *want* your damn *help*?"

Nate felt as helpless as Mat looked as he watched Mat swallow, swallow again. Blink back tears. Dougie was *furious*. Irrationally so. PTSD, Nate knew that, he'd seen the same behavior in Mat too. And what he was about to say wasn't going to make it any better. But he couldn't keep it a secret any longer, either.

"Dougie, I don't know how to tell you this, but you don't actually have a choice. Until you're cleared by your doctors, you're under conservatorship. Ward of the state. The only way you're going to be your own man again is to prove that you can care for yourself. And the only way to prove that is to do your time with a psychiatrist until he or she deems you fit."

Dougie's glare was downright withering. He threw back his blankets and, tubes and wires and flapping gown be damned, shuffled onto his knees. Into a position that Nate recognized all too well, and he felt the bile rising in his throat even before Dougie bowed his head with exaggerated flare and sneered, "Yes, Master."

And fine, maybe Nate really was a coward, but there was only one way he could respond to that.

He fled.

Two little words. That's all it was. Two. Little. Words.

Douglas had just been so fucking *angry*. Couldn't help himself, knowing that he didn't *have* to watch his mouth anymore. Could say what he wanted to say without being punished.

Still, he'd regretted it the moment he'd said it, done it. The looks of horror on Agent Johnson's and Mat's faces were unbearable to even think about. What they must think of him, what he'd just proven he *was*: a used up, broken, little jizz-covered toy no one wanted anymore. To watch a grown man scamper out of his room like that, partner on his heels . . .

He felt sick.

As bad as it was, though, Mat didn't draw back when Douglas reached out for him. Too afraid to hold hands—of what that meant between them—he closed his fingers around Mat's clammy wrist instead. "I'm sorry," he choked out. "I'm so sorry, I'm so— I'm a fuck up, I really am a fuck up, oh God, I'm sorry, I'm sorry."

He wanted Mat to leave him alone to his misery, leave him like everyone else had, like he surely would eventually when he figured out Douglas was good for nothing anymore. He wanted Mat to just get it the fuck *over* with.

He wanted Mat to never leave again.

"Shhh," Mat said, and enclosed Douglas in his arms. Douglas didn't fight off the embrace. He felt tiny and frail, smaller than he'd ever felt. Allen had starved him these past few weeks, deprived him of *everything* a human being needed to thrive. But Douglas didn't think what he was feeling right now was entirely physical.

"What's wrong with me? Why would I say that? He's right, he's right, I can't be trusted on my own, I am a d-danger."

Maybe that was really true. He'd . . . he'd *done* things, hadn't he? Things he was pretty sure weren't *right*. Things he was pretty sure would've horrified him, once upon a time. Maybe admitting that would get Mat to stay.

Maybe he'd even find some answers. Like what he was supposed to do with himself now. What the fucking *point* of it all was. Whether he really was sick, or if the rest of the world just couldn't see the beauty, the elegance, the purpose of the types of men Nikolai built.

Mat didn't acknowledge or deny what Douglas had said, just murmured in a soothing voice, "He's going to get you help. Both of us help. Just wait and see."

Douglas curled toward Mat, half on his knees again, just barely resisting the urge to press his forehead into Mat's lap. Mat wasn't a master; in the absence of real ones, Douglas had to keep reminding himself of that. "Please don't let them put me in a hospital, Mat, please! I don't . . . I just need some *time*, okay? I'll figure it out. I'll be useful. I'll be good. I promise." *I'll be a good boy. Be a good boy, Douglas.*

Mat curled a hand around the side of his head, then slowly dropped it like he'd changed his mind, laid it awkwardly atop the hand Douglas was still clutching to Mat's wrist. *Or maybe you just disgust him.* "You don't need to be useful, Dougie. You just need to heal. That's going to take time, but it's going to take help, too. I'm gonna be there with you every step—"

"You're fucking lying!" Douglas jerked his hand back, jerked his whole body back. "You heard what that agent said! He said some people would only be there for a couple weeks. They'll let you out way before they ever let out someone like me because they think I'm fucked in the head! I'll be all alone in there. They'll keep me until I die because I'll never go back to being your perfect PhD meal ticket brother. I'll wind up sucking the orderlies' dicks instead."

"No." Mat shook his head, reached for Douglas's hand again but then didn't touch. Never touched. Proving his own damn lie. "That's not going to happen. I'm going to stay with you. Nobody's going to make you . . . service them like that, Dougie. The FBI isn't going to let anyone work there who might try to exploit you."

"You don't know that! You don't know anything! And who fucking says it's *exploiting* me, huh? Maybe I *want* to suck the orderlies' dicks. Maybe what I do *matters*." The urge to leap from the bed, rip out the IV and pace and *hit something* was so strong, he nearly caved, nearly lashed out like the animal he'd once been. Nikolai might've lied to him, manipulated him, but he'd been right about that, at least. About the anger in Douglas. The desperation. The neediness. The ache to be loved. "God, you're so fucking stupid, Mat! You've always been stupid. You never— You always—" He wished he could howl, claw, fight, let out a bloodcurdling scream, but he knew if he acted out any more than he was, they wouldn't just put him in a hospital, they'd put him in a fucking padded room.

"Maybe I am stupid," Mat said, voice artificially calm even as he spoke through his teeth. "But you're sick. I don't doubt that you want to do . . . things, but that doesn't mean it's right or healthy. And you're right. You're never going to go back to the person you used to be before all this. Neither will I. Nobody expects that of you. Not me, and not the doctors. They're just going to want to see you unlearn some of the shit Nikolai put in your head. Get on the right track. Learn to ask for help. Learn healthy coping skills."

"Is that what this talk is? Healthy coping skills?"

"I don't know. I'm not exactly in the best mental health of my life, either. Maybe one day you'll be well enough to see that." Mat's eyes were wet, his voice quaking. "Maybe then, you'll take care of me a little, too."

Ah-hah. The angle. Always a fucking *angle*.

"Is that what this is about? You just want me back in good enough shape that you can lean on me? Is this about money? Nikolai said—"

"I fucking know what Nikolai said!" Mat roared. And then he flinched, tears streaking down his face. "He told you whatever you needed to hear, Dougie. Whatever he needed to say in order to twist you into what he wanted you to be. He lied. I think you know he lied, somewhere deep down inside you. I don't want to own you and I don't want to use you and I don't want to control you. I just want to see you happy."

"Then you should have left me with Nikolai."

Mat's head fell, and Douglas thought he'd won—as hollow as that feeling was—but then Mat looked up again, his face expressionless and hard. "There was no leaving you with Nikolai, Dougie. He gave you away—sold you *for money*—and he wasn't coming to get you back."

Douglas grimaced, closed his eyes. Fuck Mat for reminding him of that, for pointing out the broken trust between him and Nikolai. But maybe they could've fixed it, right? Maybe Nikolai deserved that chance. Douglas didn't even know anymore.

"So, sorry, it was either come with me, or stay with Allen." He stood. Brushed invisible dirt off his worn gray sweat suit and turned to leave. "And don't even try telling me you'd rather I'd left you with *him*."

As much as it shook him, shook everything he still wanted—*needed*—to believe in, Douglas didn't have an answer to that.

CHAPTER TWO

Douglas had become exquisitely well attuned to tension in his time at Allen's. He'd learned to read people in school, of course, and then Nikolai had honed those skills in person, but at Allen's it'd been a matter of pure survival. Know when to be invisible, to keep your mouth shut, and when to have it *wide* open.

And this car ride was one of the tensest hours of his entire life.

One that opening his mouth definitely would not fix. Which was a shame, because even he was self-aware enough to realize that was the single strongest tool in his arsenal these days.

Mat wasn't speaking to or looking at anyone. The pretty agent with those ridiculous hazel eyes (oh, how Allen would have *loved* him) was sitting stiff-backed in the driver's seat, fingers clenched around the steering wheel. He kept taking breaths, as if to say something. Kept not saying anything. He looked wrecked.

Douglas wasn't feeling much better himself.

He was exhausted just from feeling angry all the time, let alone from the confusion of not knowing who to be angry *at*: the outside world—Mat, Agent Johnson, Nikolai, God and the whole universe—or himself?

So he sat and stewed in it.

Arriving at the group home left Douglas with the same sense of unmoored apprehension he'd felt when he'd first arrived at Allen's, only this time there was no pride or determination to temper it. There was no one to impress here with his training, his skill, his cleverness or pedigree. Only doctors to convince he wasn't crazy, wasn't broken beyond repair. And somehow he didn't think Nikolai's tactics would help him there.

The home was as stately as Allen's, the grounds as large and well manicured. Carriage house, stables, servants' homes, in-law house, gardens, reflecting pool, tree-lined winding driveway, the whole nine yards. Here the English-style manor home looked well placed in its surroundings. An estate where the leaves would fall in autumn and maybe there'd even be a dusting of snow come winter. He'd have maybe liked it, if he were coming here under different circumstances.

As it was, he despaired at the fact that it was all such a fucking *waste*. What would he do here? What purpose would he serve? How would he figure out what to make of the rest of his life if he was trapped here at the whims of a whole new set of unknown masters who didn't even have the balls to call themselves what they were?

Agent Johnson pulled their car to a stop right at the curving top of the drive and cleared his throat. "This is the place," he said, sounding falsely light, like they'd just arrived at Disney.

"I'd assume so," Douglas snarled before he could stop himself. "Unless you were planning on doing a leisurely tour of stately houses?"

Mat bristled. "Shut *up*, Dougie."

"Hey, hey," Agent Johnson said. "Stand down, Mat. It's fine. It's all fine."

Protecting Agent Johnson? Is that what that was? Douglas had just assumed it to be garden variety hostility, but now that he thought about it, there did seem to be some kind of extra special tension between the two of them. Affection? Gone sour? Mat certainly didn't get protective like that with just anybody, that was for sure. Especially not an FBI agent perfectly capable of defending himself.

Agent Johnson turned in his seat to look at them both. "Okay guys, this is pretty much the end of the line for me. I've got a lot of work ahead, and so do you. I want you to know, though, that just because you won't see me around as much doesn't mean I'm not still working your case, because there couldn't be anything farther from the truth. You guys are my number one priority. I'm not going to rest until—"

"It's okay, Nate," Mat said flatly. "You don't have to give us any speeches. We know you have a trial to prep, and we're in good hands here." He reached forward, hand out like he planned on laying it on Nate's shoulder, but Nate turned at that exact second and got out of the car, avoiding the touch.

Well, well, well.

Mat fell back, expression closed off, then followed Nate. Douglas, hating himself, followed Mat.

"All I'm saying is," Mat said, trailing Nate a little more urgently now, "you don't have to defend yourself to us, okay? You don't have to make a big show of the fact that you're not abandoning us. You don't have to do any of that. Just . . . stop overcompensating and do your job."

Agent Johnson cleared his throat, shook his head. He looked *very* uncomfortable, even though Douglas couldn't see his face; the man was staring resolutely at his own hand on the doorknob. "Of course. You'll, um, see me here sometimes; I'll be doing several rounds of interviews to gather evidence." Another pause, another throat-clearing noise. "So uh, let's get you, um, checked in, okay?"

Mat said nothing. Neither did Douglas. Nobody was interested in what he had to say anyway. That wasn't, after all, what he'd been made for.

The large foyer had been converted to a lobby, complete with registration desk, but was still as grand as Allen's. Douglas had become so accustomed to such beauty that he was numb to it now. Nikolai would've said something smooth like *No marble tile compares to the treasure that is you, Douglas*, but the sentiment felt empty in his mind, rang hollow. Nikolai wasn't here, after all. Hadn't come for him. Had left him to rot at Allen's and now was leaving him to rot with the FBI. Okay, in fairness, Nikolai couldn't help it anymore—*he* was rotting with the FBI too. But whose fault was that, anyway?

Mat's, mostly.

Yeah, maybe. But that still meant Nikolai wasn't nearly as infallible as Douglas had been led to believe. That his stupid, useless beast of a brother had been able to bring such devastation down on Nikolai's head . . .

He didn't know *what* to believe, anymore. Where to put his hope, his faith.

Maybe he just didn't have any left.

"Welcome to Huntington Estates." The woman behind the registration desk smiled a warm and genuine smile, the kind of smile that said *I want to be your friend* without the *I want you to service me* caveat he was so used to seeing. He suspected it wasn't *actually* condescending, but he damn well took it that way, and it made him angry. Even angrier when Mat *didn't* take it that way, if his return smile—tiny, hesitant, but real—was any indication.

"Afternoon, Helen," Agent Johnson said. He sounded nervous. "I can't stay"—beside him, Mat bristled—"just here to check in the Carmichael brothers."

Her eyes went to her computer screen, and the keyboard clacked for a moment, and then she said, bright but not chipper, "Ah, Mat and Dougie?"

"Yep," Agent Johnson said, and for a moment Douglas let it slide because good slaves never spoke out of turn, let alone corrected their masters. But then it hit him like a two by four between the eyes that he *wasn't* a slave anymore, that his master had abandoned him, and he could damn well talk if he wanted to.

"No," he said.

Mat stared at him like he'd sprouted a second head, like he couldn't believe Douglas had it in him to reclaim even that small measure of autonomy. Well, fuck him. Douglas wasn't some hapless, brainless toy. He could stand on his own two feet.

Agent Johnson said nothing. The woman behind the counter—Helen; Nikolai had taught him always to remember people's names—was smiling patiently at him, waiting for him to speak again. Everyone was. And, okay, so maybe he wasn't hapless or brainless, but he also wasn't used to a room full of people waiting to hear what he had to say. Waiting to watch him, sure. But *listen*? No one had cared about that but Nikolai and Penny, and they were both gone.

"No," he said again, not because he thought he needed to, but because it just plain *felt* good. The word had power. A kind of power long denied him. Speaking it now was like stretching bound wings for the first time in years. "No. That's not my name. I keep *telling* you." He turned to Mat, accusing. Fuck him for being so continuously, deliberately disrespectful. "That's not my name. It's Dougl—"

But it wasn't, was it? That was the name Nikolai had christened him with. He wasn't Nikolai's boy anymore. That world was gone, and Douglas with it.

As gone as Dougie, the boy the therapists here would no doubt expect him to be before they'd declare him fit to be his own master.

"It's Doug," he said, firmly. "Just Doug."

Mat's expression softened, looked almost *happy*.

I didn't do it for you, Douglas thought reflexively, then felt sorry for it. Just because he didn't have to make Mat happy—didn't have to make anyone happy anymore—didn't mean it was right or good to get so angry when he did. Didn't mean he didn't *want* to make people happy, still.

After all, what else was he good for, if not that?

Mat nodded, as if they'd spoken to one another, and turned to the counter. "You got that down? Doug."

"Of course," Helen demurred. "You'll find while you're here that it's our number one priority to respect your autonomy. I'd never want to call any of you by a name you didn't want for yourselves, and neither would anyone else." She turned her gentle expression on Douglas. *No. Doug. Just Doug.* "Doug and Mat Carmichael. I'll just get you both some wristbands printed up, and then call someone to come and show you around. Okay? Won't take a second."

Wristbands. Wristbands for the doctors to know their names.

And to track them, probably. To keep them out of rooms they didn't belong in. To lock the place down if they tried to run away.

You're patients, not prisoners, Helen's face said as she fastened Doug's around his still bruised wrist. Definitely computerized somehow. It was too heavy to be just plastic and paper.

But there it was, typed up, official: *Doug Carmichael.*

He thought maybe, just maybe, he could get used to that. Figure out what it really meant. But not here. Not trapped like the slave they kept saying he no longer was, with masters they kept saying he no longer had, and a brother he hadn't thought of as anything but a burden for god only knew how long.

The room they brought Mat to was small—partitioned from a bigger one, by the looks of things—but clean and open. There was a window. The door was open, unless he closed it. There were no restraints on the bed.

It said a lot about Mat for *that* to be one of the high points of the room's decor.

But it was still nice. He felt safe. The common areas were monitored and recorded, but their bedrooms weren't. They had a curfew, but it was gently enforced, and clearly for their own safety. Mat watched movies. Worked out in the gym, just listening to music and jogging for hours on the treadmill and lifting weights. He didn't spar, didn't even work the bags, didn't miss it at all. He went to therapy: both group and individual sessions. He didn't talk much in group, but he listened well and gave it his all. He liked it. Dr. Tremmel—*Call me Beth, please*—was a rock-steady presence, almost motherly though she only had ten years on Mat, and she lent a shoulder at every turn but never ever let him get away with bullshit.

He didn't see Dougie—*Doug*—much, but Beth assured him that was probably for the best. They both needed a break from one another, and in Mat's case, just like on a depressurized plane, he needed to help himself before he could take care of anyone else. He knew that, he *did*. It'd been so long since he'd even *considered* his own health and safety, let alone more esoteric, seemingly unreachable concepts like happiness and fulfillment, that he was running on less than empty.

In the common rooms, there was a clear divide: those who'd been broken by slavery or even embraced it, like Doug had, and those who hadn't. Who hadn't been "trained" the way Doug and Mat had been, either because they hadn't gotten to that point yet, or because whoever'd purchased them just hadn't cared.

Mat didn't fit in with either group. He wasn't brainwashed, but he had seen what that brainwashing looked like and couldn't muster the same kind of derision the other non-brainwashed victims clearly felt for those who were. It was easy to criticize the broken slaves for "just giving up" when you hadn't seen a person taken apart piece by agonizing piece. Mat knew better, though.

He might be angry at Doug for the things he'd done to Mat, but he couldn't sit by and wholesale condemn him, either. The therapists and doctors and nurses all tried to bridge the divide, help people understand and empathize with one another, but the chasm of hurt was huge, and often personal too. Plenty of the unbroken folks had been harmed by well-trained pets. Violations like that were hard to forgive and even harder to forget. Mat knew that first-fucking-hand. Was reminded of it in staggeringly visceral detail every time he managed to track his brother down.

Which wasn't often—Doug was too busy behaving like the rebellious teenager he'd never been, testing every edict, every promise, every rule. Never attending group, skipping out on private, staying in the dining hall only long enough to gather his meal and retreat back to his room with it, stalking the grounds past curfew and tampering with his wristband. Even handing out "favors" in bathrooms and closets, if the rumors were true. Like that was the only way he knew to make friends anymore, to fit in. He'd no doubt heard how the unbroken folks talked about him, sneering down their noses like he was some bit of filth they'd stepped in. Just as surely as he'd heard how the trained pets talked, like he was some perfection to aspire to, one of "Nikolai's boys," a masterwork of art and poise who'd surely have all the answers now that their worlds had imploded. In absence of a master, they turned to the highest on the totem pole of slaves.

And maybe Mat didn't really know who *Doug* was, but he knew who Dougie was and he was pretty sure he knew who Douglas was too, and no matter which side of his little brother he looked at, he knew none of what the others thought of him was true. He wasn't scum. He wasn't a leader, either. Mat could tell in the few scant moments Doug let them spend together that the kid was desperately unhappy. Mat just didn't know how to fix it. How to help him.

Nobody did, it seemed.

And as if navigating the politics of the residents and the troubles of his brother wasn't hard enough, there was Nate to consider, too. Nate, who showed up at the facility at least a few times a week, spiriting away one person at a time for private interviews. Nate, who never spoke to Mat, not in a professional context and not in a personal one. On the rare occasion Mat tried, Nate always had somewhere else to be. Some meeting he was late for, some reason to scurry off without a word.

And more than just hurting Mat, making him feel like he was too pathetic and pitiful to endure, it fucking pissed him off.

How dare Nate just shove him aside this way? After everything they'd been through together? So what if he'd gotten hard at the thought of Nate fucking him? Nate had gotten hard plenty. Besides, it's not like he'd enjoyed the actual being-raped part. He'd done what they'd had to do, just like Nate had, just like *everyone* had. And if Nate couldn't look him in the eye after that? Didn't respect him anymore? Could only see the victim and not the person? Well, fuck him. Fuck him with a foot-long fucking horse cock and see how *he* liked it.

He winced. No, he didn't mean that. Not that part. Knew better now than to even joke about shit like that.

Mat shook his head and glanced at the clock on his little desk. Not that he really *needed* a desk, but Beth was having him keep a journal, and it was as good a place as any to fumble through his awkwardness. Speaking of Beth, he was due to his daily solo session in ten minutes. Unlike his brother, he had no intention of skipping out. Talking wasn't easy—not about what'd happened to him and *especially* not about how it made him feel—but it was undeniably cathartic. Helped to put things in perspective, even. He stood from his desk. Stretched. Snagged his gray hoodie from the foot of his bed—his own little sweatshirt-fleece security blanket, he knew, but that didn't mean he needed it any less, and Beth always said he could give himself permission to take advantage of these little comforts unless they interfered with his day-to-day life—and headed down to the first floor where all the offices had been set up.

Beth's office was in what once had been a game room. The pool and poker tables were gone, but the heavy wood paneling and fireplace and antique furniture still remained, and the whole thing reminded Mat a little too uncomfortably much of Nikolai's study. When he'd told Beth that the first day, she'd offered to relocate, but he'd turned her down. He *needed* that discomfort. Needed to face it. It kept him sharp. Challenged him in a way he could actually handle. Made him feel like maybe, just maybe, he was making progress by the mere act of voluntarily staying in that space for an hour a day.

She was sitting at her desk when he arrived, and offered him one of her even, pleasant smiles. He tried not to trust it too much; she reminded him a little of Coach Darryl—she'd work him until he cried uncle, but it was *controlled* pain, and for an obviously greater good. And she cared. She'd only known him a week, but she *cared*. Probably the kind of person who picked up stray kittens off the street.

Which was sort of him in a nutshell these days, wasn't it. Mangy and skittish and starving for things he couldn't name.

"Afternoon, Mat." She waved him into the recliner he used for his sessions, the one that reminded him of the damn branding chair.

"Heya Doc." He sat, tilted the recliner back like always, making it hard enough to get out of that he couldn't just launch up and pace whenever the urge struck. Which was often. His fingers curled tight around the plush armrests, but that was okay. Coping mechanism. Didn't make him weak. Beth had spent the first few days practically beating that through his skull. Still did, sometimes.

Beth waited a long moment for him to say something, anything else. It'd only been a week, but he knew that technique by now: leave silence for the patient to fill, and odds were they'd fill it with whatever was bothering them the most. Thing was, Mat never seemed to know where to begin. How to pick one turd off the steaming pile of shit that the last year of his life had been. Still *was*, if he was honest with himself.

"So," she finally said, shuffling through some files on her desk. She didn't get up, come around, sit closer. Knew he liked the barrier between them. He appreciated that. There were no barriers in any of the group sessions, and somehow he rarely seemed able to talk in those. Not like he did here. "I thought maybe we could talk today about getting you out of here."

"Wh-what?" Mat sputtered, fingers tightening on the armrest.

She nodded. "You're making great progress, Mat, and while I totally support you staying longer here—as long as you need—I wanted to let you know that the option's on the table for you to leave—"

"Not without Dougie— Doug. Not without my brother." He twisted his hands in the fabric of his sweatpants. "He's not doing too good here, I think you know that. I can't just leave him like that."

"I agree," Beth said. "That's why I wanted to discuss another possibility with you. Would you be open to taking on his conservatorship when you go? Now, there's no pressure, Mat, you know how I feel about you taking on too much responsibility over him at cost to you, but if it's something you want, I'd be happy to write up a letter of recommendation that you take over your brother's care in a different environment. With your permission, of course." She put up a hand when his mouth opened, although he was pretty sure he wasn't going to do anything more than gape like a fish. "Because of the trial, you'd have to be in temporary witness protection, but you could be in your own space. I'm not . . . without discussing specifics, I'm not sure this environment is all that healthy for Doug. I honestly think that with out-of-home support, he might do better just with you."

"So he *is* having sex with the other patients here," Mat said flatly.

"I think some of the other patients here are reinforcing and enabling unhealthy behaviors and attitudes," she corrected. "He needs some space."

Mat's hand went from his sweats to his face; he couldn't decide if he was rubbing frustration away or just plain hiding. How the fuck was he supposed to deal with this? Parenting a mentally stable kid brother had been hard enough. But one who hated you *and* thought every argument could be solved with his penis? And the whole time you were fucked off your rocker yourself?

"You don't have to do this, Mat. You really don't. You don't have to leave here, either, not if you don't want to. And please know that even if you do, I'd still expect you to see me an hour a day, and of course you'd have my number and could call anytime at all."

"I know," Mat mumbled into his hand. "But . . ."

"Doug's care is *our* responsibility. Your first responsibility is *your* care. If you feel you can't attend to your own well-being while also attending to his, then this matter is off the table."

"It's not that," Mat said, and realized he was still covering his face. He let his arm flop back onto the armrest. Sighed. "I'm just tired, you know? 'S no different than ever, though. Since the second Mom and Dad died. Fighting's only ever been my second job. Dougie's the first. Always has been, and I'm cool with that, I really am. I don't resent him. I don't wish it were different." Well, okay, he certainly wished his parents weren't dead, but if they had to be, he had no regrets about making Dougie priority number one. "I don't *want* his care to be your responsibility. I *want* it to be mine. I want . . ." He bit his lip against an inconvenient tremble, a tightness in his throat at a flash of memory best left buried beneath fifty tons of concrete. "I want to *fix* things between us." He raised one hand before Beth could respond to that;

he already knew what she was going to say. "And I know, I *know* that's not all on me. But I also know it's never gonna happen if he stays here, because sulking around and not talking to anybody and hiding in his room and fucking his way into people's affections isn't gonna help him get what *he* needs to be able to make things right. With me or himself or anyone."

And didn't he know that all too well. Drifting through the safe house like a ghost, miserable and withdrawn and silent, neglecting his body and his mind and throwing himself like the worst kind of manipulative slave at the one good thing to come into his life all year.

Fuck, why did he miss Nate so much? It wasn't fair that he should ache like this for someone he wanted to punch in the fucking nose, for someone treating him like a fucking leper.

"Mat?"

He jerked his eyes up to Beth's. She had this way of studying him without making him feel naked, dissected. He still squirmed a little beneath such intense attention, though. "Huh?"

"Where'd you go just then?"

Nate. Fuck. Did he really want to talk to her about Nate? About all the . . . the what? the hopes? the attraction? the potential he'd projected onto someone who'd only let him down in his own head? Nate had done everything he'd promised to do. *Everything.* So why did it hurt so fucking much to think about him?

Because he's not here. He saw what Nikolai made you and he ran as fast as he fucking could.

"Mat?"

No. He wasn't ready to talk about that yet. One clusterfuck at a time, thank you very much. "Sorry," he said. "Just . . . thinking through the angles. What would I have to do? To get the conservatorship?"

She didn't much look like she believed him, but she played along anyway. "I'd write a letter of recommendation on your behalf, vouching that I think you're well enough to take Doug into your care as long as you have a good support network in place. We clearly establish the nature of that support network and agree to binding terms: you continue to attend therapy, provide a safe environment, stay off the radar until after the trial, submit to periodic evaluation by

HHS, and so on. In the meantime, you convince Doug to come see me daily so that I can evaluate whether he'll be safe in your care."

Get Doug to finally start attending his therapy sessions. Yeah. Piece of cake.

Mat groaned.

"And he would need to continue attending sessions after he leaves here. I wouldn't push for every day like I will with you—I think we both know that's not going to happen—but twice a week at a minimum. We can even do it over Skype. I think the FBI would prefer that anyway—safer that way for everyone."

Mat let his head *thunk* back against the recliner's headrest. Said to the crown molding above Beth, too weary to be angry, "Another cage, then? Really? Can't leave the damn house?"

"It's not like that, Mat. You'll be free to live your lives in witness protection. You just couldn't come back *here*. There are some . . . most likely baseless concerns that locations associated with this investigation may be on some unsavory people's radars. The FBI arrested a lot of people in that sting, but the world's a big place, you understand."

Not big enough, if you asked him.

"You know this case has been fast tracked. The primary trial's in less than three months. You won't have to hide forever."

The crown molding blurred. Mat blinked; a line of cool wetness trailed down into his ears. "I just want my life back," he said.

Shit.

He hadn't meant to say that. What a stupid fucking thing to say. He *knew* better.

A pause, and then, "Mat, you know there is—"

"—is no going back. Only forward." He swiped at the dampness on his face, his stubbornly leaking eyes. *Way to leave a good impression on the woman trying to spring you, asshole.* "Yeah, I know. I just . . . I don't see how to get Dougie to agree to this."

Doug, asshole. You could start by respecting his fucking identity choices.

"Oh, I don't think it'll be a problem," Beth said, and though Mat was still staring at the joint of wall and ceiling, he could hear the smile in her voice. "Just tell him it'll get him out of *this* place. I'm sure he'll be all over it."

CHAPTER THREE

Getting Doug to say yes was shockingly easy. The kid had hardly said ten words to Mat since they'd gotten here, and at least nine of them had been to make it clear that just because he'd be going with Mat didn't mean Mat should be getting any funny ideas about trying to play Doug's new master, but at least he'd agreed.

Turned out the hardest part of all this was actually Mat convincing *himself* to leave. The car was due to pick them up in ten minutes, and he still hadn't finished packing what few belongings he had.

Maybe he was just nervous about spending any more time in a car with Nate again. Wasn't like that'd gone so well last time. An hour that had felt like fifty spent staring at the back of Nate's head and reminding himself of all the things he might once have been able to have with the guy if he hadn't fucked it up so badly. If he himself weren't so fucked up.

Or maybe it was the idea of swapping this isolated, safe space for a two-bedroom apartment above a knitting store in Baltimore. Sure, he'd picked out the apartment himself (or rather, Beth had given him half a dozen choices and he'd gone with the one that seemed most tolerable), but that didn't mean he was enthusiastic about actually *going* there. What he wanted was to go home, to *their* house, but that had already been sold to somebody else.

It was a pretty good symbol of everything Beth was trying to get him to accept: they couldn't go back.

Besides, if he were being honest with himself, he'd probably take one look at their old living room, the place he'd come home that night to find Dougie at the mercy of those men, the place their lives had been irrevocably altered, and flip his shit for a week.

Maybe it was better to start fresh in a place with no associations. Move forward, just like Beth kept saying.

Now if only Beth had an answer for what he was supposed to *do* with himself in this brave new world. Couldn't fight anymore, not after what he'd done to all those men in Allen's arena. Only had a high school diploma and the one marketable skill. Well, okay, two now thanks to Nikolai, but no fucking way was he going *there*. They could live off their slice of the survivors' fund for a little while—a year or two, maybe, but no guarantees after that—but even if money weren't an issue, Mat wasn't exactly built for sitting around all day doing nothing.

He didn't even have any hobbies. Started fighting so young he'd never bothered with anything else. Fuck-all knew if he was even a good student; he'd never really bothered with that either. Maybe he could become a personal trainer. Of course, then he'd have to *touch* people. Bodyguard? Hah, right. Some bodyguard he'd been when it'd really counted.

Mat sighed. *Suck it up, Carmichael. Car's gonna be here any second.*

He missed Coach Darryl. Maybe when the trial was over, they could move back to Vegas and he could beg a job teaching little kids in Darryl's gym. Kids, they'd be safe. Untainted.

Whatever. Best not to think about it now. Now he had to focus on getting him and Dougie settled in a new city. He threw his spare clothes into his gym bag. Grabbed his toiletries from the bathroom. And the picture he'd kept all this time—the one of Mom and Dad and him and Dougie he'd stolen back from Nikolai's. The one from before his whole life had gone to shit not once but *twice*.

When he was done, the duffel was still half empty. How fucking sad was that? He had nothing. Not even a decent wardrobe. Just workout stuff, built for maximum comfort. No junk; no DVDs or old cords that didn't connect to anything or pens he'd stolen. Nearly nothing sentimental, except for that single picture.

He felt like a damn ghost again. Or maybe still. Like the previous him hadn't even existed. Nothing tethering him to the world except for his duty to Dougie. *No, it's Doug now. Doug. How many times you gonna screw that up?* Without those bonds of brotherhood, he thought he'd just . . . float away.

Beth said that was normal. That it'd fade in time. That finding new hobbies, a job, building new connections would ease that pain.

But how was he supposed to do any of that when he kept getting bounced from one place to the next?

I said suck it up, *Carmichael!*

Yeah, just like he always did. Well, at least it was Coach Darryl's voice in his head today instead of Nikolai's.

He slung his half-empty duffel over his shoulder and trudged down the hall, down the stairs, found Doug in the lobby with Louise. They were talking like two normal people, Doug looking almost *animated* in her presence, some normal college kid being graced with the attention of a beautiful woman. It made Mat's chest hitch with an ache so deep he couldn't tell if it was pain or pleasure. Both, maybe. Such a rare, breathtaking thing to see Doug genuinely happy in a way that was actually healthy—excitement about the future, pleasure in another's company without power plays or expectations. But at the same time, it hurt like the fucking serum to be reminded that something so normal for most people was so rare for Doug.

He was enthusiastically chatting up a gorgeous woman, and here Mat was wanting to throw him a parade.

Mat swallowed down the tightness in his chest and made his feet move again.

"Hey," he said as he approached them, nodding and trying for a smile. Utterly failed at it, no surprise.

Well, Louise smiled for the both of them. "Hey Mat." Even Doug nodded in greeting, and not in a remotely hostile way. Mat managed that smile after all—for him. "Ready to bust this joint, boys?"

Not really, Mat thought, and then, *As ready as I'll ever be.* Except . . . "Where's Nate?"

Louise's smile faltered, just a little. "Had a meeting in the prosecutor's office he couldn't miss. Tried to reschedule, but—"

"*Are you—*" Mat realized he was shouting; had to, to hear himself over the sudden roaring in his ears. But every head in the lobby had turned toward their little group, and Doug . . . Doug had tucked himself, wide-eyed, half behind Louise's back.

Fuck.

He squeezed his eyes shut, clenched his fists, took a deep breath and counted to ten. Well, four—no way he was making it any further. "Are you *kidding* me?" he said again, quieter this time but just as harsh. He might've maybe even spit a little, but whatever, it wasn't like the situation didn't fucking call for it. In fact, he had some *choice fucking words* to go with his spittle, but if he wanted to keep his cleared functioning status—and thus his right to get out of here with Doug—then he needed to put a lid on it while anyone medical was within earshot.

And Louise wasn't the one who needed to hear it, anyway. Not her fault Nate was such a goddamned coward. Judgmental sniveling prick. Fucking liar. Wishy-washy piece of shit.

Doug was really shrinking away from him now.

This was wrong. This was so wrong. Nate might have colossally mistreated him, but that didn't give Mat the right to terrorize anyone but the man himself over it.

He took a deep breath. Another one. Louise watched him silently, her body language patient but protective.

"Let's just go," Mat said at last. "He's not even worth it."

Louise raised an eyebrow at that last bit, but she was wise enough not to reopen the discussion. Just led them to the car in silence.

They all stayed silent the entire drive.

Louise didn't attempt any small talk. Mat kept his arms folded and his gaze out the window, stewing to himself. Doug did whatever it was Doug did; Mat didn't feel much like looking at him, but he was quiet, and that was all that mattered.

Just because no one was speaking, though, didn't mean things were silent for Mat. His head was a noisy place, a million anxieties and angers all yelling at him at once.

But the one thing he kept coming back to was Nate.

Which was a terrible fucking thing to be worrying about on the car ride over to a temporary new life in pre-trial witness protection with his head-case self legally responsible for his even bigger head-case of a brother. He should be focusing on Doug. On making the new apartment livable. On making *life* livable. For the both of them. Not pining like some love-sick middle-schooler over his does-he-or-doesn't-he crush.

Love-sick, Mat? Really?

Certainly fucking felt like it, didn't it. Well, that was just one more tick in the my-life's-a-mess-and-Nikolai-fucked-my-head-forever column, wasn't it.

Louise pulled the car off the highway and onto a local road. Suburban sprawl quickly turned into the tight little quaintness of a walking town steeped in history and swarming with college kids: pre-war brick townhouses, tree-lined residential/commercial streets, little mom-and-pop shops for everything under the sun—with, of course, the requisite Starbucks on every corner. Densely populated without feeling overcrowded.

Eventually, she double-parked in front of a knitting store sandwiched between a vegetarian cafe and a high-end clothing boutique. The building they were in was four stories high, the floors above street level adorned with little wrought-iron balconies and window AC units.

"This is it," she said. "Come on, I'll give you the grand tour."

Neither he nor Doug replied. They just heaved near-simultaneous sighs and climbed out of the car behind her. By instinct Mat grabbed both duffels—his and Doug's—but Doug threw him a squinty-eyed glare and snatched his away. Mat held his hand up, placating—*I don't want to fight, little bro. Not now. Okay?*

Doug just looked away, turning to follow Louise through the front door. Mat sighed again and followed.

The grand tour wasn't so grand, but he'd certainly stayed in worse places. It was clean, old but not run down, sparsely but suitably furnished with what looked like turnkey Ikea solutions. Two bedrooms for privacy. One bathroom they'd have to share. An eat-in kitchen complete with dishes and utensils and pots and pans. A living room with windows and a balcony all overlooking the scenic street. New laptop on the desk in the corner for those Skype sessions with Beth. Every wall, every stick of furniture painted in neutral colors. Decent enough, but soulless.

Beth would've called it an opportunity to shape a blank living space into a new home. A good thing, an exciting thing. But to Mat it just felt . . . lonely and sad.

It seemed the whole fucking world felt that way, lately.

"Okay then," Louise said. "I've gotta head back, but here's your new IDs." She handed him two manila envelopes, each containing a recap of the life histories they'd been rehearsing all week, a driver's license, a couple of credit cards, a gym membership (not the kind with a boxing ring, just one of those Planet Fitness places where overcompensating guys went to supplement their steroid regimens), even a frequent shopper card for the local Weis Markets. All under the names Samuel and Jacob Senders.

"Remember," Louise said, "you're free to move about, but *stick to the cover*, okay? And keep vigilant. You even so much as *suspect* you see something, you call me. Be smart, stay away from cameras. And no hanging in places that'll give you away—no fights, no boxing gyms, no . . . wherever it is psychologists gather."

"Really?" Doug snapped. "We're going over this *again*?"

Mat winced—where the fuck had *that* attitude come from, when Doug and Louise had looked so chummy before?—but Louise let it roll right off her, nodded her head, and said, "Well, technically we're done now, but yes. If you don't make it to the trial, my boss is gonna be *pissed*." But then she smiled and winked and tossed Mat the keys, turned around, and let herself out.

Mat stood there, keys in hand and brain frozen, for several long seconds. Then called, "Wait!" and jogged out after her. Caught her at the bottom of the stairwell.

She stopped and turned when he touched her arm. "Having second thoughts?" she asked.

Mat shook his head. "I'll handle *him*. What I wanted to talk to you about—" He pulled in a deep breath, still not quite believing he was planning on saying this. "Nate. I mean, he's been avoiding me for weeks. I thought he cared. What happened between us on that island . . ."

Louise's face turned grim. "I know."

"Is that it? Does he . . . does he hate me? Or blame me, or does just looking at me make him uncomfortable? Because otherwise I don't understand why he's acting this way. I don't. Understand. It's eating me alive."

She fell against the wall, arms crossed, shaking her head. "That fucking idiot." Barking out a laugh, she opened the door and left, not even bothering to answer Mat's question. Too distracted to, maybe, because she kept muttering under her breath, "That fucking idiot. That fucking idiot."

Yeah, well, Nate wasn't the only one, because watching Louise go without a single clue what she was talking about . . . Mat was feeling like a pretty big fucking idiot too.

Once Louise was gone, Mat more or less managed to shove her, and Nate, and the trial, and all of it out of his mind, and took Doug exploring.

No car, but that was okay—this was a walking city for sure, and the public transport didn't seem terrible if they needed to venture further afield. He christened his shiny new debit card at the vegetarian cafe in their building—hey, Louise had said to vary their usual routines, right?—and both he and Doug were pleasantly surprised by how good the food was. They wandered up and down the streets all afternoon, practically *luxuriating* in that strange sense of freedom, of normalcy. Doug even seemed happy, didn't snap or slip into one of his dark moods even once.

They bought new clothes. Mat silently questioned some of Doug's choices—tight sleeveless tees and skinny jeans and a watch set in a thick black leather band—but said nothing, tried hard to keep his confusion and disapproval and . . . and *hurt* off his face. He himself went the opposite way, track pants and boot-cut jeans and baggy tees and hoodies, and like fuck he'd ever put something around his wrist again that looked like a cuff. But if it made Doug happy, he'd try—he'd really, *really* try—not to worry or judge.

They found a little shoe store, and both bought new pairs of running shoes. When Mat asked if maybe he'd want to start jogging in the mornings with him again, Doug offered him a shrug and a "maybe," but it wasn't sullen, and Mat chose to take it as a good sign. Dragged Doug into the ice cream shop next to the shoe store and let him heap more toppings than ice cream into his cup. Mat, meanwhile, hadn't forgotten Coach Darryl's speech about taking care of his body—whether he ever planned to fight again or not—so he went for frozen yogurt with fresh berries.

Which was actually pretty fucking amazing, so no loss.

The day got away from them, but that was okay. They grabbed Chinese takeout on the way back to the apartment, and browsed through the art gallery beside the restaurant while they waited. Doug seemed particularly enamored of a local artist's painting depicting two bridled horses having a graze in a field of vivid blue flowers. Mat came up beside him, forced himself to lay a brotherly hand on Doug's shoulder because Doug didn't seem to have the *thing* about touch that Mat had and normal brothers did that, didn't they? Touched each other without . . . Touched each other *innocently*?

"You really like that, huh?"

Doug nodded, eyes still on the painting, shopping bags full of clothes forgotten at his feet.

Odd. Doug had never been a horse kid before. And sure, it was pretty, but it seemed more the kind of thing you'd find hanging in the room of a teenage girl than a . . . well, whatever Doug was these days.

But clearly he liked it. *Really* liked it. Art could be strange like that, connect to people in ways they'd never considered or thought possible.

And really, the canvas wasn't that big, maybe eighteen inches square. It'd probably look nice over their couch, or maybe in Doug's bedroom. And $200 wasn't outrageous for a painting, was it? Well, maybe it was, but . . .

"Okay then." He squeezed Doug's shoulder, once, with the hand he'd made himself leave there. Doug slouched beneath him, like he thought maybe Mat was going to say it was time to go. "So let's get it."

"Really?" Doug said, sounding like the ten-year-old Mat used to sneak out for contraband.

Mat nodded, eyes stinging. Doug's answering smile—lighting up the whole damn store with pure, uncomplicated joy—would have made the two hundred bucks worth it, but then he went and threw his arms around Mat's shoulders, practically jumping on him with the force of his hug.

Happy. Free.

Hugging like brothers who loved each other.

Mat stiffened a moment, muscle memory taking their closeness in the wrong direction, but he closed his eyes and shoved that creepy-crawly feeling down somewhere deep and dark, and let himself hug his brother back.

It wasn't exactly something that was done in the middle of a store, and maybe it went against Louise's instructions not to draw attention to themselves, but just then Mat didn't give a single shit.

He was hugging his brother. His brother was hugging him. Neither of their lives were in danger, neither of them were desperate or scared or any of it. They just . . . loved each other. Had made each other happy.

He refused to let anything, even his own mind, even the polite cough of the saleswoman, take that feeling away from him.

He put his brother down when he was good and ready—Doug didn't seem to be in any hurry to break the embrace, so Mat was the one to separate them when the creepy-crawly feeling started oozing back—and tossed an apologetic smile at the saleswoman. "We'd like to buy that painting, please," he said.

One more shopping bag to add to their stack. Not that you *had* to build new lives with money, but it certainly didn't hurt. Felt damn good, actually, to pick things out again, dress and accessorize themselves and their own home.

They hung the painting and folded their new clothes into their new drawers before they settled down with their takeout in front of the TV. Mat handed Doug the remote, and somehow the kid found a rerun of *The Colbert Report* airing at 6:30 on a Tuesday. He was fairly certain they were both way too out of touch with the news cycle to get any of the references, but Doug was smiling anyway as he messily slurped lo mein with chopsticks, and seeing him smile made Mat smile.

Bellies full, hearts surprisingly warm, they fell asleep on the couch, still grinning.

CHAPTER FOUR

A knock at the door startled Mat awake.

It was pitch black in the apartment, except for the cycling light of the TV, which was airing some infomercial.

Doug, in silhouette, grasped the fabric at Mat's shoulder. "Mat—" he whimpered.

"It's okay," Mat said, heart jackhammering, already making a plan. He wouldn't open the door to them. He'd barricade him and Doug up in one of the bedrooms, put a dresser in front of the door, and call Louise. He wished they'd gotten a baseball bat or a can of mace or even a gun on their shopping trip today. How fucking innocent they'd been. How naive and stupid and—

"It's okay, Mat, it's me," a voice called softly through the front door. "It's Nate."

Mat's pounding heart plummeted.

Doug let out a shaky breath, caught between a laugh and a cry. "I'm going to bed," he announced on a wheeze.

"Okay, Doug. Have a good rest." He squeezed Doug's shoulder, silently thanking him for picking up on Mat's need to be alone with Nate.

While Doug went to his room and shut the door behind him, Mat steeled himself for whatever this conversation was going to turn into. A fight, probably. He couldn't imagine them doing anything but fighting. Was probably going to start it himself, in fact. Especially with Nate knocking on the door in the middle of the fucking night after pulling weeks of the silent treatment.

He went to let the asshole in.

Nate stood in the hall, a big tape-sealed cardboard box in his arms. He looked like absolute shit.

Mat waved him in and shut—and locked—the door behind him.

"Put that down on the coffee table there," he directed, voice flat, and as soon as Nate had done so, Mat lunged for him, giving him a hard shove that knocked him on his ass on the couch. "What the fuck do you think you're doing here at this time of night?"

"I—uh—" Nate squirmed under Mat's gaze, bloodshot eyeballs ticking from side to side. His normally crisp dress shirt was wrinkled, a coffee stain down the front. "I couldn't stay away. After Louise talked to me, I had to come. I couldn't wait. Not even until morning. I'm sorry. This is completely inappro—"

"Don't you even fucking start with your inappropriate boundaries strictly professional *bullshit*." Mat leaned down and jabbed him. "Don't you even fucking start! After all the shit we went through together, you just stonewall me? Shut me out? What the fuck is professional about that, huh? Treating me like a fucking leper? What, now that I've sucked your dick you can't even fucking look at me?" He narrowed his eyes at Nate, jabbed him in the chest again. Nate let him, didn't even hunch or put his hands up or lean away. "Or maybe you finally got what you came for and you're done now, is that it?"

"Jesus," Nate said, and pressed his fists to his eyes. "Jesus."

Mat's fists curled at his sides—he wanted to hit, to *hurt*, even knowing that if he started, he might not stop—but the tremor in Nate's voice, the evidence of tears, stayed his hand. "Why are you crying?" he demanded. He wouldn't give in to murderous impulse—how could you punch a guy in tears?—but he still got a hand through Nate's raised arms in order to jab him in the chest again. Nate *let* him again, damn the man. He wanted to shout, *Get up! Defend yourself! Fight!* but settled for, "What is this bullshit, huh? Stop it!"

"You really do think I'm disgusted by you?" Nate managed to croak. "Oh, God. Mat. Mat, Mat, Mat." He sank forward, face in his hands, and his shoulders shook. "I'm so sorry. I'm so, so sorry."

This . . . was not how he'd pictured this conversation going when he'd let Nate in. What was Nate apologizing *for*? The anger drained out of Mat, leaving weary confusion behind, and he slumped down on the coffee table across from Nate. No jab to the chest this time, just a gentle brush of fingertips across one knee. "Hey." The word came out a croak, his voice scratchy, his throat tight. He wanted to cry and didn't even fucking know *why*. "Hey, just . . . take it easy, okay? Just look at me and tell me why you're here."

Nate uncovered his face, but refused to make eye contact. "I raped you, Mat," he said to his lap. His hands were balled there, white-knuckle tight. "I raped you. I was supposed to protect you, and instead I got myself a fucking hard-on and I raped you. It wasn't even . . . I hurt you, I made you *bleed*. You *cried*. Of course I avoided you after." He sucked in a shuddery breath, scrubbed his hands over his face and let them fall, tightly balled again, to his lap. "I'm being eaten alive by guilt. Every time I look at you, I see what I did. I see how I *failed* you. And I couldn't . . . I couldn't bear the thought of looking into your eyes and seeing the recrimination there. The betrayal. The . . . the *hate*."

Mat dropped to his knees. Not in submission, not to taunt, but to make Nate understand, to be able to look him in the face even if he wouldn't stop staring at his lap. "I don't hate you, Nate. Look at me."

Nate hesitantly raised his head. He winced when their gazes met.

"I don't hate you," Mat repeated. "But yeah, you did see betrayal on my face. Not because of what you were forced to do—*forced*, Nate, just like I was forced; *you* were raped too—but because you left me hanging. I *needed* you. I needed you to tell me you didn't judge me, that you didn't think I was . . ." He shook his head, cupped his hands around Nate's fists, held on tight. Couldn't watch Nate's face when he said this next bit, because what if . . . *What if it's true?* "That I was a *victim* in your eyes, or . . . or worse, that I was dirty, *tainted* because I got it up in there just like you did, but unlike you, I didn't need to. So I needed you to be there for me. I needed to not be alone. We were together in that, and then suddenly you were *gone*."

Wetness splashed down on the backs of Mat's hands, and he looked up to find Nate crying. Not just on the verge of tears, but full-on waterworks. When he saw Mat looking, he laughed weakly. "Oh, Mat. I'm sorry." He unfisted his hands beneath Mat's, turned them palm-up and laced their fingers together. "I'm so sorry. I can't say enough how stupid I was, how sorry I am. You were right, I should've been there for you. You're not a victim in my eyes, and you're sure as hell not tainted. You're pure and beautiful and strong and I—"

He froze, mouth open. Blinked. His fingers tightened on Mat's. His lower lip trembled in the silence.

Mat lunged up and kissed him.

Licked across that trembling lip and pressed in until they were sharing breath, rasping stubble, and somehow his hands had untangled from Nate's and found their way to Nate's neck, fingers rubbing over short thick hair as he moaned into Nate's mouth, as Nate moaned back and slid his hands up Mat's arms to grip his shoulders.

There he was kneeling between Nate's knees, pressed up chest to chest and mouth to mouth, searching hands and frantic need and Mat was rock hard in his new jeans and he wasn't scared and he wasn't freaked and his skin cried for *more* touch rather than less, and when Nate broke away he had to grip Mat's face in both hands to stop him from chasing after. It was warmth, and comfort, and shelter, and yearning, and all the things he'd thought for certain he'd lost forever, would never know or be able to have again.

It was *perfect.*

So why was Nate looking at him like that? Brow furrowed, lips pursed, chest heaving, holding his face and studying it like he was terrified of what he'd find there.

Mat cupped a hand over one of Nate's where it rested on his cheek. "What?" he asked. It came out breathy; he was panting. More turned on than maybe he'd *ever* been.

Nate's mouth moved for a long moment before any sound came out. He looked like someone had just shot his puppy, like he had when he'd first walked through the door. "Are you . . ." His thumb stroked a line across Mat's cheekbone, and then he pulled his hands away, tucked them tight against his chest. "I hurt you."

"What? No. What are you talking about?"

One hand inched out, seemingly against Nate's will, to stroke across Mat's face again. Two fingertips. So gentle. When he was done, he pulled them back just far enough for Mat to see.

Damp. Devastated. "You're *crying.*"

Mat huffed a laugh, near breathless with relief. "I'm *happy.*"

And then it was his turn to grab Nate's face, and he pulled him back in for another kiss, and this time Nate didn't fight him. Smiled against Mat's lips and Mat smiled back and murmured, "I'm sorry—" *kiss* "—I didn't mean to scare you—" *kiss.*

No more words, then. Mat just kept kissing Nate over and over, rising from his knees, climbing up to straddle Nate's lap, pushing him back into the perfect, plush sofa. Kissed him some more. Never wanted to stop, never.

Nate's hands rested on his waist, his touch light, but no longer afraid. Just gentle. Perfectly thoughtful. Not like Mat was breakable, but like he was precious and awe-inspiring.

At that moment, in Nate's arms, feeling Nate's worshipful lips playing across his own, Mat felt like he actually *could* be.

Nate's next kiss landed on the corner of his mouth, then his jaw, then his neck. He felt Nate's hips rise, Nate's hands smooth inward on Mat's back, holding him more firmly. Nate's cock pressing a long, hard line into his stomach.

Mat pulled off instantly. "Nate . . ." he said, pained, and Nate stared up at him with pleasure-glazed eyes that quickly cleared.

"Sorry," Nate said, and immediately let go.

Mat winced, expecting the usual speech, the *completely inappropriate disrespecting boundaries you're a victim I'm a professional this is a conflict of interests* speech, culminating in Nate storming out of here in a cloud of shame and frustration—

But Nate just smiled. Patted Mat's sides gently. "Let's take it slow," he said with an easy grin, no hint of disappointment in it.

Mat's mortification died a blessedly premature death at that, and the heat in his cheeks faded a little. This was . . . new. This was good. He could do slow. Slow was better than *This is wrong.* Slow was *much* better than *You're a head case and I won't take advantage of you.* He sat up, settled on the empty cushion next to Nate. Kept a hand on Nate's knee, just to prove to the both of them that he fucking well could. That he wasn't *that* broken. Didn't know where to go from here, though. What to say next.

Fortunately, Nate solved that dilemma for him, sitting up straight and saying, "I got an idea. Why don't you have a look at that box I brought? It's for you."

"A housewarming gift?" Mat joked. Sitting side by side on the couch, their legs still touched—a pleasant, simple contact.

"Sort of." Nate bounced slightly. "Go on, open it!"

Feeling like a kid on Christmas, Mat ripped and tore at the piss-poor tape job, which came apart in strips. The overpacked box burst open. The first thing Mat saw was the soft burgundy fabric of a letterman jacket. That was odd. He was kind of expecting some dishes, or a waffle-maker, or possibly one of those baskets full of tea and cookies or something.

Beside him, Nate was practically vibrating.

Mat lifted the jacket up, exposing a glint of gold underneath. A trophy? He lunged for the box. Yes, a wrestling trophy: *1st Place, East Central Regionals, 1997, Mathias Carmichael.* A very familiar pair of boxing gloves. No, not just familiar—the exact ones he'd worn to victory in his first state championship, the ones Dougie had asked him to autograph and had kept ever since. A baby album, embroidered in blue thread to spell out *Douglas Carmichael.* Mat swiped his knuckles under one eye, then the other, then flipped the baby book open and ran his fingertips across the little curl of chestnut hair taped to the very first page.

And across from it, a polaroid of baby Dougie, cradled in scrawny prepubescent Mat's arms and lap. He looked slightly miffed. Mat choked out a laugh, teary and half-crazed, and ran his fingertips across the photo, too.

It took him a long, long time to put that book down and keep digging through the box.

More pictures. The framed ones from his and Dougie's bedrooms. An entire shoebox full of ones they'd never gotten around to putting into albums. The framed photocopy of Mat's first paycheck as a pro fighter. Both of Dougie's college diplomas. A whole life's worth of memories—*two* lives' worth of memories—in one messy, *glorious* cardboard box.

At last Mat finished shuffling through it, and though he wanted to touch every single item in the box again, take each one out and turn it over and over in his hands and his heart and his mind, he very deliberately replaced everything and tucked the flaps closed. Sat there for a moment, eyes closed, hands resting on the battered cardboard, just breathing and letting the tears fall down his face.

And then, just as Doug had this afternoon in that art gallery, full of joy and astonishment and, yes, even love, he turned and threw his arms around Nate's shoulders and clung on for all he was worth and whispered, "Thank you. Thank you. Thank you."

And Nate whispered "No, thank *you*" back to him, though Mat had no idea what for.

THE FLESH CARTEL

SEASON 5: RECLAMATION

EPISODE 18: THE LONG ROAD

CHAPTER ONE

Douglas woke in a strange bed in a strange room in strange clothes and tried very, very hard not to panic. Kept his eyes closed, his breathing steady, lest he tip off anyone that he was awake before he figured out where he was and what would be expected of him now.

Clothes. He was *dressed*. And not the lacy scratch of panties or the digging constriction of a corset or bra. He shifted, pretending to roll over in his sleep. Flannel, from the heaven-soft feel of cloth brushing over skin. Tops and bottoms. And . . . were those boxers underneath the pants? Yes.

Oh.

Like Dobby's sock, underwear meant only one thing: freedom. He was free. He was *Doug* now, not Douglas. Hadn't had to remind himself of that in at least a week, but then, today was the first day he'd been outside the group home. New apartment. New identity. Baltimore. *With Mat.*

It was early still, predawn light creating a gentle glow around the white blinds on his bedroom window. The apartment was silent. So was the street below, though a careful listen revealed the sporadic sounds of traffic somewhere in the near distance.

He tossed the covers back—pale blue cotton sheets and a white down comforter that'd come with the room—and sat up carefully. Muscle memory, that: expecting his body to ache, to need gentle handling. But it didn't. He felt refreshed, in fact, after a surprisingly good night's sleep born of exhaustion and a comfortable, private bed. He even felt safe, more or less; he was Samuel Senders for the next two months—*my friends call me Sam*—and nobody who might hurt him knew he was here.

Except Mat, of course.

But Mat hadn't ever actually hurt him on purpose, had he. By omission and selfishness, maybe. By recklessness and stupidity, definitely. And yet Doug couldn't help but think of yesterday, of that pure unselfish carefree *joy* in them both, if only for a little while. Of Mat dropping what'd once been ten whole weeks' worth of pocket cash, unasked, on a silly little painting Doug couldn't even explain why he liked—and this after having spent three times that on clothes and shoes and accessories and food in the span of a single day. If Mat really were only keeping Doug around to support him in his inevitable retirement, he wouldn't have done that, right? Wouldn't have done *any* of it. Not the painting, and not the fancy running shoes, and maybe not even the ice cream. Wouldn't have hugged him in the middle of that gallery, where people could look and judge and . . . and . . . and *punish*. Maybe not like Allen or Nikolai punished, but punish nonetheless. Hard stares and raised voices and derision and withheld affection and all that bullshit people everywhere always did to those over whom they wielded power.

But Mat hadn't done any of that yesterday, or let anyone else do it either. And that had to mean something, right?

Doug slid out of bed, the hardwood floor cold beneath his bare feet, and crept to the bathroom in the hall. Mat's bedroom door was open, lights off. Better not wake him. He might not beat Doug for it—he'd never had that right in any case, and Doug'd be damned if he'd let some conservatorship change that—but there were plenty of other ways to hurt someone who depended on you. Especially someone who'd been *forced* to depend on you.

So he closed the bathroom door as quietly as he could, and only then turned on the light. He'd wait to shower until Mat was awake lest he risk the noise disturbing Mat—wasn't like he had to be all neat and clean for anyone now anyway—but he emptied his bladder and brushed his teeth. Then he ran a comb through his hair out of habit. Wasn't sure what to do with himself after that. Just stood in the bathroom for a long moment, blinking into the mirror.

He looked gaunt. Tired. Not Nikolai's pretty boy anymore, not even Allen's dolled-up toy. Nobody would want him like this. No one but other slaves, anyway—his fellows at the group home had been plenty eager to sample Nikolai's goods, and he'd gone along with it, of course he had, because how else would he fit in, and what else was he good for? What else did he know? What meaning could he find if he wasn't making people happy, even if they were just slaves?

No. Not slaves anymore. Broken, discarded, masterless toys, just like you.

God, he missed Nikolai. Fuck the lies, and the scheming, and the manipulations, and the fact that Nikolai had abandoned Doug for money. It was all true—he *knew* it was true, and he didn't even care. It didn't matter. Not when there'd been such clarity of purpose, such contentment, such a sense of love and safety. All he had now were doubts, and fears, and aimless drifting. He would let Nikolai lie and hurt and manipulate him all over again if he could just have that *silence* in his mind back. That blessed, breathless conviction.

And God, what did it say about him that he'd willingly return to all of that, just to escape the harsh reality of all of *this*? Of the doubts and the fears and the uncertain future. Of never knowing what to feel or who to be or how to act. Of dissecting every word, every expression, every response to his behaviors in everyone else. Even Mat. Especially Mat.

Hiding in the bathroom forever will not help you find answers, Doug.

No, he supposed it wouldn't. But at least nothing hurt in here. Not if he didn't let himself linger.

Except, of course, that lingering was exactly what he was doing. He needed a distraction. A new purpose. Something to take his mind off all the . . . well, *everything*.

Kind of made a guy want to drink, or get high. He might have no money, but it wasn't like that'd be a problem; he had plenty to barter in the right circles, after all.

But Mat already thought he was a fuck-up, and so did the courts. And whoring for drug money wouldn't exactly help with that. If he wanted Mat's love—and to be fair, he still wasn't sure he did, but something in him just wouldn't let it go—then he needed to stay away from booze and needles. If he wanted to be master of his own life—and really, he wasn't sure he wanted *that* either, didn't know if he could ever handle responsibility like that—then he needed to stay clean.

Which brought him back to distractions. Maybe he *would* go for a run. Not with Mat, not yet. That was too . . . personal, maybe, too much like *before*. But on his own. For himself. Explore more of the city, regain more of his strength. Clear his mind with the simplicity of one foot in front of the other for as long as he could bear it.

Thus resolved, he shut the bathroom light off, then opened the door and crept back to his room in the dark, one hand on the wall to guide him down the unfamiliar hall. Bedroom door closed, he fumbled for the light switch, then pulled on a new pair of running shorts and an Adidas T-shirt. Just like Mat used to wear. Like *Dougie* used to wear, too, because big bro liked them and Dougie wanted to be just like his big bro when he grew up.

Hah. Yeah. That'd gone well, hadn't it.

Whatever. He tugged on a pair of socks and laced up his new sneakers, hoping he'd be able to break them in without blisters.

Not that a minor pain like that bothered him these days. Not likely he'd even *notice* it.

Or maybe, just maybe, you need it now. Maybe you're that twisted.

Great. One more thought to try to outrun.

He crept out of his bedroom and down the dark hall, feeling his way into the living room. Couldn't find his keys without turning on the light; hopefully this far from Mat's bedroom it wouldn't be bright enough to wake him.

Turned out he hadn't needed to worry about Mat's bedroom at all. Mat was right there on the living room couch. Curled up asleep fully clothed . . . and he wasn't alone. He was snuggled up against another man's chest—Agent Johnson's chest, the one responsible for their case. Well, that answered Doug's questions as to the nature of their relationship: sleeping with someone was intimate enough on its own, never mind sleeping with someone after going through what Doug and Mat had been through.

Doug's stomach churned. His hands tightened into fists. Why was it okay for Mat to fuck around, but when Doug did it, everyone looked down their noses at him? Even *Mat* had half lectured, half begged him to stop when he'd found out Doug had been sleeping with some of the residents at the group home.

And how fucking dare he, when he was doing the same damn thing? Worse, even. At least Doug wasn't sticking his cock into the fucking *trial.*

Neither man had woken at the lights being turned on, but Doug could certainly correct that with a yell.

But did he want to, really? Was he being too harsh here? They were both fully clothed, after all; maybe they hadn't fucked. Maybe they'd never even kissed. Maybe it was just a matter of simple human affection. God knew Doug understood *that* need well enough. He'd clung to Mat plenty of times, even in the past few weeks, even through his doubts and fears and mistrust. Did he hate Mat so much that he'd begrudge him a similar scrap of comfort and affection?

Didn't he do the same to you when it came to Nikolai?

But Doug knew that wasn't really the same. Even if Mat was wrong, his spite for Nikolai had been born of protectiveness. Doug wasn't protective of Mat, he was just plain jealous.

He wanted someone to hold him like that. Someone who wanted more than a blowjob or a willing ass. Someone he trusted enough to fall asleep with.

And maybe he even wanted to be the one to hold Mat like that. Like brothers should be able to. Should want to. Like they had, once upon a time, when life had seemed so uncomplicated, when he'd been so naive.

He wrapped his arms around himself, watching them both.

Agent Johnson must have felt his stare, because his eyes cracked open. He took Doug in and, apparently deciding he wasn't a threat, slipped back to sleep, tightening his arm around Mat's shoulder.

In his sleep, Mat sighed.

Yeah, okay, message received. Their closeness wasn't for him. Fine. He snatched his keys off the hook by the door, shoved them in his pocket. Laid his hand on the knob, but then found himself turning around, grabbing the beige throw off the back of the couch and covering the sleeping men. Too many long days of service, of anticipating needs, ingrained into his mind. Nothing at all to do with how he might've felt for Mat, before or now.

Just habit, that was all.

Mat shifted and sighed again, a contented sound, and burrowed a little deeper beneath the blanket against Agent Johnson's chest.

Doug left them to it. Closed the front door behind him as quietly as he could, and didn't bother warming up before he took off like a shot down the sidewalk.

CHAPTER TWO

Nate woke when something cracked him in the face.

Mat's elbow, he realized as he came into awareness, hands cupped around his throbbing nose.

The man himself was crouched on the living room floor in a fight stance, eyes wild and lost, looking nearly feral.

"You're okay," Nate said, extending his free hand in truce. Take care of Mat, that was the first priority, even if he was the one who'd gotten hit.

Mat blinked, and the look of fear vanished from his face. He was at Nate's side in an instant.

"*I'm* okay?" He wrapped an arm around Nate's shoulder as he tried to pluck Nate's hand away from his face. "Are *you* okay? Jesus, I'm sorry, man. Guess you shouldn't sleep with a UFC fighter with PTSD, huh?" Nate had expected him to be shaken or humiliated, but he seemed mostly concerned about Nate. He clucked and cooed, then sighed with relief. "No blood, at least. I am sorry, though."

Nate flopped back against the couch, guilt gnawing at him. Mat's words, joking though they may have been, rang true. He really shouldn't be sleeping with Mat. The guy obviously wasn't ready for that kind of intimacy, not in such an unguarded, unpredictable state as sleep.

But even awake, it was risky. He shouldn't be kissing Mat, either. The man was too raw, too conflicted, too—

"That nightmare worked up a sweat," Mat said, and gave himself an exaggerated sniff. "How about we take this to the shower?"

—fragile.

Maybe Nate was completely off base about what Mat could handle. What he was ready for. The nightmares were troubling, and sure, being elbowed in the nose wasn't awesome, but if Mat could bounce back so quickly afterward, then why couldn't Nate go along for the ride? Why couldn't he trust Mat's resilience more?

Mat stared at him, his mouth slanted with disapproval. "You're going to pull one of your speeches, aren't you? That's your pussying-out face. You're about to tell me why we shouldn't be doing this, and how I'm not ready or strong enough, right?"

"Honestly?" Mat's expression hardened all the more, and Nate's shoulders drooped. "That was exactly what I was thinking. But then I was thinking maybe I should stop underestimating you so much."

A grin cracked that stony expression. "So the big fancy FBI agent *does* learn." And even though Nate's head was still full of reasons why this was wrong—some of them profoundly compelling—when Mat extended a hand to him, Nate took it. And smiled helplessly when Mat pecked him on the lips and led him down the hall.

The bathroom was cramped, an old black-and-white tiled affair with a claw-foot tub and a round shower curtain suspended from the ceiling. The lights in here were too bright, too harsh, too damn *clinical,* so Nate turned them off in favor of the hall light outside.

It made Mat smile. Nate just hoped it was enough to lend Mat the strength to do . . . whatever it was they were about to do. Get naked together, at the very least. Maybe even more? Mat was brave, he wasn't broken, and it was true that Nate had underestimated him, but everyone needed a little help sometimes.

In the hazier lighting, Mat looked perfect, glowing but cut with shadows at the same time. Nate couldn't speak, so he didn't. He just unbuttoned his crumpled shirt. He wanted to unbutton Mat's too, but no . . . let Mat reveal himself in his own time. No pressure, no commentary, but no pitying comments either. No staring, but also no avoiding. No making Mat feel like a show, and especially no making him feel like an object of pity.

Nate hoped, anyway.

He dropped his shirt on top of the toilet. Shucked his undershirt. Glanced at Mat to find him staring openly back. He hadn't even begun to remove his clothes yet.

Shit. This was a bad idea. A bad, bad idea. He should just put his shirt back on and leave. Apologize. Not come back until the trial was over. He should—

No. He should stop fucking falling into the old damaging patterns of behavior, was what he should do. He resolutely brought his hands to the button on his slacks. Made himself meet Mat's eyes, and wiggled both eyebrows. "Enjoying the show?" he teased.

"Yes," Mat said, so quickly and firmly there was little room left in Nate's mind for doubt. Of course, he couldn't help but notice that Mat hadn't begun to strip yet. Or that no telltale bulge was tenting Mat's pants.

Still, this was when, if they'd been a normal couple—*Couple? Is that really what we are?*—he'd have started stripping Mat in return. And if he didn't want to get punched in the nose again, he needed to treat Mat like he treated everyone else.

So, smile still firmly in place, he asked, "Do I get to enjoy one too?"

He half expected to be hit for that anyway, for Mat to freak out again, but all it seemed to do was shake Mat out of his funk, like he'd only just now realized he was still fully clothed; the man's hands went to the hem of his hoodie and stripped it and the T-shirt beneath it off in a single swift motion. He let it drop on the toilet lid on top of Nate's clothes. Nate tried not to invent meaning for that, something about how mingling laundry implied intimacy or trust, but obviously he wasn't doing so well in that regard.

Fact was, he was pretty fucking hopelessly head over heels here.

And Mat was fucking beautiful. Nate had to force himself not to stare, let alone reach out and touch.

Especially when it was obvious how nervous Mat was. He wasn't hiding himself, wasn't so much as hunching his shoulders, but he made no move to take his pants off, and even in the low light, Nate could see his pulse hammering away in his throat.

So was he or wasn't he supposed to remind Mat now that they didn't have to do this? That Mat didn't have anything to prove to him or anyone else? Would that make things better or worse?

He wished there were a guide for all this. Maybe, if they stuck it out, they could see Mat's therapist together sometime.

In the end, it was Mat who broke the awkward tension, thankfully taking the decision out of Nate's hands. "So," he said, chuckling weakly. "We gonna shower with our pants on or what?"

At least fifty separate muscles unknotted in Nate's back. His smile wasn't forced at all when he said, "Well, we should probably at least take our socks off. Wet socks are gross, man."

And then he lifted one foot and did just that. Mat followed suit. Somehow, after the socks, the pants were easy; Mat visibly tensed when Nate unbuckled his belt (which in turn had Nate wondering if he should make the switch to suspenders—he was pretty sure Nikolai had never beaten Mat bloody with *those*), but that moment passed too.

Nate didn't hide his erection when he slipped out of his briefs. He didn't draw attention to it, either.

Mat took a deep breath, let it out, and then he was naked too.

Gorgeous. Top to bottom, no exceptions. Nate drank him in. *Let* himself drink Mat in. Avoiding looking at Mat's body was the behavior of a man who still saw that body as evidence, no more erotic than a crime scene photo.

And that just wasn't true. Whether or not Nate felt guilty or conflicted, there was no denying the rush of pleasure from looking at the hard lines of Mat's body. The defined pecs, the ridges of his abs, the perfect shadows etched by his Apollo's belt. His heavy, hanging dick, soft though it was. No missing that.

"Sh-shower," Nate said. "Please tell me you like them hot."

Mat let that little bit of unintended innuendo pass without comment. He turned away shyly to fiddle with the taps, like he was grateful for the excuse to hide himself. Nate's eyes went immediately to the collection of fading scars on Mat's back and flanks, the places where belt buckles and whip crackers had met the thinnest flesh, where the bones were closest to the surface. Not as bad as when he'd first escaped, but still impossible to miss. Some Mat would no doubt carry forever.

"Hot's good," Mat said, back still turned and shoulders tight, testing the water with his hand. "I'm stiff from the couch."

Nate let *that* little bit of unintended innuendo pass without comment, too. Just stepped over the high lip of the tub when Mat did. Left plenty of space between them as he drew the curtain closed, shrouding them in dimness.

We don't have to do this, Mat. It's fine. I won't think any less of you.

But he kept those words locked behind clenched teeth. Wouldn't do that to Mat. Not again.

Instead, he'd trust Mat. Trust Mat to know what he wanted and what he was ready for, how much discomfort he could handle and whether or not it was worth it. Trust him to speak up if he changed his mind.

"I can *feel* you brooding back there, Nate."

The words were judgmental, but his tone was light. Okay, maybe a little frustrated, too, and definitely tense, but he didn't sound angry, at least. He stuck his head under the spray. Turned around to face Nate. Water plastered his hair to his head and ran down his face and neck and shoulders and— *Ahem.* Clung to his every curve and hollow, just like Nate wanted to. God, if any more blood ran to his cock, he was going to pass out.

"Sorry," he croaked. "Are you—" His hands flapped up in some aborted gesture he couldn't even identify, fell back to his sides. *Don't ask if he's okay, don't ask if he's okay.* The bathroom was beginning to steam up; a drop of sweat ran down Nate's temple. "I mean, um . . ."

Mat held out a bar of soap and a washcloth, and his smile was clearly amused, but his hands were trembling. "Wash me?"

"*God yes,*" Nate gushed before he could stop himself. He took the soap and washcloth. And then lowered to his knees at Mat's feet.

He wasn't sure why he'd done that. His face heated. Mat gave him a bewildered stare, but Nate wasn't going to ruin this. He *wasn't*, so he went along with what his body had started and washed Mat's feet. Focused really, really hard on them, because otherwise he was going to wind up hypnotized by a faceful of dick.

It was kind of appropriate too, in a way. Washing Mat's feet, he pictured biblical stories, stories about faithfulness and willing servitude and humility and reverence and ritual cleansing. Every last one of those things rang true in his heart, in his head, as Mat lifted one foot and then the other to allow Nate to run the soap over the arches and under the soles.

Even over his brand. *Especially* over his brand; to avoid or glance over that scar too quickly was to treat it as something shameful, when it wasn't. It was a part of Mat now, and while Nate could hate that it had happened in the first place, he wouldn't let that hate get in the way of loving Mat, all of him, just as he was.

He didn't touch Mat skin to skin, though he ached to. Soap. Cloth. Up his calves. Behind his knees. His hard, curving thighs, tense and twitching a little beneath Nate's ministrations, though whether from ticklishness or . . . something else altogether, Nate couldn't tell.

Come on, Nate. What are the odds he has such ticklish thighs?

But it didn't matter because Mat was standing still for it. Head down, eyes tracking every movement of Nate's hand. Breathing hard, though by the looks of his soft cock, not for the same reasons Nate was breathing hard. But Mat wasn't giving up on them, and neither would Nate.

He worked steadily. Front of thighs. Back of thighs. Inside thighs. Which led him, inevitably, to Mat's groin. Cock and balls. He washed them tenderly, as tenderly and thoughtfully and reverently as Mat's feet. It was a privilege to touch Mat this way, and he felt that sense of gratitude from his overflowing heart right down to his fingertips.

He kept eye contact the whole time. To show he wasn't ashamed, yes, but also to give Mat a face to look at. *His* face. No anonymous hands pawing at him. *Nate's* hands.

Through the barrier of the cloth, he felt Mat's cock stir and thicken. A part of him wanted to linger, coax that nascent erection to life, but to do so would disrupt the ritual, and Nate needed—*needed*—to see that to completion first. So he moved on, sweeping his hands around Mat's stiff body to the plusher curves of his ass.

No surprise, Mat clenched. Nate touched him anyway—gentle, questing touches—holding his gaze the whole time.

Mat didn't shove Nate away, but Nate saw him swallow.

You're so damn brave, he wanted to say, but to speak seemed taboo.

He stood, and Mat turned without being directed. Nate scrubbed his back, once again affording his scars the same reverence as the unmarked flesh. All beautiful. All lean and hard and most importantly, unbowed.

Nate was ruined for anyone else.

Maybe he always had been. What man could possibly compare to this fighter at his peak?

He washed Mat's shoulders, from the blades over to his arms, one by one. When Mat turned around again, the arousal was plain on his face. Huge pupils, flushed skin. He even bit his lip. His hand caught Nate's wrist. Pushed it low, never breaking eye contact.

But Nate didn't touch him, not where he wanted to be touched. Not . . . yet. He moved forward, until they were in each other's space, skin glancing skin as they shifted and breathed. He washed Mat's abdomen. Circled the soap over his chest. Mat gasped, head tipping back, when Nate swiped the washcloth over his nipples. The urge to lean in then, to put lips and teeth to that strong neck or those tender pink nubs, was nearly overwhelming, but he just tightened his grip on the washcloth and soap and reminded himself of every tense, trembling muscle, every nervous flutter of Mat's pulse up until now.

He wouldn't screw this up. Not again. It was too fucking important.

So's the damn trial. You shouldn't be doing this. If anyone finds out . . .

He couldn't even make himself believe that no one would. Not really. One look at the two of them in the same room and the defense would *know*.

But there'd be no way to prove it. And I'm just one agent of many. He's just one witness of many. He needs me more than the prosecution does.

Mat's hand cupped his cheek. Glassy blue eyes, hazed with arousal, met his. "You okay, Nate?" Mat whispered.

The irony, the injustice of that—that Mat should be the one to ask after Nate's well-being. Nate nodded. Cleared his throat. "You?"

"Better than I thought I'd be. But maybe I can't freak out when there's no blood in my brain to fuel the panic." He gestured to his erection with a lopsided smile.

"We really shouldn't have sex," Nate blurted out.

Mat's face shuttered.

"Okay," Nate said, instantly regretting it. There he went taking control again, deciding what was best again, shoving Mat out again. "Okay, let me try that again. I know you think that the whole . . . the trial, the conflict of interest thing is just an *excuse*, a way for me to . . ." He shook his head, wishing he weren't so unbearably turned on so he could *think* straight. "To . . . to run away from this, from you. And though I'm ashamed to admit it now, maybe that was true once." He put the soap back on the holder, let the washcloth plop to the floor of the tub, and reached for Mat's hand with both of his. Mat tensed but went along with it, though Nate thought maybe the tension had nothing to do with bad memories this time. "But it isn't anymore, you get me? Whatever—" He squeezed Mat's hand, pulled it to his own chest and held it there. "Whatever *this* is, I want it. You have to know that, man. You have to . . . after we just . . ."

"Yeah," Mat said, so softly Nate almost missed it over the hiss of the water.

"But I can't just abandon my responsibilities, either. I swore an oath, Mat, and even if I hadn't, all those people the Cartel hurt . . ." He shook his head, squeezed Mat's hand tighter. "I *have* to make that as right as I can. Even if that means . . ."

"Yeah," Mat said again. He dropped his gaze to the floor, toed the wet washcloth. "I get it, man."

Disappointment, but no anger, thank God, at least not that Nate could tell. "It's only two more months, you know? Two more months, and then we can . . ." He pried one hand away from Mat's, gestured broadly. "Whatever this is. We can figure it out."

Mat turned his hand in Nate's grip, grabbed on to Nate and tugged him forward hard enough to send him stumbling. He bumped into Mat, chest to chest and thighs to thighs and, oh God, hard cock to hard cock. Nate groaned. Mat's arm snaked around his back and held him tight.

"And what am I supposed to do in the meantime, huh?" Mat growled in his ear. Half need and—ah, there was the anger. "How'm I supposed to just . . ." All the strength went out of his grip, and he sagged against Nate, dropped his head on Nate's shoulder. Tucked his face into Nate's neck and murmured against the skin there, "I don't think I can do this alone."

Nate's arms came up around Mat's back, held him tighter than he would've dared even five minutes ago. This time, Mat didn't tense, and though he did pull away a few seconds later, he left less than a foot of space between them.

Nate kept his hands on Mat's shoulders, held Mat's gaze. "You don't have to." No hesitation. He meant every word of it. "Just because we can't have sex doesn't mean I'm not going to be here for you. I know

I fucked up in the past, Mat, but I'm not going to do that anymore. I'm not going to run away from you. I'm going to be . . ." He nudged forward, bumping their bodies together. "Right here."

Mat huffed. "Well, if we can't have sex, can we at least jerk off?" he joked, then paused. "*Can* we? Here, I mean? Now? I haven't touched myself *for* myself in over a year." He curled a hand around his own dick, but Nate didn't miss the part where his knuckles brushed Nate's erection, too.

"Oh God," Nate said, when he was supposed to say *no*.

He didn't say no.

He pushed off Mat's body, weathering the disappointed look Mat leveled at him, then braced one hand against the bathroom wall and wrapped the other one around his own dick.

I haven't touched myself for *myself in over a year.* How could he possibly say no to that? Deny Mat that?

He looked Mat in the eye—stared at him hard, like he was trying to use X-ray vision or something—and licked his lips.

"Jesus," Mat breathed.

"I mean, guys masturbate all the time, right? Perfectly normal. No conflict of interests there."

"Exactly." Mat's hand on his substantial dick moved a fraction of an inch. His eyes fell half-closed, then snapped wide open again. "Talk to me," he said, and Nate couldn't tell if it was an order or a plea. "Don't want to forget who I'm here with."

Plea, then.

Or maybe that was just Nate's overprotectiveness talking. Why couldn't it be both? Why couldn't Mat be sensitive, needing support, and still be hot as hell and take-charge, the kind of guy who'd ram Nate up against a wall and keep a hold on his throat while he fucked him from behind?

Damn, that mental image made it easy to get back to the task at hand.

Mat was staring at him, nostrils flaring, his strokes slow and determined.

Talk to him.

"I like to think about you fucking me," he managed to say. "Like to think about that big dick in your hand teasing my hole until

I'm begging. In my head you always take mercy on me in the end, though."

Mat made a low sound in his chest, pumping himself in earnest. His eyes never left Nate's face.

Nate felt like the best kind of whore. Pushing through the vague humiliation of exposing himself this way—really, what was a divulged fantasy in the face of all Mat had shown *him*?—he took hold of that hungry look in Mat's eyes and spilled all his secrets. "Now that you're here in front of me, I think I was wrong. You're a bastard, aren't you? A sexy one, I mean." He flushed. "I think, when we have sex, you're not gonna let me off easy. You're gonna take control and you're . . . you're . . ."

Whatever the expression that settled on Mat's face at those words, it wasn't arousal. Mat's hand stilled on his cock. So did Nate's.

"This is all wrong," Nate moaned. He shuddered, revulsion and orgasmic pleasure clashing inside him and setting off sparks. Not good when you were in an enclosed space with a man made of gunpowder.

"I won't control you," Mat said, that strange expression slipping away, his hand beginning to stroke again, nice and slow. "But I won't go easy on you either."

Okay, okay. He hadn't fucked up entirely yet. His eyes were drawn to the slide of Mat's foreskin, stretched taut now, the glans almost fully exposed. Mat's palm circled over it, slid back down again. Mat groaned.

So did Nate. "I don't want you to go easy on me. Or hold back. I want . . ." *I want your good days and your bad days and your rage and your weakness and your tender lovemaking and your wild sex I'll feel in my ass for a week.* "I want you to be yourself. Whatever you need to give me or make me take or ask of me. That's what I want."

That didn't sound nearly as sexy as what he'd started with, but it was true.

"I mean, I want to *share*—"

"I know," Mat said, voice somehow breathy and tight all at once. The hand not stripping his cock reached out toward Nate—toward Nate's cock—then drew back just an inch or two shy of its goal. Was it the trial, propriety, Nate's ground rules stopping him? Or was it memories?

They could make new ones, if only Nate could figure out *how*.

"I want to ride you," Nate said, his hand moving at lightning speed now just imagining his own words coming true, the two of them playing it all out without encumbrance, without fear or doubt. Mat's hand picked up the pace to match. He'd tilted his head back, exposing his throat, and Nate wanted to latch onto it but didn't. Kept his distance. "With your hands all over my body. Want you to look at me when you're inside me. See even a fraction of how you make me feel every fucking minute of every day. See how much I—"

Mat's head snapped forward, eyes zeroing in on Nate's, expression so intense, so . . . *desperate* that Nate choked back the truth he'd nearly spilled. Maybe Mat wasn't ready to accept that yet. Maybe he didn't know *how* to yet.

"—I worship you," he amended. "I never stopped. You in the ring. You at the after-parties, chatting everyone up but me. You standing here now." He had to stop, breathe a moment—the pleasure was growing, growing, and if he wasn't careful, he'd blow soon. "I can barely stand to look at you because—" No, no, no, this was veering away from sex again, but he couldn't fucking stop himself, not here on this precipice, so desperate to connect. "I feel like I don't deserve you."

Mat's brow furrowed. At some point he'd stopped stroking himself altogether, but his fingers were still curled around his very hard dick. "You don't deserve me? You *saved* me."

"You saved yourself."

"No, I *escaped* by myself."

Weren't they supposed to be jerking off right now? Wasn't this supposed to be dirty talk? Neither of them was even moving anymore. They were just standing here, half under the miraculously still-hot spray in a little apartment tub in the semidark, holding their dicks, and Nate knew it was absurd and he should get shit under control, but he couldn't fucking stop himself. Sometimes the opportunity came, and it was the wrong time, but you still had to reach out and grasp it. It needed to be said.

Nate needed to say it.

"And then you got yourself back on your feet. You rescued your brother and all those other people. You saved them. *You.*"

"And you think I could have done that if you'd given up on me?" Mat's expression was tender. "Don't you think for *one second* I don't realize what you gave me. What you did for me. And you don't even feel like I owe you anything for it. You don't consider yourself the hero of this story. You just—" He bit his lip. "That's how much you love me."

All that struggling to hide it, keep it unspoken, and Mat had known and accepted it all along. That desperation Nate had thought he'd seen, maybe that'd been because Mat had *needed* it so much—no, not *needed*, just . . . wanted it, craved it—not because he'd feared it. Nate should've known better; Mat wasn't the kind of man who succumbed to his fears. Unlike Nate.

So Mat had said it first.

And no matter how afraid Nate was, no matter how much he shouldn't do this until the trial was over . . . Well, sometimes an opportunity came, and it was the wrong time, but you still had to reach out and grasp it.

"That's how much I love you," Nate echoed, letting the weight of the confession go, and stepped forward, pressing himself to Mat's body. Closing the artificial distance between them at the same time he closed his hand around both their dicks—or as much of them as he could manage to fit, at least—kissing Mat as hard as he craved to. Mat's mouth opened up beneath his, and Mat's hand curled around his own—not to push away, as he'd feared for a moment, but to encourage Nate to grip tighter, to move.

Didn't need to tell him twice.

He moaned into Mat's mouth, felt Mat's answering moan buzzing against his lips. Their joined hands sped, sped, and despite the heavy talk, they'd both obviously been closer than they'd realized because half a dozen strokes later, Nate's hand was clenching hard on Mat's hip and Nate's own hips were thrusting up furiously into their grips and he was bursting into a million glittering pieces, would've fallen if not for the strong arm wrapped around his waist, holding him in place as Mat's hand pumped furiously, drawing Nate through his orgasm and past it to a brittle edge that left him teetering again as Mat stiffened, shouted, spurted into their hands and up their bellies.

They clung to each other, after, Nate needing to be held nearly as much as he imagined Mat did. He resisted the urge to ask Mat if he was okay, *knew* it would ruin the moment . . . at least assuming the moment hadn't already been ruined by Nate's disregard for Mat's demons. He shuddered—no, that was his teeth chattering. The water had finally gone cold.

Mat kissed him again, running the discarded washcloth between their bodies as he did, then turned off the taps.

Not ruined, then. Thank fuck.

Mat wrapped a towel around Nate's shoulders. Kissed his forehead, every inch the caretaker.

And Nate . . . Nate found himself strangely in need of caretaking. Coming down hard off his high, acutely aware of how much he might've just fucked up. Not even necessarily between him and Mat, but for the case, for the trial, for the unbiased testimony he was supposed to deliver in eight weeks.

Emotions flooded him. Shame and disbelief at what he'd done. Fear they'd be found out. Stubbornly, irrationally hurt that Mat hadn't said he loved him back, even though Nate knew, in his saner moments, that that was fine and to be expected. That to pressure Mat into *anything* was abhorrent. That a man who was still struggling to love himself wouldn't know *how* to love someone else, someone new, couldn't be expected to figure out how to fit someone who'd been a stranger a few months ago into his own too-strange new world.

But Mat didn't let him fall into that abyss. He rubbed Nate's shoulders with the towel and kissed his face again—chaste, playful kisses, a sweet unassuming kind of affection Nate would never have never expected from someone as passionate and intense as Mat—and then grabbed another towel to rub over Nate's head.

The sense of innocence that gesture imparted—that feeling of boyhood reclaimed, of the purest, sweetest kind of love—made Nate's eyes burn with happiness.

Mat was going to be okay. *They* were going to be okay.

If Mat could teach Doug to feel this way again, maybe he could be okay again too.

I love you, Nate mouthed to his reflection in the mirror while Mat was busy toweling himself off.

"Hey," Mat said, roughing a towel over his hair. "There's a nice little cafe downstairs. You wanna grab some breakfast?"

Nate turned around to answer and cracked up. Mat's hair was sticking out at every conceivable angle, and the confusion on his face at Nate's laughter only made him more adorable. Nate wanted to kiss him again. Run his fingers through that hair to smooth it down—or maybe mess it up more.

Fuck it, why not? He'd already crossed the line, might as well enjoy it over here on the other side. He reined in his laughter, pecked Mat on the lips, smoothed both hands over his head. "I'd like that. Can't stay too long, though; I have a meeting at nine and it's an hour's ride in."

That seemed to sober Mat a little. "Is this . . . I mean, did we just . . ."

"Screw things up?" Nate asked, but he smiled to soften the blow of it.

Mat nodded.

Nate smoothed a hand across Mat's hair again. Wasn't sticking up anymore; he just wanted to touch him. "I mean, it's a given this can't get out. People *can't* know, you get me?" Mat nodded again. "But I don't plan to tell anyone, and neither do you, and it's not like this'll be my first time testifying with my emotions involved. I know all the tricks by now. It'll be okay. I'll make sure of it."

Mat nodded again, but he didn't seem so convinced. Maybe because Nate was a little nervous himself. Sure, he'd felt personally entangled in cases before—hungry for justice, for vengeance even, for victims he'd grown close to—but *never* like this.

He sighed, stepped out of the little bathroom, skin pebbling as the cooler, drier air in the hallway hit. "Come on," he said, turning and holding his hand out to Mat. "Let's go get dressed and have that breakfast. My treat."

CHAPTER THREE

Doug ran until his lungs burned and his calves ached and every footfall in his new sneakers felt like he was running on a bed of nails. It . . . wasn't very far. A couple miles, maybe. He'd spent the last year developing a whole different kind of stamina and this one had fallen by the wayside.

Or maybe he should've just paced himself better.

Well, whatever the case, he found himself in what was clearly a more . . . *adult* area of Baltimore. Nightclubs with edgy names. Shop fronts with mannequins dressed in leather and latex. Bars with names like the Bear Cave and PussyCats. All closed now, of course—it wasn't even seven yet on a Wednesday morning—but it wasn't so hard to imagine the life on this street when the sun went down. The thoughts disgusted him, yet at the same time he found them . . . comforting, maybe. Familiar, at the very least. No question there'd be men here who knew how to master, pets who *wanted* to be slaves. Nobody would question Doug's desire to make people happy, to avoid conflict, to feel loved. No one would even look at him twice.

Unless he wanted them to. He'd never been cocky before, but he was one of Nikolai's boys now—or at least he *had* been—and he had no doubt he could turn every head in the room if he tried. Have his pick of them, even. The kind of men who drank in a place called the Bear Cave would recognize lips made for sucking cock when they saw them.

But was that really what he'd been made for, after all? Did he really want that? Did he even *like* it? So hard to separate his own desires from the ones that'd been forced inside him via pain and loneliness and fear. Impossible, actually. Fuck, he didn't even know if he wanted to go home again—not just back to Mat, but back to Vegas, back to school, back to that tidy, straitlaced, academic life he'd once planned for himself. He'd held on to that dream so tightly for so long. Now he couldn't even tell if it'd make him happy.

Only way to find out was to try, he supposed. Scientific method. Theory, testing, hypothesis.

His stomach growled. He was thirsty, too, but he didn't have access to his own money, and Mat obviously hadn't considered the possibility that he'd ever let Doug out of his sight—*you mean out from under his thumb*—long enough to have given him even a fucking five-dollar bill. Let alone a debit or a credit card. Doug tried not to be hurt by the implication that he couldn't be *trusted* with something like that—what'd they think he'd do, buy a plane ticket and flee? No, probably they just hadn't thought about it at all. Hadn't even occurred to them. Because, hey, what's a slave need with a credit card?

Not a slave anymore, Doug. Not *a slave.*

Okay, fine, then what's a head case need with a credit card?

I need to buy fucking breakfast, is what. Maybe someone should've thought of that. *At least Nikolai never forgot to feed me.*

Well, he'd just have to go home to eat, was all. The city was coming to life around him, bustling with commuters and morning joggers and fuck-all knew what else. For all that he was exposed out here on the sidewalk in his jogging shorts and tee, he felt strangely safe. Invisible. Nobody paid him any mind. He was nothing special out here—no makeup, no fancy clothes, no collars and cuffs, no ornamentation on his naked flesh, no perfect posture on his knees. Even his brand was hidden inside sock and shoe, and no one would know what it meant if they saw it anyway.

Christ, and he thought he'd been lonely at Allen's.

With a sigh, he turned around and started shuffling back the way he'd come. He'd run in a more or less straight line lest he get lost, so finding his way back was easy. Except for how tired he was, how sore his feet were. He'd have to work on that. Shameful, is what it was. His body was valuable; he should've been taking better care of it.

Not your fault. Allen's.

Yeah, except Allen wouldn't have chained you like a dog for two months if you hadn't been such a bad fucking slave.

He froze in the middle of the sidewalk, squeezed his eyes shut and pressed his fists to them. *I'm not a slave anymore, I'm not a slave anymore. I'm my own man now. And I don't regret it.*

He gave up walking and broke back into a run. Exhausted he might be, but maybe, just maybe if he moved fast enough, none of those hurtful, confusing thoughts would be able to catch him.

He thought he'd run right up into Mat's arms, let his brother hold him and coddle him like he always had, let himself take strength and solace from it like he used to before Nikolai had opened his eyes to new truths (lies?), but their paths winded up intersecting earlier than he expected.

In that vegetarian cafe on the ground floor of their building, sitting in the back of the tiny restaurant, unavoidably in view through the front window . . . was Mat, with Agent Johnson. Chatting over coffee and breakfast, and, by their body language, obviously not in a case-related meeting, either.

Doug might've been completely out of touch with the outside world, but he could still recognize flirting when he saw it—fuck, he practically had a PhD in flirting. And sexual attraction, too. He definitely saw that in the way Nate clasped Mat's forearm across the table. The way Mat didn't just allow it but actually *encouraged* it.

How fucking dare they? How fucking dare they flaunt their perverse fucking relationship, their undeserved happiness, the fact that they were having a fancy fucking breakfast while Doug couldn't even be trusted with enough pocket change to buy coffee at a gas station?

Before he could stop himself, he was shoving through the cafe door.

The cheerful jingle of the bell sounded like a taunt.

In his anger, he forgot Mat's fake name, so he just yelled, "Hey, you!"

Mat's head snapped up—as did everyone else's in the cafe—but Agent Johnson startled so hard he sloshed his coffee. *That's right, fucker. You* should *feel guilty. Caught with your dick in the cookie jar.*

"*Sam,*" Mat said through his teeth, his surprise giving way to that special brand of condescending, mortified outrage that seemed the sole domain of meddling older brothers who thought they knew better. He stood from his chair, waving apologetically at the handful of other patrons and the employees behind the counter. Hooked Doug around the arm in a distinctly ungentle grip and dragged him outside, Agent Johnson close on their heels. Doug didn't fight. It wasn't that he didn't want to, or that he was any less furious than he'd been a moment ago—more, in fact, now that Mat was manhandling him like he owned him. It was just how thoroughly he'd been conditioned, how sickeningly his heart tripped in his chest and stoppered up his lungs with the instinctual fear that he'd misbehaved, that he'd be punished, that he'd failed his master.

Because sure, they kept telling him he was masterless now, but he was still being hauled out onto the sidewalk to be put in his fucking place, wasn't he.

Except Mat didn't stop outside. Didn't hit him or shout at him. Even his grip eased—still insistent but no longer painful—as he tugged Doug through the foyer of their building, up the stairs, and into their apartment. He placed Doug firmly on the couch, held out a warning palm to keep him there. Turned to Agent Johnson and said, voice deceptively gentle, "Could you go downstairs and pay the bill, please? Apologize to them?"

Agent Johnson licked his lips, eyes darting between Doug and Mat. "Sure. Yeah." He looked like he wanted to ask if Mat would be okay, but he didn't. Just stepped out into the hall and closed the door behind him.

As soon as he was gone, Mat turned to Doug again, arms folded over his chest. "Okay." He gave Doug a level look. "Say what you need to say."

Doug's anger was rapidly slipping through his fingers, and he didn't even know why. He didn't want to have to explain himself—didn't even think he could. He didn't want to make excuses. He didn't want Mat to be so fucking *gentle* with him after the show he'd just put on downstairs, the way he'd just endangered their safety. He wanted . . .

He wanted to be *punished.* Put in his place and then be forgiven. Be told what to do next. What to say. How to feel. Couldn't handle that look of *expectation* on Mat's face. The weight of it. The responsibility.

Like what he wanted mattered. Like he was capable of deciding that anyway, like he'd *ever* been, like he hadn't gone from sheltered son to sheltered little brother to sheltered pet and had never once so much as *played* at taking control of his own life.

He couldn't handle *any* of this. He needed to get out of here.

"I just wanted to say . . ." He cleared his throat. Spoke up. "I just wanted to say you should at least give me some spending money. So I can go out and live my life."

Mat's eyes widened. "Oh! Oh, oh, of course. I'm so sorry, Doug, I should've . . . I mean, it's as much yours as mine anyway, right? I'll give you the debit card and you can get some cash out."

"*Cash*," Doug said, holding out his hand. "I wanted breakfast. A fucking drink after my run. I got—" *stuck*, he didn't say. Was too ashamed to admit he'd pushed too hard, too fast, worn himself out miles from home. Like the stupid slave he was. Like someone who had no fucking idea how to take care of himself.

"Right." Mat looked chastened, distracted. He reached into his back pocket for his wallet. Pulled out a pair of twenties and the debit card and handed them to Doug. "Of course, bud. I'm sorry I didn't think of this earlier."

Doug took the card and the money, shoved them in his pocket. "I'm gonna shower and change, and then I'm going out."

Mat's struggle not to ask *Where?*, not to police Doug, was visible on his face. Instead he swallowed and nodded and said, soft like he was fighting not to choke up, "Maybe we can run together tomorrow?"

"Yeah, maybe," Doug said, not meeting Mat's eyes. They both knew he was full of shit, but he wasn't angry enough anymore to cope with the disappointment he knew he'd see there. "I've got my phone," he added by way of concession. "S'not on, but I'll call you if I need to."

Mat looked like he wanted to argue with that—*turn your damn phone on, don't you know I'm going to sit here worrying about you all day?*—but he just pressed his lips together, nodded, and said, "Be careful, Doug. Er, *Sam*. Be careful, Sam."

It almost made Doug mad, how hands-off Mat was being. What was the point of this rebellion if Mat wasn't going to push back even a little? He wanted to fight, damn it.

"Don't wait up," Doug said, but couldn't quite make himself slam the bathroom door behind him.

"I didn't even worry about him being gone," Mat said. Nate kneaded his shoulder, listening intently. Silent, supportive. Mat just wished it were enough. "I noticed, but I didn't, you know? What if someone had found him on the street and taken him away? I'd have been sitting there eating breakfast with you just—"

"Okay, stop." Nate turned sideways on the couch, drew Mat's head up with gentle fingers under his chin. Their knees touched, and Mat felt sick for even noticing. Selfish, it was selfish, *he* was selfish and Doug could've gone missing right under his smitten fucking nose—

"I said *stop*," Nate said, voice as gentle as his fingers but no less commanding for it. "I can see the hamster running in your head. You can't live like that forever, Mat. You're safe now. Nobody knows you're here but me. The bad guys are in jail. Life's not going to end if you let your guard down just for a second."

Except it had once already, hadn't it. And he and Doug would probably still be fighting to cope with the consequences of that lapse fifty years from now.

Nate's fingertips left his chin, swiped gently across his cheek. Mat noticed the wetness there only as Nate wiped it away. God, he was a fucking mess.

He sniffed back the urge to let himself fall into it, to full-on cry, to let Nate comfort him. Tugged his face from Nate's hand. He couldn't be touched like that right now, so gently, with so much forgiveness. He'd left Doug helpless. Alone. Penniless out on the streets of a strange city and all because he'd let himself get too fucking *comfortable.*

"It's okay. You're okay. You didn't do anything wrong, okay? Let Doug find his own way. Let him make some mistakes. Let him figure out who he is. He needs his freedom, Mat, and you need yours, too. He'll come home."

Mat was hearing what Nate was saying, but he wasn't feeling it. Couldn't let the panic go. The *weight* of everything. It was true, he knew, he *knew*, he needed not to hold on so tight, would end up choking them both. Maybe already had. It wasn't like he hadn't considered a million times the possibility that if he'd let Doug stand on his own two feet a little more before this whole mess had happened, then maybe Doug wouldn't be such a mess now. Maybe Doug could've fought it better, held out longer, if he hadn't been so used to being taken care of, told what to do, watched after his entire life.

But look what'd happened when Mat *had* left him to his own devices. Those men had come and destroyed *everything*.

He was breathing too fast. The room was starting to tilt.

Hands on his face. Gentle, firm. For half a second Mat was sure he'd gotten his bell rung, that Coach Darryl was leaning over him, patting his cheek, telling him to focus.

But it was Nate—as warm and steady and familiar and comforting as Coach Darryl had always been. And Mat hadn't been hit in the head—he was fucking *panicking*.

When his eyes finally focused on the face in front of him, Nate drew him into a hug. "If you can't trust yourself, then trust me, okay?"

"I do," he murmured into the side of Nate's neck. Without thought, without hesitation. The adrenaline drained away, left him shaking and sticky with cold sweat. He huffed a nervous little laugh. "It's the rest of the world I'm worried about." And Doug. He *wanted* to trust his brother not to do something stupid, but . . .

But he stayed behind once already. Chose them over you.

"I can't promise he isn't going to make any mistakes, Mat. I can't promise he's always going to make healthy choices. But he'll make it through okay. And whatever mistakes he makes, they *aren't your fault*. All you can do now is be there for him, accept him, love him, all the things you're already doing. You've been through too much together for him not to come home to you." He kissed Mat's forehead. "Trust, babe."

Mat's lip wobbled at the pet name, the way it rolled so unconsciously off Nate's tongue, how heartfelt he sounded, how *sure* of himself. If Nate could believe in them all so much, well, maybe Mat could too.

Or at least fake it till you make it, right?

He shuddered bodily at the ring of Nikolai's voice inside his head, and Nate leaned forward to kiss it away again, lips pressed to Mat's furrowed brow.

"I'm sorry, I have to go," he murmured against Mat's heated skin. He pulled back, gripped Mat's shoulders in two steadying hands. Dropped his gaze and bit his lip. "I have to be careful about coming here. I don't know if . . ."

"It's okay," Mat said, even though it wasn't, because it'd always been his job to be strong, to take the punches and stay on his feet. He didn't know how to do anything else anymore. "I understand. I'll be fine."

"I'll call you," Nate said. Pecked Mat on the lips, then changed his mind and went full-in, hands circling behind Mat's back and neck, fingers carding into his hair. One more peck when he pulled back, and then he touched their foreheads together and added, "I'll miss you."

"Yeah," Mat choked out, because if he tried to say anything else as he felt Nate's hands leave his body, as he watched Nate stand and slip into his dress shoes and head to the door, he'd just end up bawling like a little kid, begging *Please don't leave me alone.*

He'd had enough of being alone to last him a fucking lifetime.

Doug spun the face of his cuff-like watch until it rested on the inside of his wrist, then smoothed a hand down his skintight leather vest and the seat of his equally skintight jeans before approaching the Bear Cave. Tried not to think about the . . . the *reproach* on Mat's face when he'd bought these clothes. Not that Mat had seemed to notice when Doug had left the apartment wearing them. *Slut in his natural habitat and all that.* Why should he have noticed?

Except it was way too early in the day for the Bear Cave to be open yet. And probably not a whole lot of respectable places he could pass the time at in these clothes. There were surely at least a handful of *un*respectable places he could go, maybe even make a few extra bucks that Mat wouldn't be keeping track of. Down by the water, probably, in the maze of old industrial docks and warehouses away from the polite veneer of the Inner Harbor. Madame had sold his body, after all. So had Nikolai. Allen might not've taken cash for his services, but he sure had *used* Doug like a whore.

It was different, though, wasn't it? What he'd done for them? It hadn't been . . . it hadn't been *cheap*. Or amateurish. He hadn't been made to be disposable, forgotten about. Even if that was exactly what'd happened in the end. No, he didn't want that. Didn't deserve to be treated like some ten-dollar hooker. Nikolai had made him better than that. The man might've been a monster, full of lies, but at least he'd taught Doug his value.

So Doug spent his day at a little second-run movie theater watching back-to-back matinees instead. Bought popcorn and soda and a huge box of Junior Mints and let himself not care, for a few hours, about keeping the perfect figure. He had no one to keep it for anymore anyway, so what did it matter if he lost himself for a while in sensory pleasures? Indulged? Did something for *himself*?

Dangerous thought, that. Halfway through the second movie—some ridiculous bit of garbage full of explosions and car chases and assholes just generally acting like the animals he'd come to realize most people were—he began to realize how quickly he could get used to this. To stuffing his face with contraband and lazing in dark theaters all day doing nothing, being good for nothing. Thinking nothing, feeling nothing but the slow simple pleasures of good food and mindless entertainment. How tempting it was.

He forced himself out of the theater before the movie had ended. Left his half-eaten box of candy behind, though he wanted to keep it, remembering too many days of going hungry. The debit card in his pocket wasn't endless, and he only had fourteen of the forty dollars left that Mat had given him just this morning.

Maybe he should find a job. A real job. Not one on his knees or his belly, but one that'd remind him not to get too comfortable. Something he could do to be useful. To not have to depend on Mat's tenuous generosity anymore. God knew *that* wouldn't last forever.

Maybe the Bear Cave needed a new server. He could do that. He'd waited hand and foot on more men than he could count. He was *good* at it. He could even mix the damn drinks; Nikolai had taught him so much.

But the Bear Cave wasn't hiring. The burly guy behind the bar gave him a shrug and a halfhearted "Sorry, kid." And Doug must have looked completely pathetic, because the bartender poured him a shot of vodka and pushed it across the bar. "On the house," he said with a gentle smile.

Doug hesitated. He wasn't supposed to—

Who's going to stop you, huh? Nobody here to give a fuck.

The last time he'd gotten drunk, Allen had beaten him until he couldn't stand. Hadn't even been his fault—a group of his guests had emptied half a bottle of wine up his ass, laughing like hyenas the entire time.

Yeah, well, Allen's not here now. And it's only one shot.

Besides, what was the worst that could happen? Even if the bartender roofied him, it'd be just another Thursday afternoon.

He picked up the shot and tossed it back in one tear-inducing gulp.

Four hours later, he was still perched on that same stool, picking at a bowl of pretzels and licking the residue of his . . . fifth? sixth? . . . beer off his lips. The place was a lot more crowded now, packed with bodies and music and voices. He hadn't bought at least the last four drinks. Opened his mouth like a good boy when somebody tipped a fresh bottle to his lips. Closed his eyes. Swallowed. Moaned and let his tongue catch a stray drop before it could run down his chin.

Someone was touching him. Maybe several someones. Didn't matter. He let the hands go where they would, like he was supposed to, like a good boy. Shivered at the words whispered in his ear, followed by a graze of teeth: "What a good boy you are. So pretty."

"Than' you, Masser." The words rolled off his tongue easy, without thought. He flushed with shame at slurring them, but the man just pulled back and grinned and tipped the beer bottle to Doug's lips again, so obviously he didn't mind Doug being drunk.

A hand drifted up his thigh, squeezed his cock through his leather pants. "You here alone, boy?"

Doug nodded, splayed his knees open. Felt a flash of fear when the man *tsk*ed, but it poofed away when the hand squeezed gently at his cock again and the man said, "A boy like you should be collared. Leashed up. Not out here by yourself, no one to take care of you, no one for you to worship."

Doug nodded, head loose and sloppy on his shoulders. He knew that. Tried to say he had been until recently, that he'd been taken away from his old master, let go, sold for money, but he couldn't quite seem to make his tongue work anymore.

"You want to come in back with me, boy?"

He nodded again, bigger this time. Yes, he did want that. Wanted to worship. To serve. To be told what to do and make people feel good and not have to think or worry. To feel secure, to do what he'd been made for. To be a *good boy* again, even if it was just for a little while.

Mat waited for hours. Sure, he'd tried his best to take Nate's advice to heart. He'd put on a movie. Skipped some rope. Looked up some new recipes on their new computer, in case Doug came home for dinner.

Mostly he sat on the couch staring at his phone, waiting for it to ring.

Dreading that it would ring, because if Doug called him, it would only be for something terrible.

On the other hand, maybe something had happened that was so terrible he *couldn't* call.

No. He had to let Doug explore his freedom. He had to let Doug explore his freedom. He had to let Doug explore his freedom.

He chewed on his lip. Stared at his phone. Turned the TV on, then turned it off again.

Texted Nate, who texted back, *Can't talk now but hang in there.*

As day turned to night, he grew too worried to sleep, so he wrapped himself in a blanket and sat vigil on the couch. If he passed out from exhaustion now, at least he wouldn't be too uncomfortable.

Doug came in at around three in the morning. *Fell* in, to be specific.

He could barely walk. He reeked of booze and . . . *other* things. His shirt was torn. His hair mussed. No mistaking the stain on the front of his vest, even in the low light. The crusty smudge on his cheek, the stiff tufts of hair, the bite marks and bruises blooming on his exposed skin.

Oh God.

Mat launched up from the couch, caught himself halfway across the room and forced himself to go slow, be gentle. His baby brother had been attacked. *Again.* On Mat's watch. Rushing him now would only make things worse.

"M'off duty," Dougie slurred, nudging Mat's questing hands away when they landed on his shoulders, ran down his arms, looking for injury.

"Who did this to you?" Mat asked, keeping his voice soft. He couldn't panic. He needed to stay calm. For Dougie. "Dougie, Dougie look at me. Who did this?"

Dougie's eyes dragged up from his feet to Mat's face. Widened, briefly, then settled back down. "Mat?" he asked.

Mat nearly choked on the alcohol fumes streaming from his brother's mouth. Grasped his shoulders again, gentle, gentle. Couldn't bear the thought of hurting him. "Yeah, Dougie. Yeah, I'm here."

"Jus'some guys at the club." Dougie listed out of his grip. "Calm down. S'not like I didn't aks for it. Just havin' some fun."

He pinballed toward the hallway to their rooms.

Mat chased after him, couldn't decide if he wanted to hug Dougie or hit him.

It's not just fun, *not for you or me. It can't be* just fun. *Even if you asked for it, they should have known better than to say yes. You don't have to do this if you need approval or love or whatever; I'm right here.*

But he found he couldn't say any of it. Was horrified, in fact, by what *did* come out of his mouth: "You're *smashed,* Dougie."

"S'*Doug,*" he said, whirling around like a wobbly top and poking a finger into Mat's chest. Or trying to; he missed, poked Mat's arm instead. "'N' sowhat?"

Hit, not hug. Definitely hit. Mat tore a hand through his hair instead, clutched at it until he made himself wince. "You can't . . . you have no idea what you're *doing* when you're this drunk. It's not consent, Dougie. Those guys *raped* you!"

"*You* raped me!" Dougie spat, then gave a high, shrill laugh that cut through Mat's defenses as brutally as any whip. "Or did *I* rape you? Errybody raping errybody!"

"Dougie, *please* . . ." He didn't know how to finish that sentence, didn't know what to *do,* only knew that this was so much worse than what he'd spent all day fearing, that it hurt so much more he wasn't sure he could bear it. He hitched a breath, choked back a sob. Clutched at his brother, half in desperation not to lose him, half to keep himself from collapsing right there in the dim hall.

"Leamme 'lone, Mat." Dougie shoved at his chest, but there was no strength behind it, no coordination. Mat couldn't even remember *how* to make his fingers unclench from Dougie's arms. "You don' own me."

"Of course I don't," he whispered, voice still choked, every inch of him so brittle he was *sure* he'd crack. "I don't *want* to. You know that. Please, just—"

Dougie managed to shove away. Turned his back and stumbled into his room, stripping his single layer of clothes as he went. Had he been wearing underwear when he'd left? If so, it was gone now. Mat's eyes were drawn to the raw welts covering every square inch of Dougie's ass and thighs, and he had to bite his lips against puking.

"They hurt you," he choked out.

"So?"

"*God*, Dougie."

Dougie whirled on him, and the poking finger came back, this time on his left hip. "S'no big deal. Made 'em happy."

Mat caught Dougie's wrist in his hand before the kid could poke him again or pull away. Gave in to the fear, the fury, and jerked him until he met Mat's eyes. "Did it make *you* happy?" he demanded.

All that drunken defiance drained out of Dougie's face in the blink of an eye. His arm went slack in Mat's grip, and he dropped his eyes to the floor, and when he spoke it was so quiet Mat almost didn't hear it. "Doesn't need to, does it?"

The kid was downright gentle as he extricated his wrist from Mat's shock-slackened hand. He touched his fingertips to Mat's forearm, the briefest caress—a wordless apology, or maybe a plea for understanding. "Imma go shower," he said. "Go to bed. You look like shit."

Yeah, no kidding. He felt like shit, too. *Was* shit.

How the fuck had he let this happen?

No way he'd ever go to bed until he could figure out how to make sure it would never happen again.

CHAPTER FOUR

Doug woke to sunlight drilling a hole through his eyelids and every last nerve in his body throbbing. He groaned, rolled over, and buried his face into his pillow. The alarm hadn't gone off yet; he still had time to sleep before prepping for the evening's entertainment. God, he dreaded the thought of trying to salvage the wreck of his ass. Just shifting in bed had him sticky and dribbling. He'd have to be liberal with the shower shot before lubing himself up all over again.

And Christ, someone had beaten the crap out of him. Had he been bad? Why couldn't he remember?

Because you're hungover, asshole.

. . . wait. Why was he hungover?

He pried his eyes open with a quiet groan, and cautiously lifted his face from the pillow. Blinked until the light stopped slicing at his eyeballs and—

Not Allen's. Baltimore.

His apartment.

No.

Mat's apartment.

Mat, who'd been furious when he'd come home last night. Pushing him around. Shouting. Shaming.

You damaged what he thinks is his.

Doug's stomach lurched.

No, it's not like that. You damaged what he loves.

Doug snorted, shook his head, sat up carefully. The room took a lazy spin, then settled.

Yeah, that's a nice convenient truth to believe in, Doug. You know better.

Did he, though? *Was* it all just a soothing lie?

Fuck it, he was way too hungover to contemplate life's mysteries without at least a cup of coffee first.

He stumbled to the bathroom, pissed, showered, brushed his teeth. By the time he'd managed to worm damp skin into tight pants—they hurt like hell against all those welts but the satisfaction, the *need*, to see Mat's reaction to them made it all worthwhile—he felt almost human again. Ready to paint on his game face.

Literally, in fact. He'd bought one tube of eyeliner at the shop that'd sold him his pants. Fuck Mat anyway; he put some on. Used the tip of his finger to smudge it around a little.

When he sauntered into the kitchen, Mat looked up from his newspaper, startled, and immediately looked down at it again. He didn't bury his nose between the pages fast enough; Doug still saw the blush creeping up his neck and cheeks.

"I . . ." Mat mumbled, "I made some coffee." Still avoiding eye contact, he pointed at the pot steaming on the counter.

Curious. Mat almost never drank the stuff—Coach Darryl disapproved of caffeine (and sugar, and cream, and basically everything else in life worth eating or doing). Which meant he'd made it for Doug. A peace offering, perhaps? An apology for last night? Not what Doug had been expecting, but whatever. It didn't change anything. He headed toward the pot, provocatively swaying his hips as he went. Testing the sincerity of Mat's contrition.

He wondered if Mat was staring. Wondered if Mat was analyzing his movement, worriedly trying to decipher from his gait what he'd gotten up to last night. Or glaring, hating him for being such a filthy, desperate slut.

Maybe Mat was turned on.

Doug's hands shook when he tried to pick up a mug. Shook hard enough and clasped tight enough that the handle of the mug snapped clean off in his hand. Vibrating, he gently set the handle down on the countertop. Poured coffee into the broken mug regardless, deliberately not turning around to meet the worried stare he felt on the back of his head.

The hot porcelain scalded his hands as he carried his drink back to the table.

"You have a therapy appointment today," Mat said coolly. "Over webcam. One o'clock. I'd really appreciate it if you could make time for it."

"Can't."

Hot anger slashed through Mat's piercing gaze.

"Why not?"

Hmm. Doug hadn't thought that far ahead. Was he desperate enough for a fight to say, *Because I don't fucking want to*? Desperate enough for Mat's kindness and pity to say, *Because it'll never work, not on me*?

He finally settled on, "I'm going out again."

Mat's face went a sickly gray-green, like he was going to puke on the table.

"I need a job," Doug snapped, the resentment he felt rendering it true.

Mat's head snapped up. "What? No. The survivor's fund—"

"Won't last forever." Even if Mat weren't controlling every penny of Doug's share, he'd still need a job. He needed to make his own way and get out of this apartment and out of Mat's care. Make his own life. Not be Mat's little toy or project anymore. His own money, his own place, where he could do what he wanted with *who* he wanted.

Mat would appreciate it, too. Maybe not at first, but eventually. No more tiptoeing around, no more waiting up all night. He and Nate could move on. Be happy. Doug would stop being Mat's problem, and it would be such a relief that Mat wouldn't try to claw him back. Not once he realized how easy it was to forget about Doug. Like Mike had. Like Nikolai had. Like Penny had.

Except right now, Mat was still staring at him like he'd sprouted a third nipple. And also maybe like he wanted to chain Doug to the bed and never let him go again.

That shit wasn't happening. No fucking way.

"Yeah, so, thanks for the coffee," Doug said in a tone that wasn't thankful in the slightest, and stood from the table—coffee three-quarters untouched—before it could occur to Mat to grab him, not let him go.

He had to get out of here. Had to escape. Run, and never stop running.

He couldn't be a prisoner anymore. Not Allen's prisoner, not the government's, and not Mat's.

"Don't wait up," he added, snagging his keys and stuffing his feet into his sneakers.

"Doug?" Mat pleaded, eyes huge and glistening in that way they so often seemed to nowadays. "Just . . . look, you can have your freedom. I'm not going to try to stop you from figuring this out. I don't want to control you; I just want you to be *safe*. So please. Please, *please*, don't go to that bar again."

Doug felt the hate wash over him. He smiled sweetly. "Oh, don't worry, Master. I won't."

No skin off his back. Not like there weren't a million other leather bars in this city, anyway.

Doug was nursing his third beer—courtesy of the third handsy but disappointing leather daddy to try his luck with him tonight—and a basket of fried everything—courtesy of the fourth—when he saw her. A woman in a tight red dress and tall black heels with red soles. It wasn't her outfit that caught his attention, though; it was her hair. Blonde, done up immaculately in a chignon.

For the first time in a long time, he thought of Penny. Of Penny's hair done up that way so perfectly, and Doug standing behind her, zipping her dress or clasping her necklace or just rubbing her smooth pale shoulders.

Was it Penny?

Had Penny been arrested during the raid with her husband? Or had she been allowed to go free? Or simply gotten away?

Doug's body began to respond to her as it always had. The way he sat up straighter, the way his smile softened, the way his cock filled and curved, ready to slide into her at a moment's notice.

But then the woman turned, and Doug saw her in profile, and the illusion shattered.

Didn't stop him from smiling in invitation, though. *This* was a woman who could take control. Lead him, guide him, pet and praise and fill him with purpose. Like Penny had. Nothing like the poser Doms who'd plied him with food and liquor tonight.

No, she was the real deal. An honest-to-God mistress. He could feel the confidence, the power, the God-given *right* radiating off her from across the room.

She smiled back tightly, sharp eyes alighting on his meal, then his greasy fingers.

He grabbed for a napkin so fast he spilled his beer.

She glared, disapproving, at the evidence of his clumsiness dripping off the bar and onto the floor, and Doug had visions of all the punishments to come. Of being shoved down in the puddle face-first, made to clean it with his tongue as she beat him until his tears mingled with the grit and beer. Doing his penance, earning his forgiveness. Pleasing her. Becoming a *good boy* again. Maybe even *her* good boy.

Even if just for a little while.

She strode in his direction as he fell to his knees, using napkins to sop up the mess. Not his tongue. They were in public, after all. Maybe she'd have him put his tongue to service later.

On his knees, he watched her shoes come into view.

"You're a messy little boy, aren't you?" she asked, firm but with a trace of good humor.

Teasing. So why did he respond as though she was furious and about to unleash hell on him?

He cowered as if it were Allen looming above him. He felt like fucking *crying*. Yet still somehow he remembered his tongue, remembered his training. *Flatter with that sweet mouth, my beautiful boy*. He managed to stammer out, "N-no Mistress, I mean, yes Mistress, but it's just, you're so beautiful and I wanted to impress you and—"

"Oh dear." She stilled his tongue with a single touch to his shoulder as she crouched beside him. He had no idea how she managed it in such tall heels. "Did I spook you? It's all right. It was an accident. More endearing than anything, really." She cupped his cheek, turning his face until he met her gaze. "Glad to know I can still have that effect on such pretty young things."

Yes. Nikolai's beautiful boy. I'm still useful. Still desirable. Still have something to offer, not useless, not used up and broken.

"How about I take you somewhere more private so you can recover?"

Recover. Not make it up to her. Not prove his worthiness. Not apologize properly.

Recover.

Her kindness made him want to cry all over again. "Oh, yes please Mistress thank you Mistress I promise you won't regret it, I promise, I—"

"Shhh," she said, petting his head. "None of that. I can see for myself what a good boy you are."

"Yes," he breathed. Leaned into her petting hand. Would've crawled right into her if he could've. *Disappeared* into her. "*Yes.*"

"That's better." She stood, extending a hand to help him up.

Her palm wasn't as soft as Penny's. She had calluses in odd places, like she did physical labor for a living. Maybe she did. Maybe she was a tradeswoman, transforming by night into a polished society mistress. Maybe she couldn't afford one of Nikolai's boys, but what did it matter when she so clearly *deserved* one?

And what did Doug care, so long as she chose him?

After talking quietly with the bartender and exchanging a folded bundle of bills for a single key on a ring, she led him into a quiet back room, not much different from the one at the Bear Cave where six men had taken their turns with him.

Nobody waited for him here, however. They were alone. As soon as the door closed, she smiled and took down her hair. Gentled him by the shoulders onto the edge of the modest bed—the centerpiece of the room. "Let's take a break and talk limits," she said. "Can you do that for me, cutie?"

Doug sat where she placed him and posed in a way he thought she'd like. "Anything you want, Mistress. I can do anything you want."

She sat beside him, toeing out of her shoes. Her pedicure was attractive, but not expensive looking. "For now you can call me Corinne. I'll let you know when it's time to pick the formalities back up. What's your name?"

Boy, he wanted to say, or maybe *Whatever pleases you, Mistress*, but somehow he knew that would upset her. "D—" No, wait, that was wrong. Giving out real names, telling the truth even if it could hurt them, was the sort of thing slaves did, the sort of thing people who couldn't take care of themselves, couldn't be *trusted* with themselves, did. "Um, Sam, Mis— Corinne. My name's Sam."

"Nice to meet you, Sam. I haven't seen you around before. Are you new to the scene?"

New, yes, but more experienced than any other boy you've had. His heart rate ratcheted up, thinking that she'd leave him over this. Thinking he was green and unskilled, that he didn't deserve her time or attention. "I'm still good," he promised, abandoning his pose on the bed for proper position at her feet. "Really good—I'll make you so happy. I've had a lot of practice, considering. And what I don't know yet, I— I'm a quick learner. Please, I promise."

She looked slightly pained.

What he wouldn't give to be allowed to slip between her legs and prove himself. But no. You never touched a master or mistress without explicit permission. Only slaves could be touched without consent.

"Sam," she said, squatting down to eye level with him again, and suddenly she looked so much like Mat in her expression that Doug found himself fighting back tears. "Be honest with me, okay? You seem really high-strung right now. Are you under the influence of anything? Are you . . . are you safe with me right now?"

"I've never been more safe," Doug insisted. He wanted her off her knees. *Needed* her off her knees; she didn't belong there, down on the floor with the likes of him. She was supposed to be taking control, not . . . not *this*. His hands reached out to clutch at her, but he pulled them back, balled them on his thighs. "Please let me show you. Please let me show you I can be everything you want. I'm skilled, I promise."

"I don't doubt that, sweetie. What I'm doubting is whether you're in the right headspace right now to be doing something like this."

"I'm not *crazy*," he snapped. Why did everyone keep *saying* that? He was fine, damn it. He was *fine*.

Except here he was, mouthing off to a mistress.

"Oh God." He dropped his head. Ground his teeth. "I'm sorry, Mistress," he whispered. He really, really was. But maybe this was a good thing. Maybe she'd stop asking so many questions now and punish him like he needed. Punish him and let him earn her good graces and be her good boy.

She cupped his shoulders. "Of course you're not crazy, Sam. And you have nothing to be sorry for. *Nothing*." She sighed. "But I'm afraid I'm not going to be acting as your mistress tonight."

"No!" Doug cried, louder than he had any right to. "No, please!"

She didn't let him go. Didn't strike him. Didn't shove him away in disgust.

Didn't pull him close, either, didn't tug his face between her legs.

She just held him right where he was.

"I'm sorry, Sam. I really am. I don't want you to take this personally, okay? I just . . . being a Dominant is a huge responsibility and right now, with you, I'm not feeling confident that I'd be living up to my own ideals if I pushed this situation further."

He squeezed his eyes shut, trying to keep tears from escaping.

It didn't work.

"Oh, sweetie." She hugged him to her chest and stroked his hair with one hand. "Oh, sweetie, really, don't take it personal. You're beautiful. You have no idea how sweet and lovely you are. But I don't think BDSM is what you really need right now, and I'd be really, *really* wrong to try to pretend it was."

Was that what he was doing? *Pretending*? Broken toy pretending he was still useful? Discarded pet pretending he could still be loved? Masterless slave pretending he could run his own life, make his own choices?

Be a real boy?

"It doesn't mean I don't like you, okay? Hey, what if I go back to my car and get my flats and my purse and I take you out for a milk shake? I know a great place that has like fifty flavors. You can tell me a little about yourself."

A milk shake. Like some fucking *child*. Like he needed to be cared for, *coddled*.

Then again, he *was* crying into a strange woman's shoulder. And how many times had Mat and Beth and everyone else under the sun told him these last few weeks that there was nothing wrong with needing a little help?

"Okay," he said. Sniffled. Swiped his hand across his nose lest he snot up her beautiful dress. "Okay. But only if you let me buy."

"We'll go dutch," she said with a radiant smile.

After a short detour to her car as promised, Corinne walked him to a nearby greasy spoon with so much neon it kind of hurt his eyes. She eased his nerves with stories of her job as a freelance photographer, and how her sexual role as a Dom helped her get ahead in her career because she was so well versed in coaxing subjects into the emotions and levels of comfort she needed. Over decadent malted milk shakes, she asked Doug about himself. He told her half-truths. That he'd dropped out of his PhD program. That he lived with his overbearing brother.

"Does he know where you are right now?" she asked gently.

He liked her so much, trusted her so much, that he couldn't help but tell the truth. "If he did, he'd be fucking furious."

She leaned back in the booth. "Oh, I see. Well, how about you just text him and let him know you're out for a nice platonic dinner with a lady? Might cool him off a little. Tell him you'll be home by midnight."

"But I won't," Doug protested.

"Yes, you will. Because when we're done here, I'm telling you to go straight home. No more bars. No more back rooms. Whatever you're seeking, you won't find it there. You're only going to get hurt."

Her tone brooked no argument. And frankly, he was glad of it. It made him feel less lost. More cared for. That someone would bother to take the time to make decisions for him. To worry about him.

Even if sometimes he thought getting hurt was maybe kind of half the point.

He took out his phone. Waited while it booted up.

"And while we're at it, Sam, from now on, I want you to keep your phone on when you go out. I'm not going to tell you to stop playing, but I want you to be safe. When you go out, you tell your brother when you're going to be home, and you stick to the curfew you set for yourself. A boy as eager to please as you . . ." She shook her head, looked genuinely pained on his behalf. "I hate to say it, but not every Dom out there is as responsible as they should be. We try to make it as safe as we can, but people are unpredictable, and when you're in that headspace, you can't always watch out for yourself."

Not *You can't take care of yourself,* but *You can't always have your own back.* The distinction was subtle, but important, and something about it made Doug tingle, warm all over. She didn't . . . she didn't doubt him, and she didn't pity him, and she *didn't* think he was a child.

He sucked at his milk shake to hide his smile, and nodded.

"I understand if you don't want to give your brother that much control, so if that's the case, you can text me instead. Just tell me where you're at and who you're with and when you're planning on getting home. No judgment. I'm not your mother and I'm not trying to run your life. I just . . . I don't want to see you get hurt, okay, cutie?"

Doug nodded again, feeling warm and fuzzy and safe. "Okay."

She smiled. A genuine, beautiful smile. God, maybe one day, if he were good enough, if he were strong enough, he'd actually deserve her. Be good enough *for* her.

"Good. Thank you. That makes me feel much better. Now text your brother."

She watched him do it.

Safe, out w/ friend. Her name is Corinne. Be home by midnight.

"Tell him where you are. The Starlight Diner."

At the Starlight Diner, he typed, and hit Send.

Mat's reply came not fifteen seconds later; he must've been hovering over that damn phone all day and night. *ok. be safe. call if u need me, im here.*

And then, fifteen seconds after that, *I love you. Have fun.*

All those capital letters and careful punctuation hadn't escaped his notice.

"There, that wasn't so bad, was it?" Corinne asked.

He shook his head sheepishly.

"You've got to learn to pick your battles when it comes to overbearing sibs, Sam. Me, I grew up with three older brothers . . ."

CHAPTER FIVE

At quarter to midnight, Doug and Corinne said their good-byes. He refused a ride home, saying he could use the fresh air—and the exercise, two and a half milk shakes later. Corinne agreed, so long as he promised to text her when he was safely back at the apartment.

They parted with a chaste kiss on the cheek and a long, heartfelt hug. He hadn't for one moment stopped fantasizing about burying his face between her thighs, but this was okay too. Good, even. *Normal.* The sort of thing real boys did, he was pretty sure.

Which was probably a big part of why he was feeling stronger and more stable than he had in ages. So much so that even when his walk took him past the leather bars, he didn't feel any need to go in and lose himself in service.

He couldn't stop thinking of what Corinne had said about ethics and responsibilities, about how there was a right and a wrong mind-set, a healthy and an unhealthy way to go about the game. She hadn't rejected him because he wasn't good enough, she'd rejected him because she didn't want to hurt him or take advantage of him. She cared.

So what did that mean about the men from last night? They'd seen the same Doug, except sloppy drunk to boot.

They'd still gone ahead and used him, though.

Used him.

"Hey," a man on the sidewalk with a cigarette in his mouth called. One of the handsy "Doms" from earlier tonight who'd bought him beer.

Doug bristled. Ignored him. Kept walking. After an evening with Corinne, there was no question in his mind about what kind of person deserved his service and what kind didn't.

Well, okay, maybe a *little* question—*just a broken boy, a discarded slave, you deserve nothing but what your betters deign to give you.* But he was capable of ignoring it tonight, basking in the afterglow of Corinne's care. He wasn't a slave anymore. He *wasn't.*

"I said hey! Boy!"

"Sorry, sir," he mumbled, feet stilling of their own accord. Reflex, that was all. Instinctive reaction to that commanding tone. But no. Not a slave anymore. *Not a slave.* "I'm off duty."

"Off duty? No such thing. Come on." The man closed the distance between them in a couple of paces, hand clamping around Doug's upper arm. "I bought you a drink. You owe me. Don't give me trouble, cunt, or so help me I'll give *you* trouble. But maybe you'd like that, huh? Yeah, I bet you would." His fingers tightened to bruising around Doug's arm. "Hole like you, *wants* to be pounded."

Hole. The shock of that word had him frozen in place, shivering in a cold sweat. Unable to think or speak.

Unable to do *anything.*

"That's better, you little tease. Just need a firm hand, huh? Sorry I didn't figure that out earlier. Wouldn't have wasted my cash on courting you." He took a final drag on his cigarette, looked for a second like he might put it out on Doug's arm, but then flicked it to the sidewalk and ground it beneath his heel. *Like he's going to do to you, Hole. Like you're going to let him.* "Can't say I was sorry watching those cocksucking lips nurse that bottle, though."

He tugged Doug along, around the corner and down a dark side street. Doug didn't fight. *Couldn't* fight. Could barely feel his own body, remember his own name. "Maybe I'll buy you another one. Fuck you with it. Bet you'd like that, yeah?"

He nodded numbly, wondering what the fuck he was doing. *Hey, not like you can pretend you haven't gotten off on that before.* Allen's guests had been big fans of liquor-bottle dildos. It'd be par for the course for Doug. This man had sensed it. Sensed his need to be controlled and roughed up and fucked like a toy. Corinne's high-mindedness had been awfully tempting, but in reality, it was quaint and naive. So was her assumption that he'd be home by midnight.

Hole. That's all you've ever done right in your life. Only thing you were ever good at. Only thing you ever will *be good at.*

And sure, maybe he'd learned to ignore Allen's voice in his head, but even Nikolai had called him that.

Precious pet or no. He'd still been a hole.

He whimpered as the man shoved him face-first into the wall. Squeezed his eyes shut, waiting for the inevitable rush of cold air as his jeans were yanked down.

His skintight, fuck-me jeans.

This was what he'd wanted, wasn't it? What he *needed*? The only thing he was good for. And if he was good *enough*, he wouldn't have to try to make sense of his clusterfuck of a life—at least not for a little while. Wouldn't have to worry about anything but service and doing his master proud. Would get to be a good boy. A flawless, empty vessel, no worries, no fears, no thoughts, no responsibilities but the one.

Be a good little hole.

Yeah. He could do that. *Had* to. Was the only way he knew to survive.

Pants down. Shirt up. Doug obeyed every command, but the man hurt him anyway, whistled at the sight of all those welts and bruises painting Doug's skin and then got to work adding some of his own.

Doug pressed his forehead to the rough wall and squeezed his eyes shut, taking it like a good boy.

It went on forever. *Forever*. Doug sobbed openly. Unlike Nikolai, this master obviously wanted his tears, and it was so, so easy to give them. Felt natural. Right. Who knew—maybe the man would soothe Doug when it was over. Maybe he'd even let Doug come.

Or maybe he'd leave him lying there, covered in cum, without so much as a touch or a word of praise.

Wouldn't matter, though. Doug would know he'd been good. That'd be enough. Would have to be; it was all he'd ever be allowed to have.

At long last the master paused, seemingly for breath, but then he shouted, "Find your own fag!"

Pounding footfalls, someone running fast and hard.

And then the sound of a fist hitting flesh. Deep, heavy punches, punctuated by grunts and gasps. Doug just faced the wall, eyes shut, wishing it would be over soon and that the victor would take him fast and then leave him the fuck alone.

At last, one set of footfalls limped down the alley in retreat.

Doug braced himself.

"Pull up your fucking pants."

Mat.

Oh God. Mat. He's not supposed to see me like this. It's supposed to be over; I'm supposed to be convincing him it's over.

Disgust dripped from Mat's voice even after he stopped speaking. Doug flinched and sniffled, but did as he was told. Hands shaking. *I'm a free man now. I'm a free man.* How was it that Mat's mere presence could so powerfully remind him of what a *failure* he was, how weak and pathetic and lost?

Doug had no doubt that in Mat's eyes, this had been a rescue. Even Doug knew that "Dom" had been mistreating him, abusing him. So easy to see now, through Mat's furious glare, that Doug hadn't really wanted this. Had been too weak to stop it. Had lied to himself to make it okay.

And Mat had saved him.

But Doug didn't feel saved.

"Out with a fucking friend!" Mat spat, grabbing him roughly by the arm—fingers finding the bruises the last man had made. "You even fucking named her! God, I'm so stupid. I'm so fucking stupid!"

Doug didn't struggle. Didn't fight.

Just like he hadn't with the last master.

Mat frog-marched him the whole way home. Mat would punish him, and then it would all be over. He'd never get to be his own man. Wasn't strong enough.

Just a hole. That's all you are, boy.

Was there even any point in telling Mat the truth? That yes, he had been out with Corinne, and he'd had the best of intentions, but then—but then he'd stopped kidding himself about who he was and what he deserved and so of course it had come to this in the end?

"I can't believe you even thought you had to lie," Mat raved as he shoved Doug through their apartment door. "What, did you think I was gonna police you? Did you think I was gonna try and— God *damn it*, Doug!" He slammed the door closed behind them. Punched the wall with so much force it buckled under his fist, left a smear of blood and plaster dust across his knuckles, still white with tension.

Doug cowered away. He'd been hit so many times tonight already. Hurt so much already. And Mat would make it so, *so* much worse.

He'd seen his brother *kill* men with those hands. Men stronger than Doug. Men he wasn't even angry with.

What would he do to Doug?

"What the hell do you want me to do, Doug? What are you trying to fucking achieve? First you go out to punish me because you want me to be worried sick about you. Now you go out and lie so I *don't* worry, and I find you in a fucking back alley with some scumbag? A back fucking alley! Did he even have a fucking *condom*? Did you even ask? Don't you have any fucking self-respect?"

You needed a *self* to have self-respect. Didn't Mat understand that?

At Doug's cowering silence, Mat whirled with a shout and punched the wall again. The smear of blood was bigger this time, and it was so, so easy to picture it across Doug's face, pouring from his nose, choking down his throat. His fingers pulsed with pain where Allen had broken them. His nose throbbed with a phantom *crack*.

No. Not again. Please God not again, I can't.

He needed to stop this. Calm Mat's anger. Bring their home back into order.

Good thing he was a world-class expert at relieving tension.

Good boy. Good hole.

Maybe that's why Mat was so angry: even strangers were getting to have what he couldn't.

Doug pushed through the fear. Laid a gentle hand on Mat's arm to still him. Then he sank to his knees, still holding Mat's elbow—keeping Mat in place—as he did. He pressed a soft kiss to the fabric of Mat's sweatpants, right where they were heavy and full. And musky from the fight. Doug shivered, trying to lose himself in the smell and the taste and the sensation of service.

Mat stood stock-still. Frozen in place.

Doug thought that meant permission, Mat's acquiescence, but when he leaned in again for another kiss, Mat snapped back to life.

Roared.

Kicked him right in the center of his chest and sent him sprawling into the coffee table.

He couldn't breathe. Couldn't— couldn't— He wheezed, tears streaking down his face, back a line of fire where he'd hit the table, chest as fragile and crumbling as the walls Mat had hit.

"What the fuck is *wrong* with you?" Mat shrieked. "God fucking *damn* you! I can't, I can't—" He paced in circles, shoulders shaking, hands fisting and unfisting.

How had Doug gotten everything so wrong? "Mat," he whispered, or tried to, as hard as it was to suck in air.

"Don't even fucking talk to me. Don't even, don't even—" He yanked at his hair with both fists. "Just— I have to get out of here. I can't be here. I can't be around you. I—"

He stopped his pacing. Stared down at Doug. "I . . . I *hurt* you." His eyes widened, watered. "Oh *God*." When he blinked, one tear streamed down each cheek. His mouth hung open like *he* was the one who couldn't breathe through the pain in his seizing chest. "I'm so sorry, Dougie, I'm— Are you okay?"

Doug nodded dumbly, even though he was pretty sure he wasn't. Like, cracked ribs kind of not okay. But Mat was already babbling over him.

"God. Christ. I really do need to get out of here. I need to get away from you. I should have never let them talk me into taking you out of the group home. I can't take care of you, I can't do this, I—"

His hands twitched at his sides, and his feet shuffled, like he couldn't decide if he should go to Doug or flee from him. The brotherly instinct must've won over; he knelt beside where Doug still lay sprawled, clutching at his chest with one hand and trying to reach the pain in his back with the other. Mat nudged both hands aside and replaced them with his own, lifting Doug's shirt, palpating his chest and back. Never once meeting Doug's eyes, which was maybe a good thing because that meant he couldn't see Doug grimace.

"Jesus," Mat murmured, to himself, Doug thought, and then, "Okay, I think you're okay. Fuck. Okay. I . . ." He stood abruptly. Backed away. "I'll go, okay? I'll leave you alone. I'll just . . . I'm gonna go. I'll leave you the debit card. God. I'm as bad as that asshole. I'm as bad as him . . ." He put his face in his hand. "I'm as bad as him. I'm as bad as fucking *him*."

Still repeating it, he slipped out the front door and was gone.

For a long time, Doug just sat against the coffee table, too pained and shocked to even move. He thought maybe he'd sleep right here, but then his phone buzzed with a text.

It's Nate. Mat's on his way to my place. He will be home tomorrow a.m. Just stay indoors. If you need help, call me. I'm here for you too.

Mat had gone to Nate. Of course he had. He was upset. Traumatized. *Yeah, like a* normal *guy would be when his brother tries to suck his cock and he kicks him hard enough to rattle his teeth.* There was no missing the fact that Nate had become Mat's rock. The person Mat could lean on anywhere, anytime.

The jealousy didn't make Doug mad. It just made him want to cry.

Who did Doug have? Certainly not Nate, no matter what he said. Once Mat told him what had happened, Nate wouldn't want anything else to do with him.

Fuck, even *Doug* didn't want anything else to do with himself. He wasn't so fucked up that he didn't know just how *extra* fucked up he'd been tonight. What he'd done. What he'd tried to do. How he'd really, truly *believed*, even if only for a moment, that it was the right thing. The only thing.

No wonder nobody trusted him.

He thought of Corinne, but he barely fucking knew her. There *was* a text from her—must've come in while that so-called Dom was beating him, or maybe when Mat was beating him, who knew—and he took a moment, hands shaking, to text her back (*Im home ok thank u. Sorry i forgot to text before. Was talking to bro*) because no fucking way was he going to fail her too, near stranger or no. But he couldn't *go* to her, not like Mat had gone to Nate.

Mat was probably crying on Nate now. Or raging to him. Or just fucking him, to get the bad image, the bad *touch*, of his bad brother out of his mind.

As kind as Corinne was, he could never tell her the whole truth, or even a meaningful part of it. Not when he was in witness protection. Nobody could know what he'd been through, not even Corinne. Hell, could he even trust Corinne? What if she was a part of the Cartel, even if she didn't seem like she was? She could be one of those bounty hunters.

Or she could just be an outsider, well-meaning but completely unequipped to handle the vast pile of shit Doug was drowning in. Unable to even *understand* it.

Doug was completely alone. No one to trust. Not even himself—*especially* not himself. God, he was such a fucking *head case.* He needed to talk to *someone.* Fuck, maybe even Beth, their court-appointed counselor . . .

Or maybe someone who actually cared about Doug. Who understood what he was going through. Who maybe even loved him, even if it wasn't the way Nate loved Mat.

He picked up the laptop they were supposed to use for their webcam counseling appointments and opened the search engine.

Typed in *roger petrovic.*

Wasn't even sure if he'd get any hits. Maybe the guy was in deep hiding, like Mat and Doug were. Or going by his birth name, whatever that was. Maybe he was just in a facility somewhere, but the database of who was living where was classified. Maybe he was on trial, or a witness. Doug didn't know. He only knew that Roger had been taken into custody when the FBI had raided Nikolai's.

Roger hadn't been in the group home with Mat and Doug, though Doug had secretly hoped—many a time when he was on his knees in some closet giving head—that one day he might miraculously be transferred there. He'd been desperate for an ally then.

Yet he hadn't even checked up on Roger since they'd gotten to Baltimore. So much for love.

Better late than never? He wasn't sure. But it had to be worth a fucking try.

There were several thousand results. A few Facebook pages for other men, and then . . .

Investigation into Sex Trafficking Victim Care Facilities Launched after Patient Suicide.

Grisly Discovery Has Human Rights Groups Demanding Stronger Mental Health Oversight.

Brainwashed Sex Trafficking Victim Takes Own Life While Under Care.

Doug's stomach felt like it was going to drop right out of his body. Just the headlines made him want to be sick, and he wished he could slam the laptop shut, but he had to know for sure. Maybe they were talking about someone else. Maybe it was just the group home where Roger was staying. His Roger—the Roger he knew . . . he was so strong, so perfect, so happy. He'd *never* . . .

Nikolai said I was strong and perfect and happy too, and look at me now.

Nausea creeping up his throat, he clicked the first link.

Roger Linden, AKA Roger Petrovic, a rescued victim of the biggest sex trafficking bust in recent history, was found dead today in his room at a Victim's Fund facility.

In 1988, after disappearing without a trace at the age of 18, Linden was presumed dead, until he miraculously resurfaced earlier this year thanks to an FBI sting.

After spending over twenty years in captivity, he was deemed not of sound mind and committed to the Ansalem VF Group Home in Wytheville, VA, where he was to receive counseling and round-the-clock care. However, on the morning of October 2, he was found by facility staff, hanged with a bedsheet from a light fixture. His death is presumed to be a suicide, though an investigation is underway to rule out foul play.

This latest tragedy has all eyes on the facilities where these vulnerable victims are currently being housed. "Although we have high hopes for many victims' eventual recoveries," a representative of the Ansalem facility said, "others like Roger coming from long periods in captivity—and especially those who were forced to participate in the victimization of others—are facing much more challenging odds. The priority of staff in these cases has been finding the balance between monitoring them for their own safety and respecting their autonomy. We can't treat them like prisoners after what they've been through, even for their own good. Sadly, with Roger, that balance was not adequately maintained. We'll be launching an internal investigation to make sure another tragedy like this doesn't happen again."

Linden was 44 at the time of his death, and is survived by no known family. If you would like to contribute to his burial fund and to future recovery efforts for other victims like him, please

Doug shut the laptop. Numb. Even the pain in his rib cage was gone, replaced by a yawning vacuum that sucked the air out of his lungs and the beat out of his heart.

Roger couldn't be dead.

He *couldn't*. This had to be . . . some kind of joke or cover-up for his safety or, or . . . or . . .

The sob that ripped out of Doug left him as stunned and breathless and agonized as Mat's kick to the chest. Somehow, he was on the floor again, too.

He curled up tight. Let the tears soak into the rug.

Seemed as good a place as any to lie down and die of his misery.

It was an awkward, uncomfortable position, but damn it, Mat didn't care. He needed to be close to Nate right now. Needed comfort, wanted it, and knew Nate had it to give.

Even if it meant spending the long ride back to Baltimore flopped sideways with his head crammed into Nate's lap as he drove.

One-handed, because his other hand was gently stroking Mat's hair.

Nate had been pretty on edge last night. Not exactly pleased to be picking Mat up from a very public train station, not under the circumstances. It had been dangerous. Reckless. He could have been seen and captured by rogue agents of the Cartel. He could have exposed their relationship at the time when they most needed it kept quiet. He'd endangered himself and the case.

And yet, despite his frustration, Nate had still pulled him into a gentle, careful hug. Shushed him when he'd wept. Held him the entire night.

Nate loved him. Loved him enough to overlook his mistakes, his failures. Loved him enough to forgive him, and to convince him to forgive himself. Yes, he'd hurt Doug. Yes, he'd acted inappropriately. But Nate still loved him. Still sympathized with him.

He was also still driving Mat home where he belonged.

But after a night in Nate's bed, just holding each other, Nate wasn't angry anymore. Neither was Mat. Upset with himself, yes, but the hatred—of himself, of his brother, of himself again for hating his brother in the first place—had given way to regret.

He'd go up the stairs, he'd apologize to Doug, he'd insist that they both do a joint session with Beth to talk about what'd happened. He'd actually stop and listen to Doug's side of the story about what had happened in that alley. He had assumed Doug had lied to him about Corinne, and assumed that he'd been at the bar, and assumed that he'd led that bruiser out into some back alley to fuck him and fuck him up, but that was just how Mat had seen it. It wasn't necessarily the truth.

Probably the truth, but not necessarily. He still should have let Doug explain. He shouldn't have yelled, or been so rough.

And yeah, Doug shouldn't have tried to suck him off, either, but . . . well, one problem at a time.

They'd left at the ass-crack of dawn, but still hit the start of rush hour traffic on the way into the city. Mat was glad of it. More time to gather his strength, steel himself, plan his approach. More time with Nate, too, who—if he dared to allow himself to look too closely at it—he knew beyond a doubt he loved just as much as Nate loved him.

But, yeah. One problem at a time.

The car crawled along the highway. Mat shifted his head on Nate's thigh with a sense of contentment he had no business feeling right now, and very deliberately did not contemplate another urge he had no business feeling right now: to turn in the other direction and bury his mouth in Nate's crotch.

He was simultaneously disappointed and relieved when they finally arrived.

The apartment was dark and still when he let himself in—without Nate, who gently but firmly declined Mat's invitation for breakfast—shades drawn and the door to Doug's bedroom firmly closed. Again with that sense of disappointment and relief; he wanted so badly to reconcile with Doug, but he was also so tired and on such uneven footing and so glad to have a couple minutes to compose himself and get his shit together before he had to face the music. Maybe even time to sleep a little.

Good plan. He shucked his shoes, then his jeans and shirt, and crawled into bed in his boxers. Suspected maybe he should take a run instead—he'd skipped yesterday, waiting anxiously for Doug to come home—but was half-asleep before he'd even completed the thought.

Then startled *wide* the fuck awake at the sound of a creaking floorboard nearby, at the feel of the mattress dipping behind him, the blankets being pulled back, a body slipping into his bed.

It's just Doug it's just Doug it's just Doug . . .

Strange—no, fucking sad and terrifying—how that knowledge brought him exactly zero comfort. His heart was thrashing, his skin clammy, his throat locked shut. He couldn't even make his body uncurl, his head turn, his teeth unclench to ask *What are you doing?* as Doug slid in behind him and tucked in close, turning Mat into the little spoon.

Mat slammed his eyes closed and waited, dread building to a cloying ball of nausea in his gut as one of Doug's arms slid around his waist and the other wiggled between him and the mattress, as Doug's very naked chest and thighs plastered to Mat's own very naked back and legs, and then . . .

Nothing.

No lips pressing to his skin. No erection digging into his ass. No poisonous words. Just . . . stillness.

No. Not quite. He realized, as his own pounding heart and rasping lungs began to quiet, that Doug was crying. Softly, nearly soundlessly. But that moisture on the back of Mat's neck wasn't all sweat, and those snuffled little breaths were a million miles away from arousal.

Mat lay still, breath held. Waited. His fingers itched to close around his little brother's back, to card through his hair in soothing strokes. But he couldn't, not yet. Not after last night.

The best he could offer right now was no resistance.

That seemed good enough for Doug, who cried and clung for a good five minutes before whispering, so low Mat almost missed it, "I don't want to die, Mat."

What? What on earth had brought *that* up?

Maybe you screaming at him about condom use in back-alley fucks and then kicking him square in the chest.

Moist air puffed across the nape of his neck, and then, "I don't . . . that's not what I want to become."

Mat sighed, rolled from side to back and tucked an arm around Doug's shoulders, drawing his brother's head onto his chest. Letting his hand give in to the urge to rub a soothing circle on Doug's bare back. Just a big bro comforting a little one. Nothing sexual about it.

"I know, Doug. I never actually thought— I shouldn't have said those things last night. I'm so sorry."

Doug's arm tightened around his middle, face burrowing deeper into his chest, smearing tears everywhere. God, what Mat wouldn't give to know how to ease his pain, to stop the crying.

"I don't know why I . . . I lost control, Doug, and I *hit* you, and I can't . . . I can never undo that and I'm *so sorry*, but I can promise I'll do my best to make it up to you, and to make sure that it never hap—"

"Roger's dead."

Mat felt like *he'd* been kicked in the chest.

"Wh— Roger? How? *Roger* Roger?"

Doug nodded wordlessly, hiccupping, and started to cry all over again. "He's dead. They set him free and he killed himself. Without Nikolai he . . . He killed himself. They say—" He sobbed.

Mat knew the right thing to do was say something comforting, be the big brother, pull Doug close and tell him it was all going to be all right. But he just didn't have it in him. He was crying too.

Didn't even understand what this emotion was. Whether he was mourning Roger—Roger who'd been kind to him, who'd made love to him, who'd been just as much a victim of Nikolai's machinations as Doug had—or despairing because Roger had harmed them, had been a part of Nikolai's plan, and yet Mat still couldn't hate him enough to be happy he was dead.

Whatever he was to them, he was gone now.

Mat thought back to that last conversation with Roger. That last time they'd sat together on Mat's bed in the hotel, right before the raid. Roger had already been adrift, even then.

Mat had told himself Roger could be helped. Could get better. Could heal. Had needed to believe that because if *Roger* could, then surely Doug . . .

But he hadn't.

"What if I'm like him?" Doug moaned into Mat's chest, mirroring Mat's thoughts. "What if I don't get better? What if, what if all this therapy and all this 'justice' and all this freedom can't save me? I don't want to die. I don't want to die. I don't want to die!" His fist weakly pounded Mat's chest as his voice grew more strained. And then he stilled. His hand fell slack on top of Mat. His breathing, shaky, slowed and calmed. "But maybe I should," he whispered. "What happened yesterday, what I did to you . . . maybe we'd *all* be better off if I just—"

"*No*," Mat growled, even as he felt choked by his tears. Unlike with Roger, there was no confusion here. No hesitation. "No. Doug, you're fucked up and I'm not going to pretend you're not, but if I have to choose between you fucked up and alive or just . . . d-dead, l-like him, then I choose alive. Every time. No matter *what*, Doug. Remember? No matter *what*."

He realized he was holding on so tightly that he *had* to be hurting Doug, but his brother didn't complain or try to pull away. Mat's heart ached far too much in far too many ways to try to contemplate the meaning of that now; he just lightened up a little bit and let himself cry on Doug and let Doug cry on him. Because no matter how fucked up they were—and they *both* were, no doubt about that—no matter how much they hurt each other or how difficult things got, he was never letting go of Doug again, never letting Doug fall victim to his past or his despair.

And he wasn't ever going to let Doug let go of him again, either. Was never going to give Doug another reason to want to walk out that door and not come back.

CHAPTER SIX

The sun was high in the sky when they finally untangled from one another and wiped their tears. Neither of them had slept, Doug didn't think—last night *or* this morning. He felt bone-tired, but cleansed. There was an aching hole in his heart that Roger had left, but Mat had forgiven him. Didn't hate him. Wasn't going to let him fall. Or worse.

And Doug was surprisingly okay with that. There was no shame in needing help—he'd dedicated his whole adult life to learning to help others, after all, and even Nikolai had made that much clear. Didn't mean he was a child, or a pet, or a slave. Just meant he was loved. Really loved, and not just for what he could provide.

Now if only he could remember that all the time. *Believe* it all the time.

It wasn't going to be easy; he knew that. Far too easy to slip into despair instead, into Nikolai's web of lies and mind-fucks and deceit. But today was fresh, and he felt strong and untainted and steady, and even if he might not feel that way tomorrow, well... *One day at a time, Doug. You can do this.*

Mat made them breakfast, just like he had the day after their parents had died. They'd shared a bed that night, too. Holding each other and crying, just like this. Things had felt as uncertain then, but the one thing they'd been sure of was their love for each other.

Today felt about the same.

"I have a therapy session in a couple hours," Mat said tentatively as he sliced his egg white omelet into tiny pieces. "I was thinking maybe you could sit in with me? You know, you don't have to say anything, no pressure, but you can be there, see how it is. Maybe ease you into it?"

Doug found himself nodding. "Yeah. I'd like that. Maybe talking about it would help." All those years of learning talk therapy, the principles behind it, the psychology of it—of *course* it would help. But only if he was ready for it. Open to it. He thought maybe he was now. Hoped he was, anyway. "You know, the woman I was with last night, Corinne, she was really nice to talk to. Felt really good, actually. Made me . . . made me *think* about things, you know?"

Mat blinked—Doug could see him thinking, *Corinne is real?*—but then nodded.

"About how people treated me. About . . ." So hard to get the rest of that sentence out, fear and shame clogging his throat. He cleared it away with a long sip of coffee. "About how I've been treating myself."

Mat nodded again, nothing but sympathy and understanding in his eyes. No judgment. No anger.

"But I couldn't tell her so many things."

Couldn't even tell her his real name.

Yet another nod from Mat. *Like a bobblehead*, Doug thought unkindly, but the mean impulse fled in an instant, replaced by the sort of warm glow he hadn't felt since Nikolai had kissed him good-bye. Mat was *listening* to him. Understanding him, even.

"Beth's really nice too," Mat said. "She doesn't judge. And you can tell her anything at all. She knows what really went down."

"You tell her things?"

"Yeah." Doug watched his brother cave in to the impulse to hide behind his walls—he turned his eyes to his plate, cut his omelet into even smaller pieces, but didn't eat any. Then Mat put his fork down, decisive, and met Doug's eyes again. "Even the stuff I'm really ashamed of. Moments like . . . like last night, when I—" His eyes misted over, but he blinked the moisture back, never looked away. "When I hurt you."

Doug offered a tentative smile—*I forgive you, brother. Like you forgave me. Like maybe one day I can figure out how to forgive myself.*

Mat gave the same little half smile back. Cleared his throat. "She puts it in perspective. Helps me start to forgive myself. I made a lot of mistakes, Doug, and I'm still making them."

"You made fewer mistakes than me," Doug said, even though he *knew* this wasn't a contest—pain never was. But Mat was still *himself*, after everything. Doug could hardly say the same. Had no idea what he was now except a total disaster zone of a human being. Maybe not even a human being.

But he was learning, wasn't he? He was *trying*. At least he was now, anyway.

"I'm not just talking about when we were . . . in captivity," Mat said. "I'm talking about before that, too. I haven't always been a good brother. I kind of got thrown off the deep end when Mom and Dad died, and I'm not sure I quite landed on my feet. I . . . I clung too tight. I was too scared to let you fly without a net, make your own calls—what if something happened and I lost you too? Nikolai exploited that."

"You were always there for me," Doug said fiercely. "Just like now. No matter what."

Saying it aloud made him realize how true it was. And how intense that truth felt. Nikolai *had* exploited that—exploited *him*. Exploited *them*. Found every chink and weakness and filled them with lies close enough to real life to feel like truth.

Except they hadn't been, had they. Doug realized now, cheeks flushing, stomach churning, that maybe somewhere, deep down, he'd known that all along. Had "forgotten" that to survive, but never *really* forgotten.

"No matter what," Mat repeated with a smile. He was like a calm island at the center of Doug's raging storm. He looked . . . at peace. He finally took a bite of his omelet. "So can I count on you to give therapy a try? For Roger? For me?"

Doug nodded. Added, because he knew how important a truth it was, "For *me*, too."

THE FLESH CARTEL

SEASON 5: RECLAMATION

EPISODE 19: PROMISE

CHAPTER ONE

Outside the courtroom was a media circus—news vans and microphones and camera flashes—and even with a security detail, Doug felt cornered and exposed.

Inside the courtroom, cloistered away from the nosy crowds, his hand gripped tight in Mat's, he felt even worse.

He'd thought . . . well, he wasn't sure *what* he'd thought. That seeing Madame (real name Dana Hewlett, apparently) and Allen and the bounty hunters and the procurement team and everyone else who'd hurt him sent away to rot in cages for the rest of their lives would feel good. Vindicating. Satisfying. Safe. A reclamation of a life cruelly stolen. That knowing they couldn't hurt him anymore would make moving forward somehow easier than it'd been these last few months. That all his hard-won progress would seem like peanuts in comparison to the leap he'd take after finally putting this all behind him.

That he'd even be *able* to put this all behind him.

And yes, in some way, some pale-shadowed, deep-down imitation way, he really *did* feel all those things. But mostly what he felt was *weary*. Scared and hollowed out and wrung dry. From his testimony. From having to face his abusers again.

Strange, too, how impersonal, how distant, his so-called closure felt.

Mat squeezed his hand as the judge read out the next sentence. Penny's, oh God, and what the fuck was *wrong* with him that he wanted to weep all over again—Jesus, hadn't he done that *enough* the last two weeks with the trial?—at the thought of her going to jail. For one hundred and forty-seven years, apparently, with no hope of parole. He knew better now than to say she was innocent. Far from it; she'd sat back and let it all happen, had done plenty of it herself, even if she'd never inflicted physical pain. Yet still he felt love for her, and what was it Nikolai had once said? That emotions are by their nature irrational? Yeah. That.

Doug turned his gaze to Nikolai, flanked by guards in the front row on the other side of the aisle. He'd made a deal, wasn't going to prison, but that didn't mean he could waltz off into the sunset, either. The feds couldn't quite figure out what to do with him—he was, after all, a victim of the Cartel himself—so they were carting him home, deporting him to a country he hadn't seen since he'd been, what, five? Six? Did he even still speak the language? How would he get by there?

Not your problem anymore, Doug. And fuck him for ever making it so to start with.

His eyes slid back to his brother, grim-faced and taut on the bench seat beside him. Listening, cold and intent and darkly satisfied, to every pronouncement the judge made. He looked . . . fierce and terrifying and beautiful and strong, and Doug felt a surge of pride and blessedly uncomplicated love. No worries or fears or quid pro quos, just *family*.

Mat met his eyes and squeezed his hand again, and it occurred to Doug that Mat was clinging to him just as much as he was clinging to Mat. That this had all been hard for him too. Beyond hard. Doug's pillar was as shaken as he was.

Doug just hadn't seen it before. He'd been blind to how much Mat had been hurting. How confused and frightened he'd been. Couldn't see beyond his own nose back then.

But that was before their joint therapy sessions. He'd only listened in at first, but that had been a journey in and of itself. Hearing Mat say things he'd have never assumed, never even dreamed. He'd seen a side of Mat he never knew existed. A side of Mat that needed Doug's care and nurturing as much as Doug had ever needed Mat.

Not selfishly, though. Not an exchange, or a transaction, or a demand.

Just family. Love. *Real* love. Not Nikolai's twisted concept.

Doug would never let himself forget that again.

It was amazing, what they could get through when they were on each other's side.

And with others on their side as well. To Doug's left, Beth, watching them both surreptitiously as she listened to the sentencing, ready to support them if they needed it (okay, if they flipped their shit, but still). To Mat's right, Nate, looking satisfied enough for all four of them at the words coming out of the judge's mouth: *multiple lifetime sentences; one hundred and eighty years; ninety-seven years; no chance of parole; consider yourself fortunate there is no death penalty here.* To Nate's right, Coach Darryl, his face a near mirror of Mat's. And four rows back and to the left, Mike, here without his new family to support his old one. He wasn't staying at Nate's through the trial like everyone else; Doug just . . . wasn't comfortable with that yet. Still wasn't sure how he felt about Mike—it wasn't a topic they'd touched on much in therapy yet; too many other more immediate issues to discuss—but the little boy inside him was glad he was here. Doug hadn't worked up the courage to say much more than hello to him yet, but he was glad that Mat had pressed him to let Mike come.

Even if he was afraid that Mike was only here for show. Or because he felt *obligated* somehow. Like maybe he was afraid the world would condemn him if he didn't come, that the talking heads on the nightly news would blather on about how the man who'd raised him for four years couldn't be bothered to support him when things got tough.

Just like Nikolai had said.

Just like *Nikolai.* Only hanging on to him as some kind of *investment*—put in the time, cash the checks while your good little boy keeps your house clean and your dishes washed (and your dick sucked—not that Mike had *ever* looked at him like that), say good-bye and never think of you again.

Doug didn't want to believe that. He really, *really* didn't. And Nikolai had lied about so many things, and of course it'd been in Nikolai's best interests to lie about this too. To twist Doug's insecurities, to convince him he'd never truly been loved. He *knew* that. And yet . . .

Stop it, Doug. Don't let him hurt you anymore. Mike loves you. He loves *you.*

And yet it was to Nikolai, rather than Doug's loved ones, that his gaze kept being drawn. The one criminal in this whole mess who *wasn't* getting his comeuppance.

Being deported to Russia ain't exactly a yacht party, you know.

Yeah, but nor was it three lifetimes in the slammer surrounded by people who thought you had a big hand in putting them there.

It wasn't fair.

But by the same token, if Nikolai hadn't taken the deal, then where would they be?

Stuck back at Allen's still, Doug was willing to bet.

Just the *thought* of that sent a cold shiver through him, and this time both Mat *and* Beth squeezed his fingers.

Like it or not, as much as Nikolai had had a hand in stealing his life, he'd also had a hand in giving it back.

Doug hated that. He didn't want to feel conflicted about Nikolai. He didn't want to feel thankful—after all, the plea bargain was as much self-preservation as it was any act of altruism—but he still couldn't hate Nikolai the way Mat did. Mat looked at Nikolai and saw a monster. Doug looked at him and saw a monster *and* a lover.

And now he couldn't even have the closure of a sentence.

Russia was awfully far away, but it wasn't a jail cell. It wasn't penance for his wrongs. It wasn't . . . it wasn't *safe*.

It was a nonanswer. A stay. Nikolai wasn't going to pay for his crimes, he was just going to leave them all behind. Leave Doug behind with his wounds. Leave Roger behind in his donated grave.

Doug realized he didn't want Nikolai to just walk away from any of this. From him. If the law couldn't have a say, then shit, at least Doug could. Roger couldn't speak for himself anymore, but Doug damn well could.

"Hey." He leaned over Mat, toward Nate, extricated his hand from Mat's to tap Nate on the knee. "Hey," he whispered again, careful not to draw the attention of those around him, to distract them from the judge's endless pronouncements.

Nate's hard hazel eyes fell on Doug and softened immediately. He leaned over Mat's other side, and Mat leaned back—not to avoid touching them, like he might once have, but just to be polite, give them room.

Doug whispered into Nate's ear, "I need to talk to Nikolai before they send him off."

He knew Mat had heard him by the way Mat's chest stilled, the way the weight of his gaze landed heavy on the side of Doug's head.

But Mat said nothing. Two months ago he would've railed, overprotected, controlled—*bad idea, Doug; I'm not gonna let you do that, Doug*—but now he held his tongue.

Nate didn't say anything either. Didn't ask why. Didn't ask if he was crazy. Just thought it over for a moment, then nodded. Slipped his phone from his pocket and typed away for several seconds.

The guard to Nikolai's left checked his phone. Met Nate's expectant gaze. Nodded.

Nate gave Doug a wary thumbs-up as the judge sent one of the bounty hunters who'd tortured Mat to jail for eighty-five years. Doug loved Mat, he did, and the thought of someone having hurt him like that—even himself; he had no illusions now about what truly unforgivable things he'd done to Mat, how blessed he was that Mat *had* forgiven, if not forgotten—absolutely enraged him. Yet somehow he was more focused on the prospect of getting his face time with Nikolai than he was with hearing that sentence passed.

Closure. That was what watching the sentencing was all about. Closure. As witnesses, they weren't even required to attend the sentencing. Nate and Beth had given them a choice, and Mat and Doug had both decided it was something they needed to see through to the end.

Now, he would see this thing with Nikolai through to the end too.

Closure.

Nikolai thought they would escort him directly from the courtroom to the airfield after the last sentence had been read, but he was brought to a holding cell instead. A frisson of excitement mingled with terror ran up his spine like a fault line. Had the terms of his deal changed? Was there new information in play? Or had some last secret remnant of the Cartel, not ferreted out during the investigations or the trial, paid an assassin to deliver one very final good-bye?

He wouldn't cower or cry, not like some of the men and women he'd seen today. Pitiful in their defeat. Nikolai would be—had been—dignified in his.

Assuming, of course, that it was to come. Despite all the so-called counseling and therapy, all the agents and lawyers, the threats and the insults these last few months, he still knew exactly who and what he was: Better. Smarter. A trainer of immeasurable skill. A master in every sense of the word. Concession was not defeat, his mentor had taught him that early and often, and if he were still permitted to get on that plane to Russia today, he'd show every last one of his naysayers just how strong he still was.

How quickly he could rebuild.

How *well.*

In that respect, it lessened the pain of Roger taking his life. After all, he could hardly start anew on the frontier with a remnant of his old dead life tethering him to his past.

He'd hoped, once, that Roger would be able to wait for him. Nikolai had given up so much in the name of being free to care for his pets, after all. And now he had no pets to care *for*. He'd almost thought the man weak when he'd heard the news, but then he'd realized Roger's suicide was not weakness, it was limitless loyalty: rather than speak ill of his master, of his master's work and life's purpose, Roger had given his life. Nikolai had sacrificed, and Roger had honored that sacrifice in the only way he could. Nikolai both deserved and respected such selflessness.

He knew the public and the FBI and his guards resented how little remorse he'd shown, even in the wake of Roger's death, even when hearing Mathias and Douglas Carmichael tearfully recounting his supposed "crimes."

Let the fools be resentful. Let Nikolai be hated and despised.

He was still free. He'd won.

Even if he did miss Roger terribly sometimes. Well, perhaps one day he'd make them pay for stealing the man from him.

He smiled as his guards cuffed him to the sturdy interview table. They didn't offer him a refreshment. He didn't ask for one. The animals would probably urinate in it anyway.

"Watch your fucking mouth," the baser of the two guards said. "Don't give me any reason to concuss you on the tabletop before we send you back to Mother Russia."

Such showy impotence. Nikolai was tired of the performance. Months of threats and posturing. Soon it would all be over.

As soon as whatever was about to happen in this room came to pass.

"We'll be listening in. Watching."

Nikolai nodded, smirked. "Of course. Far be it from me to deny you whatever small pleasures you can find in your meaningless lives."

"Don't take the bait," the other guard consoled, patting his partner's shoulder.

They left. Shut the door behind them. The only door, of course, and no windows, either. Just a buzzing overhead fixture and a camera mounted in the corner. A cage the likes of which the world would never need again if only more people like him were left to lead.

He sat. Waited. Straightened his shoulders and lifted his chin when the door finally opened.

And in walked Douglas.

So strange to see him clothed, wearing a shirt buttoned to his throat, a tie and jacket. He'd cut his pretty curls into what Nikolai could only label a hipster shag. His expression was gaunt and exhausted, nothing like the sweet face of the boy Nikolai had known.

"What a pleasant surprise," Nikolai said, and meant it.

"Can it," Douglas barked back. He scraped his chair and threw himself into it, unconsciously mimicking his brother's body language. "This isn't one last chance for mind games—" He paused, like he'd intended to address Nikolai some way: By first name? By last name? By a slur? Or was it *Master* on the tip of his tongue? "It's a chance for me to get some closure with you. So I'm gonna talk and you're gonna listen."

Nikolai made a welcoming gesture with his chained hands. "By all means, Douglas."

"Just Doug." Douglas's pretty pink tongue flicked out to wet his lips. He didn't meet Nikolai's gaze. "Are you sorry that Roger's dead?"

"I thought you were doing the talking and I was doing the listening."

"J-just answer the question!"

Nikolai leaned back in his chair with a smile, savoring the panic and confusion in Douglas's voice, even as he wished so very much for the opportunity to quell it. To soothe Douglas. The boy was terribly unmoored without his guidance, that much was evident.

But all Nikolai said was, "It will be an adjustment, having to iron my own shirts."

Hit. Douglas reared back like he'd been slapped across the face.

"That *is* what you wanted to hear from me, isn't it, Douglas? That I have no remorse, that I didn't care for Roger at all, that I don't mourn his untimely death?"

Douglas's hands balled into fists on the table. Trembling. Nikolai wished he could cover those delicate, furious hands with his own. Hold them until they were still. "The truth, Nikolai," he ground out, voice tearful.

"You already know the truth. I loved Roger deeply, with my whole heart, much as I love you now—even after you betrayed me so. Of course I mourn his loss."

"Betrayed you! *Betrayed* you? You sold me! You gave me up! You l—" His voice locked, beautiful blue eyes watering. "You l-left me there with that *monster* while he . . . while he . . . You *left me*! There was nothing to betray!"

"Oh my. That doesn't sound like the hurt of a man conscripted into sexual slavery by an inhuman monster. That sounds much more like a jilted lover to me." Nikolai smiled again. He'd missed this. It made him feel himself again. Powerful. Like perhaps his future in Russia wouldn't be bleak at all. All he needed was a project. All he needed was *this*. "Yes, Douglas, I sold you. I never lied to you or betrayed you. I did exactly the thing I had promised from the beginning. And every moment you were away was physically painful to me. I was trying to be a professional, honoring my commitment to my client, fighting my desires. In hindsight, I wish I'd given into them instead. Even knowing you'd come back to me one day, I wish I'd never let you go. But while I freely admit to selling you, Douglas, I *never* gave you up. Didn't your brother tell you what lengths I went to in order to see you freed from Allen's clutches?"

"You made a fucking plea deal. You're going free after watching a line of people you once rubbed elbows with get locked up forever and then some. Don't pretend it's an act of altruism."

"It didn't have to end this way, Douglas. Do you really think I didn't have fail-safes in place to prevent my own fall and the fall of the Cartel? Do you really think my only option was to give up everything?"

Douglas recoiled. His expression shuttered. He said nothing.

"I fell on my sword, Douglas. I had a way out. I didn't have to cooperate, but I did. For *you*."

"No. That's a lie. That— It's just more mind games."

"I suggest you ask Agent Johnson and your brother again how my assistance was obtained. Somebody is lying here, but it most certainly isn't me. You know I never li—"

"*Don't*," Douglas growled, slamming his fist on the table. "Don't say you never lied to me. You know damn well that's not true."

Nikolai canted his head, a gentle demur—*Perhaps you and I have different definitions of the truth, my dear boy.* "Ask for yourself, then. Go on. Ask them." He held up his cuffed hands, emphasizing the chain through the bolt on the table. Raised an eyebrow and quirked his lips. "I'll wait. But I *did* do this for *you*, Douglas."

"S-so what? So maybe you were looking out for me, in your sick head." How quickly he acquiesced to Nikolai's truth. Still so biddable, even as he labored not to be. "Doesn't change the fact that you kept me hostage and tortured me and raped me and brainwashed me. Doesn't change the fact that Roger is dead because of what you did to his mind."

"Everything I did, Douglas, every last thing, was out of love. For you, and for Roger, gods rest his soul. Can you say the same of your brother, with his oh-so-keen sense of self-preservation?"

"Yes," Douglas answered, a little more forceful than strictly necessary.

"Can you still say so now that he's entangled with that agent of his? For whom, I might add, he risked the outcome of the trial itself—conflict of interest, you see?"

Another hit. Douglas might not have physically recoiled this time, but there was no mistaking the impact of that truth in his eyes.

Perhaps this day would go well, after all.

"Mathias is a man of hot passions, Douglas. He isn't like me. He doesn't have room for more than one great love. Will you make him choose between his duty to his brother and his desire for companionship? Or will you fall on *your* sword?"

"You want me to *kill* myself? Like Roger?"

"Hardly." Nikolai wished more than ever that he could reach out. Wanted badly to touch his poor floundering boy and guide him home. "I want you to come with me. You're a free man. I'm a free man. We can start a new life together. I'll show you what I mean when I say I live and breathe for you. You'll be my greatest love. You are. In fact—" Yes, yes, yes. "In fact, I see now that you were always more to me than just a pet. You were more to me than Roger."

Another hit, accidental. Clearly the boy mourned for Roger as deeply as Nikolai did. More so, perhaps. He backtracked, explained: "Roger was a servant. A deeply loyal and loved one, but a servant just the same. No mistaking the power dynamic there, who loved and gave more than whom. But you!" He stared into those huge, disbelieving eyes. "I *tore down the world for you*, Douglas."

He paused, waited for that to sink in. Waited. Hardly dared to admit, even to himself, how desperately much he wanted this. Needed it, even.

"And I'd do it again." The boy shivered, nearly imperceptibly, but oh, Nikolai could read him so, so well. Hatred in those eyes, yes, but vulnerability, too. For all the arguments that spewed forth from Douglas's perfect lips, there was no denying the seed of love, of devotion, of hunger and *need* buried deep. Fragile, true, but Nikolai could nurture it back to life again, he was *certain* of it. "You could be my partner, Douglas. My protégé. You have the aptitude. The giving nature. The understanding of the human psyche. I've clearly made mistakes, but you could teach me to overcome them. Together we could make *art*, Douglas. We could open the eyes of a whole new generation of beasts in need of a gentle hand. In the rubble of our old lives, we could build anew. All this pain and confusion you're feeling now, this rootlessness, this humiliation, this loss, I can take it all away. You could be at peace, Douglas, and so could I. We could learn to love one another all over again, in a brand-new way."

Say yes.

Nikolai's heart scarcely beat.

Say yes.

Douglas didn't blink. Didn't speak. Nikolai wasn't even sure he was breathing, he was so still and quiet.

Say yes.

"You really do love me?" he asked, barely above a whisper.

"Forever and always, above all others," Nikolai promised. *Just say yes.*

For a moment—a perfect, fleeting moment, so beautiful it couldn't survive—Douglas's expression softened to Nikolai, softened like the face of a man about to be kissed.

But then the moment ended. Douglas's face was a mask, as impenetrable as the one Nikolai had worn over a year ago at their first meeting. He stood. "You don't even know what love *is*, Nikolai. And you never, ever will. You're going to die alone, just like Roger, and it serves you fucking right."

For the very first and, gods willing, last time, Nikolai Petrovic found himself at a loss for words.

Douglas was gone before he'd gathered his wits enough to say good-bye.

Mat and Doug had spent a lot of sessions with Beth talking about how Mat needed to trust Doug to make his own decisions and build his own life and generally live his own life. It wasn't actually an issue their time in captivity had created so much as one that time had drawn into sharp focus.

Mat was going over those conversations in his head, drawing on them for strength, while he waited in a row of uncomfortable plastic hallway chairs for Doug to finish up his meeting with Nikolai.

As far as Mat was concerned, he had nothing to fucking say to the guy and he hoped his plane crashed into the ocean, but Doug had obviously thought he could get something—some scrap of healing—out of one last confrontation, and Mat wasn't about to deny him that.

Even if it made him sick with worry.

There was a camera in the meeting room, and a microphone too. A small handful of people were listening in on the fateful conversation, with Doug's full knowledge and permission.

Mat wasn't one of them.

It felt good, actually. Like he was doing right by Doug. Letting him grow. Doing a bit of growing himself, too. He was excited to tell Beth about their progress.

He was also excited to get the fuck out of this courthouse and back to Nate's apartment for some much-needed rest.

It felt like he was finally getting air again after months of holding his breath.

He just needed to get the fuck out of here. He was ready to not be in the same building with the people who'd brutalized him and Doug. He was ready to not be in the same *state* as any of them.

He was ready to finally put this behind him, even if only for a few blissful hours of peaceful sleep, before facing up again to the reality of what they'd survived.

The door to the interrogation room opened, and Mat launched to his feet, bracing himself for whatever Doug might need. To either side of Mat, Nate and Coach Darryl stood, too, but they hung back, let Mat take point. He wished Beth were still here, but she had so many others to care for, especially now. Doug had made his choice, even knowing she couldn't be his safety net today.

Or Mat's.

The first thing Doug did was pull Mat into a long, tight hug. "Thank you," he said into Mat's shoulder. "Thank you for letting me have that."

"I didn't let you," Mat replied, not letting go. "It's not my place to *let* you. I just . . . supported you letting yourself."

Doug's arms actually got tighter around Mat's middle. Mat nuzzled his nose into Doug's hair, smiled against his scalp. For just a moment, he felt so warm and fuzzy his eyes watered.

He cleared his throat, loosened his hold. Realized they'd been hugging close as could be for a good thirty seconds, and he hadn't once thought of darker times, hadn't once felt the urge to let go. "So, are you ready to get out of here?"

Doug slipped out of Mat's arms. Nodded. "Yeah. It's done."

He made it sound as final as death. Mat . . . appreciated that.

He never wanted to come back here—or face Nikolai—again.

They walked through the halls together, Nate steering them to a back entrance out of reach of reporters, where a uniform was waiting with Nate's car. Everyone piled in, looking as worn and weary as Mat felt. Such a huge victory, so long in coming, and yet they were all too raw and exhausted to enjoy it. It barely even felt real. Beth had told them to expect this, that it was normal, that when they'd had a chance to rest and heal and reflect and accept, peace and closure would finally come.

God, was he ever looking forward to that.

Of course, there'd never quite *be* closure for Doug if he couldn't reconcile his feelings about Mike, that low-level mistrust and insecurity that Nikolai had blown wide open. Doug's family was tiny—no aunts or uncles, no cousins, no grandparents, no birth parents, not even a foster mother. Only Mat and the man who'd stepped in to raise Doug for four years remained. Doug had clawed his love for Mat back from Nikolai, but Mike . . . Mike remained a casualty of Nikolai's isolation and brainwashing. A casualty Doug could *not* afford to lose, not only because he was the only family Doug had apart from Mat, but because it was a blemish on his far-too-fragile sense of self-worth, one that had needed healing even before Nikolai's interference and was even worse now.

Mat rolled his head to look at his brother beside him on the backseat. Too damn tired to turn his whole upper body. Doug must've felt the same, because his eyes slid sideways to meet Mat's, but nothing else.

Mat mustered up the beginnings of a smile. "Hey, little brother."

He got the same smile back. "Hey, big brother."

God, so nice to be able to say that, hear that, without thinking about . . . *things*.

"So I was thinking," Mat began, pushing said *things* far, far from his conscious thoughts. Every day it got a little easier to banish those memories. "I know we're all just gonna crash tonight, but maybe tomorrow, to celebrate, you know? Maybe we invite Mike over for lunch."

A look of hurt came over Doug's face. "I dunno. He probably wants to go home. Already spent two weeks here. Don't want him to feel obligated."

Mat still didn't understand why it was so hard for Doug to accept that Mike loved him just like Mat did. The kid knew what family meant now—did he really not believe that Mike was family too?

"He wouldn't feel obligated, Doug. No more than I feel obligated. He wants to see you. That's why he was at the hospital . . . after. That's why he's here now. He wants to be with you and support you. He just doesn't want to push you. An invitation would really bridge the gap."

"He has a family to go home to," Doug mumbled.

"They'll still be there a couple days from now. You're his family too."

"His *foster* kid."

"Who he raised for four years. Whose college graduation he came to—both times. Who he *still* sends birthday and Christmas presents to. Who he saved by not letting your case drop even after it went ice cold." He nudged Doug's knee with his own, gentle affection. "Come on. Look, I know the way you feel about Mike isn't *all* because of what Nikolai put in your head, but how about you use how *completely wrong* Nikolai has been about everything else as evidence that maybe when it comes to Mike, your personal insecurities are wrong too?"

"Did Beth coach you to say that?" Doug said with a soft laugh.

"Yeah. Too headshrink-y?"

"Takes one to know one." Doug's eyes had slipped closed, but he was smiling. "Okay. Invite him. At least then I tried."

"That's all anyone wants," Mat said, and reached over to take Doug's hand.

CHAPTER TWO

Doug was nervous. Just as nervous as he'd been in those minutes leading up to his conversation with Nikolai. But Mat was here at his side. They'd gone for a long run this morning, climbing a tree into the neighbor's yard and then sneaking out their back gate to avoid the press. Mat had made them a big breakfast when they'd returned, and after touching base with Beth for a morning mini-session, they'd spent the last couple of hours debating the pros and cons of moving to various cities.

Money was going to be an issue—the survivor's fund would cover modest rent but not much else, and wouldn't last forever anyway—and there was no denying the . . . whatever it was between Mat and Nate that was obviously influencing Mat's favorite choices. But they were *free* now, weren't they. Nothing to hold them anywhere, or dictate anything. Strange, the sensation of knowing you could just . . . go wherever you wanted. He'd never, ever had that before. Really, neither of them had. Even Mat, the big responsible adult, had always been bound by where he'd trained and fought.

Except he wasn't going to fight anymore, not ever again. Doug damn well knew why. The things he'd had to do . . . No, they'd find something else. Doug had two degrees; maybe he *would* take care of both of them for a bit while Mat figured his life out. Not as a meal ticket, not as an obligation, not because Mat expected (or worse, demanded) it. Just . . . out of love.

Together, they'd figure it out. As long as they had each other, they had everything they needed.

Even if Doug maybe sometimes did, just for a brief moment every once in a while, contemplate the idea of getting his *own* place.

Even if Doug suspected that Mat maybe sometimes, for just as brief a moment, contemplated the idea of moving in with Nate.

They had their whole lives ahead of them to find their own paths. For now, they'd make something together. Repair their broken bond. It was getting better every day.

And who knew. Maybe Mike really did want to be a part of his future somehow.

Maybe.

Mike was going to be here in a few minutes. Alone with Doug and Mat. Nate was away at work and Darryl had pleaded some excuse about wanting to pick up a wedding gift for his daughter that he could only find in DC.

All going well, they'd all meet up here later and Nate would bring home a big dinner for them.

All going well.

"Relax," Mat said, dropping a hand on Doug's shoulder and giving it a rub. Doug leaned into it—all this casual touching, it was still pretty new. And nice. Really nice. He got teary-eyed just thinking about it sometimes, how much Mat had been able to forgive, how they'd managed to reclaim a healthy, familial intimacy for themselves. "It's gonna be okay. Better than. You'll see."

"I trust you," Doug said.

A knock sounded at the door. They both startled—that was one hurdle they hadn't cleared yet. Mat still put Doug behind him before looking through the peephole.

"Let me in!" Mike cried. "I'm gonna get trampled by paparazzi!"

Mat undid the latches, and Mike tumbled through the door, huffing and puffing and grinning.

Doug had forgotten that. His smile. It made Mike look like a father right from first glance. Good-humored, but weary. Loving, but a little cheesy.

Doug smiled back.

"Are you two okay?" Mike asked, putting down the shopping bag he was holding to pull them both in for a simultaneous hug, one in each arm. "Can you even sleep with those choppers going all the time?"

"Learned to sleep through a lot," Doug said without thinking, then winced when Mat did.

But Mike didn't let the awkward moment last. He picked up his bag, fished inside it. "I brought that awful pie you like." Said with that same loving, cheesy smile. "Rhubarb, Jesus Christ. Who eats *rhubarb* pie? Sour celery, more like."

"Oh, thanks," Doug said, taking the pie. Remembering all the teasing Mike had done. But he'd always still bought it. Even eaten it with Doug, making a show of how sour and stringy it was. "Are you here because you feel like you have to be?" he blurted out.

Mat *blinked* at him.

Yeah. That was *so* not how they'd planned this.

Mike's smile softened. Didn't falter, just softened. Became sincere in a whole new way. "Of course I'm not, son."

"Am I?" Doug choked, because apparently his carefully rehearsed speeches were out the window now. "*Am* I your son? I mean, I don't mind if I'm not, you don't have to say that just to make me happy, I'm a big boy—"

"Doug." Mike sighed, clasped a hand to Doug's shoulder—or rather, hovered fingers over him and waited for permission to touch, which Doug had to admit he really appreciated—and walked Doug over to the couch. Sat him down. Mat, ever supportive, sat on one side of Doug, and Mike took the other. Only then did he continue. "Boy, you're really making me wish Pattie was still here."

"Don't catch your new wife saying that," Doug mumbled.

"Why not? Loretta knows I miss Pattie. Doesn't mean I love Loretta any less. I got lots of room in my heart."

He looked pointedly at Doug, who scrunched his nose at how corny that last line was. Corny, cheesy dad.

Mike said nothing more, just kept blinking at him. Doug knew that look: he was waiting for Doug to figure something out. Something super, super obvious by the expression on his face.

Finally Mike rolled his eyes and added, "Just because I've got two new kids doesn't mean I love my old one any less."

Doug's palms were sweaty on his thighs. He wanted to believe what Mike was telling him, but he just . . . he couldn't *trust* it. Couldn't help but think again of Nikolai, of that frighteningly similar arrangement: raise a kid, get some cash, then send 'em on their way, so long, good-bye, don't let the new master torture you on the way out.

Nikolai hadn't come for Doug. Mike had fallen in love with someone new, moved to Florida, raised two new kids.

Stopped calling. Stopped checking in. Sure, those Christmas and birthday presents still came, but . . .

"I'm not your kid, though," Doug mumbled. "I'm not a minor anymore. I aged out of the system. Your contract ended." *The government checks stopped.*

Now Mike look pained. "I think maybe I made a mistake with you." Doug's heart clenched—*a mistake, you were a* mistake—but Mike pushed on before he could reply. "Pattie and I, we talked it over and agreed to let you go your own way. You'd always held yourself so carefully *apart*. So skittish. You were a good kid, Dougie, and we loved you, but . . . Well, 'If you love something set it free,' and all that." He paused, rubbed a hand across a day's scruff on his chin and cheek. "But maybe that works better for captive birds than insecure kids. So look, if it's a legal contract you want, I got one of those right here."

Doug's heart thudded too loud in his ears as Mike dug into the plastic bag he'd brought the pie in and produced a manila folder. He pressed it into Doug's shaking hand.

"Go on, open it."

He didn't want to. But he *needed* to. Because all of Mike's talk . . . it didn't sound like he regretted fostering Doug, it sounded like . . . Well, Doug wasn't sure, exactly, but something good, he thought. Dared to hope.

The stack of papers inside the envelope was old and wrinkled, the ink faded. It was dated: Doug's eighteenth birthday. Both Pattie and Mike had signed it.

Doug ran his fingertips over Pattie's signature, like by touching it he could touch her hand just one more time. Memories flooded back so fast and warm they brought tears to his eyes.

So did the realization of what he was actually holding.

Adoption papers.

All they needed were Doug's signature.

"Why?" he asked, holding the papers so tightly in his hand that they crumpled.

Mike's fatherly smile wobbled, but not with sadness or doubt. "It was always in the cards, son. But you were becoming a man, and we wanted you to make the choice. Then Mat came and got you and you went away to college and Pattie died . . ." He took a shuddery breath, swiped a hand over his mouth. His eyes, locked on Doug's, began to shimmer. "And I kept the papers the whole time, but it never felt like the right time. And then you were gone, and they said you were dead or you were never coming back, and you know, I couldn't even bring myself to throw them out *then*. They're probably expired."

"I never knew," Doug choked out, feeling his own eyes water. Mat's hand was on his shoulder again, but he wasn't saying anything. Wasn't trying to control the conversation or make Doug's decisions for him or push him one way or another. He was just there. Supportive. Present.

"The thing is, Doug, Pattie and me, we got your file and then we met you and we brought you home and brought you up those few precious years, and in our hearts you were already our son." He sounded choked up. Doug couldn't bear to look at him. "We'd already chosen you. We just wanted to give you the chance and the time to choose *us* too."

Wet splatters hit the page. Doug couldn't speak with the thickness in his throat and the tears streaming down his face, so he just nodded. Fumbled on the coffee table for a pen. Signed the papers right then and there, expired or no.

Then left them on the table because who cared about this shit anyway, *contracts* weren't what mattered, Nikolai had taught him that even if it was the exact opposite of the lesson he'd meant to impart. No, *people* were what mattered. Imperfect, hurtful, dutiful, giving, insecure, loving people. Family.

He threw his arms around Mike and just . . . held on.

I'm sorry, he wanted to say. *I'm sorry I misunderstood you. I'm sorry I didn't trust you. I'm sorry I doubted you, let Nikolai poison the well, let my own insecurities and fears come between us.* But Mike wasn't Nikolai, and neither was Mat, and Doug didn't have to say any of that because Mike *knew*, because he'd never hold it against him or lord it over him, because family forgave.

And Doug's family, right here for him the whole time, had forgiven *him*.

No matter what.

They cried and ate pie. The three of them, even Mat, ate the whole fucking thing. Right there at the coffee table, getting rhubarb goo on Doug's tearstained adoption papers.

Mat was so fucking happy for Doug—and for Mike, who'd always been kind and welcoming and inclusive with him—that he couldn't stop himself.

They cried so much they kind of lost track of time. Mat couldn't speak for the rest of them, but by the time the pie was gone, he was pretty sure he was crying about *way* more than just this afternoon. It was cathartic as hell, but it also meant they were taken by surprise when Nate came through the back door with an armload of fancy takeout.

Doug quickly wiped his cheeks and jumped to his feet. "I'll set the table," he announced.

"Let me help," Mike added, and followed him into the dining room.

Mat stood staring at Nate, still snuffling, and waved. "They're good tears," he said before Nate could worry too much.

Nate's shoulders sagged with relief. He dropped the bags of takeout to the floor. "Oh, thank God."

"Welcome home," Mat said, and opened his arms.

Nate stepped into them, wrapping his arms around Mat and laying a soft kiss on his mouth. "Thanks, handsome official boyfriend."

"Been waiting for this day?" Mat asked against his lips, realizing with shocking suddenness that, yes, the trial was over and, hello, no more conflict of interest. Heat rushed to groin so fast it made him dizzy.

"Um, yes, but for more than just that one reason because I'm not completely self-involved. But let's focus on that one first."

"Agreed," Mat said—okay, maybe kinda purred a little—and nuzzled Nate's nose with his own. He wanted to put the trial and thoughts of justice and testimony and all the rest of it aside. He was booked for a debriefing session about his post-sentencing feelings with Beth tomorrow, and until then, he was just going to enjoy himself.

He realized how much he *wanted* to enjoy himself. Like *enjoy himself* enjoy himself. Like, get Nate's pants off enjoy himself.

He kissed Nate again, deeper this time, really tasting him, one hand clasping the nape of his neck.

"Shit." Nate tried to pull away from Mat's greedy suction on his lips. "Before I forget, I have something for you."

The last time he'd brought something for Mat, it had been the box of their memories. Their life. Mat would never stop being thankful for that.

"Well, you *and* Doug, actually." Nate extricated himself from Mat's embrace, reaching into his back pocket as he called, "Hey Doug, can you come in here for a minute, please?"

Doug poked his head around the corner, cautious, eyes still red from all their crying, and after seeing Mat and Nate not naked on the living room floor, came the rest of the way into the room. Stood next to Mat.

Nate cleared his throat and shook his shoulders, clearly trying to make himself look official. "So, as you both know, Allen Smythe-Kennedy was on the FBI most wanted list." He looked between them. Bounced a little on the balls of his feet. Made himself stand all official and impartial again. "Well, his placement on that list came with a pretty generous reward for information leading to his capture. Similar rewards were on offer for seven other members of the Cartel who went to prison yesterday. And by generous rewards—" he thrust an envelope at them, grinning like a loon "—I mean three point nine million dollars all together."

Three point nine . . . *what*?

Mat blinked. Turned to Doug, whose expression of stupefied shock no doubt mirrored his own. Had he really just heard . . .?

Nate waved the envelope at them again, grin still splitting his face. "I got a bonus for my part, not to mention about five hundred new job offers, but this check in my hand here is for you two. Your bravery and sacrifice helped set into motion the biggest sex trafficking sting of the last two centuries. Nobody's kidding themselves that there's no more sexual slavery in the world. We're not even kidding ourselves that this particular ring is dead for good. But damn, we dealt them one huge fucking blow. Rescued over four thousand victims. Put away several hundred scumbags for life. Thanks to you."

"Us?" Mat asked. Nate was still waving that damn envelope. Mat finally worked up the hand-to-brain coordination to take it.

It was so fucking *light*. He half believed that big sums of money like this could only be given to you by giant novelty check and balloons. Half believed someone had made a mistake somewhere, accidentally tacked on two or three extra zeroes.

But when he opened the envelope, there were two checks, one made out to Mathias Robert Carmichael, the other to Doug.

Three point nine million dollars in total. All those zeroes—those very accurate zeroes—on the checks began to blur.

"Yeah, so, they wanted to do some big ceremony, media circus, you know. But I figured you'd had enough of that by now."

"Had enough of it on the first day," Doug said, then laughed a little hysterically. "Are you sure this isn't a joke?"

Mat nodded carefully—his head felt too big for his neck, like if he nodded too hard it'd just snap right off—and passed both checks to his brother.

God, his heart was pounding.

Doug studied the checks, one after the other, over and over again. But Mat . . . Mat only had eyes for Nate.

"Dinner can wait," he growled, and grabbed Nate's hand and dragged him down the hall and into Nate's bedroom. No, *their* bedroom.

From behind him, as he closed the door, he heard Mike saying, "Hey, what'd I miss?"

Mat laughed. And laughed and laughed.

CHAPTER THREE

Nate had expected an extreme reaction from Mat one way or another—whether that was doing cartwheels across the living room or just falling to the floor crying in relief—but he definitely hadn't expected this. Hadn't expected Mat pushing him into the bedroom and hooking a finger into the knot of his tie, yanking it clean off in one motion.

"I love you," Mat announced as he made his way to Nate's buttons, his fingers shaking but still effective. "I love you," he said again as he stripped Nate's shirt from his shoulders with focused determination. And again—"I love you"—as he tugged Nate's undershirt over his head.

Only as he attacked the button of Nate's dress pants did Nate get his head together enough to lay a hand over Mat's, stilling his frantic energy, and say, "I love you too. So much, Mat, God . . . So much." He almost said *You have no idea*, except he knew that was wrong. Knew Mat knew *exactly* how much because he felt the same. He gripped Mat's face in both hands, planted a firm but brief kiss on his lips, then stepped back and stripped off the rest of his clothes himself.

Christ, he was so hard already that just the brush of fabric over his erection had him leaking.

Mat growled low in his throat and *stared*, muscles tense, practically vibrating as he took Nate in. Nate had the sudden image of a big cat waiting to pounce, and for a moment the intensity *literally* took his breath away, but then he thought of T'Challa's pre-pounce butt wiggles and then thought of *Mat* doing pre-pounce butt wiggles and just burst into laughter instead.

As intense as Mat looked, he didn't get annoyed at that. He broke out in a grin instead.

They'd come so far, that they could be in the middle of a moment like this and still laugh, smile. It was *normal*, and that was what made it extraordinary.

Nate sat on the edge of the bed, stroked his erection, just once. Any more and he'd burst. "C'mere," he said, and beckoned. Not an order, but not a timid *Are you sure?* either. "And for the love of all things holy, *please* get naked."

Mat laughed as heartily at that as Nate had at the butt wiggles, stripping his shirt off with total abandon and tossing his pants and underwear aside a second later.

Not one—not *one*—hint of self-consciousness or panic or fear. Maybe they'd get lucky and it'd last.

"You are the most gorgeous man I have ever or will ever see," Nate said, quite plainly talking about more than Mat's body or face. He wasn't exactly operating at a high-enough mental capacity to be smooth. "Would it be wrong of me to say I've been waiting a long fucking time for this?"

"Me too," Mat said, and lunged forward between Nate's spread legs, pushing him back onto the bed. They hadn't touched since that time in the shower, when they'd both lost themselves. They'd had more self-control since, but that wasn't necessary anymore.

Their cocks glanced together. Nate's eyes rolled back, the pleasure of it was so intense.

"Not only am I gorgeous," Mat said, kissing Nate's neck, rocking his hips. "I'm also rich."

This time they laughed together, full and hearty, and it felt just as amazing as Mat's cock rubbing up against Nate's, as Mat's lips nipping at his collarbone.

"How far you want to take this, rich man?" Nate couldn't help himself. It had been two months, and they'd done nothing but kiss, and even before then the boundaries hadn't exactly been clear. He hoped Mat wouldn't find it insulting that he'd asked.

He didn't. "Dunno. So far so good." Mat licked a swirl around Nate's left nipple and added, "Great, even."

"Fuck," Nate cried, back arching. How could something tickle and feel so good at the same time?

Nate didn't know, but Mat did it again with his other nipple. Lapping at it this time, and then sucking it into his mouth in a slow, teasing draw.

"Shhh," Mat chided when Nate groaned. "Got company, remember? Make too much noise, I'll have to shush you with my cock."

"Oh *God*," Nate moaned, at least six times louder than the last time. *Yes. Yes, God yes. Yes yes yes.* Nate wanted—*needed*—to test that threat. To see how assertive Mat would get—and wasn't that a miracle all on its own, that the man could order him in bed and not . . . not *remember*. Nate couldn't wait to suck Mat off, taste his foreskin and his pre-cum, play with his balls, everything he'd ever fantasized about since that very first fight years ago. Couldn't wait for Mat to enjoy it.

"Tsk tsk," Mat teased, nipping his way up from Nate's nipple to his collarbone to his ear. Sitting up, *God yes*, shifting forward. His smile was downright *filthy* as he loomed over Nate, singsonged, "I warned you . . ." But oh how *gentle* he was as he raised up on his knees, straddled Nate's face, hovered overtop him, letting Nate choose to come to him or not.

Hah. Like there was any question about what Nate would choose.

"Wanna watch you do it," Mat said softly, the teasing gone from his voice. "Just watch you the whole time, okay?"

He sounded . . . vulnerable. So beautiful and strong. Nate nodded. "Whatever you need." He reached out with both hands, gently stroking Mat's muscular thighs. "Gonna give you everything." He kissed one thigh, then the other. Kept a grip on the back of Mat's legs as he raised his head up to kiss the head of Mat's cock.

Could hardly believe he was getting to have this. To be the one special enough, trusted enough, lucky enough. Could hardly believe he deserved it.

But oh, he'd make it *perfect* if he could.

He kept his eyes open. Looked into Mat's eyes. *I'm here. Whatever you need, I'm here.* Mat bit his lip. Never looked away. Drawing strength, and that was fine, because Nate needed strength sometimes too.

Releasing one of Mat's steady thighs, Nate wrapped his hand around the shaft of Mat's dick, gently drawing the foreskin back. Suckled the head as it came into view.

Mat's moan was soft and sweet, and there was nothing apologetic about it, either. Nothing apologetic about how he thrust his hips, not fucking Nate's mouth so much as begging for more.

Nate certainly wasn't apologetic about giving it to him. He sucked and licked and worked Mat's dick with his hand, and God, it was so good, it was better than his fantasies. His fantasies where Mat, still sweaty from the fight, pushed him roughly to his knees, gave him a chance to get Mat's dick wet before Mat crowded him up against the wall and shoved that dick right into Nate's willing ass. This was gentle. Impassioned. *Fervent.*

Better.

"God, I want you to fuck me," Nate moaned in between licks and kisses and sucks.

It was only when Mat stilled that he realized he'd said it.

He let his head drop to the pillow, his fingers drop from Mat's cock. "I mean, if you want. When you want. You don't have—"

"No takebacks, Nate," Mat growled, both hands tightening with warning against Nate's scalp. "Let's do it." There was no mistaking the bravado in his voice, but damn, Nate admired that. And still really did want Mat inside him.

"Okay," he said, determined not to ruin this for Mat. For either of them. If Mat could power through his fears, so could Nate. "How, uh, how do you want me?"

Mat sat back on his haunches, resting most of his weight on Nate's hips. His hands trailed down Nate's chest, one splaying across Nate's stomach, the other going to Mat's own erection, which, Nate couldn't help but notice, was not quite as proud as it had been a few moments ago in Nate's mouth. Nate didn't mention it.

"Like this," Mat said, his eyes locked on Nate's like their lives depended on not even fucking blinking. "Just like this." He shimmied back further, gaze still drilling straight into Nate's head, hand trailing down Nate's hip, thigh, as he knelt between Nate's legs. Took gentle hold of Nate's knees and nudged them up, back. Nate didn't need to be told twice; he spread his legs wide, tucked his knees to his chest, held them there one in each hand. Ass exposed. Eyes on Mat's. Not looking away for a second, no matter how much he itched to see if Mat had gone softer or gotten hard enough to fuck him again.

For a long moment nothing happened—no movement, no words, not even any silent communication. Just Nate and Mat staring through each other, Mat's chest heaving, nostrils flaring, pupils blown—by good or ill, Nate didn't know. Nate's hands trembled behind his own knees.

The moment stretched thin. Brittle. Finally, Nate couldn't help it, whispered, "We can st—"

"*Don't.*" Not cruel or angry, exactly, but hard. Emphatic. Mat still hadn't moved a muscle below his neck. Above it, the lines around his eyes were tight. Jaw clenched and flexing.

It was a near thing, but Nate somehow managed to not talk himself out of this, to let it play out how it would instead of pulling his old *We shouldn't be doing this* bullshit. *He* wasn't the one who should be making that call. It was Mat's choice, Mat's needs at play here.

Even if he couldn't stop his mind from straying back to the first time they'd been naked together. To Mat on his knees, tears streaming down his face as Nate's cock split him open.

But here, now, Nate wanted this anyway. He'd healed; they both had. He'd long since learned to forgive himself for that day—maybe even learned he'd had nothing to forgive himself *for*.

Still, it was no wonder he couldn't help saying, just to be safe, just to make sure Mat really, really *understood*, "You know it's totally okay if y—"

"*No*!" Mat shouted loud enough to startle Nate, fists pounding into the mattress. No mistaking the anger this time. The *anguish* on his face. "No, it's *not* okay! It's *not*!"

Nate waited, breath held, tongue pinched hard between his teeth, to see what would happen next. If Mat would storm out or cry or break some furniture or who the fuck knew what else. But whatever he was going to do, whatever he *needed* to do, Nate was there with him. He held Mat's gaze to let him know that, watched those big blue eyes shimmer with tears, with the kind of pain nobody could ever soothe for him. But God, how Nate wanted to try. To wipe it all away.

The best he could offer, though, was his understanding. His acceptance of Mat with all his scars and triggers and imperfections. And himself; he kept his knees tucked up, his legs spread wide. Let Mat decide.

Finally, without a word, Mat sniffed hard, nodded, and reached over to the bedside table. Opened the drawer. Nate supposed that was where all guys kept their condoms and lube, and sure enough, Mat came back with both.

"No one ever used condoms," Mat said, soft and distant as he squeezed some lube onto two fingers, watching his hands intently. "There, I mean."

Like he needed to clarify. Like Nate didn't know what he'd meant. Like he didn't remember shoving in bareback himself.

"You're not sick though," Nate said. Not a question. They'd been tested half a dozen times since they'd gotten home.

"I still want to use one with you. Because I respect you. Because it's . . ."

Different, he didn't say. *Not like it was with them.* But Nate knew what he meant here too.

"Thank you," Nate said, because damn if he knew how *else* to respond to that except with every ounce of the gratitude he felt at the idea that Mat could love him this much, find him this worthy, *trust* him with this. The words felt so right that he said them again, touching fingers to Mat's arm to get his attention, to make Mat look him in the eye again. "*Thank you.*"

For everything. For the condom. For loving me. For trusting me. For forgiving me all my trespasses and stupidities and flaws. For being you.

Mat held his gaze a long moment. Nodded. Yes, he understood—the text *and* the subtext, the spoken and the unspoken. He blinked back tears as he dropped his chin, took a shuddering breath and licked his lips. Oh yes, Nate was ragingly hard again, and there was no question of where Mat's attention had just gone.

Or those two slick fingers, which slid teasingly down the shaft of his cock, over and around his balls, and settled, far too lightly, against his hole.

"*Yes,*" Nate hissed. Mat liked him to talk. Liked Nate to keep him present, remind him who he was with. "Feels so good, Mat. Want you so much."

"You do," Mat said. He rubbed slowly, in small, tentative circles. He didn't sound quite *relaxed* yet, or particularly aroused, but at least neither his voice nor his touch were mechanical. And when he said, "I want you too," Nate didn't doubt it for a moment. Knew that Mat just needed to take his time, find his headspace. Fight his demons.

Well, he wouldn't be fighting them alone. Never again.

"You have no idea how long I've been dreaming about this, Mat. The fantasies I've had. The things I want to give to you, share with you, make you feel." He gasped as those two fingers pressed inside him, just the tips, moaned as wantonly as he ever had as Mat wiggled them a little. Nodded furiously when Mat looked up from his fingers to Nate's face, eyebrows raised in question. So careful not to hurt him like so many had hurt Mat.

Mat licked his lips, slid his fingers in a little deeper. Panted softly, open-mouthed. He looked half-stunned, half-confused, and yes, definitely aroused now. "Keep talking," he said, rocking those two fingers in and out. "Please."

"I want y— *Oh God.*" Prostate. Mat'd found his prostate. "I want you inside me," he panted. "All of you, every inch, *oh, oh, God* . . . I want . . . I want you pressed up against me, my dick trapped between our bellies while you rock inside me, your—" Another finger. Straight back to his prostate. *Christ.* "Your face hovering over mine, your breath on my chin, fucking me with your eyes while you fuck me with your perfect cock." Not exactly the most original or romantic stuff he'd ever said, but Mat seemed to like it. He kissed Nate's chin. Jaw. Lips.

"You really want me . . ."

Nate laughed, breathless, so turned on he feared he'd pop untouched. "You can't . . ." *Fuck*, how was he supposed to think when Mat kept doing that *thing* with his fingers? "You can't seriously doubt that, Mat, can you?"

Mat's smile was soft and sneaky, fingers relentless even as his lips gentled over Nate's and he whispered against them, "No. No, I guess not."

"So stop doubting." He stretched his neck to kiss Mat, quick and sloppy, then added, "And stop teasing, God, *please*, stop teasing. I've been a bottom for twelve years, Mat. You're hung, but I can handle you. I *want* to feel it tomorrow, you get me? Fuck me already. *Please.*"

Mat twisted his fingers. Stroked and crooked them, and Nate let out a desperate yelp.

"I *mean* it, Mat."

"Okay, okay, okay." Mat chuckled. Kissed Nate again softly. And then his fingers were gone from Nate's ass and a condom wrapper ripped and fresh lube squelched and before Nate could even form the words *God please hurry,* Mat's hands were pressing at the backs of his thighs, urging Nate's ass up higher, and that glorious cock was sliding hot and tight into his hole.

It was *such* a fucking cliché, but Nate kind of felt like his heart had stopped and he'd passed out all at once.

"Wow," he moaned aloud.

Above him, Mat's shoulders shook. "You are one of a kind," he said, half-laughing, but the laughter stopped for both of them when he drew back and thrust.

Nate locked his legs around Mat's waist, pulling that fat dick deeper inside. Pulling Mat closer to him so that Mat's sweat-damp abs raked his cock and Mat's pecs rubbed his own. So that hot moist breath puffed across his face and, when he arched his neck up off the bed, he could mash his lips to Mat's. No finesse, not with all the rocking and thrusting and moaning and clinging, not with the way Mat's tongue drove into his mouth and Nate's fingers dragged through Mat's hair and down his exquisitely muscled back. But fuck finesse anyway. Finesse was *so* overrated.

All Nate wanted was passion. Closeness. Love.

He and Mat had those in spades.

"Can't believe—" Mat panted, hips jackhammering, cock slamming into Nate so hard and fast he was seeing stars "—I'm doing this."

"Can't believe how *lucky* I am," Nate panted right back. He was close, God, *so* close, never felt a six-pack quite like that grating so hard and fast over his dick, never had such strong, sure hips pounding against his ass.

Never *loved* a man quite so unreasonably fucking much.

That was it—that was the thought that pushed him over. He blew like a fucking flash-bang, hands digging into the muscles of Mat's back, legs locking so hard around Mat's waist not even a crowbar could've pried them apart. Cum painting both their abdomens.

Mat must have felt all those muscle spasms on his end, too, because he roared and crushed his forehead against Nate's, found some leverage from somewhere and pressed the advantage of all that fighting strength to thrust his hips in one last frantic burst despite Nate's locked heels.

And then he froze, cock pulsing, muscles trembling, his whole body steel-hard for one long moment before going slack.

He fell, hot and heavy and pliant, on top of Nate. Panting into the side of his neck, hard cock still buried inside him.

Nate had exactly enough energy left in his quaking, fucked-out limbs to wrap his arms around Mat's sweaty back, to turn his head and kiss Mat's ear.

And then whisper into it, "Christ, you're heavy."

Mat barked a laugh, reached down between them to pinch the condom to his softening cock, pulled out and tucked in tight beside Nate, limbs tangling back around him. "Such a fucking romantic," he murmured.

"Only for you."

"Fuck." Mat's laugh sounded strained this time. "Thank you, Nate. Really, I mean it. Thank you. I . . . I didn't think I was gonna be able to do that again. I mean, like, *ever*." He lifted his head, rested his suddenly very pointy chin on Nate's chest to meet his eyes. Dead serious, now. "You helped me reclaim that."

"Wasn't exactly a hardship for me, to be honest." Despite the glib words, Nate felt his throat thicken. "But I'm glad."

They lay there like that a while longer, letting the sweat cool, lazily kissing whatever bits of skin each of them could reach without moving too much. Mat's fingers traced slow, ticklish patterns over Nate's chest. Nate's did the same over Mat's back, up his neck, into his damp hair, back down again. Until Mat squirmed a little and said, "Ugh, ew, I gotta take care of this condom, man."

Nate tightened his arm around Mat's shoulder, kissed the top of his head. "Let me. You stay."

But Mat snagged his wrist as he tried to get up. "Tell you what. Let's both go. Shower. Yeah?"

Hell yeah.

They traded inevitable handjobs in the shower—inevitable because no way in hell could Nate just stand there watching every perfect muscle glisten and drip and *not* want to chase each drop of water with his tongue—and it struck Nate as the perfect mirror of their first real touches in Mat's shower two months back, a perfect bookend for the victory they'd clawed from Mat's tragic past.

Eventually, actual washing happened, thankfully before the hot water ran out, and by the time they were toweling off and getting dressed, both their stomachs were growling.

"So," Mat said, pulling on a pair of pajama bottoms and a tee—no socks, no hide-everything hoodie. "You *did* have takeout, right?"

"Yeah. Not sure how good it's gonna taste microwaved, but yeah."

Mat headed for the door, and Nate followed on his heels, already itching to touch him again. "Man, at this point I don't care whether it tastes—"

Doug, Mike, and Darryl were all sitting together on Nate's couch, eating Nate's fancy roast-with-all-the-trimmings takeout directly from the containers, and smirking like a bunch of little shits.

Darryl looked up at Mat from his container of roasted herbed vegetables and said, "So I see you got your workout in today."

Mat froze, absolutely rabbitlike, and for a second Nate was sure he was going to have to defend his boyfriend's honor or, God forbid, his mental health, even if that *did* mean trying to beat up a hugely successful UFC coach. But then Mat untensed and rolled his eyes and shook his head and said, "I hate you so much right now, oh my God," and snatched the takeout container right from Darryl's hand.

Doug snickered quietly behind a chicken leg.

Nate flicked him on the ear as he walked by, and settled in the armchair. Mat, takeout in hand, draped himself over Nate's lap and fed him a spear of broccoli.

Nate didn't like broccoli. But right now? He couldn't possibly have cared less.

CHAPTER FOUR

"At the moment? For me?" Doug cast his gaze around the room. Twelve sets of eyes were looking back at him: some haunted, some confident, some peaceful. A couple months ago when the wounds from the trial and the witness stand were still fresh, having all this attention focused on him would have had him scrambling to perform. Now, he just took a deep breath and spoke on, from the heart. "Right now, celibacy feels good. I tried having sex, but it wasn't healthy. It was with people who were exploiting my vulnerabilities. And then I met someone—a woman—who wouldn't have sex with me specifically because she *saw* those vulnerabilities, and that kind of made me question whether maybe it might be better if I just took care of myself first."

Lots of sympathetic nods. They'd all been in his shoes, to one degree or another. All had had their own vulnerabilities exploited.

"And then when I caught myself . . . you know, with Mat . . ." He nodded toward his brother, who nodded back. This was a truth he still had trouble facing, one that made the shame flare particularly bright, but the group knew the sordid details already anyway. And none of them judged him for it. "Well, that was when I *really* understood how deep my issues ran. And while I *do* feel like I've really worked through a lot of those issues—thanks to all of you, by the way—" he flashed a smile at the group, at Mat, at Beth "—I'm still not feeling any particular urge to rush back into things."

Another round of nodding. Doug's cheeks heated, and he rubbed at the back of his neck, chuckled nervously. "I mean, that's not to say that I don't have, you know, *urges*. Just . . . I dunno, maybe I don't quite trust myself yet, you know?"

Ivan, a skinny young man sitting to his left, nodded especially fervently. "Do you think it . . . changed you? I mean, you were straight, and then . . ."

"And then being in captivity trained me to respond to men. I've thought about that a lot. Before we were taken, my brother was gay, and I'd always thought of myself as straight. But after everything, I started to wonder if maybe I hadn't been bisexual all along. But now? My brother's still gay, and even after everything, I still think I'm straight. I mean, yes, I look at men differently now, but that's not a part of me the way being gay is a part of Mat. It's something that was forced on me. And it's a . . . a residue, I think. Part trained physical response, part trained mental one." Just like he still got off on the idea of being dominated, being hurt, being *used*—the way so many of them here had rape fantasies now. But he knew it was normal and expected and could maybe even be healthy, all of it, and nothing to be ashamed of. Still, he fidgeted in his seat, cheeks too hot. Knowing something and *knowing* something weren't exactly the same thing, and this was a sensitive subject, definitely.

But Ivan's eyes were on him, so intent, so . . . hopeful, Doug thought. And it wasn't that Doug had any obligation to the kid—he didn't have to serve anymore, he knew that now down to his bones except on his very worst, darkest days—but he still *liked* to help people. Always had. And as Beth had told him over and over, that was only a weakness if he let it be. So he pressed on.

"Responding to men, *liking* men, it was a thing I had to convince myself was true to survive, you know? I couldn't . . . I couldn't fake it, not with Nikolai, and not to myself and still get up every day. So that programming went *deep*. Who knows, maybe it'll never go away. But at least now I know it for what it is. And you know, if a man asked me out right now? Like, wanted to date and he was nice and even wanted to take it slow, I don't think I'd say yes anymore. It wouldn't be fair to either of us, because even if I can't know for sure, I do believe one day that programming's going to fade away completely."

Doug felt scoured raw and a little nauseous after all that inner prying, but Ivan looked so utterly relieved that Doug was glad he'd done it. Glad for himself, too—these were demons he knew he had to face head-on in the moments, like now, when he felt strong enough.

Never mind how proud and pleased Beth and Mat both looked at all he'd just said. True he didn't do it for them, didn't *need* their approval, but it sure did feel nice.

"So if a girl asked you out, you'd be interested?" Leslie asked with an impish smile. She and Mat had crossed paths at the auction house, and Mat had described her as brave and fierce. She seemed to be carrying that same attitude into her recovery, too, with just a dash of cheekiness that simultaneously invigorated and unnerved the others in their group.

"A girl did ask me out," Doug replied. "Serena Chang. My college crush, actually." He huffed a breath through his nose, quirked his lips. "Guess she likes a project, you know?" A few self-deprecating chuckles were the only answer to his equally self-deprecating question. "But I couldn't . . . I just couldn't. Not anymore. Probably not ever, not with her."

Leslie tilted her head with a sad, understanding smile.

Someone else piped up. "I had a boyfriend before all this. I haven't even called him. I don't even know what I'd say. He knows I'm alive and I'm safe now, but I feel like honestly, even though *I'm* alive, the me *he* dated is dead. The me I am now . . . I don't know if she and him even have anything in common anymore."

Beth's turn to speak now—and Doug was expecting it, after that particular line. "There's no denying your experiences changed you, Maddie, and in some profound ways. But they don't *define* you. You've grown, yes, but the things you loved before, the things that made you who you are? Those things aren't gone. That other you isn't dead. She's just stronger, more aware—scarred, yes, but more prepared for life's challenges. Her priorities may have shifted, but her core is there. For instance, you still enjoy classic movies, and crocheting, and mystery novels, right?"

Maddie nodded weakly. Hearing, but not understanding. Doug knew that feeling. It wasn't always easy, and some days movies and novels and crocheting all seemed like such frivolous, meaningless things, dwarfed by the realities and horrors and dangers of life.

But other days, *good* days, they were simple pleasures, meaningful pursuits. Ways to connect and create and even self-actualize. Things to bring meaning and love into life. His morning run with Mat. Kurt Vonnegut. Stephen Colbert. Contraband. His schooling, even. He'd told himself those things were meaningless, once, but now he realized how very necessary and crucial and important they really were. How they combined to form who he was just as much as his past did, as his actions did, as the people he loved and who loved him back did. And that was a truth that even Nikolai couldn't twist or take away.

Still, he wasn't sure he'd *ever* be able to share his life intimately with someone who didn't understand his bad days as well as his good ones.

But intimacy *would* be possible again. Some day, with the right woman—a love of his own as pure and powerful as the one Nate and Mat shared, even though he'd once believed himself broken beyond repair. He knew that now.

Maybe even Leslie, once they were both further along the path to recovery. There was no denying that her inner strength and charm were as goddamn magnetic as her outer beauty.

Mat would definitely approve. Doug cast her a quick smile, and she smiled right back.

Too bad he was leaving.

"Well, Doug, thank you so much for sharing on your last day with us. I'm so glad to see the growth you've achieved in these last months. You've really been a positive part of this group, and we're all going to miss you." Beth turned to Mat. "And you, Mat? It's your last session, too. Anything else you'd like to say?"

Mat cleared his throat. Actually stood. Didn't look anyone in the eye as he said, simply, "I'm proud of my brother. I'm proud of myself. I'm proud of all of us." He sat.

Doug applauded him. And Beth, and Leslie. They all did, and then it was time to go. To leave this part of their lives forever.

Before they got out the door, Leslie stopped Doug with a gentle but unhesitating touch to his arm, slipped his phone from his pocket, blew a kiss at the camera, and then programmed in her number.

Hell, maybe one day he'd even call her.

Mat drove them back to their little apartment to shower and change before meeting up with everyone for one last dinner. He let Doug have the first wash—their hot water heater was nothing to write home about, and frankly Mat could use a cold shower before spending two hours sitting next to Nate in public—and took a last slow wander around while he waited. Just like their safe house in Baltimore, this place had come furnished, bland, and serviceable, rented for its proximity to their therapist and to Nate more than anything else. Completely impersonal except for Doug's horse painting over the couch. He wouldn't be sorry to see it go, but if he let himself dwell too long on the *people* he'd be leaving behind, well . . .

Well, who knew? Maybe they wouldn't be moving very far after all. The Eastern Shore was still on their list of finalist locations. Actually, it seemed like everywhere other than major cities full of reporters and remote mountain forests that reminded them of Nikolai's was still on the table.

The water shut off, and from the bathroom Doug called, "Your turn!" As Mat turned down the hall, he caught just a flash of Doug streaking butt-naked to his bedroom—the kid had never really redeveloped a sense of modesty, and after months of therapy Mat knew better than to push it on him, to shame him like that, as long as his behavior stayed healthy—but it still twinged something uncomfortable in Mat, still made his heart beat and his palms sweat a little.

Well, Doug hadn't meant to do it in front of him, he knew that too. And like Beth and Nate kept reminding him, he was still the same fighter he'd always been; he could knock that discomfort right the fuck aside.

So he did, and twenty minutes later, showered and shaved and wearing the one business casual outfit he owned, he stepped a little shyly into the living room. Stupid to feel that way, he knew, but both pants and shirt were fitted, and he wasn't exactly blind about the way people had eyed his body even before he'd become a sex slave and then the media hero of the decade, and now he just . . . Well. Nobody could blame him for plucking at his shirt a little, could they?

"No tie?" Doug asked, straightening his own. He was about a hundred degrees more put together and formal than Mat, but that was pretty normal by now. Doug liked to dress up in tailored suits, beautiful and knowing it and completely unattainable. Mat understood that kind of personal power, even if he didn't want it himself.

He hooked a finger under his collar, where the top button was undone, and tugged a little self-consciously. Hated, *hated* things touching his throat. No big mystery what that was about, huh?

"No," he said, quietly. "No tie." Then added, because he was absolutely fucking *determined* not to let this one last night of celebration turn maudlin, "You look great, man. Smell good, too."

Doug beamed. "Colors for Men," he said. "Nice, yeah?"

Mat snorted. Regular little metrosexual his brother had become these days. Not that Doug wouldn't slug him in the shoulder if he said that aloud. Besides, Mat wasn't going to rain on his new self-confidence parade any more than Doug was going to rain on Mat's self-comfort parade. "You any closer to being able to make an announcement tonight?" he asked. "Or are we going to wind up just packing our stuff up in a van and driving in whatever direction the wind takes us?"

Doug shrugged. "I was thinking we could flip a coin or play Rock Paper Scissors for it. Let's go; I'm starving."

The ride to the restaurant was comfortably silent. About halfway through, Doug fiddled with the radio awhile, then turned it off again with a sigh. They'd both missed a year's worth of new trends, and Mat knew well that strange, unpleasant *out-of-time*ness that came from facing the subtle but undeniable shift of the world around you, the way things had changed while you were . . . gone.

At the restaurant, the host gave Mat's open top button and tieless neck the side-eye, and if the steak weren't so damn outrageously good here Mat would've just left—better option than starting a fight, which was his other urge. But then the man led them to their table without further criticism, and seeing everyone already waiting there, Nate and Coach Darryl and Mike, made Mat forget all about his self-conscious irritation.

A hearty round of hugs and polite small-talk like "How was your flight?" were exchanged, and then they sat down to already-waiting drinks, a Manhattan for Doug and a Jack and Coke for Mat. Neither of them drank, usually, but this was a special occasion. Beth had given them the go-ahead to indulge, and taking that into account, they'd both agreed to limit themselves to two.

The waitress materialized with menus the moment they'd all settled. Stilled as she was handing Mat his. Even in the dim fancy-restaurant lighting, he saw her pupils dilate. He sighed internally. Waited for it.

"Oh hey," she said, breathy and eager, "are you—?"

"I get that a lot, but no." Mat flashed a big, fake smile at her and took his menu from her frozen hand.

Her return smile said she didn't quite believe him, but she was a professional in a high-end restaurant and she wasn't going to push the issue. "Sorry, sir," she said instead. "My name is Dahlia, and I'll be taking care of you this evening."

She rattled off specials. They ordered. Mat decided *fuck it all*—but in a fit of pleasure rather than self-destruction—and ordered a steak the size of his head with onion rings and garlic mashed potatoes instead of the asparagus and roasted root veggies. Nate teasingly poked Mat's belly. Darryl raised an eyebrow, but he was smiling. Then he ordered the same damn thing.

They managed to chat about nothing of even the slightest import—Jenny's wedding plans, the soccer tournament Mike's stepdaughter had just won, Stephen Colbert taking over for David Letterman, the reading habit Mat had developed lately (no wonder Doug liked Vonnegut so much)—until the food came.

Darryl, ever dispensing the tough love, waited until Mat was crunching into an onion ring to ask, "So, where you boys headed on Monday?"

"It's that soon?" Doug asked in a fake whine, looking to get a rise out of him. Darryl didn't take the bait, but Mike did.

"You could always postpone," he said. "If you're having trouble deciding."

Mat shook his head vehemently. "Not deciding is a decision all by itself." How many times had Beth reminded them both of that? "And a cowardly one, at that." Which, okay, maybe Beth *hadn't* said, but Mat had heard it anyway. "We're always going to be hanging on to the past if we stay here. You know that."

"We need to put down roots somewhere," Doug added. "No more furnished apartments. No more foot out the door living. We want to find a town we love enough to buy a place in. Make it ours. Start our lives." He cast a hesitant look in Mat's direction. "Maybe even buy *two* places."

The kid looked downright scared all of a sudden, and no, Mat wasn't having that. Wasn't going to let Doug keep thinking, however subconsciously, that his life wasn't his own to lead, that Mat would hold him prisoner in any way, that they couldn't be a family without also having their own lives. So he crooked a downright dirty smile, bumped his shoulder into Nate's, and said, "Yeah, you know, it *would* be nice to be able to have hot monkey sex on the kitchen table sometimes."

Nate kind of choked on his drink a little, and Mike blushed furiously, but Doug laughed, pure and clear and relieved, and that was all that mattered to Mat.

Coach Darryl, dry as ever, took a sip of his beer and said, "I hope you won't expect us to *eat* at that table when we visit."

"We'll have separate sex and dining tables," Mat replied with a grin.

"So," Nate said, clearing his throat and taking another long swig of his beer. He looked uncomfortable, and Mat wished he could say it was just because of the teasing, but he knew better. They'd talked about this, the whole *them* thing, the possibility of having to cope with long distances, and no matter how they sliced it there were no easy answers. "Is the Eastern Shore still a possibility?"

Okay, *one* easy answer. He and Doug could have their nice yuppie suburb on the water, quiet and peaceful without being *too* quiet or peaceful, and still be only an hour or so from Nate.

"Yes," he said, because, God, part of him wanted that—wanted a life, a future, *forever* with Nate—so badly he felt sick with the need of it. "But so is Lauderhill, Florida, and Henderson, Nevada," he added, because another part of him—maybe even a bigger part, and certainly a *louder* part—couldn't help but put his loved ones first, even still. And why should Doug be so far away from Mike just so Mat could have more sex on tables? And as for a Vegas suburb, what if Doug really *did* want to go back and finish his PhD program at his old school? Sure, he was waffling now, but Mat suspected the waffling would stop if he were actually close enough to go.

Nate looked like he was trying so hard not to let his broken heart bleed all over the table that Mat almost couldn't bear to add, "And so's Oahu."

"Mat . . ." Doug began, but Mat cut him off before he could start in about how *impractical* Hawaii was and how expensive and what would we *do* there, anyway?

"We can afford it," he said emphatically, "and there's just . . . there's so many happy memories there, you know? I mean, I know we've only ever been there once, but it was so important to both of us, and after Nikolai's"—so nice to be able to say that name without cringing, without wanting to break something or puke—"it became even more so. I think maybe we need that. Real bad. Hell, even if we don't wind up buying a place, just rent there for a few weeks and decide against it, it would still count as a pretty damn nice vacation." He turned to lock eyes with Doug and added, "And if we do decide to stay there permanently, we can work out the *practicalities* later."

Doug looked for a second like he'd run out of ways to argue this, but then he said, "There's no group in Hawaii. You might be okay, but I . . ." For a moment he looked sheepish, ashamed, but then he squared his shoulders and met Mat's eyes again and said, "But I still need it. The support. The therapy. The people. All of it."

"So start one," Mat said without thinking. And then realized—hey, that was actually a damn good idea. "You're a licensed social worker. You have half a clinical psych PhD. And let's face it—nobody's gonna understand a survivor's experiences more than you do."

Doug's eyes had gone huge, but not from fear or shame this time, no. No, this was *excitement*. Mat pushed the advantage. "Beth always said you were a huge help in group. A calming force. And most of us, we've got no roots. We can go anywhere. I'm sure plenty of folks could think of worse places to recover than in Hawaii."

Doug said nothing—Mat knew how vehemently he didn't want to take Nate away from him by moving them so far—but there was no denying the spark he'd planted in the kid's head.

"And I can work there too. I mean hey, if I can open a gym for underprivileged kids in Vegas or Florida or Maryland, I'm sure I can do it in Hawaii."

Silence for a long moment, everyone digesting their thoughts as surely as their fine meal. Mat chewed a bite of steak while he waited for someone, anyone, to say something.

Predictably, it was Coach Darryl who had the balls to break the silence. "You know," he said, "I always thought it'd be nice to retire in Hawaii."

Mat's head shot up. "*Retire*?"

"Why not? I got a daughter getting married and striking out on her own who could use a business to take over. God knows she's as good with the fighters as I am—probably better at kicking their asses. I'm getting on in years, and now my best fighter's out of the business, too." Ha. Like Mat had *ever* made Darryl real money. "'Sides," he said, winking at Mat, "I've got a soft spot for underprivileged kids. Feels like a sign from on high, all of that happening at once."

He was talking lightly, but there was no mistaking his intention, the real truth behind his words: *I lost you once and I got you back and I'm not taking that gift for granted.*

It seemed so crazy, now, that Nikolai had ever talked Mat into moments of believing that nobody cared for him, that nobody was looking out for him, that nobody wanted him, that everyone in his life only bore him as a burden.

Coach Darryl was none of those things. He loved Mat like his own kid. Wanted to take care of Mat as surely as Mat and Mike wanted to take care of Doug.

And you know what? Why not let him. Mat didn't have to be the big brother, the fighter, the strong one *all* the time. He could lean on people, too. It didn't make him a burden or a deadweight or the one responsible for the shit the world hit them with while his guard was down. It just made him a deserving human being. After being treated like a dog for so long, taking a little more care of himself, acknowledging his own humanity, seemed like a downright necessity.

"I could use an experienced hand at the new gym," he said, a little surprised at how shy it came out. "Don't know the first thing about keeping books."

Coach Darryl's eyes narrowed. "I ain't gonna be your secretary, Carmichael."

Everyone laughed. Even Coach Darryl. Even Mat.

"Speaking of Hawaii," Nate put in when the laughter had died down somewhat, "I—"

Just over his shoulder, a camera flash went off.

Once upon a time, that wouldn't have bothered Mat in the slightest. Somebody's birthday party, somebody's anniversary, heck, a fan from the UFC or someone just wanting to share their dinner plate with the internet.

But it wasn't once upon a time, and the cell phone was pointed directly at Mat and Doug, and Mat knew, fucking *knew* it wasn't a UFC fanboy behind the lens.

Bile rose in Mat's throat. Red spots—nothing connected to the flash—danced in front of his eyes.

This wasn't the first time Mat and Doug had been recognized in public. No, more like the thousandth, probably, not counting that moment with the waitress at the beginning of their meal. It also wasn't the first time some scummy photographer or rubbernecking civilian had tried to take their picture. Talk to them. *Touch* them. Ask for sordid details of their time in captivity. Use it for some shady news rag or inspiration porn or just plain porn-porn. No matter how harrowing their stories had been, no matter how much they'd cried on the stand, some people just couldn't seem to separate fantasy from reality, porn from real-life trauma. Mat had no issue at all with people jerking off to whatever bit of fiction turned their crank—fuck, even Doug had admitted in group to needing it sometimes to get aroused, the rape fantasy, the assault fantasy. But to use personal, traumatizing details, to superimpose Doug and Mat's very real faces onto porn, to be unable to muster up enough basic human fucking empathy to realize that for them this wasn't a fantasy, it was their *lives* . . .

This wouldn't be the first time Mat had slugged someone for it, either. Broken a camera, a phone. Broken a fucking *nose*.

He was out of his chair before his brain could catch up with his legs.

"Mat," Doug murmured, fingers closing gently around Mat's wrist, but all Mat could think of was smashing that guy's phone right through his skeevy fucking face. Calling him sick pervert trash, no better than the men who'd raped him and his brother, *tortured and raped* them, damn it, this wasn't a fucking game, this had ruined their lives, ruined them, ruined—

But they weren't ruined yet. No, they weren't ruined *at all*. They'd beaten it. Gotten so much better. Here they were, out to dinner with their family, sharing a nice evening, dreaming of the future.

Was some human scum with a cell phone worth ruining what they'd so very carefully constructed?

Mat lowered himself painfully back into his seat. Doug laid a hand on his arm, a silent comfort and thanks, a silent show of pride.

"I'll go talk to a manager," Coach Darryl said, and stood.

Nate took Mat's other hand and squeezed. "They'll make him erase the photo. He'll be kicked out. Or do you want to leave?"

Mat shook his head. A couple of tears leaked, but they were gone as quickly as they came. "No. I don't want to leave. I want to stay here and finish our dinner and enjoy our night. I want *dessert.* Now—" He turned to face Nate with a smile, like none of it had ever happened, and it felt like the bravest thing Mat had ever done. "What were you saying before you were interrupted?"

Nate ducked his head, looking bashful. "Well, uh, I was just gonna say that, you know those five hundred job offers I got after the trial? Well, one of them was in Oahu. PI stuff. Big-money reward cases."

He . . . Wait, *what*?

Nate smiled in the face of Mat's blinking confusion. "I could be like Hawaii Five-O. Because, you know, all joking aside, I've been feeling kind of dissatisfied with the FBI for a while. They didn't even want me to pursue your case. Had to do it on my own time. Of course *now* they're kissing my ass, but the damage is kinda done. Even Louise thinks a change of scenery would do me good."

"But moving to follow me? Don't you think that's a little . . ."

"Don't you pull some 'I'm a burden' crap now, Mat Carmichael. *Yes,* I think it's a little serious. In fact, I hope it's *very* serious." He turned in his chair, leaning his whole body into Mat's space, gripping Mat's hand in both his own and staring him in the face. "Permanent, even. Like, same-sex marriage is legal in Hawaii now kind of serious and permanent. You feel me?"

"O-oh," Mat said, because Jesus. *Jesus.*

"Not that we have to get married the minute we get there—we got nothing but time, and I know you need yours, we both do—but I'm not going to pretend it's not on my mind. That it hasn't been for a good couple months now. That it won't be in a year or two years or five years or whenever it is you'll be ready."

Mat's hand was trembling in Nate's, and those fucking *tears* were back, but this time he couldn't have cared less, didn't want to wipe them away, didn't care if the whole world snapped pictures right now. Nothing he could do but close that tiny distance between them and kiss Nate, nothing else he *wanted* to do, just taste and touch and feel and smell and hear him, melt right *into* him, and good God table sex was really starting to sound like an *amazing* idea—

"*Ahem*," Coach Darryl coughed, and suddenly Mat remembered: Restaurant. Not alone. Nate not, in fact, the only other person in the entire world.

How long had they been lip-locked that Coach Darryl had already come back from talking to the manager?

He pulled back with a nervous laugh, sniffed and wiped his lips.

"So Hawaii, then," Doug announced to the table.

"I like Hawaii too," Mike piped up. "Loretta and the kids will definitely be on board for visiting at least once a year."

Coach Darryl nodded. "Hawaii."

So did Nate. "Yeah, Hawaii."

Seemed like as good a place as any to build a new life with the people they loved the most.

AUTHORS' NOTE

This is it! Two years and almost four hundred thousand words later, you're finally reading the very last episode of The Flesh Cartel. Thanks so much for sticking with us! (Or if you're reading this after mainlining the whole series now that the last episode has been released: Hi and welcome! Hope you enjoyed the ride!)

As corny as it is to say, this series has been a labor of love for both of us. For years, we'd each wanted to write a story that had been eating at us but that neither of us quite had the means to publish before Riptide—or the tenacity to tackle without each other. Considering the sheer volume of words and the nature of the subject matter, this series wasn't easy for us to write, and we don't imagine it was easy for all of you to read, either. But we made it, and we're so glad we did.

On so many levels, The Flesh Cartel was an experiment—one that wasn't without missteps and setbacks—but we couldn't be happier that it's resonated with so many people. We knew going in that the content was controversial and extreme, and that the writing would require the utmost care, consideration, and respect, and even then that we wouldn't always get it right. It was both a surprise and a pleasure—and a little overwhelming too, if we're being honest—that so many of you came out of the woodwork to put time and emotional energy into the story of these two lost brothers broken but healed and made whole again.

Whether you were reading for thrills or for chills, we sincerely hope our efforts delivered and that you fell as deeply in love with Mat and Doug as we did. We've done our very best to leave Mat and Doug—and Nate, and even Nikolai, and everyone else—in a place where they can rest easy in our hearts and yours.

For authors, saying good-bye to our characters at the end of a project is always a bittersweet experience, and considering how big a project Flesh Cartel was, that feeling is multiplied a thousandfold.

We're excited but sad to be moving on to new things, but when you've spent as much time with characters as we have with Mat and Doug, invested as much life and hope and depth into their lives and their futures, you can never really leave them.

And we've spent all that time with you, too, readers. We've read every tweet and Tumblr post and email sent to us, even peeked at a couple reviews. We've felt so privileged to meet you at conventions, to sign books and take selfies with you, to hear your thoughts and opinions on this massive undertaking, to see your enthusiasm and your philosophic musings and your speculations and hopes and frustrations and your transformative fan works.

It goes without saying that this series would not exist without you. Original plans were for roughly nine episodes, and of course it didn't pan out that way—characters and worlds have a way of getting away from their creators—but our ability to *finish* this sprawling saga, all nineteen episodes of it, came down to you. To your endless support and generosity and enthusiasm, without which we may not have been able to persevere. Every inch of our success is thanks to you—with an especial thanks to those readers who supported the series so vocally when certain retailers refused to carry it.

Special thanks as well to our editor, Sarah Frantz, who was with us from the very first, plotting back and forth; to our brilliant cover artist, Imaliea, who brought Mat, Doug, and Nikolai so beautifully to life; and to all the other Riptide staff past and present who helped to polish and format and cover and market these books.

Now that the series *is* done, stay tuned for some exciting new things. (Did someone say a revised and illustrated edition?), as well as some non–Flesh Cartel releases from the both of us.

Thank you for taking this journey with us. We hope it was as satisfying for you as it was for us.

With love and respect,
Heidi and Rachel

Dear Reader,

Thank you for reading Rachel Haimowitz and Heidi Belleau's *The Flesh Cartel, Season 5: Reclamation*!

We know your time is precious and you have many, many entertainment options, so it means a lot that you've chosen to spend your time reading. We really hope you enjoyed it.

We'd be honored if you'd consider posting a review—good or bad—on sites like **Amazon**, **Barnes & Noble**, **Kobo**, **Goodreads**, **Twitter**, **Facebook**, **Tumblr**, and your blog or website. We'd also be honored if you told your friends and family about this book. Word of mouth is a book's lifeblood!

For more information on upcoming releases, author interviews, blog tours, contests, giveaways, and more, please sign up for our weekly, spam-free newsletter and visit us around the web:

Newsletter: tinyurl.com/RiptideSignup
Twitter: twitter.com/RiptideBooks
Facebook: facebook.com/RiptidePublishing
Goodreads: tinyurl.com/RiptideOnGoodreads
Tumblr: riptidepublishing.tumblr.com

Thank you so much for Reading the Rainbow!

RiptidePublishing.com

MORE EPISODES OF THE FLESH CARTEL

The Flesh Cartel, Season 1: Damnation
The Flesh Cartel, Season 2: Fragmentation
The Flesh Cartel, Season 3: Transformation
The Flesh Cartel, Season 4: Liberation

ALSO BY HEIDI BELLEAU

Bliss, with Lisa Henry
King of Dublin, with Lisa Henry
The Professor's Rule series, with Amelia Gormley
Rear Entrance Video series
Blasphemer, Sinner, Saint, with Sam Schooler (Bump in the Night anthology)
Mark of the Gladiator, with Violetta Vane
Cruce de Caminos, with Violetta Vane
The Burnt Toast B&B, with Rachel Haimowitz (coming soon)

ALSO BY RACHEL HAIMOWITZ

Power Play: Resistance, with Cat Grant
Power Play: Awakening, with Cat Grant
Master Class (Master Class, #1)
Sublime: Collected Shorts (Master Class, #2)
Counterpoint (Song of the Fallen, #1)
Crescendo (Song of the Fallen, #2)
Anchored (Belonging, #1)
Where He Belongs (Belonging, #2)
Break and Enter, with Aleksandr Voinov
The Burnt Toast B&B, with Heidi Belleau (coming soon)

ABOUT THE AUTHORS

Heidi Belleau was born and raised in small town New Brunswick, Canada. She now lives in the rugged oil-patch frontier of Northern BC with her husband, an Irish ex-pat whose long work hours in the trades leave her plenty of quiet time to write. She has a degree in history from Simon Fraser University with a concentration in British and Irish studies; much of her work centred on popular culture, oral folklore, and sexuality, but she was known to perplex her professors with unironic papers on the historical roots of modern romance novel tropes. (Ask her about Highlanders!) When not writing, you might catch her trying to explain British television to her newborn daughter or standing in line at the local coffee shop, waiting on her caramel macchiato.

You can find her tweeting as @HeidiBelleau, email her at
heidi.below.zero@gmail.com, or visit her blog:
www.heidibelleau.com.

Rachel is an M/M erotic romance author, a freelance writer and editor, and the Publisher of Riptide Publishing. She's also a sadist with a pesky conscience, shamelessly silly, and quite proudly pervish. Fortunately, all those things make writing a lot more fun for her . . . if not so much for her characters.

When she's not writing about hot guys getting it on (or just plain getting it; her characters rarely escape a story unscathed), she loves to read, hike, camp, sing, perform in community theater, and glue captions to cats. She also has a particular fondness for her very needy dog, her even needier cat, and shouting at kids to get off her lawn.

You can find Rachel at her website, rachelhaimowitz.com, tweeting as @RachelHaimowitz, and on Tumblr at rachelhaimowitz.tumblr.com.

She loves to hear from folks, so feel free to drop her a line anytime at metarachel@gmail.com.

Enjoy this book?
Find more unconventional kink at RiptidePublishing.com!

Bump in the Night
ISBN: 978-1-62649-063-5

Strain
ISBN: 978-1-62649-070-3

Earn Bonus Bucks!

Earn 1 Bonus Buck for each dollar you spend. Find out how at RiptidePublishing.com/news/bonus-bucks.

Win Free Ebooks for a Year!

Pre-order coming soon titles directly through our site and you'll receive one entry into a drawing to win free books for a year! Get the details at RiptidePublishing.com/contests.

NIKOLAI

His mastery of the language definitely left something to be desired. Which was why it was so gratifying to meet a young American man with whom he could speak in English.

"So you're from the States too?" the young man asked, drinking deep from the refreshment Nikolai had purchased him. Plush pink lips around his cup. Eyes big and blue beneath a fringe of dark hair, gently curling.

"I spent some time there, yes, but I'm putting down new roots now."

"Huh, cool. Me, I don't have any roots to speak of. Not anymore. My parents disowned me when they found out I was gay. We'd had this whole trip planned through Eastern Europe, but now I'm alone, so . . . I'm just backpacking around, hitching rides and doing day work. Living rough off the grid. No TV, no phone, no bills. It's pretty great, actually. But I'm thinking I should probably move on to, uh, more friendly countries anyway. Haven't gotten laid in weeks. Maybe you should think about putting *your* roots down somewhere else, too. Considering."

He seemed so relieved to have met Nikolai, a man of similar proclivities, in such a terrible, backward place while the sting of cruel rejection was still so fresh. One bright light in a vast, vile darkness. Just this conversation must feel so *safe* for him. Nikolai would gladly be this vulnerable young man's safe harbor. "Oh, I don't think that will be necessary for me. I keep to myself, mostly. No fear of angry villagers when you keep your distance and keep their noses out of your private life. Nothing better than privacy, in my opinion. And a nice, remote location. It's why I purchased such a large country estate on the outskirts of Moscow."

The boy's ears perked at the mention of Nikolai's money. Not as much as he'd once had—all his US assets had been seized—but his mentor had taught him well; over the years, he'd squirreled away many a nut for the winter in warmer climes. And he had a feeling his spring would be arriving again soon.

"Would you like to see it, perhaps? Stay awhile before you move on? I've many an odd job to be done by a strong young man such as yourself, not afraid of a little hard work. I'm quite certain I could help you get to exactly where you were meant to be."

The boy nodded again, eyes gone bigger, dreaming, no doubt, of better days.

Oh yes, better days indeed.

www.ingramcontent.com/pod-product-compliance
Lightning Source LLC
LaVergne TN
LVHW091115080826
845145LV00008B/1927

* 9 7 8 1 6 2 6 4 9 1 1 8 2 *